# Before, After,
## and Somebody in Between

# Before, After,
## and Somebody in Between

### Jeannine Garsee

**BLOOMSBURY**

Published by Bloomsbury U.S.A. Children's Books
175 Fifth Avenue, New York, NY 10010
Distributed to the trade by Holtzbrinck Publishers

Library of Congress Cataloging-in-Publication Data
Garsee, Jeannine.
Before, after, and somebody in between / by Jeannine Garsee. — 1st U.S. ed.
p.     cm.
Summary: After dealing with an alcoholic mother and her abusive boyfriend, a school
bully, and life on the wrong side of the tracks in Cleveland, Ohio, high school sophomore
Martha Kowalski expects to be happy when she moves in with a rich family across town,
but finds that the "rich life" has problems of its own.
ISBN-13: 978-1-59990-022-3 • ISBN-10: 1-59990-022-X
[1. Alcoholism—Fiction. 2. Drug abuse—Fiction. 3. Family problems—Fiction. 4. High
schools—Fiction. 5. Schools—Fiction. 6. Cleveland (Ohio)—Fiction.] I. Title.
PZ7.G1875Bef2007        [Fic]—dc22        2006027975

First U.S. Edition 2007
Typeset by Westchester Book Composition
Printed in the U.S.A. by Quebecor World Fairfield
2  4  6  8  10  9  7  5  3  1

All papers used by Bloomsbury U.S.A. are natural, recyclable products
made from wood grown in well-managed forests. The manufacturing processes
conform to the environmental regulations of the country of origin.

*For Chuck, Beth, and Nate, with love,*
*and for Joan Garsee, my second mom*

## 1

Okay, I'm sitting on the edge of my bed, listening to Beethoven and scribbling in my notebook, when Momma shuffles up behind me and smacks me in the head. Not hard, mind you. Just enough to get my attention. "Ow!"

"Will you get up off your butt and *do* something already?"

"I am doing something. I'm writing in my journal."

"Well, I don't care if you're rewriting the damn Constitution. We still got boxes to unpack and I ain't doing it all myself."

"Hey, I *am* unpacked," I remind her, waving my arm around at my puny new room. Ugly brown walls, paint cracks now hidden by all my Elvis posters, a tower of books stacked by the door because Momma won't blow any money on a bookcase. My old black trunk is shoved in one corner, one key secretly taped to the bottom, the other stashed in a hole in the windowsill.

"Hmph. I see." Momma clumps over to the window to survey my breathtaking view of the driveway and rusty fire escape. "Dang, how can you think with all that racket?"

At first I think she's talking about Beethoven. Then it dawns on me she means the Lindseys, the family upstairs. We've lived here less than a week and I haven't officially met them, but I've seen the kids playing outside. Brothers, I guess—a boy about my age with geeky black glasses a lot like mine, plus a shorter, heftier kid, and a curly haired baby. There's an older, scarier guy, too, maybe sixteen or seventeen, with baggy pants, chains, and a stud through his bottom lip.

The Lindseys are black, by the way. I'm not. In fact, except for Momma and Wayne, I'm probably the only white person on the block. On the next fifty blocks, as a matter of fact. I'm surprised Wayne lives here since he's such a bigoted redneck, but his grandparents or somebody left him this house, so he rents out the upstairs. Now Momma and I are sharing the downstairs with him.

I'm not thrilled with any of this, but what can I do? Face it, Momma's crazy. The craziest thing she'd done before this was ditch me last June for two whole days with nothing to eat but a bag of Fritos. When she finally showed up, dead drunk and with two black eyes, she ranted and raved half the night about how all men are scumbags, then barfed in my lap and passed out cold. Well, when she didn't wake up the next morning, I ended up in a so-called group home for adolescents, surrounded by the biggest weirdos and losers on the face of the planet.

Anyway, Momma was shipped to detox, and from there to rehab, and that's where she met good old Wayne. According to Momma—*eew!*—it was love at first sight. With both of them originally from West Virginia, maybe they bonded over a bowl of pork rinds or something. Now here I am, stuck in the bottom half of a roach-infested dump in one of the worst neighborhoods on the east side of Cleveland. The eleventh place I've lived in the past six years, but at least it's not another trailer park or a room over somebody's garage.

"Well, it gets on my nerves," Momma complains, still hung

up on the Lindseys. I think they're using the ceiling over my head for basketball practice. "I don't see how Wayne puts up with it. Maybe I oughta head up there myself and tell 'em to knock it off."

"Go for it, Momma. Better ask Wayne for one of his guns."

Momma turns, folds her arms, and sends me one of her looks. "I'm not so sure I like your attitude, missy. Now, you gonna help me finish up with those boxes, or what?"

I sigh and slap my notebook shut. "Yeah, yeah. Be right there."

The second she's gone, I spring up, tuck my journal under my arm, slide open the screen, and swing my legs over the windowsill. Hmm, can I do it? Tossing the notebook ahead of me, I manage to scramble onto the last rung of the fire escape, then climb halfway up to where I can sit and write in peace. Ha! She doesn't like *my* attitude? Well, I'm not wild about the fact that we're now playing house with some hulking, tattooed, gun-crazy Neanderthal I never even laid eyes on till last week.

I barely write two words when something small and hard whacks the back of my head. I jerk my face up to see that hefty kid leaning out of a second-floor window.

"Who you spying on, bitch?" he bellows down, tossing another marble.

"I'm not spying on anyone," I snarl back, rubbing my head. "And don't call me 'bitch'!"

The boy starts to mouth off, but he's elbowed out of the way by the kid with the geeky glasses. "Back off, Mario! Or I'll tell your old lady you're throwin' crap out the window again."

Mario growls something not very nice and immediately vanishes. The geek leans over the sill with that chubby, springy-haired baby balanced on his hip. "Hey, don't mind him. He looks big, but he ain't even twelve yet."

"I thought you two were brothers."

"Naw, cousins. His mom's my aunt Gloria. Anthony's his brother."

"That scary-looking dude?"

"Yeah, that's him."

"So who's that?" I ask, pointing to the baby, who grins at me around all the grubby fingers in his mouth.

"My brother De'Andre. We call him Bubby, though. Who're you?"

"Martha. Who're you?"

"Jerome. Hey, wait a sec . . ." The kid disappears to dump the baby somewhere inside, then hops through the window and plops down a few rungs above me. I hear the baby howling in protest, but the boy doesn't seem concerned. "So, like, are you related to that guy or something?"

Wayne? Puh-lease! "No, he's just—he's a friend of my mom. Why?"

"Just wonderin'. I ain't seen him bring many people around. Girlfriends, maybe."

"Well, I guess he won't be bringing them around now. Unless he wants my mom to slit his throat in his sleep." I giggle, imagining Momma's reaction.

When Jerome smiles, his gorgeous white teeth make him look a bit less like the world's biggest nerd. "She sounds a lot like my aunt."

"Nope, nobody's as crazy as my mom."

"That's what you think."

"Trust me. She's crazy."

"How crazy?"

On one hand, I'd like nothing more than to keep everything a secret. On the other hand, if Momma falls off the wagon anytime soon, things could get very unpleasant around here. "She drinks, she takes pills. She even OD'd a while back, and she had to go to rehab—that's where she met Wayne—and now she's sober, and, like, goes to AA meetings all the time, and—" Okay, time to shut up.

Jerome doesn't seem the least bit disturbed. "So where's your dad?" he asks, banging his heels on the metal rung.

"Dead," I blurt out.

"Dead how?"

"Promise you won't tell?" He nods rapidly, and I admit, "He got stabbed to death in prison."

I wait for Jerome to run screaming in the opposite direction, which is what people normally do when they find out about my dad. But all he says is, "For real? For what, drugs?"

"No! He just gambled a lot, and I guess he wrote some bad checks, and then he stole some money, and—"

"You serious?"

"Duh. Why would I make it up?" As he soaks this in, it occurs to me that he hasn't said a word about himself. "What about *your* mom and dad?"

"Nothing. They're just gone." He nods at my notebook before I can beg for the details. "So what're you writing?"

"It's my journal. I write down everything that happens."

"Wow, that sounds . . . boring."

"No, it's not. I have fifty-two of them so far." And all of them locked in my black trunk in case Momma decides to poke around. She'd kill me if she ever read some of the stuff I've written about her. I don't do it to be mean. I do it because, well, I've always done it. A habit, I guess, like biting my nails.

Jerome eyes my notebook a bit more critically. "So what are you gonna be, a writer or something? A journalist?"

"Um, I think you have to go to, like, college for that?" No point in telling him what Momma thinks about college.

"Well, I'm going to MIT," Jerome says loftily. "Nuclear physics."

"What are you, some kind of genius?"

"Got a four-point-oh GPA," he replies with a smug grin.

I pat my mouth in a fake yawn. "Well, so do I. And I'm a sophomore this year 'cause I got to skip a grade."

"Get—out! Me, too." Jerome scoots down one step closer. "You starting at Jefferson tomorrow?"

"Yes," I say slowly, and we stare at each other in speechless wonder.

Jerome finally says it. "Wow. This is weird."

"Totally weird!" I burst out. Jeez, I didn't realize till this second how freaked out I am about starting a new school. A big city school, too, unlike my *other* ten, way-out-in-the-boondocks schools. "Hey, I wonder if we'll have any classes together."

"C'mon up later," Jerome offers, "and we can look at our schedules. Maybe—"

"Mar-*tha!*" Momma's howl blasts through the window below me.

I almost fall through the railing. "I'm coming! Shit." Reluctantly, I drag my seminumb butt up from my perch.

"Yup, just like Aunt Gloria." Jerome shakes his head mournfully.

"Trade you," I offer, only half-kidding.

Jerome snorts. "Right. That's what you say *now*."

## • • • • • **2** • • • • •

I unpack the rest of the boxes in less than an hour while Momma sprawls on the saggy couch, sipping Pepsi and watching a soap. Fifty or sixty pounds overweight, with megableached hair that crackles like shredded wheat, she looks nothing at all like the mom who walked me to kindergarten, or braided my hair. Sometimes when she smiles, I'll see a flash of that old Momma, but she doesn't smile very much, unless she's smiling at Wayne.

"I'm all done," I announce. "Now can I be excused?"

"Excused for what?"

"I want to go upstairs and hang out with Jerome."

Momma squints intently at a Monistat commercial, then swivels her head in slow-motion back to me. "I don't think Wayne wants you hangin' around up there."

"Why not?"

"Wel-l-l, it's all boys up there, for one thing. I don't want you getting into no trouble."

"God, Momma! What do you think we're gonna do?"

"I know what *you* ain't gonna do. I just don't know what them *boys* ain't gonna do."

I blow out a sigh. Best way to handle Momma is to butter her up, then turn around and do what I want. "You want me to make dinner tonight?"

"Naw, don't bother. Wayne's gonna pick something up, so . . ."

I lean closer. "Momma, you okay? You look kinda—" Out of it?

"I'm fine," she answers, mashing her thumb on the volume control.

I take the hint and slink off to my room. *Not* fine, when it comes to Momma, can mean either "drunk" or "depressed." Personally, I prefer drunk. At least I know she's alive.

A roach skitters across the floor and boinks into my toe. I leap back with a scream, snatch up my handy can of Raid, and blast the little critter with a lethal dose of foam. I grab my school schedule and rush out to avoid the fumes, and Momma pays no attention as I duck through the back hall and up the narrow staircase.

A tiny silver-haired lady with a soft, wrinkled brown face answers my knock. Eyes enormous behind inch-thick glasses of her own, she leans on a four-footed cane and shakes her free fist. "Child, you either a Jehovah Witness, or you selling Girl Scout cookies—and if it ain't the cookies, you better haul your heathen self outta here before you rile me up again!"

"Grandma, that's Martha," Jerome explains over her shoulder.

"*I* know who she is," the old lady snaps with a not-quite-guilty smile, hauling me into the kitchen. "This great-grandbaby of mine got no sense of humor," she adds sideways to me as Jerome rolls his eyes. "Be nice to have a little girl round here for a change. You got a granny of your own?"

I shake my head.

"Mm, mm. Well, you can call me Grandma Daisy. My momma, she named all of us after flowers. Daisy, Rosie, Violet . . ."

"Mar-tha." Jerome shuffles impatiently.

Grinning, I say good-bye to my new "grandma" and follow Jerome to his room. Swear to God, it looks like a war zone with peeling wallpaper, falling plaster, and moldy food scattered around. Well, now I know why we have roaches, but what's with that falling-down ceiling? If I belonged to this family, I wouldn't pay Wayne a dime till he got his ass up here and fixed it.

Bubby, huddled in his crib in droopy training pants, stretches out his arms with a blood-curdling shriek of joy. Omigod, snotty face and all, he is just too cute! I swing him out of the crib while Jerome watches uncertainly. "Aunt Gloria wants me to keep him in his crib. He keeps messing his pants and won't use the toilet."

"Duh! What is he, like, one?"

"Just put him back, okay?"

"In a minute." I tickle Bubby's fat brown thighs and blow raspberries into his belly, and he laughs so hard he chokes on his own spit.

With a big old sigh, Jerome digs out his schedule. We sit side by side on the bed with Bubby in my lap, and compare notes. "Damn, only two classes together," he says in disgust. "Science first period and English second."

"I hate science."

"Not me. I like it."

Well, he would, Mr. Nuclear Physicist.

Bubby glances up with a stricken expression, and at that exact moment something very warm and very wet gushes into my lap. It takes me a second, but then I fly up with a yelp, a river of pee dripping down my legs. "Damn, I told you, this kid needs a freakin' *diaper*—"

"*What the hell you doin'?*" the infamous Aunt Gloria screams from the doorway, her long, cadaverous face twisted with rage.

My vocal chords shrivel up into raisins.

"Auntie," Jerome begins as Aunt Gloria stalks over and yanks Bubby out of my arms.

"Didn't I tell you to use the toilet?" Bubby pedals his short legs, trying to escape, but she flips him over, smacks his butt, and dumps him headfirst into the crib.

"Hey!" I shout as Bubby, sobbing, stuffs a sock monkey into his mouth. He gazes at me in shock and misery, like I'm the one who betrayed him.

"You stay in that bed till you quit pissing in your pants," Aunt Gloria warns him, then whirls on me so fast I almost fall over. "Look, I don't know how your momma be raisin' you, but my boys do *not* entertain girls in their bedroom."

"But we were just—"

"Out! And I catch you up here again, I'm gonna whup *all* y'all's butts!"

I look hard at Jerome, expecting him to argue. But all he does is jerk his head toward the door, then glance away like he's ashamed. Why doesn't he stick up for his baby brother?

I duck out of the room and clatter back down the steps to find Momma parked in the kitchen, wolfing down a Big Mac. She points to a wilted bag. "There's a cheeseburger for you, sugar pie. Wayne remembered you like 'em. Wasn't that sweet of him?"

"Yeah. Sweet."

Momma knows I don't like Wayne. She likes it even less when I let her know it, but doesn't comment this time.

"So where is he?" I ask.

"Out in the garage looking for a wrench. Sink's leaking."

Well, about time he fixed that. This kitchen reeks of mold, and I'm sick of standing in a puddle every time I wash a dish. I nibble on the burger, but the food is cold, and I don't have much of an appetite now anyway.

"Momma, you oughta see the way they treat that poor baby upstairs. That aunt of his hit him for no reason, and she, like, never lets him out of his crib, and—"

"Martha," Momma interrupts, munching a french fry, "didn't I tell you not to go up there in the first place? You don't need to be locking yourself up in some boy's bedroom, anyway."

"Hello, we were looking at our schedules."

"I don't care. It ain't fittin'." I splurt out a giggle, and Momma slaps a hand on the table. "Now what's so funny?"

"You sound like Mammy in *Gone With the Wind*."

She almost—*almost!*—cracks a smile at this. But then Wayne clomps in, swinging a wrench, tracking mud all over the floor. "You do what your momma says, little girl," he commands, giving Momma a big juicy kiss before he drops to his knees and crawls under the sink. His pants sag dangerously low, and I never saw such a furry back on any living creature that wasn't safely behind a ten-foot electric fence. "No reason for you to be up there with them people."

*Them people*, huh? Well, he could've said worse. He usually does. "What? Am I not supposed to have any friends around here?"

"You heard your momma." His voice, muffled under the sink, still comes across loud and clear. "Keep your butt downstairs."

Oh, by the way, Wayne's not too fond of me, either.

"You can be friends with 'em, sugar pie. Just not up there." Momma's all lit up and dreamy now that Wayne's in the same room. "And don't worry about that baby so much. Ain't nothing wrong with a smack on the butt every now and then."

"But, Momma—"

She points to my greasy wrapper. "You gonna eat that, or what?"

I shove my half-eaten burger across the table. "No. I'm going to bed."

"Already? It's only seven."

"I'm tired, okay? And I got school tomorrow."

I can tell she doesn't remember that, but she tries to cover it up with, "Well, good. I hope you make some new friends. You weren't all that sociable last year, were you, sugar pie?"

How can you be sociable when your mom makes you move every time the rent's overdue or when her latest boyfriend dumps her?

"You got something to wear tomorrow? Didja check the box?" Momma means the Goodwill box, a treasure chest of mostly unwearable, smelly rags.

I flutter my eyelids. "Yes, Momma, I checked it. And yes, it's still crap."

"Beggars can't be choosers," she says breezily, licking salt from her fingers. "Things'll get better."

Yeah, I've heard that one before, too.

Two crummy minutes into homeroom the next morning and all I can think is: No way will I survive the next three years in this hellhole.

Legs splayed in the aisles, spitballs sticking to my hair, a boom box in the back of the room blasting hip-hop. The teacher's name is Miss Fuchs—"That's *Fee-yooks*, please. Fee-yooks, Fee-yooks." She says it like nine times so we don't mistake it for something else, then rattles off the cardinal rules of Jefferson High: No drugs, no cigarettes, no cell phones or pagers. No weapons of any kind including nail clippers, hair pins, and probably even toothpicks. Oh, and by the way, no inappropriate sexual conduct.

What, is she blind? There's a major grope-fest going on in the back of the room, and I can smell cigarette smoke from the john across the hall. So far no sign of any weapons or drugs, but the guy next to me—Jamal?—reeks of booze as he snores, facedown, into a puddle of drool on his desktop.

Except for two scuzzy dudes off to one side, mine is the only white face in the room. I'm not surprised, but wow, how weird is this? I sneak another look around as Miss Fuchs rattles off names: Aiyisha, Monique, Kenyatta, TyShawn, and omigod, *Chardonnay*? Isn't that some kind of wine? That poor girl's mom must be crazier than mine.

My sympathy fades as Chardonnay twists around to spread her lips in a demented grin. Her long yellow teeth probably haven't seen a toothbrush in months. I take a chance and smile back, and what do I get? A pudgy middle finger jabbed under my nose.

My next thought is: Shit. I may not even survive homeroom.

"Martha Kolsky . . . um, Kro-waw-ski, um . . ." Miss Fuchs stammers cluelessly.

I raise my hand to correct her with "Ko-*wal*-ski" just as a broken pencil zings off my lip. Some guys in the back chant "Yo, Ma-ar-rtha!" while the idiot behind me hammers my chair with his foot. Miss Fuchs pounds on her desk, screaming for order, and a blackboard eraser whomps her in the chest. Too nosy for my own good, I glance around to see who threw it, and notice a boy picking his teeth with a wicked-looking penknife. He winks when he sees me, and I whirl back around, nibbling the raggedy pink stump that used to be my thumbnail.

Oh-h-h, God, this is a dream. Or a movie. Or temporary insanity.

As soon as the bell rings, I snatch up my stuff and join the mad rush while Miss Fuchs teeters near the door, whimpering with relief. Without any warning, a hurricane force hits me from behind and I'm half knocked off my feet by a single swing of Chardonnay's massive arm.

"Outta my way, bitch," she snarls, plowing me into the wall.

Face-to-face, I'm shocked by her mammoth size—torpedo boobs, WWE shoulders, and a butt big enough to plug up Lake

Erie. I scream bloody murder as she grinds her heel into my sneaker, but she only smirks and lumbers out the door.

And my third brilliant thought of the day is: I am so-o-o freaking screwed!

## ••••• 4 •••••

Hugging my books, sneaking looks over my shoulder, I hobble through the halls in search of the biology room.

Some old dude with a shabby suit and overgrown nose hairs flags me down as I wander aimlessly along the science hall. "Biology lab?" I nod, and he points to the door behind him. "I'm Mr. Finelli. Hurry up and find a seat."

Jerome waves from a black-topped table in the back, and I gratefully slide in. "Took you long enough," is his unsympathetic greeting.

"Not my fault. Some bitch in homeroom just stomped on my foot."

"Yeah, and I bet that bitch's name begins with a C."

I stare. "How'd you know?"

"Oh, she beats up anybody who pisses her off."

"I didn't piss her off. She attacked me for no reason."

Jerome shakes his head. "Oh, she had a reason, that's for sure."

"Why? Because I'm white?"

"No, 'cause you were *there*."

I rub my throbbing foot under the table while old Mr. Finelli starts yammering about some project I am so not interested in. All I can think about is Chardonnay, and that boy with the knife, and how much I miss all my little hick schools where the worst that could happen might be a wad of bubble gum in my hair.

After biology, Jerome, who was here for ninth grade, too, acts as my guide dog and leads me easily to English without getting us lost in the crowded maze. We find two seats together near the front, and one girl from my homeroom, tall and skinny with a thousand long braids, throws herself down on my other side. I pretend not to see her. Nobody's flipping me off again.

"Martha, right?" She stretches long brown legs across the aisle, forcing everyone else to climb over them. She is thin, thin, thin with amazing cheekbones and slanted dark eyes that slice into your brain. Her bony wrists are covered with jangling bracelets, and she's wearing a skimpy leather skirt, and tight black boots with bone-crunching pointed toes and stiletto heels. And all those earrings! My God, how did she ever survive the piercings?

I nod curtly. Yep, Martha, the Amish farm wife. Martha, the Wal-Mart greeter. What I need is something classier, like Genevieve or Sophia or Lydia. A name that belongs to the rich and famous, to the order-givers, not the order-takers.

"*Ps-st!* We gotta read *Romeo and Juliet* in here." Like an old TV gangster, Braid-Girl mutters out of the side of her mouth. "You wanna buy last year's test? I know somebody who got it."

"What for? It's not like I don't know the story."

"Well, ex-cu-use me, Miz Wonder Bread." She crumples up a piece of notebook paper and pops it in my face.

"Way to go." Jerome sniggers on my other side.

I glance at the girl's rigid profile, sorry I said anything at all. I hate this day! I'll never make a single friend.

After English, Jerome and I have no more classes together. I say good-bye sadly, squint at my crumpled schedule, and then fumble my way through the halls of insanity, hitting the locker room of the gym at the same time as Braid-Girl. She pointedly ignores me. I ignore her back. Then, to my horror, I spot Chardonnay, looking meaner and bigger than she did two hours ago.

"Hey, honky bitch. 'Sup?" Not answering her back, unfortunately, only pisses her off more. "Hey, I'm talkin' to *you*!"

I try to squiggle around her, but she pushes me up against the lockers. She's a mile wide and about as big as a wild boar, so huge in fact that she could smother me with her chest by moving a single inch closer. The mere idea of dying with Chardonnay's boobs in my face, cutting off my light, my oxygen, and even my screams, seriously makes me want to pee down my leg.

"Hey! Leave her alone."

Chardonnay ignores the voice—Braid-Girl's, maybe?—and shuffles even closer. Our noses almost touch, and she has zits on hers, plus zits on her chin and on her forehead and on her thick, sweaty neck. I stare, morbidly fascinated.

"Hey, Blubber Butt! You deaf? I said let her be."

Yes, it's Braid-Girl, and I can see her inching over till she's right within punching distance. Good! With any luck at all, Chardonnay'll turn on *her* instead.

Chardonnay sneers. "Who's gonna make me?"

Sweat spurts from my armpits like a busted hydrant because I'm positive I'm about to die here in this locker room. Then, incredibly, the voice of God booms from the other end of the room: "What's going on back there?"

No, not God. The PE teacher.

"Ain't nothin' going on, Miz Lopez." Chardonnay keeps her

voice pleasant, but her face twists with rage. She waits one last second before stepping back, and I gasp with relief at the blast of fresh air.

"Then get your butt into the gym. I had enough trouble with you last year."

Chardonnay sends Braid-Girl one last menacing glare, and Braid-Girl bares her teeth in a taunting smile. With hatred hissing from her pores like some kind of secret biological weapon, Chardonnay flips Lopez the bird and plods out of the locker room.

Lopez ventures over for the first time. In spite of her tough butchy haircut and bulging biceps, even she was smart enough not to get too close to old Blubber Butt. "What's the problem here?"

I open my mouth to explain, but my legs turn into pudding. I slide down the locker, hitting my butt hard on the floor, and Braid-Girl jumps forward as I let out a squeak of pain. "She's sick! You want me to take her to the nurse?"

Unconvinced, Lopez asks my name, and Braid-Girl answers for me while I sit there, trying not to cry, totally humiliated.

"And who are you?" Lopez asks irritably as Braid-Girl crowds into her space.

"Her friend."

"Yes. I see that. What is your *name?*"

". . . Aiyisha Simms."

"Okay, Simms. You can take Martha to the nurse, but I want *you* to come back here. Understand?" Braid-Girl lifts her hands and rolls her eyes, and I can see Lopez's lid is about to blow. "Is—there—a—problem—with—that?"

"No, ma'am," Braid-Girl says sweetly. "I ain't got a problem at all."

Lopez points a finger in her face. "You watch yourself, then. I'm giving you ten minutes." Braid-Girl hauls me to my feet, and Lopez calls after us, "And take off some of that lipstick, Simms. You're starting to look like a hooker."

"What a bitch," the girl says calmly when we're out of earshot. "Maybe I wanna look like a hooker, she ever think of that? Dumb-ass heifer."

"You're not Aiyisha," I manage to croak. "Aiyisha's in our homeroom."

"Yeah, well, won't this make her damn day?" She winks.

"So who are you?"

"Shavonne Addams."

"Well, why'd you lie about your name?"

Shavonne withers me with a look of outrage. "Hey, I had that bitch last year, okay? She don't know my name by now, that's her own damn problem." Ignoring my protests, she shoves me into a restroom, climbs up on the sink, and whips a mangled pack of Marlboros out of a purple lace bra. "Want one?"

Nervous glance at the door. "You nuts? What if we get caught?"

Shavonne lights up and inhales deeply. "Man, you always such a baby?"

"No," I lie.

"Bull. You about shit your pants back there."

True. I fan away fumes as she sends a blast of smoke rings spiraling up to the ceiling. "Well, thanks. You saved my life."

"Just stay away from that psycho. She eighteen years old and ain't even a junior, and guess what she done last year? Stabbed some girl through the eye with this little Bic pen, and got her fat ass thrown out the rest of the year. That girl got a glass eye now, and ain't nobody seen her since."

"Why'd she stab her? Was she white?"

Shavonne eyes me narrowly. "No, she wasn't white. Chardonnay's pure evil. Back in eighth grade she tried to kick my ass, too. Ain't touched me since, though," she adds with a vicious grin.

"How come?"

" 'Cause now she knows I kick back."

I eye Shavonne's long bony frame. "*You* kicked Chardonnay's butt?"

"Well, I broke her pinky finger. She couldn't do nothing to me after that."

Impressed, I pull off my glasses, splash water on my face, then wriggle out of my shoe and peel down my raggedy sock. No blood. Guess I'll live.

Shavonne wrinkles her nose at the purplish bruise on my foot. "Damn, girl. You lucky that cow didn't break every last bone." Flinging back her braids, she takes another puff of her cigarette. "So, you're new, right?"

"Oh, how can you tell?" I demand, twisting the sock back over my aching foot.

"Where you from?"

"Spencer."

"Where the hell's that?"

"Cow country. Anyway, we move, like, twice a year. So far this is the first place that has sidewalks."

"So how'd you end up here?"

Sigh. "My mom's shacking up with some dude. We live down on Ninety-third."

"He black?"

"Who?"

"Your mom's dude."

"No, he's a hillbilly slumlord." Shavonne giggles, and I ask,

"Where do you live?" because, with any luck, we might be neighbors.

"You know those projects down by the hospital?"

Hey, I thought you had to be on welfare to live in the projects. Shavonne doesn't look poor. Her clothes are stunning, her hair and nails perfect. Even her skin is flawless, smooth and dark as the bottom of a Hershey bar. I feel drab and juvenile next to her in my fugly glasses and *South Park* T-shirt, my long, frizzy brown hair springing madly out of a scrunchie.

"We have roaches," I say stupidly for no particular reason.

"Roaches?" Shavonne sticks out her tongue. "That ain't nothin'. I got junkies in my building and you can't even call the cops 'cause if they find out who done it, they come blow your damn brains out. They be pissin' all over the hallways, too. Girl, I got to jump over puddles when I leave outta there in the morning."

She smokes in silence, and I begin to get nervous again. "Um, maybe we ought to go see the nurse?"

"What for? All she gonna do is tell you to take a load off. You already done that."

"Maybe she'll send me home?"

"Nope. Only way she'll do that is if you puke on yourself. Or if Aunt Flo shows up and messes up your clothes."

I haven't met Aunt Flo yet. I must be physically retarded.

A bell rings and both of us jump. I ease my shoe back on as Shavonne jams the Marlboros into her bra and buttons up her blouse. "I got lunch next. How 'bout you?"

I consult my schedule again, and almost collapse with relief. "Me too!" And I follow her swinging braids out to the hall, pushing my way semiexpertly through the noisy, jostling mob.

So far today, one enemy and one friend. Now all I have to do is make it to the last bell alive.

Jerome and I wade home together through broken glass, litter, and empty beer cans. Halfway there, I remember something. "You pissed me off yesterday, I hope you know."

"What'd I do?"

"You didn't do *anything* when your aunt smacked your brother."

His guilty gaze slides away from me. "She only smacked him one time."

"He's a baby, okay? You shouldn't let her smack him at all."

"So you want me to fight with her so she can beat my ass, too?"

"Well, why do you let her? I'd never let anybody beat me up." Aside from Momma's occasional whack upside my head.

Jerome stops short in the middle of the sidewalk. "You know something? You just running your big mouth and you don't even know what you're talkin' about." He struts off, leaving me to wander home alone, wishing he weren't so touchy and my mouth weren't so big. But if Bubby were my brother, nobody'd lay a finger on him!

Momma greets me in the kitchen, a bit brighter than usual. "Well, how was your first day?"

"Sucked. Big time."

"I sure wish you wouldn't use that word, sugar pie."

"I'm not kidding, it really did suck. Some kid brought a knife to school."

"Did you tell someone?"

"No-o-o . . . but then there's this girl, Chardonnay? And she, like, shoved me into a wall, and then she stepped on my foot, and—"

"Well, I hope you shoved her back."

"Momma, she's humongous! She's about as fat as a—" *Oops!* I clamp my jaw shut. Weight's a touchy subject where Momma's concerned.

"You gotta learn to fight back. Can't go through life letting people knock you around."

*Ha,* easy for her to say. She probably could ram Chardonnay through a brick wall.

"I don't suppose," I say, oh so casually, "I could go to a Catholic school or something."

"We ain't Catholic," she announces, in case I don't remember.

"So? I'll convert."

"Those schools cost money. You're staying right where you are."

"For how long?" I whine. "Momma, this house sucks, this neighborhood sucks, that whole school sucks, and everything sucks, sucks, *sucks!*"

"*Stop saying that word!*" she roars, spinning around as fast as somebody her size can possibly spin. "You oughta be grateful Wayne took us in like he did. You wanna be livin' in a box under a bridge somewhere? You know, the problem with you is, you're just like your daddy was. Spoiled rotten, always puttin' on airs,

always actin' like you're so much better than anybody else—"
And on and on, blah, blah, blah. Everything I've heard a thousand times before.

I slam into my room and grope under the windowsill for the
key to my trunk. So what if I'm like my dad? My dad was smart.
He even went to college for a while down in West Virginia, till he
hooked up with Momma who never made it past the ninth grade.

I dig through my cluttered trunk till I find my latest journal.
I keep all of my journals in here, plus old report cards and birthday cards, and a few old toys I can't part with. Lots of photos,
too, but none left of Daddy. Momma slashed them all up during
one of her drunken frenzies.

Once, when I was little, we were all riding in the car, and I remember passing an old factory. Thick, pure white smoke poured
out of the stacks, and I poked Daddy in the back to point it out.
"Look at the clouds!"

Daddy said, very seriously, "Yep, that's a cloud factory, honey.
That's where God makes all the clouds."

Wow! I stuck my head out the window to get a better look,
but then Momma had to ruin it with, "Don't lie to the kid, Ray.
She believes every word you say." To me, she added, "It's smoke,
sugar pie. Nothing but dirty old smoke."

But when Daddy winked at me in the rearview mirror, I knew
the truth: that Momma was wrong about the clouds, and this
would be just our secret.

Times like this, I really do miss my dad. He's the one who got
me hooked on Beethoven. He liked to play classical music in the
car just to drive Momma nuts. He played it at home, too, on his
violin, till Momma put an end to it.

I stare at the blank page of my journal, but no way can I concentrate. All I've done today is fight, fight, fight. I'm utterly sick

of it, and Jerome is right: I'm always running my big mouth, always pissing people off.

I lock my trunk back up, stash the key, take the screen off the window, and scale the rickety fire escape. Jerome's sprawled on the bed, his nose buried in *Romeo and Juliet*, and I can hear Bubby snoring in the crib. That other kid, Mario, is nowhere around.

I scratch on the screen and whisper, "Hey!"

"What?" he grumbles without looking up from the book.

"I take it back, okay? I had a really sucky day."

He drops the book into his lap and turns his head to the window. "Yeah. Me, too."

"Can I come in?"

"You wanna get us killed?"

"I'll be quiet. I swear."

With a dramatic sigh, Jerome crawls across his bed to unhook the screen. I jump over the sill, plop down beside him, and point to the book. "I can't believe you're reading this already. We've got, like, six weeks."

"I don't like to wait till the last minute."

"Duh, I can read it in one night. Are you always such a grind?"

"You always such a stuck-up bitch?"

"Are we always gonna end up fighting like this?"

"Probably," he admits, but at least now he's smiling.

###### •••••• **6** ••••••

While Miss Fuchs races through attendance the next day, Shavonne shoots me a note from three rows away: *Come over after school, k?* Knowing that today *has* to be better than yesterday, I send her a thumbs-up. I relax even more when I notice that old Blubber Butt, happily, seems to have lost interest in me. A couple of homeroom homies harass me off and on—*Ma-a-artha, yo, Ma-a-artha, hey boo, gimme some sugar, baby!*—but at least they're nice enough to keep their hands to themselves.

At lunch, Shavonne and I sit with Kenyatta and Monique. Kenyatta's dark, tiny, and smart, with straight black hair hanging into her eyes. Monique, on the chubby side, even flashier than Shavonne, acts like an airhead, but still, she's sweet. I'm just glad I don't have to eat alone in this freaking cafeteria. Food flies through the air, fights break out every minute, and the music's so loud you have to scream to be heard.

When they announce over the PA that there's a music assembly last period for anyone interested in joining the school orchestra, Shavonne slams down a fist. "Alri-i-ight! Let's bail!"

I blink. "You mean cut?"

They break into hysterics, and Kenyatta whaps me on the back. "Girl, you gonna be hangin' with us, you better get your shit together fast!"

"My shit *is* together, and I'm not cutting. Anyway," I say loudly over their shrieks of laughter, "maybe I want to go to this thing."

"Eew, what for? It's or-ches-tra!" Shavonne taunts.

"So what? I like classical music. I listen to it all the time."

"You?" Shavonne hoots, and adds as I glare at her, "Well, you don't look the type to me. More like . . ." She pauses, then lets out a shrill, "Yee-*haw!*" that makes Kenyatta and Monique laugh even harder.

"Hey!" I snap, hugely insulted. "For your information, my dad had a violin. He taught me how to play it when I was, like, five, okay? And I was good at it, too."

Shavonne smirks. "Heh, this I gotta see."

"Well, you can't. I don't have it anymore," I confess.

"Why not?" Monique asks from behind her compact, dabbing a lung-clogging dose of powder on her greasy nose.

All three wait expectantly for my answer.

"My mom burned it," I finally admit.

"She burned your violin?" Kenyatta says in disbelief. "Why?"

"Oh, she was pissed at my dad about something, so she took some of his stuff, threw it in a barrel, poured gasoline all over it, and tossed in a match. She burned the garage down, too," I add carelessly, wondering, how secretly twisted do I have to be to utter this story? "The fire trucks came and everything."

"Wow," Shavonne says in wonder as they all sort of look at me with new respect. "Remind me *never* to fuck with Martha's mom!"

Monique speaks up as she twists open a tube of scarlet lip gloss. "Well, my mom burned my head with a curling iron once.

Gave me a bald spot for a year." Shavonne hurls a half-eaten muffin at her head, and I laugh, really laugh hard, for the first time in days.

Miraculously, Shavonne agrees to come with me to the assembly. We sprawl out in the top bleachers of the gym while the orchestra plays something I actually recognize—"Spring" from *The Four Seasons*. This is the first time I ever heard it played by real people, and the orchestra sounds great, not what you'd expect from a bunch of kids. High-pitched violins shoot out notes so rapidly, I have no idea how anyone can move their hands that fast. The lower-pitched cellos draw the rest of the music together with a deep, soothing hum I can feel deep inside my chest.

"Wow," I whisper, glancing sideways at Shavonne who, already bored, saws at the tips of her gem-studded talons with an industrial-sized emery board. Rubbing away goose bumps, I lean as far forward as I dare without falling out of the bleachers, hypnotized by the stunning sounds below. As the last notes fade away, it strikes me without warning, a mental explosion of truth: Maybe *I* can do this, too!

Shavonne looks up long enough to eye me nervously. "You gonna puke? 'Cause you look sick to your stomach."

My limbs spring back to life. "I'm doing it!"

"What? Wait—"

But I'm already halfway down the bleachers, knocking my way through the crowd. Violin, violin! I wish I could fly over the crowd and be the first in line, because—yes, yes, yes—*I know this could be me!*

But by the time it's my turn, like a hundred kids have already picked the violin. So Mr. Hopewell, grand pooh-bah of the string section, falls all over himself trying to dump a cello off on me.

"No fair," I moan. "I used to *play* the violin."

He squints, reminding me of Dr. Huxtable from *The Cosby Show* with his craggy dark face and lame checkered sweater. "You took lessons?"

"Um, no, but—"

He holds a cello up hopefully, and I think: that big clunky thing? Then I start to remember those low, spooky notes, and cautiously reach out to touch a string . . . *plunk*! And that one single sound, so warm and so beautiful, sends a jolt up my spine, smoldering my brain stem and rippling the skin on my arms.

Never mind Mr. Hopewell's speech about how playing an instrument is a major commitment, blah, blah. Never mind when he says it costs like twenty-five bucks a month to rent one. By the time that note from the cello string has quivered off into thin air, I've made my mind up.

Shavonne shakes her braids. "Girl, you off the hook. That thing's bigger than you."

"No. It's perfect." Now if I can just figure out a way to wring some money out of Momma.

After school, I head off to the projects with Shavonne. Her building, sprayed with graffiti and unnervingly dark in the hall, reeks like a toilet, so I guess she wasn't kidding about the junkies. Inside her apartment, though, everything's bright and colorful, not at all what I expected.

An ancient fluffy cat, purring noisily, rubs her chin on the toe of my shoe. I love cats, but Momma's allergic, and Wayne would probably use the poor thing for target practice.

"That's Josephine. She's even older than me." Shavonne dumps her books and grabs hold of my wrist. "C'mon."

Josephine chases my shoelaces as I follow Shavonne to her room. It's bigger than mine, and she has her own TV with every cable station on earth. One big worktable, cluttered with art supplies, and a tall wooden easel take up most of the space.

I study the paintings and drawings that decorate her walls. "Man, these are awesome! You oughta go to art school or something."

"I know," Shavonne says smugly. None of that aw-shucks stuff for her.

We play around with her makeup and jewelry and hairpieces, and spill our guts with music videos blasting in the background. Shavonne's dad is dead, too, and her mom cleans for some rich family in Shaker Heights. All this makeup and stuff was given to her by her cousin Rodney, a professional drag queen who's halfway through a sex change and now insists on being called Rashonda.

Well, I can't beat the Rodney story, but I do tell her about Momma and how she's missing a few stars from her Lucky Charms. We're having so much fun, I don't even look at the clock till Shavonne's mom rolls in after work, and by then it's seven thirty. "Oh, man. I gotta go."

Mrs. Addams, a shorter, sourer, skinnier version of Shavonne, shakes her head when I tell her where I live and shoves a couple bucks into my hand. "Child, I *know* you ain't walking home by yourself in this neighborhood."

So, wedged next to a sleepy, smelly old lady on the overcrowded bus, I ride to the end of my street, fingering an imaginary bow, plucking invisible strings, and humming snatches of *The Four Seasons* under my breath.

What's funny is that the raggedy lady hums along with me. Every single note, exactly in tune.

## 7

At school, Chardonnay remembers I'm alive, and calls me "bitch" or "ugly girl" whenever she sees me. To be perfectly honest, I'm not the only person she picks on, but, unlike Shavonne, I'm too much of a wuss to fight back. Who wants a ballpoint pen drilled through their eye socket?

But now it's Friday night, start of Labor Day weekend. Wow, no Blubber Butt for three glor-i-ous days! Wayne fires up the grill in the driveway for barbecued chicken, and the cool evening air smells fresh and autumny. I haul my boom box to the garage and play "Hound Dog" over and over till Wayne makes me change over to some stupid hillbilly music.

Wayne's in a surprisingly jolly mood and doesn't seem to mind when Jerome shows up with a pot of baked beans. "From my grandma," he announces, cautiously handing it over to Momma.

"Well, ain't that sweet of her!" Even Momma sounds cheery for once, considering how she's been moping around here for the last few days. "Why don't you ask her to come on down? We got plenty of food. Right, Wayne?" Like she has to check with him first.

Wayne shrugs, poking at the chicken with a giant fork. "Hey, the more the merrier."

Now this makes me suspicious because, as far as I can tell, Wayne never hangs out with the Lindseys. I've never heard him say one nice word about them.

"Um, thanks," Jerome says, equally wary. "But my grandma goes to bed kinda early these days."

We load up our plates to a roaring Garth Brooks, and I mouth Shavonne's *Yee-haw!* when I see how Jerome cringes. We're not the only ones who don't care for this hillbilly soundtrack, either, because a few seconds later an upstairs window grinds open.

"Turn that shit off!" Aunt Gloria screeches down.

Wayne bellows back, jabbing the barbecue fork at the house, "Don't you tell me what I can do in my own friggin' backyard!"

Well, Aunt Gloria proceeds to tell him where he can put his own friggin' backyard, and Wayne tells *her* what she can do with her *own* black ass, back and forth, back and forth, till Aunt Gloria gives up and slams the window shut.

"They do that a lot?" I ask Jerome as we head wisely for the front porch.

"Huh, all the time."

I see a bearded, shriveled old man with missing legs rolling his wheelchair along the curb. He waves feebly at Jerome. "Y'all seen my dog? Seen Ole Marvin 'round?"

"Sorry, Mr. Washington," Jerome calls back, sinking his teeth into a chicken leg.

"Who's that?" I whisper.

"Luther Lee Washington. He stays drunk all the time."

"Maybe I'd stay drunk, too, if I didn't have any legs." I wave my own dripping hunk of chicken. "You want something to eat, Mr. Washington?" He just looks so sad.

With a shake of his grizzly head, the old man pushes off on his wheels. "Naw, thanks, baby. Think I'll keep on lookin' . . ."

"Pitiful," Jerome comments around a mouthful of meat. "That old one-eared dog of his been dead for a month. Got run over downtown."

"Didn't anybody tell him?"

"*You* wanna tell him?"

"Well, no," I admit. "But isn't it kinda mean to let him go on hoping like that?"

"Maybe." Jerome sucks the last bit of meat off a greasy bone before tossing it over the porch rail. "Or maybe not."

The music in the backyard switches over to "Boot Scootin' Boogie," and I can hear Momma and Wayne just a-whooping it up by the garage.

"Oh God, I can't stand this," I wail softly to Jerome.

"Aw, c'mon. They just having a good time."

"Yeah, well, if it was your mo—" I snap my lips shut in the nick of time. No point in bringing up the fact that he doesn't *have* a mom to boot-scoot down the driveway in full view of the whole neighborhood.

Anthony picks that moment to stroll around the corner of the house, all baggy pants and dangling chains, his hair twisted in tight rows from one end of his scalp to the other. "Yo, JoMo, my man! Hangin' with the white chicks now?"

Jerome stops chewing, but stays silent.

"Mind your own business," I suggest, hoping I sound tougher than I feel.

Anthony sends me a dark, dangerous smile, then jams his

hands into his pockets and swaggers off—probably to the Eagle Deli at the end of the street where all the rest of his future convict buddies hang out.

"JoMo?" I poke Jerome with my elbow.

Jerome finally swallows the chicken. "It's like a street name."

"You mean like a gang name?"

"What do you think?" he demands, rolling his eyes.

"Well, you're not in his gang . . . are you?" I ask suspiciously, even though the idea of Jerome in a gang is funnier than hell. Kind of like trying to picture Sister Mary Shavonne taking her final vows.

"I ain't in no kind of gang," he insists, highly offended.

We rock on the squeaky glider and devour the rest of our food while inventing gory, creative ways to annihilate Chardonnay. As the sun begins to sink over the telephone wires and rooftops, sending soft slashes of lavender and pink across the sky, we gather up our trash and wander to the back of the house where we find Mario crouched on the steps, a tear-streaked Bubby squirming on his lap.

"Where you been?" He thrusts the baby at Jerome. "I'm sick of watching this kid. I got stuff to do, man!" And he takes off down the driveway, swaggering like Anthony.

"Damn. I was gonna study," Jerome says with a hopeful lift of his eyebrows.

"Yeah, yeah. I'll take him." I hold out my arms and Bubby climbs into them happily. Jerome, with a grateful glance, rushes up the back steps and into the house.

"Ba-ba-ba," Bubby babbles, snatching my glasses off my nose and jamming them in his mouth. Yikes, just what I need. I shove them back on, then swipe a hunk of chicken from the cooling grill, shred it, and feed it to Bubby one piece at a time. He gobbles it up like he hasn't eaten in days, but I know that's not true. Jerome takes good care of him when he's not in school.

We plop down into the overgrown, weedy grass where Bubby pulls at my ears and my hair and jumps on my stomach. The music is low for a change, something soft, old-fashioned, and kind of yodely . . . oh yeah, Patsy Cline, out a-walkin' after midnight, in the moonlight, yada, yada—and Momma and Wayne sit together in lawn chairs, their hands entwined, heads close together. Momma sees me and waves, and I wiggle my fingers back. Even Wayne sends over what could possibly pass for a smile.

It hits me then how truly happy Momma looks, a whole lot happier than she's looked in a long time. Cheeks pink, crispy yellow hair bouncing in the breeze, her toothy smile bright and beautiful. Wayne slings a tattooed arm around her shoulders as she takes a dainty sip from a can of Pepsi, and then leans into him, giggling, as he whispers something in her ear.

"Ba-ba-*bah!*" Bubby insists, lunging for my glasses again.

I catch his arms and hug him tightly, breathing in his sticky, barbecue baby scent. He squirms and squeals and finally settles down, growing heavier and heavier till he conks out cold. I stretch him out in the cool grass, his head warm on my lap, and watch the sky turn colors, the moon grow bright, the lights blink on in the surrounding windows. Just listening to the music, and wishing like crazy that this one single night could go on forever.

## 8

Momma stays in her jolly mood all weekend, which, strange as it sounds, is why I don't mention my cello. Nothing sets her off like asking her for money. But by Tuesday morning I've put it off long enough, and of course she stares at me like I've suddenly sprung an extra head. "Twenty-five bucks a month! Where am I supposed to get that?"

"I don't know, but—c'mon, Momma, please. I really want to play!"

"Oh, you don't need to be wasting your time like that. You got schoolwork, and your chores, and—"

"No fair! I make straight A's. And look, look! This place is spotless."

She hems and haws. "Mm, I don't know, it's an awful lot of money, and I'm not so sure I want to listen to all that screechin' again."

"What screeching?"

"All that screeching you did on that old fiddle we had."

Yeah, the one you burned! "I didn't screech," I remind her stiffly. "I was good. Everybody said so."

"Well . . ." Momma pauses, and then shocks me with, "Maybe so."

Okay. Suck-up time.

I sidle closer and drape my arm around her fleshy shoulders. I'm not the huggiest person in the world, and she eyes me suspiciously. "Momma, I swear, if you don't like it, you won't even have to hear it. I'll play it in my room. I'll only play when you're not here. But ple-ease let me, please!"

Momma twists her lips and puffs out a sigh. "Well, okay. You can try it. But," she adds before I can rejoice, "you gotta ask Wayne for the money, 'cause I ain't got it."

Damn, damn, damn. Why do I have to go crawling to Wayne?

I bitch about this all the way to school, till Jerome finally says, "So what's the big deal? Go ask him for the money."

"But he's such a creep!"

"Well, either ask him or don't ask him. Just quit whining about it."

So much for moral support.

Shavonne doesn't show up for homeroom, and Chardonnay trills, "Hey, ugly girl! Where's your big-mouthed friend?" when she sees me.

Nervous twitters from the people around me. Gritting my teeth, I pointedly flip open my copy of *Romeo and Juliet*—and a split second later, the book thunks against the chalkboard. I stare at my empty hands, trying to figure out what happened.

"Hey bitch, I'm talkin' to you!"

A red-hot, imaginary curtain drops in front of me as Miss Fuchs flits in and stops, shocked at the stillness. She has no idea how she just saved my life. Chardonnay faces front, the picture of

innocence as I suck air back into my lungs. Now I think I understand why somebody would carry a knife to school. Screw zero
tolerance! Three more years in this snake pit, and I might have to
carry one myself.

Shavonne shows up for English, claiming she overslept.
"Well, thanks a lot," I huff. "I could've used some help."

No sympathy from her, either. "What am I, your body-
guard?"

"No, but—"

"Girl, you want that skank to quit risin' on you, you gotta get
right up in her grill, you know what I'm saying?"

"Um, actually I have no clue what you just said." Sometimes
I think I need a pocket translator around here.

"I'm telling you to fight back."

She makes it sound so easy.

. . .

Jerome, aka Mr. Nuclear Physicist, joined the chemistry club, of
course, and abandons me after school to hit the first meeting.
Miserable and depressed I walk home by myself, my stomach
ripped up from all the stress. I don't even notice Anthony and his
posse hanging out in front of the Eagle Deli till one of them
whistles at me and makes me dodge around a telephone pole to
avoid his grimy paw.

Anthony smacks him. "Cut it out, man. That's JoMo's bitch."
With a shake of his crotch, he adds, "You like dark meat, baby,
don't you?" as his homies fall all over themselves, laughing.

"Freaks!" I blurt out before sprinting off. Ugly boarded-up
buildings rush by me in a blur. Rusted fences, junk cars, and broken pieces of sidewalk. Trees that don't even look like trees anymore, just sad, spindly pieces of wood. I hate this neighborhood!

Gasping for breath through a clog of hair in my mouth, I fly into the house, dive into bed, hug my stomach, and refuse to move for the rest of the day.

. . .

By morning I'm no better. I try to stay home, but Wayne couldn't care less that I might be slowly dying from some massive internal rupture. "Aw, you look fine. Go take a pill or something."

Right, go take a pill. The old Kowalski family motto.

"Where's my mom?" I demand.

"Still in bed. Leave her alone."

"Why? Is she sick?" I glance nervously around, knowing full well that they went out last night after AA and didn't get back till after I was asleep. No beer cans or whisky bottles, so that's a good sign. And yes, I still search for them, every day, everywhere.

Wayne frowns when he notices my gaze. He wouldn't be a bad-looking dude if he lost the tattoos. Oh, and washed his hair, shaved, and bought himself a toothbrush. "What're you looking for?"

"Nothing."

"She's tired out, that's all. We went out dancing last night. Why do you always think the worst about your momma?"

Habit, what else? I make a face and slouch back toward my room, then stop when I remember the most critical thing. This might not be the best time to ask, but if I wait for him to be in a better mood, I might be waiting the rest of my life.

Casually I back up and give him my sweetest smile. "Hey, Wayne? By any chance did Momma talk to you about me taking cello lessons?"

The cigarette almost jumps out of his mouth. "Huh?"

"Cello lessons," I say very slowly. "I need twenty-five bucks a month to rent a cello. Momma says it's okay with her if it's okay with you." I cross my fingers so hard, my knuckles snap.

Silence. Wayne blows a tornado of smoke toward the yellow ceiling. Noticing his empty mug, I trip over my own feet to pour him some fresh coffee. He grins then, and remarks, "You know, I used to play the gee-tar, myself. Had me a band and everything."

I teeter hopefully, faking interest.

"Twenty-five bucks, huh? Well, I reckon we can swing it."

Wow! This just goes to show you, you never know about Wayne. Every now and then, he can really act human.

Outside it's beautiful—warm sun, blue sky, just a hint of a breeze. Jerome trudges beside me, talking incessantly about Mr. Finelli's stupid science project, but all I can think is: I'm getting my cello, I'm getting my cello!

During English, my stomachache grows worse. Maybe I should've eaten breakfast. Maybe I'm getting the flu? Maybe I just need to throw up except, well, it's not exactly *that* kind of sick.

After class, Shavonne and I make a pit stop, and omigod! My mangy old cotton undies are soaked with blood, plus I find a big, obvious splotch on the back of my jeans. How could I not have felt this? And did anyone else notice?

"You stuck?" Shavonne rattles the stall.

"I just got my period." I can't believe it. I've been waiting for this for years. Why did it have to hit me in the middle of English?

"Need a Tampax?"

"Um, don't you have a pad or something?" Shavonne throws one over and I miss the catch, and smack my head on the toilet while I'm groping around. "I gotta go home. It's all over my jeans." Shavonne snickers, and I yell, "Hey, it's *not funny!*"

"Jeez, chill out. What do you want me to tell Lopez?"

"I don't care what you tell her. Tell her I dropped dead."

The halls are almost silent, but halfway to the exit I hear a guard yell, "Hey, you!" I bolt through the door, my back crawling with a sensation of being pummeled by rubber bullets. My beautiful morning sky clouds over rapidly as I rush home on wobbly legs, this weird foreign object shifting between my thighs like a soggy brick.

Wayne's already left for work, and yes, Momma's still in bed. Rummaging through the john, I come up with only two pads. Great.

I jiggle the humongous lump under Momma's covers. "Momma, wake up. I need money." She only grunts. Bending over, I sniff, but all I can smell is her morning breath and the perfume she wore last night. "Momma?"

"Go 'way," she grumbles. "I feel like shit."

"Are you sick?"

"I said get outta here!" She rolls noisily to her other side, yanking the sheet over her matted blond curls.

Okay, not sick, not drunk, so what does that leave? Depressed, dammit. And nasty on top of it.

I give up and raid her purse, but only find two bucks. How much do I need? I have no idea. I picture myself at the store with a bunch of people in line behind me, a box of pads in my hand and a few cents short. Haven't I been humiliated enough for one day?

Well, Aunt Gloria might have some, not that I want to mortify myself any further. Upstairs, I knock softly on the Lindseys' kitchen door. No answer. After a minute I let myself in, wondering if Aunt Gloria keeps a shotgun handy, and how quick she'd be to use it.

Nobody's home. Under the bathroom sink, I find a full box

of Always with Wings, and stuff eight or ten of them under my shirt—and then nearly leap out of my skin when the back door bangs open and heavy footsteps pound up the stairs.

Shit, shit! I fly into Jerome's room but there's no time to hit the window. I squeeze into the cluttered closet one split second before Anthony erupts into the room. Through the crack, I see him slide into home base and shove an arm under Jerome's mattress. He rocks back on his heels, and I hold my breath till he jumps up, rushes out, and stumbles back downstairs.

I count to sixty before slinking out of the closet. Jerome's mattress is crooked, and I tell myself no, I am *not* going to look. I've seen way too many movies about people, usually girls, who can't mind their own business and end up dead. And yet—

I squat next to the bed, hoist the mattress, and feel my eyes pop out at the wad of cash. At least three inches thick, hundred-dollar bills. And sitting right next to it? A gun.

Damn, I knew that guy was up to no good! But now what do I do? Tell Aunt Gloria? Excuse me, ma'am, but I snuck into your house to rip off some pads, and . . .

I'm afraid to leave the gun there, but I'm more afraid to touch it. Why, oh why did I even have to look? Careful not to leave a trail of pads behind me, I clutch my loaded T-shirt, swing my legs over Jerome's sill as thunder cracks overhead, and make it to my room, soaking wet, in record time.

Cramps are coming in waves now, shark's teeth sinking into my innards. I soak in the tub for a solid half hour, then pop three Tylenols and stretch out on the couch.

Momma's in a "mood," I'm on the rag, and I bet everybody in English saw that big red stain on my butt. On top of that, thanks to the rain, the cable just fizzled out.

Life, in general, pretty much sucks.

## •••••• 9 ••••••

I wake up sweating in the middle of the night, jerked out of sleep by the worst nightmare I've ever had—an ear-shattering explosion of springs, stuffing, and flying limbs. Can guns go off by themselves, or is that only in the movies? I picture Bubby poking a chubby arm under the mattress . . . oh, I never should've left it! How stupid was that?

I watch my window turn lighter and lighter, then blow out a sigh when my alarm finally rings. No clean clothes, of course. If *I* don't do the laundry, nobody else around here will. I paw through Momma's musty Goodwill box till I find a top with no stains, no rips, and only slightly yellow armpits.

Momma's sipping coffee in the kitchen. "Nice shirt," she comments sincerely.

I slop coffee into a mug. "Gee, thanks. I like it, too. Especially the BO stains."

Okay, now she notices. "You feelin' okay, sugar pie?"

"Nope. I feel like crap."

"You sick?"

"I'm on the *rag*," I announce, with the right touch of drama.

Momma gasps. "You are? When? Why didn't you say something?"

Boy, you'd think I just got accepted to Harvard. "Well, I'm saying it now, okay? And I need some damn pads."

"I'll pick some up today. You got enough to get you through the day?"

"Barely." No thanks to you.

Momma tilts back in her chair. It creaks dangerously under her weight, and I wish she wouldn't do that. "You're all grown up now, sugar pie, and you know what that means."

"Yeah, it means I'm gonna bleed like a butchered hog for the next forty years." Why does she think I'd be happy about this?

"It means you gotta be, you know, careful. With the boys, I mean. I'm way too young to be raisin' any grandkids"—I roll my eyes—"and what with all those diseases you can catch nowadays"—I roll my eyes even harder. "If you're as smart as you think you are, you'll stay away from the boys. Especially the black ones," she adds, obviously meaning Jerome.

If I roll my eyes any harder, they might pop like a couple of grapes. "Ooh, does that mean I gotta give him back his ring?"

Momma scowls. "You're pretty mouthy today, missy, and I don't like it one bit."

Finally it all rushes out. "Well, you were no help at all! And you didn't have to yell at me and throw me out of your room!"

Momma taps her sugar spoon against her mug of black coffee. "I get down sometimes," she says in a voice I can barely hear. "Some days I don't even like to open my eyes. That ain't nothin' new."

I feel a stab of guilt. "I know, but—well, you stayed in bed all *day*. If you get that depressed, then why don't you . . . you know, go see somebody?"

*Clunk!* The chair drops forward, and she's out of it in an instant. "See who? You mean one of them quacks?"

"Well, maybe they can give you pills or something—"

"They tell me in AA I ain't supposed to take any pills."

"Is that true? Even stuff from doctors?"

With a dirty look instead of a straight answer, Momma clumps off in a snit just as Jerome bangs on the front door.

"I'm running late," I lie through the screen. "Go on without me."

"I can wait," he offers, trying to see behind me.

"No, you can *go*."

"Jee-sus!" He clatters off down the porch steps.

So now that makes two people in a row I've ticked off today.

I wait another few minutes, then scale the fire escape. Jerome's room is empty except for a snoozing Bubby and another juicy roach waddling along the wall. I scoop my arm gingerly under the mattress, hoping not to pull back a bloody stump. I can feel the money, the whole fat wad of it, but nothing else. Heart thudding, I flop up the mattress to be sure.

Nope, it's true. The gun is gone.

. . .

I lurch into homeroom ten minutes late, and Chardonnay greets me with: " 'Bout time you hauled your honky ass in here."

"Shove it, bitch." This from Shavonne, of course.

"Who you callin' a bitch, bitch?" Chardonnay snarls back.

"Ladies! Enough already!" Miss Fuchs glares at me like this is somehow my fault. "Take your seat, Martha. I'm marking you tardy."

The whole class goes, *Ooooooh!* which sends Miss Fuchs into another book-banging hissy as I slide into my seat and slump my chin in my hand—and then *wham!* Chardonnay's gargantuan arm knocks into my elbow, and my jaw almost hits the desk.

My shout startles even me. "Get your freaking hands off of me!"

"Then quit looking at me, bitch."

"I'm *not* looking at you!"

Turning back around, Chardonnay says to the room in general, "One thing I can't stand? Some damn honky-dyke-polack bitch mad-doggin' me all the time."

Honky-dyke-polack bitch. Wow.

Ignoring the fact that doing what I'm about to do means I have a death wish, I poke her three times in the back: "Kiss." *Poke.* "My." *Poke.* "Ass." *Poke!*

The class goes ballistic. Chardonnay tries to leap out of her chair, but the tiny desk gets stuck around her enormous hips. She shakes it loose like a bucking bull. "Whadja say to me? Whadja say to me?"

Shavonne's between us in a flash. "Hey, what's wrong with you? You deaf, too? Or just fat, ugly, and stupid?"

Even slack-jawed Jamal's wide awake for this one. Miss Fuchs snatches up the wall phone, hollering for help while Chardonnay and Shavonne circle like a couple of bulldogs. Even the homeboys in the back are superglued to their seats.

"You best start mindin' your own damn business," Chardonnay snarls. "Or I'm gonna mess you up so bad, your own momma ain't gonna know you."

Shavonne shoots back, "Yeah, so what? You still gonna be uglier."

The door bursts open, two guards rush in, and Miss Fuchs starts to point with a trembling finger: "Her. And her. And that one, too." That last one being me, the innocent bystander—well, except for that one little old slip of the tongue.

They separate the three of us like POWs and I get marched over to my counselor for the official interrogation. Mrs. Bigelow, way past retirement age, frowns at me from the other side of a desk so obsessively tidy, it's obvious they pay her to do squat around here. "I'm very disappointed to see somebody like you down here, Martha."

Somebody like me? I watch her flip through my record, silently moving her frosty pink lips, wondering what would possess a woman this old to dye her hair that particular shade of red, no magenta, no . . . fuchsia? And a plunging neckline might look great on Shavonne, but Mrs. Bigelow's saggy, freckled cleavage makes me want to gag.

"Straight A's, no disciplinary actions . . ." She snaps the folder shut and surveys me sternly. She pencils in her eyebrows, I notice, but apparently missed one today. "However, you seem to have started off on the wrong foot. You left school yesterday without permission . . ."

"I was sick," I butt in.

". . . and now I hear you're picking fights with your class-mates and using profanity."

What—ass? "I used one bad word, and she started it anyway."

"How did she start it?"

"She called me a name." Four of them, actually.

"That's no excuse. This isn't kindergarten, and I'm sure you're mature enough to figure out how to ignore certain people."

"But this isn't my fault! She's been out to get me from day one."

Her turkey neck quivers, and her one eyebrow flies up. "Martha. Now I know you might feel as if you, uh, don't quite fit in here, but . . ."

Blah, blah, blah, and bla-a-ah! She gives me everything except the old sticks-and-stones routine.

". . . so consider this a warning. Next time it'll be a detention. And—!" She raises a pointy fingernail as I raise my butt up off the seat. "If you leave school again without permission, Martha, you may very well be suspended."

Well, fine with me. I deserve a vacation!

## · · · · · **10** · · · · ·

Wayne's waiting in the kitchen when I get up in the morning. He went out last night, without Momma, came home late, and slept on the couch. Shoot me if I'm wrong, but I swear I can smell rancid whisky leaking out of his pores.

"What?" he barks when he sees me sniffing.

"Nothing."

He looks like crap, and it serves him right. He had no business drinking! So much for rehab, right? No wonder Momma's still in bed again. Now she has a *reason* to be depressed.

Biting my tongue, I put on a pot of coffee, go brush my teeth, come back to the kitchen, pour him a cup, and drop it in front of him with a significant *clunk*. He slurps noisily, and lets out a blissful "Ah-h-h!"

I can't be quiet any longer. "Does Momma know you were out drinking?"

"Yep, and I already heard it from her, so don't you start in on me, too."

What I want to do is ask him about that money he promised

me, because Mr. Hopewell wants us to have our instruments by Monday.

"Um . . . Wayne? Remember that cello we talked about? Well, I kinda need it by Monday."

It takes him forever to answer, like he's busy thinking about something else. Then, half in a trance, he whips out his grimy wallet and holds out a pile of green. "Here. This oughta do it."

Wow! I snatch the money out of his hand before he can change his mind.

Mr. Hopewell told us to get our cellos from a music store downtown at Tower City. It's cheaper there, but on Saturdays it's only open from ten till four. I call Shavonne who makes me wait two hours because her mom's braiding her hair, and then we meet halfway and hop the bus to Public Square.

First thing she says is: "Talked to Kenyatta this morning, and guess what? Guess what fat, ugly, foul-mouthed skeeza got her ass knocked up?"

"Shut *up*!"

"Swear to God. Can you even picture it? All that naked, sweaty blubber rolling all over some poor guy . . ."

"Eew, stop." Like I don't see enough of Chardonnay's blubber rolling around in the locker room.

"I mean, how'd he even know where to stick it?" Shavonne screeches as the horrified lady next to us flees to a safer seat.

They say there's someone for everyone. I guess it's really true.

. . .

Down at the music store, the snippy clerk digs up a cello, and only then does she inform me I need a "responsible adult" to sign the contract. "Just routine, dear. In case anything happens to it."

I say in my most responsible way, "Well, ma'am, my mom

couldn't come down here, but I do have the money." I rustle it in her face. "So, like, can I take the contract home and bring it back next week?" It's already two fifteen, and they're not open tomorrow.

"Sorry, dear."

"But I need it by Monday."

"Sorry, dear."

"Sorry, dear," Shavonne mimics. "Yeah, you sound real sorry."

The lady shoots us a granite smile. "Excuse me, but if you don't have any further business in this store, I suggest you leave."

"Hey, we been thrown outta better places than—"

I wrestle her out to the sidewalk. "Sha-vonne! You're gonna make it so that lady never lets me in there again!"

"Yeah, well." She shouts over my head in the direction of the door, "This ain't the only music store in town, ya know!"

Sometimes I wish she'd learn to shut her mouth.

"Come on, come on." I push her along. "Let's go back and get my mom."

Because it's Saturday, we have to wait forever for a bus. I squirm on the curb in front of Tower City, eyeballing a beautiful black coat in the department store window. Oh, I hope Wayne stays in this generous mood for a while. A new winter coat would really be sweet.

I twist Shavonne's wrist so I can peer at her watch: two fifty-five. "Oh Go-o-d! We'll never make it back."

"Chill already."

"I don't want to chill. I want my cello!"

Finally the bus chugs along, but when we get back to my house, Momma and Wayne are nowhere around. I scream my lungs out while Shavonne tries to shush me. "Jeez! No big deal, just go back there on Monday. Whole damn orchestra ain't gonna fall apart."

"Yes, it will!" I kick a chair halfway across the kitchen, then snatch up Wayne's coffee mug and heave it against the wall. Damn him anyway! How come *he* didn't know I'd have to sign a stupid contract?

Shavonne jumps aside as Grandma Daisy hobbles into the kitchen. "Lord have mercy! What's all the racket down here?"

I hug myself, too upset to even speak, as Shavonne blabbers out the problem, and next thing I know, Grandma's jangling her car keys and ordering us into the car "right quick."

She has to slam on the brakes when Aunt Gloria rushes out. "Y'all get outta that car, you hear me? Granny, you know what the doctor said, you too blind to be drivin'!"

"It's an emergency," Shavonne begins, but Grandma Daisy can hold her own.

"I ain't that blind," she snaps. "And girl, I'm gonna run over your foot, you don't step outta my way."

Laughter explodes from Shavonne. Aunt Gloria ignores her, and points a finger at me instead. "You hear what I said? She ain't drivin' you nowhere—now *get out of that car!*"

Grandma Daisy winks at us, then guns the motor and slams the car into reverse. Aunt Gloria has to leap into her own petunias to avoid certain death, and in less than fifteen minutes we're back at Tower City. Ignoring the No Parking signs, Grandma Daisy crunches the front tire against the curb and then limps through the revolving doors, jabbing her cane, poker-faced and dignified.

"I am this child's grandmother," she informs the gawking saleslady. "Now where's that contract at?"

The lady looks at me, then back at Grandma Daisy who

stares right back, eyes fierce and hugely magnified behind her bifocals. "May I see some identification?" She squints at Grandma's driver's license. "Ma'am, this expired four years ago."

Grandma Daisy thumps a bony fist on the counter. "You see that picture? That look like my face? Good, that's all you need, 'cause I ain't here for no driving test. Now you hand over that paper and give this little girl her cello, or things're gonna get ugly around here fast."

The saleslady believes her, and Grandma Daisy signs her name to the three-month contract. At the very last second, I spy a blond girl with a cello on the cover of a CD, bow frozen in mid-air, so I snatch it up and pay for it out of what's left of Wayne's money. Then I wrap my arms happily around the big plastic cello case—*a coffin with a handle* is Shavonne's opinion—and lug it to the car.

"Thank you, thank you!" is all I can say, but Grandma Daisy waves me off, wrenches the steering wheel, and aims the car into a snarl of horn-blowing traffic. Shavonne shrieks as we barely miss the front end of a Hummer, but I hardly notice. I'm too busy hugging my cello case, and thinking about Monday.

Momma and Wayne have been gone all night long. To keep myself from totally freaking out, I spend Sunday on the couch listening to my new CD. The blond girl is somebody named Jacqueline du Pré and wow, the music almost has me gasping for breath. Edward Elgar's *Cello Concerto in E Minor*. So beautiful, and so sad, it actually hurts me to listen—but is it the music itself or just the amazing way she plays? Is this something you can learn to do, or do you have to be born with it?

Born with it, I bet. But how do you know if you are?

By the next morning, still no sign of Momma or Wayne. To Jerome's immature amusement, I lug my new cello the whole thirty blocks to school and store it in the music room where Mr. Hopewell swears it'll be safe. Well, it better be safe or Grandma Daisy'll skin me alive.

Instead of a last period study hall, I now have music class. This is just for strings, and there's only like ten of us in the room. So what happened to the other thousand who signed up for the violin? Guess that twenty-five bucks a month weeded most of them out.

Mr. Hopewell, the Bill Cosby clone, goes over each instrument piece by piece. Then he walks around, and, one by one, twists our limbs into the correct positions for our instruments. Mine goes between my legs, so lucky thing I'm wearing jeans.

"Relax," Mr. Hopewell says with a chuckle, but when I lean into the chair, he pokes me in the back. "And sit up straight. No slouching." So which is it, relax or sit up straight?

We try a few notes, and the first ones sound *awful*, like a garbage truck, maybe, rolling over a raccoon. But the stuff my dad taught me dribbles back into my memory, and—wow—I'm playing this thing! Actually churning out real notes. Well, sort of.

Mr. Hopewell notices. "Not bad, Martha," is his only comment, but it's the way he says it that thrills me to the bone. "Okay, people, listen up. I want you all here every Monday, Wednesday, and Friday one hour before the first bell. This is not negotiable." He gives me a thumbs-up, probably because I'm the only one not groaning.

Back home the house is still deserted, and I'm having visions of an orphanage right out of *Oliver Twist* with cold gruel, vicious bedbugs, and nightly beatings. Jittery and distracted, I try to concentrate on my cello, holding it with perfect posture, applying the exact amount of pressure to the heavy strings. But now the bow feels clunky and awkward, and my notes screech eerily in the silent house.

I heave the bow onto my bed. "Goddammit. Where *are* you guys?"

My mind spits out the worst-case scenarios: Car accident? Kidnapping? Murder, or even worse, one of those murder-suicide things? I check Wayne's gun cabinet to see if anything's missing, as the black hole in my stomach grows bigger and deeper.

What'll I do if they never come back? Last time she dumped

me, I ended up in that group home with all those freaky, pathetic kids. Oh, please, no way do I want to go *there* again!

. . .

Tuesday and Wednesday pass without a word. Wayne's job calls twice, and I put on a fake-Momma voice and jabber about some family emergency. A suspicious Grandma Daisy starts inviting me to dinner—good thing, too, since we were low on groceries even before Momma took off—and Aunt Gloria glares at me, biding her time, setting traps. Every night when I go to bed, I lie there in the dark, trying to sleep, but imagining the worst.

Finally, Wednesday night, I can't stand it any longer. Leaving the TV on to ward off burglars, I sneak up the fire escape to spend the night upstairs. Bubby cuddles with me on Jerome's bed, while Jerome takes the floor with minimal bitching.

"You sure your aunt won't come in?" Already I'm shaking at the thought.

"She never comes in here at night."

"Who takes care of Bubby if he wakes up?"

"Who do you think?"

I tickle Bubby's belly. "Are you my wittle baby? Are you my wittle cuddly-wuddly baby boo?" Bubby giggles and wrenches my nose hard. "Ow!"

"Can't you go stay with some relatives?" Jerome's voice floats up from the floor.

I snort. "I don't know any of my relatives, and they wouldn't want me, anyhow."

"How come?"

" 'Cause my dad had to drop out of college when my mom got pregnant with me. He was gonna be a music teacher, and he ended up working in some factory. I guess they disowned him or something." That's what I've always been told—that, and that my dad always thought he was so much better than Momma. The same thing, I might add, she always accuses me of. "Anyway, I never met my dad's family. My mom hates their guts."

"Do you miss your dad?" Jerome asks unexpectedly.

The only sound is the ticking of the clock, and a tiny snore from a suddenly limp, heavy Bubby.

"I can't hardly remember him," I say at last, curling my arms around Bubby and snuggling him close. "But yeah, I think I do. You miss your folks?"

"Well, my mom, yeah. It's stupid, but I do."

"Why is it stupid?"

Another long silence. "My mom's a junkie. She had Bubby in jail, and then, when she got out, she just never came back. And I don't even know who my dad is. I never met him in my life."

Man! I prop myself up on one elbow. "You never told me that."

"Maybe I don't feel like broadcasting it, okay? Bad enough I gotta put up with Aunt Gloria and Anthony and all that drinking they do, and all that pot and other stuff they think I don't know about, and—"

We hear a sound in the hall as someone, maybe Aunt Gloria herself, struts past the door. She stops, like she's listening, and we both hold our breath so long, it's a miracle we don't suffocate.

By the time the footsteps fade away, neither of us feels like talking anymore. Besides, Bubby just peed on me, so what do I do now?

## ●●●●● 12 ●●●●●

Thursday evening I ferret through Momma's room, looking for money. I find some change in a coat pocket, a couple of singles on the dresser, and a Ziploc bag full of pot under a pile of Wayne's undershirts. Wow, what a shocker.

Friday after school, I load up on books at the neighborhood library, avoiding anything with a picture of a screaming woman on the cover, or anything by Koontz or King, my two gruesome favorites. A fantasy trilogy and a couple of old-lady mysteries ought to take my mind off of Momma for a while.

Back home, I find the Lindseys' rent check taped to the kitchen door. I peel it off, then instantly freeze, sensing a demonic presence.

"Where they at?" Aunt Gloria demands in my ear.

I spit my heart out of my mouth. "W-Who?"

"You know who!" Jostling me aside, she barges in, searching for body parts and traces of blood. All she sees, though, is a very clean kitchen, bright and sparkling and smelling like lemony Pine-Sol. "I ain't paying no rent money to some smart-mouthed child, that's for sure."

I force myself not to look at the check. Rent money! Wonder if I can cash it . . .

Squinching her forehead, she marches into the living room to survey Wayne's gun cabinet, hands on her hips. "Mm, mm, mm."

I decide not to bring up the fact that she's trespassing, and that if Wayne does show up, he'll pump her full of buckshot. "They're out of town," I say lamely.

"Till when?"

"Till, um . . . till Monday."

"Fine. They ain't back by Monday, I'm reporting this bull-shit. I don't need no child burnin' the whole damn house down around my head." She snatches the check out of my fingers. "And I'll give this to your *daddy* when he gets back."

"He's not my daddy," I snarl, forgetting to be scared.

Aunt Gloria sails out with a snort. The instant she's gone, I slap the chain on the door, then ball up on the couch and munch my nails. First the cops, then the social workers, and then I'll be adopted out—to who, some pervert with a photo studio in his basement?

Where is she? *Where is she?* Oh, I can picture Momma perfectly, laid out in a satin dress, in an ivory-colored coffin, pale hands folded sweetly over a wooden cross—no, wait, not a cross, maybe a single white lily . . . omigod, omigod! Please let her be okay!

The evening drags like a crippled rabbit. I listen to Elgar again, then put on some cartoons, conk out around midnight, and by four a.m. I'm hopelessly wide awake. I take out my cello and work on my notes, but the screeching of the strings makes the roots of my teeth throb. Still, I keep at it, ignoring the occasional warning thump on the ceiling, till my body aches, my fingers flare into torches . . . and just as I'm getting the hang of it, I hear the front door clatter open, and Momma's "Yoo-hoo!"

She's alive! I race to the living room where she sweeps me into a hug. She kind of stinks, but not like booze. More like someone who hasn't seen the inside of a bathtub in a week.

I hold my nose as she smothers me, then chisel her off when it gets to be too much. "Where *were* you all week? Why didn't you call me? I was freaking out! That bitch upstairs wanted to call the cops, and there's no food in the house, and *I can't believe you did this to me!*" Seconds ago I was so happy to see her. Now I'd like to punch her lights out.

"Oh, sugar pie, I'm so sorry. But Wayne, he took it in his head to drive down to West Virginia to see his daddy, and I thought we'd only be gone a couple days, but . . . well, Wayne, he and his daddy got into a fight and then he kinda went off on a bender, and then I couldn't get back, and his daddy don't have a phone, and . . ." She stops to blow her nose. "I'm real, real sorry."

"Momma, you can't just take off whenever you feel like it!" Why do I always feel like I'm the mom around here? "And where's Wayne anyway?"

Momma's face crumbles again. "Last I heard, he got picked up for drunk driving and was lookin' for somebody to bail him out. Not me," she adds, lifting her chins. "I hooked up with some real nice AA folks down there, and they passed the hat to get me the bus fare home. And you'd be proud of me, sugar pie, 'cause when I saw Wayne like that, and how damn nasty he got? Well, I told him it was me or the booze. And he picked the booze."

I start to ask why the AA folks didn't let her use *their* phone—but then her bottom lip quivers and she heaves out a shuddering breath. Poor Momma. It's not her fault Wayne turned out to be such a pathetic jerk!

"Well, never you mind," she insists, squeezing my hand. "We can do without him just fine. First thing today, I'm gonna go look for a job. There's a nursing home right close. Maybe I could be a nurse's aide again." I wait for her to notice how nice the house looks, but she flips back her dirty hair and trudges to the kitchen. "So what's to eat around here?"

Duh, if there wasn't any food here a week ago, why would we have any now? So she roots around in her purse and hands me a food card. "I'm not using that! Don't you have any real money?"

"No, I don't. A lady from AA gave me this, and it's just as good as money."

"But—"

"No buts. And if I don't find me a job real soon, we're gonna end up on welfare anyhow, so you might as well get off your high horse and get used to the idea." Ah, there she is, the Momma I know and love.

"What if Wayne doesn't come back?" Worse, what if he comes back and kicks us both out?

"I ain't worryin' about that now. All I know is, money's gonna be tight for a while. No more luxuries, sugar pie."

Luxuries? What luxuries? Food? Hot water? Toilet paper?

I spin the card across the table. "Forget it, Momma. I'm not using this thing in public."

With a hefty sigh and a pitiful shake of her head, Momma says for the thousandth time, "Martha, Martha. I swear, you are just—"

"Like my dad," I finish glumly. "Yeah, I know."

## •••••• **13** ••••••

Crusty-eyed and exhausted from lack of sleep, I show up for cello practice at six forty-five. Mr. Hopewell stares in horror at my swollen fingertips. "What've you been doing?"

I yank away my hand. "Practicing, like you said."

"I didn't tell you to turn your fingers into ground meat. And stop biting your nails. People'll see your hands, and nobody wants to look at that."

I'm starting not to like this man very much.

We work for a while on tuning our instruments. I seem to be the only one in the room who doesn't need the piano to do it—"perfect pitch," Mr. Hopewell calls it, which doesn't win me any friends. Then, one by one, we have to show him our "progress." He listens to me for an extra minute, and changes his tune. "Well, well. Very good. Keep it up, Martha."

I get dirty looks from the kids around me, but I just smile and forgive him for picking on my nails. When the bell rings, I gather up my stuff in a daze and lock up the cello. Wow, does he mean it? Does he really think I'm good?

Lost in a daydream, I forget to stay alert. A foot hooks my

ankle, my books go flying, and then I'm staring at the floor an inch away from my nose.

"Sorry 'bout that, ugly girl." That same foot pokes my ribs. "Next time get outta my way."

Chardonnay's halfway down the hall by the time I figure out what happened. Knees throbbing, I gather up my scattered books and stagger to homeroom—and there she is again, lurking outside the door. Grinning, she flicks a pen against her mossy teeth. No dinky little Bic for this honky bitch, baby. This one's a super-sized, industrial-strength, eight-buck Dr. Grip, chiseled razor-sharp, no doubt, and laced with cyanide.

"This ain't a good day for you to be here," she says conversationally. "Maybe you better take your skinny ass on home."

I take my skinny ass down to the office instead, and Mrs. Bigelow is not thrilled to see me. "Chardonnay tripped me in the hall and now she's threatening to stab me."

"Stab you? Did you see a weapon?"

"Yes. I mean no. I mean, she's got a pen in her hand."

"A pen." Good thing teachers can't smack us. "Martha, go back to class."

So I go back to homeroom, and peek through the door to see Chardonnay slouched at *my* desk, her big, smelly feet propped up on her own. Well, that does it! Keeping an eye out for the guards, I slink out a door. I am not spending another second in this asylum.

"What're you doing home?" Momma demands when I limp in.

"Um, it's a holiday," I stammer. "I forgot all about it."

"What holiday?"

National Save-A-Honky's-Chicken-Ass Day? ". . . Kennedy's birthday."

Momma nods wisely, gulps her coffee, and waddles out with me on her heels. She pulls on a bright pink dress, then peels it off in disgust. Next she tries to squeeze into a purple pantsuit, split-ting the back seam. "What am I gonna wear today?" she wails.

"Where you going?"

"I already told you. I gotta find me a job, remember?"

Squirming with embarrassment, I watch her stuff her rolls into a foofy green frock that might've been fashionable when Elvis ruled the airways. She rips this one off, too, and then glow-ers at me like it's my fault she's about as big as Jabba the Hut. "What?"

"Momma, I hate that school!" I burst out. "Do I have to go back there?"

"Martha, everybody hates school. Why do you think *I* dropped out?"

Well, that's reassuring.

"If those black kids are giving you a hard time, you just let me know. I'll go down to that school myself and set 'em straight."

"It's not that. It's just one person, that girl I told you about."

"So why's she picking on you?"

"How would I know?" I yell. "Because she's a fat ugly bitch?"

I never should have used the word "fat."

"People can't help what they look like, missy. Maybe if you tried to get along with this girl, she wouldn't be houndin' you all the time."

Oh, gee, now why didn't *I* think of that?

. . .

When Jerome gets home that afternoon, I sneak upstairs for a lit-tle sympathy. He's no help, either. "Well, you can't keep cutting school. You want to flunk out?"

"So what am I supposed to do, let her stab me in the eye?"

"Maybe talk to Mr. Johnson?" Mr. Johnson's our principal, a bald-headed troll with hideously bad breath.

"Great. Then I'll really piss her off."

"Either that, or *you* stab *her*. Hell, I'll even hold her down," he offers, and I'm nice enough not to point out that Chardonnay undoubtedly could mash him flat with one thumb.

Bubby, tired of being ignored, crawls into my lap, pinches my neck, gives me a sloppy kiss, and manipulates my face. I squeeze him close, and that's when the door blasts open.

"You again?" Aunt Gloria bellows. "You get back downstairs where you belong!" She descends on us all, rips Bubby away from me, and throws him roughly into the crib. "And how many times I gotta tell you to stay in there?"

"Stop!" My body lunges forward, propelled by an alien force, but Aunt Gloria hauls off and slugs me in the head. I never saw it coming, and it stops me cold. Jerome leaps between us, but that only makes her madder.

"You in for it now, fool!" She grabs a hanger and starts swinging, and even though I duck, I get a good whack on the shoulder. Jerome, on the other hand, isn't as fast, or as lucky. With Aunt Gloria's next wallop, he gets it in the face.

"Get—out!" she screams at me.

Jerome shoves me toward the window as the coat hanger whizzes. "Go, Martha. Go, go, *go!*" I'm barely over the sill before Aunt Gloria slams the window hard enough to crack the glass, and I land in my own room with my skull still vibrating.

I sink to my knees and stick my fingers in my ears, trying to block out the sound of Bubby's screams. Is she hitting him, too? I don't want to know! Hell, all the times Momma smacked me around in the past, at least she never used a freaking weapon on me.

Something has to be done about that bitch! But what can *I* do? Momma will tell me to mind my own business, and Wayne doesn't give a rat's ass about the Lindseys.

God, I wish we were back in our old house. I don't mean that last slum we lived in, or the one before that, or before that. I mean our real house down in Spencer, way out in the country where we used to live before Daddy gambled everything away. Big house, big rooms, and a big backyard. And best of all? We didn't share any of it with anyone, and especially not with some crazy person who beats her kids with a wooden hanger.

. . .

In the morning, I scribble a note for Miss Fuchs—*Please excuse Martha for her absence yesterday. She was very ill!!!*—then dress quickly and grab a stale donut. Outside, the bump on Jerome's cheek gleams like a lavender golf ball.

All he mumbles is, "She was high again. She didn't mean it."

"You oughta report her to someone! Can't your grandma do something?"

"She's scared."

"She doesn't act scared to me," I argue, remembering how Grandma Daisy almost mowed Aunt Gloria down with the car.

"Well, she is. Everybody's scared. Well, not Anthony," he adds truthfully. "He ain't scared of nothin'. And he knows his mom's crazy."

Yeah, 'cause he has a gun, I almost say—but then I'd have to explain what I was doing in Jerome's room.

I sigh. "Well, I guess we all have crazy moms. Maybe we oughta start a club."

"Mine's not crazy," Jerome says testily. "She's an addict, okay?"

"Sor-ry." What the hell's the difference?

"She used to take me places, you know, like to the park, to the pool. Man, I wish she'd come back," he adds fiercely, "and kick Aunt Gloria's ass. She never did drugs till Aunt Gloria got her started. And she never once hit me, not one single time."

We're almost to school when, like an omen, a bus rumbles by with a sign on the side: Report Child Abuse. Call 1-800-4-A-CHILD. I look Jerome straight in the eye, but he doesn't say a word. He really doesn't have to. That silence of his is a whole lot worse.

## ••••• **14** •••••

Good news: Momma did get that nurse's aide job, so now she works till midnight every night and goes to her AA meetings every morning. For the whole month of October, there's no word from Wayne, not even a phone call warning us to get our butts offa his land. What do they call people like us? Oh, yeah—squatters.

Momma's mad because Aunt Gloria refuses to hand over the rent check. And when Momma's mad, I'm the one who suffers.

"I ain't shelling out another dime for that thing!" is what I get one morning when I mention, quite nicely, that my cello contract expires in twenty-two days.

"Momma, I can't just quit. Can't you make it, you know, kinda like an early Christmas present for me?"

"Early, late, it don't make no difference, I ain't got the money, and I sure ain't thinking about Christmas. Now I don't want to hear another word about it!"

"Fine!"

. . .

At lunch, Shavonne and Kenyatta and Monique exchange class pictures, and I have nothing to give them because Momma didn't buy mine. Even Aunt Gloria paid for Jerome's, and she's not even his mother.

"Jerome gave you his picture?" Shavonne whips the wallet-sized photo away before I barely have it out of my backpack. "Damn, that is one fine-lookin' dude when he take off them ugly glasses." She flips the picture over and scribbles XOXO on the back.

"Hey!" I grab it back. "Not funny, Shavonne!"

The whole table cracks up, and Kenyatta insists, "Oh, c'mon, we all know he likes you. You bringing him to the party tonight?" Her Halloween party, she means.

"That is so not true," I argue, my face growing hot. "And no, I'm not bringing him." Jerome can't come anyway. Friday nights are Aunt Gloria's binge nights. He can't trust her around Bubby, not even with Grandma Daisy in the house.

After school, Jerome dumps me for Chem Club again, and I must look like a bag lady tromping down the sidewalk, lugging my cello case and grumbling out loud. I didn't even *want* my class picture, but that's not the point. Shavonne's mom, I bet, spends every nickel she makes on Shavonne. All those clothes? All that art stuff? I'm lucky to get lunch money. Momma ought to be glad I'm playing the cello, and not screwing around with guys or jabbing dirty needles into my veins.

The air is crisp and smells of burning leaves, and for once this shabby old neighborhood doesn't seem quite as shabby, or even as old. Afternoon sunshine glints on each house, bathing every witch and every pumpkin in a splash of gold. I love Halloween, and man, do I need this party tonight!

Anthony's hanging out on the front porch when I make it home. He squints at my cello case. "Yo, girlfriend. Whatcha got there?"

I am so-o not in the mood. "Excuse me. I'd like to get into my house."

He spreads his legs, blocking my way. Patiently, I wait. Why should I have to go around back?

"C'mon, Anthony. I got a ton of homework to do." At his puzzled look, I add, "You know—*homework*? That's the stuff you do when you go to school. You, like, get graded on it and everything." Blabber, blabber. God, what am I saying?

"Smart girl. Betcha make straight A's." He grapples for a cigarette and nods at my cello. "How much that cost you?"

Losing patience, I try to push past him. Unfortunately, he gets right in my face.

"Hey, don't you go shoving on me. All I done is ax you a question, so why you gotta act all ugly and shit?" Smoke curling into his nostrils, he pushes a twenty-dollar bill into my chest. "Give you twenty for it."

I say nothing.

"Okay. Forty."

"It's not for sale. I'm only renting it."

"What? You think 'cause I ain't no white-bread smart-ass like you, I can't appreciate good music? Dang. And you a stone fox, too." He reaches out, but his hand stops in midair as his gaze locks into mine. Too late I remember that when you meet a mad dog, the last thing you want to do is make threatening eye contact. "Now why you gotta act like such a cold-hearted bitch for? You gonna hurt my feelings."

I gauge the distance between myself and the door. Three feet, maybe four . . .

"Double or nothin'." He whips out more bills and dangles them under my nose.

"Are you deaf? I said it's not even my freakin' cello. Now get out of my way and let me into my house!"

With a knowing smile, he steps aside in a leisurely way. "Ain't your fuckin' house no way," he reminds me as I squeeze past, accidentally thunking him with my case. With a piglike grunt, he jerks on my ponytail. "Better watch yourself, girlfriend—and keep your skeezy ass out of my brother's room."

Does he know I saw the money? That I know about the gun? Where is it, anyway? Does he have it on him right now?

Ripping my hair away, I scramble into the house, smash down the deadbolt, and then scream with shock when his face pops up in the window. After a slow, significant smile, he dissolves out of sight.

## ⦁⦁⦁⦁⦁ **15** ⦁⦁⦁⦁⦁

Momma's working tonight, so I scarf down a pizza pocket and race through my homework so I won't be stuck with it over the weekend. I grab my stuff and head over to Shavonne's who, by the way, came up with the most spectacular idea for our costumes—we're going as each other!

I make it there before dark, and we have the place to ourselves because her mom's at work, helping to cater some big fancy dinner. Shavonne spends two full hours twisting my hair into long braids and slathering me with pitch-black mascara. Her cousin Rodney/Rashonda, the ultimate drag queen, generously donated a few tubes of professional greasepaint, guaranteed not to melt under the hottest of stage lights. I paint her a peachy-pink, and she paints me a chocolate-pudding brown.

"I can't believe I'm gonna wear this thing in public," she complains, pulling my *South Park* T-shirt down over one of Rodney/Rashonda's curly wigs and tucking it into her jeans.

Me, I'm in a low-cut sweater and skimpy skirt, the best things I've found in that Goodwill box so far, topped off with

Shavonne's black, lace-up, high-heeled dominatrix boots. I gloss up my lips for good measure, and gape at myself in the mirror.

"You need to accessorize," she informs me critically. "Hey, let's pierce your ears! Lemme go grab some ice—"

"Do I look like an idiot?" I duck as she throws me a pile of colored Mardi Gras beads followed by a bracelet, a leather choker, and a tarnished silver ring with a big black stone. "Wow. This is, um, pretty ugly."

"Hey, it's a mood ring. I found it in a junk store."

I slip it on my finger and wait. The stone stays black. "Well, you got ripped off."

"Naw, black just means you in a real shitty mood. Let's booze you up and then see what color it turns."

"I don't drink," I say quickly, knowing Momma would kill me if she knew I was even thinking about it.

Shavonne flips a pair of her mom's glasses, minus the lenses, onto her newly-pink nose. "Yeah, you do," she insists, shoving me toward the door.

. . .

Kenyatta lives in a huge, crumbling stone house a few blocks away. Her folks, if they exist, are nowhere in sight. Made up like an exotic African princess, she waves a bottle of vodka in my face. "Help yourselves, sluts," she offers, and grins at my plunging neckline. "Dang, you got titties! I never woulda guessed."

I spy a keg of beer on the kitchen table, surrounded by liquor bottles. "Um, you got any pop? I took an antihistamine."

Shavonne glares. "Bullshit. This is a party, okay? Not some Girl Scout meeting."

"Yeah, c'mon," Kenyatta argues. "Live it up for once!"

Monique, in skintight gold spandex and a bone-chilling blond

Afro, cheerfully swats my back. "Yeah, get down! I'm five drinks ahead of y'all!"

Boy, all that peer pressure stuff they warn you about. Just say no, Martha. Be your own person, Martha. Well, I am my own person, but I still want to try it. Believe it or not, I've never even tasted a beer. Besides, *I* am not Momma. I, at least, know how to exercise self-control. I came here to have fun, dammit. Who wants to drink Pepsi?

So, armed with two vodka and orange juices, I follow Shavonne down to the crowded basement where we're greeted by deafening music and wall-to-wall bodies. It's dark as hell, not that I can see much anyway. I left my glasses at Shavonne's so I wouldn't destroy the illusion.

Shavonne immediately jumps into a dance with TyShawn, one of our homeroom homeboys, so I gulp my first drink down and then stand there alone, wobbling in my boots, sipping daintily on the second.

A vampire materializes, spits out his fangs, and tucks them secretively under his black vinyl cape. "Wanna dance?"

I'd rather not touch the hand he just spit into, but luckily this is a fast dance. I swallow the rest of my second drink as he pulls me over, and I rock and shake and really get into it. Dizzy or not—wow, I feel great!

The music switches to a slower song, and I find my nose smooshed into the vampire's sweaty chest. "What's your name, baby girl? I'm Maurice."

Trying to avoid his onion-dip breath, I scream over the music, "*Martha!*"

"Martha, yeah baby, you look swe-e-et to-o-night!" He strokes my long braids, then drops his hand down to grab hold of my butt.

Whoa! I shove my plastic cup under his nose. "Do you mind getting me another screwdriver?" Maybe I can hide while he's gone.

With a stupid grin, he dashes off. Tugging my pantyhose out of my butt, I wonder what the chances are of stealing TyShawn away from Shavonne. He's way cuter than Maurice—square-jawed, puppy-dog eyes, big, sexy lips to die for—and I bet he has nicer breath.

Too late. Maurice is back, dragging me into another dance. As I hold my plastic cup high, I can feel him rubbing against my skirt, and—holy shit, tell me I'm imagining something hard and strange knocking into my hip bone.

Do I panic? Do I scream? Do I slam him with my knee? Nope, and here's why: because the liquor kicks in, and suddenly I don't care.

Don't care that Maurice is blowing onions into my nose.

Don't care that his woody's whacking my thigh.

Don't care about anything except dancing my butt off. I gulp the last of my drink, flip the cup over my head, and grab Maurice's skinny shoulders—and the next thing I know, I'm down on a couch with an extra tongue in my mouth, and omigod, I am so—not—*that* drunk! I hammer his head and pull at his ears, and a second later I'm on the floor with no idea how I got there.

"You sneaky bitch! What you doin' with my babydaddy?"

Music rips to a stop. Lights shoot on. I'm still not sure who threw me on the floor, but I think it's very likely my tailbone's busted. Towering over me is one wildly irate Chardonnay. Maurice, right on cue, babbles like a lunatic. "You got it all wrong, baby, this ho come on to *me!*"

"Why, you lying little shit!" I yell up from the concrete.

Confused, Chardonnay freezes. "What the fuck?"

Should've kept my mouth shut.

"Girl, I *know* that ain't your honky self under all that shit," she growls, squinting down into my face.

"Hey," Kenyatta interrupts. Bravely, she gives Chardonnay one teeny-tiny push. "Ain't nobody invited *you* here, bitch!"

Well, that sets her off, and she starts F-ing this, F-ing that, saying stuff like, How dare I mess with her baby's daddy, huh? Astonished, I stay glued to the floor, trying to absorb this, till Chardonnay grabs my braids and hauls me to my feet. Outraged, and strangely unafraid, I snatch a handful of her own ratty weave, and let go in horror when I feel it tear away from her scalp.

Mightily pissed, hair askew, Chardonnay tosses me aside with no effort at all. I see the knife in her hand before I even catch my breath—but then TyShawn steps forward along with his posse. "Hey, didn't you hear what our hostess said?" he demands as Shavonne darts over to jerk me to my feet. "Your name ain't on the guest list, ho."

"I ain't lettin' no white girl mess around with *my* man!" Chardonnay screams.

"White?" Dead-meat Maurice stares first in my direction, then down at the greasepaint all over his hands.

Ignoring Chardonnay's rapid-fire threats and obscenities, TyShawn and his homies hustle her upstairs with naughty Maurice following far behind. Nobody comes back. And now that my happy buzz has been obliterated, all I want is to get out of here myself.

Dodging trick-or-treaters, keeping our eyes peeled for trouble, Shavonne and I kick our way through the crunchy leaves back to the projects. At the door of her apartment, she whips open her jacket to show me the full bottle of Kahlúa she ripped off from Kenyatta.

"Man, what are you? Some kind of klepto?"

"You see her stash? She ain't even gonna miss it."

Inside, she dumps the Kahlúa into a pitcher of milk, and we curl up on her bed, arguing over which movie to watch. She wants *The Color Purple*—*the* most depressing movie ever made!—and I want *Lord of the Rings*, one of my favorites. We grudgingly decide on *When Harry Met Sally*, and by the time we get to the part where Sally fakes an orgasm in the restaurant, we're plastered again.

"Heh, that could've been me tonight, with TyShawn. Or you and Maurice!" Shavonne lapses into a fit of evil laughter.

"Gross!" I yell, slopping more Kahlúa into my glass. The memory of Maurice's tongue snaking over my teeth makes me want to run to the bathroom and gargle with bleach. And what was with that rock in his pants? Do guys do that all the time and not even care if we notice? "Hey, did you know Maurice was Chardonnay's boyfriend? You could've warned me, you know."

"Girl, I was busy with TyShawn. That heifer hadn't shown up when she did? I mighta gotten me a real piece of that fine brother's black booty." She smacks me on the back as I sputter Kahlúa. "You okay?"

Oh, I'm more than okay. I feel warm and happy, and very, very heavy, my arms and legs filled with liquid sand, and everything we say only cracks me up more. I tell her about Aunt Gloria, how she chased me with a hanger and then busted Jerome's window trying to slam it on my ass. I even act it out, and Shavonne laughs so hard she rolls off the bed. That gives me a perfect view of her alarm clock: ten thirty-five. "Crap. I better go." I reach down to pull off a boot, but she waves me off.

"Naw, you can gimme 'em back on Monday. Heh, let your

momma wonder what you *really* been up to tonight. You can keep that ugly-ass ring, though."

"Really? Aw-w, thank you!" Ugly or not, what a sweet present! I throw my arms around her and squeeze her neck till she chokes. "Oh, I *lo-ove* you, Shavonne!"

"Girl, you wasted! Want me to walk you halfway?"

"Why, so both of us can get raped and murdered?" Again we lose it, howling with laughter as she follows me outside where I instantly plunge down the steps.

Shavonne drops beside me. "How you gonna walk home like this?"

Dizzy and sore, I check for damage as a pair of headlights swoop by, and two car doors slam. Seconds later, I hear footsteps approaching.

"Shit, my old lady and her boss." Shavonne jumps up, trying to block me from view. "Hi, Ma."

Silence. All I can see are two pairs of feet—clunky white work shoes and men's shiny black loafers—that seem to multiply in front of my eyes. My glasses are in my purse, but I don't think that's the problem.

"I ain't even gonna ask what devilishness you two been up to." Mrs. Addams's tone is highly constipated. "Child, you get up offa the ground before I haul you up by, well, whatever you call that mess on top of your head."

I try to say "braids" but hiccup instead. I picture myself all covered in brown paint, smelling like Momma after a two-day bender, and start to giggle—but then my stomach cramps up and the giggle turns into a groan.

"Hey, Mr. Brinkman." Shavonne nudges me with her toe but I refuse to budge. One false move and I'll puke for sure. "This is my friend, Martha, um . . . Martha . . ." She can never remember my last name.

Mrs. Addams stares pure poison down her nose at me. "Your momma picking you up?"

Still counting the shoes, I shake my head, and then two large male hands fling me up off the ground. The world spins. The puke rises even further. "Never mind. I'll drive her home after I pick up Nikki."

Mrs. Addams whirls on Shavonne who's trying to skulk back into the house. "Sweet Jesus, I oughta wear you out!"

Gripping my sticky brown arm, the man leads me to his car and opens the back door. "I'm not allowed to do this," I mumble, collapsing into the leather seat. "Go for rides with strange men."

"Well, tonight you don't have much of a choice." Switching on the light, he stares at his brown-smudged hand. "What *is* this stuff?"

"Makeup," I answer meekly, squinting against the glare. "Sorry."

"Well, try not to get any on the upholstery." Too late, mister. Over his shoulder he asks where I live, and it takes me a second to remember my address. "First I have to run by the Palace to pick up my daughter. I'll drop you off on the way home."

Palace? I topple over onto the seat, picturing a castle with a moat . . . and then I'm jolted back to semiconsciousness when the car rolls to a stop. I lift my head long enough to catch a painful glimpse of flashing gold lights—oh, the Palace *Theater!*—then tighten up in a ball, my face stuffed into the soft leather, hoping my tiny skirt at least covers my rear end.

A door opens, a moment of dead silence, and then I hear a voice whisper, "Daddy, please tell me that's not a hooker in the backseat."

"Just get in," the man says tiredly.

"I smell booze," the girl argues, lagging back.

"For Christ's sake, it's not me!"

Hmm, kind of testy there.

The door slams, splitting my head in two, and I flap a hand over my mouth as a spasm hits my stomach. One thing's for sure, a rich guy like this will not take too kindly to me spewing in his car.

"How was the show?" the man asks. The girl doesn't answer, and I can feel her gawking at my curled-up back. "Nikki, please turn around and put your seat belt on."

"Who is she?"

"A friend of the Addamses. I said I'd give her a ride home."

After a reluctant pause, this Nikki chick launches into a blow-by-blow of the ballet she just saw, describing every detail of the story, the music, even the tights on some of the more well-endowed male dancers. Her dad chuckles disapprovingly, but he laughs at her jokes and listens attentively, and I'm sucked into a lull by the drone of their voices.

Then Nikki gasps. "Daddy! You're not *really* going down *this* street, are you?"

"Hush."

I peek up through the window. Yep, my street, alright. The car stops, and I throw open the door, hop out, and promptly trip on the curb, landing face first in a mountain of dead leaves. After fishing for my purse, I crawl to my feet and totter up the driveway. Once I'm safe on the porch, the big elegant car glides soundlessly away.

I jiggle the doorknob. Damn! Locked out. Teetering, I wonder what to do next—and that's when it hits me, and hits me good. I hang over the railing and throw everything up: vodka and OJ, Kahlúa and milk, even the pizza pocket I had for supper.

Dripping snot and puke, I sink to the floor, the world twirling and swirling like a demonic merry-go-round.

"*Martha!*"

I leap out of my skin. Am I asleep or awake? Through a roaring haze, I hear a way too familiar voice: "Looks like that kid of yours had a little too much to drink, Lou Ann."

Oh, no-o. Not Wayne.

"Martha, you get up this instant!" Momma explodes.

I roll over instead and hide my face, tortured by the porch light and Momma's shrill twang.

"Aw, let her sleep out here," Wayne suggests. "Teach her a lesson."

Yes, please do. Please let me sleep.

And that's all I remember till I wake up at dawn, soaking wet and shivering under the rusty glider, one dead leaf sticking out of my mouth.

## •••••• 16 ••••••

At two in the afternoon, I wake up stinking to high heaven with puke in my hair and the mother of all headaches. I rub my naked finger in dismay. I lost the ring, maybe in those leaves last night. I hope Shavonne won't notice, especially after the big gushy deal I made.

After a long hot shower and double shampoo, I peek into the living room to see Wayne parked beside a pyramid of beer cans, polishing a gun, chuckling over two screaming, half-naked chicks on TV. When he booms out a belch that I can smell across the room, my esophagus slams into reverse and I launch back into the bathroom.

My face is still in the toilet bowl when Momma throws open the door. "What the hell were you thinking, comin' home drunk like that last night?"

"Sor-ry," I growl, coming up for air.

"You don't sound sorry to me!"

"Why're you yelling at me? Go yell at Wayne. He's the one out there getting shit-faced again." I climb to my feet long enough to run cold water over a washrag, and collapse back down with it plastered to my face.

"Never mind Wayne. I'm talkin' about you! You pull a stunt like this again and you're gonna be in big, big trouble!"

"Momma," I moan, "you're not even supposed to be *around* people who drink."

"I ain't drinkin', okay? You see a drink in my hand?" She whips the washcloth off my face. "I don't know where you get off tryin' to judge me all the time." Her voice cracks on the last word, and she pitches the washcloth into the greasepaint-stained tub.

"Momma, I'm not judging you, I just—"

"Just what?"

"I don't know why you want to stay with him. Why can't it just be you and me for a change?" I know I sound like a two-year-old, but honestly, I don't get it.

Momma softens, and her green eyes shine down at me. Fat or not, I forget how pretty she can be when she's not shrieking in my face. "I love him, sugar pie," she says simply. "And he loves me, too."

Right. "So where was he for a whole month if he lo-oves you so much?"

I half-expect a smack for that one, but instead she says, "He just had some things to work out, things with his family. Sometimes they don't always treat him so good."

Huh, wonder why. "So did he?" I ask, to be nice, only because she's trying to be nice.

Momma sighs, one elbow resting on the towel rack. "Some things you just can't work out, sugar pie. He had it rough his whole life. His daddy's a big, mean, nasty old man who never did nothin' except treat him worse'n a dog. And now he's really feelin' low, 'cause he can't go back to work."

"How come?"

Momma whispers, "They fired him, said he took off too much time. But everything's fine between us," she insists in a happy, hopeful way, and before I can add my two cents, she pats my damp head. "Gotta run now, 'cause he's driving me to work. Now you get up and behave yourself. See you when I get home."

As soon as they leave, I swallow some Tylenol, put on Beethoven's *Ninth*, and throw myself across my bed to wait for the pain to go away. Just as it starts to ease up, though, I hear Wayne tromp back in.

I jump up to slam my door, but I'm a fraction too late. He stops it from closing with the toe of his king-sized boot. "You got a bad attitude, little girl."

"I don't even know"—I grind my shoulder into the door— "what you're talking about!"

"No? Well, what was it you called me in front of your momma? Shit-faced?"

I change my mind and swing the door toward me instead. As he catches his balance, I plow past him and snatch up my hoody. No way am I staying home alone with this dirtbag!

Wayne beats me to the front door by a nanosecond. "See? This is what I mean by bad attitude. In case you forgot, little girl, this is *my* house, okay? Now I'm gonna do my best by your momma, but you remember one thing—the only reason you're here is 'cause *I'm* letting you stay." I inch along the wall till he barricades me with an arm, then lock my eyes to the faded words on his sweatshirt—Gun Control: Use Both Hands—and don't move a muscle. "But that's gonna change, you don't start showing me some respect. If I didn't respect my daddy, he'd whup the hell outta me, and make me thank him for it, too."

I've seen Wayne crabby before. I've even seen him get nasty.

But I've never seen him look this evil before, and that's because I never really saw him drunk before. Now I know what people mean when they say booze brings out the very worst. I can see the worst in him right now, like staring a devil in the face.

"Okay," I say nervously, flashing a final glance toward the door.

"Okay what?"

I force the words out. "Okay. I respect you."

"You don't sound like you mean it."

"I *respect* you! Now let me out of here!"

This doesn't satisfy him, and he pokes me hard in the shoulder. "See? That's what I mean. No goddamn respect." He steps back from the door. "You watch your mouth from now on, 'cause the way I see it? Your momma needs me right now a whole lot more than she needs you."

The smell of the beer on his steamy breath—the same beer he's been drinking right in front of Momma who's trying so hard to stay sober—rips away my fear and makes me spit out my next words as I reach for the door. "Oh, yeah? What for? You don't even have a job anymore, *loser.*"

Next thing I know, Wayne grabs my hair exactly the same way Chardonnay grabbed it last night. I can hear it crunch in his fist as the phrase "kick him in the balls" comes to mind, but it's like watching a slasher film, starring me as the doomed bimbo. I'm petrified with horror.

"I ain't tellin' you again—*you watch your fuckin' mouth!*"

With that, he flings me outside, and the momentum sends me flying down the porch steps and into the grass. Then I'm up and running—down the sidewalk, down the street, around the corner, past old Luther Lee Washington in his wheelchair. As long as I'm running, as long as I'm moving, I don't have to think about

Wayne's fist in my hair. Or about Momma, goddamn her. How, how did she ever hook up with this maniac?

When I run out of breath, I trudge the rest of the way to the projects, shivering in the chilly air. Shavonne's hungover worse than me, but perks right up when I give her the gory details. "What—a—psycho!"

"Can I spend the night? My mom doesn't get off till midnight."

"I guess. My mom's kinda sick, so we gotta be quiet."

"What's wrong with her?" She looked fine last night.

"She's sick," Shavonne repeats. "Been working too hard."

We sprawl on her bed and watch a sappy Lifetime movie while Shavonne works on a disturbingly realistic drawing of Chardonnay's skull with her brain fully exposed.

"Nice hearse last night, huh?" she comments. "Lucky you didn't end up in a morgue."

"Real nice," I agree. "I almost puked in it, too."

"Whadja think of Nikki?"

I draw a blank. Leftover alcohol poisoning, I guess. "Who?"

"Didn't you guys go pick her up or something?"

"Oh, her. I think she thought I was a hooker."

"Bitch, right?" I shrug, and Shavonne adds, "Ma dragged me over there once to pick up a check she forgot, and man, you oughta see that place. Damn garage's bigger than this apartment, and they've got this yappy little dog, and man, that Nikki girl's a trip."

"Trip how?"

"Oh, you know. Nice to my face, but she's, like, lookin' at me all cross-eyed like she wants to shove a finger down her throat. So I go, 'Hey, what's the matter with your face?' and she's like, 'Whaddaya mean?' and I go, 'Girl, you don't start looking at me straight, ain't no way you gonna get them beady eyeballs apart.'

So *she* goes"—Shavonne tries to mimic an English accent, and my head hurts worse when I laugh—"'Rah-ly, I have no clue what you mean, and please don't speak to me again.'"

"Oh, no she didn't."

"Oh, yes she did. I swear, I don't see how she can work for that triflin' bunch of fools."

The movie's back on, and I can hear Mrs. Addams at intervals, hacking up chunks of her lungs. Eventually, I have to comment. "Man, I hope she didn't do that all over the food last night. Some party, huh? All those rich people coming down with TB."

I meant it as a lame joke, but Shavonne shoots me a one-more-word-and-I'm-gonna-tear-your-face-off look. Out loud, she says shortly, "I'm taking a shower." She whips her shirt over her head, kicks off her sweatpants, then pauses, stark naked in the flickering light of the TV. "It's not TB, asshole. She's got HIV."

I nearly strangle on a rope of my own breath, too shocked to apologize.

"She's had it for years. It ain't never made her sick before, but now she been coughin' all week."

"Sorry," I squeak.

Shavonne grabs a towel off the back of her door. "Just keep your mouth shut, okay? Nobody else knows." And she streaks off to the john.

I never knew anyone with HIV. I never even knew anybody who knew anybody with HIV. I'm awake half the night, wondering how she got it. Does Shavonne have it, too? Would she tell me if she did?

. . .

At least Wayne's truck is gone when I get back home the next day, wrapped in a heavy sweater of Shavonne's that reaches my knees. Hopefully I can sneak in without Momma noticing.

Wishful thinking

*Thwap!* A smack in the head the second I step through the door. "What in the sam-hill do you mean, not comin' home all night long? I was ready to call the cops!"

"So why didn't you ask Wa-ayne why I didn't come home last night?" I yell back, slightly dizzy from the unexpected slap.

That throws her for sure, but not in the right way. "What're you talking about? He didn't . . . you know, try to get funny with you, did he?"

Oh, yu-u-uck! How could she even think something that gross? "No, Momma, he just threw me off the damn porch!"

"So where were you all night?"

"Hello, are you even listening? I said Wayne threw me off the porch!"

This she totally ignores. "You get in your room. You're grounded, missy!"

Grounded from what? It's not like I have a life. I open my mouth to protest, but she rushes at me like an underwater torpedo, so I bolt for my room and barricade the door with my dresser.

"You're crazy!" I scream through the wood.

"Crazy," like "fat," is another one of those words I should never use around Momma. Roaring like a rabid elephant, she pummels my door for like thirty seconds before she gives up and stomps off.

I've neglected my cello over the past couple of days, but now an irresistible urge forces me to open the case. I wipe my face and blow my nose, then lift the cello out, and yes, I even hug it for a sec. Positioning myself perfectly on the edge of my bed, I rest it against my leg and lift my bow. Scale up, scale down. Scale up, scale down. All my exercises over and over, plus the three real pieces I now know by heart: Schubert, Brahms, and a little thing by Mozart. I play and play till my fingers are raw again, till every note sounds perfect. Peace and joy overtake me—but then I start crying, and my tears drip off my chin and skitter through the strings.

Now I know why Momma won't pay for this cello. It's not the money at all.

She just doesn't like me very much. I don't think she ever did.

## ●●●●● **17** ●●●●●

For the next week or so, I stay out of Wayne's way, and Chardonnay, by some miracle, chooses to ignore me. But the best thing of
all? I just know I'm going to be a star because today, after practice, Mr. Hopewell, his smile bright against his wrinkly dark
face, says, "Well, you think you're ready to join the orchestra,
Martha?"

Tingling inside, I smile back. "You serious?"

"You bet. I think you've come a long way."

Well! I guess all those hours of practicing over the past couple
of months, and all those bloody fingertips are starting to pay off.

"And I think you ought to talk to your folks about taking
some private lessons, too."

I feel my grin get sucked off my face. "Huh?"

"With a private instructor, I mean. I know you have talent,
but that's not going to be enough. You need one-on-one instruc-
tion, so you can grow as a musician." He waves at the empty room.
"You need a mentor, someone to help you develop your skill.
You're light-years ahead of everyone else, but there's only so much
you can learn in a class with thirty other kids."

"How much do they cost?" I ask suspiciously.

"I won't lie, they're not cheap. But," he adds as I open my mouth, "if there's any way you could swing it, it'd be the best thing you could do. Now, I'm not trying to blow up your ego or anything, but yes, you've got something special."

"Well, do you think—" God, I'm afraid to ask. "You think I could, like, ever do this for a living?"

Now he's cornered. "Uh, most professionals start out a lot sooner than this. Still, you're only, what? Fifteen? Sixteen?"

"Fourteen." He squints, like he doesn't believe me. "I skipped a grade."

"Well, I think you've got the potential. And I know you've got the passion, so—well, you never know."

Then he hands me this brochure from the Great Lakes Academy of Music, a private high school right here in Cleveland. You have to audition to get in, plus it's very expensive, and I mean thousands, okay?

He reads my mind. "You can always apply for a scholarship. I'll even be the first one to write you a letter of recommendation. But there's more to playing an instrument than just playing an instrument, you know. There's a whole culture out there, a world of people who devote their entire lives to their music. I'd sure like to see you become a part of that club." He winks. "Think about it, okay?"

Wow, picture it! Me, center stage in a spotlight in a long black gown, cello poised between my knees, while a hushed, expectant audience waits for my first note. Me, a member of this exclusive musical "club," with other musicians for friends, sharing our music, and—oh, how can I talk Momma into this, how?

. . .

Momma's working and Wayne's in his usual spot, drunk, when I get home from school. Ignoring him, I cart my cello into my room, anxious to practice for that imaginary audience I can't get out of my head. If I play very, very softly, maybe he won't wake up . . .

"Hell, you sound like a cat that got caught up under my engine one time."

My bow screeches to a halt. I didn't even hear him come in. "Excuse me? I don't believe I heard a knock."

"I don't buh-*leeve* I heard a *knock*!" he mimics, swaying. "You paying the bills around here? No? I didn't think so."

Okay. I'm out of here.

His radar kicks in, though, and his bloodshot eyes narrow. "You ain't going nowhere till you fix me something to eat."

"I'm not your maid. Go fix it yourself."

Wayne's face undergoes this weird transformation. Oddly enough, his voice stays soft. "What'd you say? I don't think I heard you right."

"You heard me just fine." I will not, will *not* let him intimidate me this time. I'll pretend I'm Shavonne. She'd never think twice about kicking him in the balls—

But before I can lift a foot, I'm flying into the wall like one of his crushed-up beer cans. "That's to help you remember our little talk the other day. Now get your ass out there and *fix me some supper!*"

Refocusing my eyeballs, I vault over the bed and rush for the phone so I can call Momma right now and *make her come home!* But Wayne wrenches the receiver out of my hand. Pieces of it zing as he slams it to the floor, then jerks his belt out of his jeans.

"What are you doing?" I scream.

"You just don't get it! When I tell you to go do something, you damn well better do it. Why's everything gotta be such a big goddamn deal with you?"

Fear surging through every fiber of my body, I scream and lurch away, but he swings the belt fast, and—*whomp!*

"So you wanna give me a hard time, huh?" He chases me down, cornering me by my closet, every blow of the belt like an explosion of fire. I hunker in the corner, my mind a nauseous blur, waiting for him to murder me in cold blood, here in my own room.

Finally he stops. "Ain't so smart anymore, are you? You don't want to follow my rules? You can find the door yourself." He grabs a jacket and heads out, whistling cheerfully. I just lie there like a puddle, my heart hammering so hard I can feel the floorboards vibrating under my chest.

Get up! Do something! But I can't even move.

Why didn't I fight harder? How could I let this happen? How could *Momma* let it happen?

Once I recover, I decide not to be here whenever Wayne gets back. I layer on my sweatshirts, top them off with Shavonne's sweater, and fly to the door, where I bump smack into Anthony, lurking in the back stairwell. Not doing anything in particular, just . . . lurking.

"Hey, baby," he whispers, slurring the words. "Lookin' for me?"

Horrified that I even touched him, I leap through the door and zoom to the library, nagged by the vague realization that I'm surrounded by psychopaths twenty-four hours a day.

Only hunger forces me to go home when the librarian locks the doors behind me. I stumble into the house, half-dead from frostbite. Momma's already home, and I know her shift doesn't end till eleven thirty.

"Why, hi-i-i there, sugar pie!" She grabs me, hugs me, and slides a sloppy kiss over my face. I push her away, sickened by the stench of booze.

"You're drunk!" I screech, rubbing spit off my cheek.

"Yeah!" she screeches back. "I just quit my job!"

"What? Why?"

"All those damn nurses, always accusing me of stuff I didn't do. I finally told 'em where to get off, and now I'm celebratin'!"

She quit her job? Now we'll never get away from Wayne!

With a half-scream, half-roar, I lunge into my room and start heaving stuff against the walls—and that's when I notice it.

My cello's gone.

Did I leave it at school? No-o, I remember practicing, and then—shit!

My feet come alive and I fly from room to room, searching everywhere and anywhere, but my cello is gone. *Gone, gone, gone!*

Fear has no place in my panic-stricken fury. I race back out to the kitchen where Momma's fishing for munchies. "Where is it? Where's my cello?"

Momma stares blearily. "What're you talking about?"

"Did Wayne take it? Did he?" Who else would do something this shitty?

"I don't even know where he is! He's been gone since I got here."

"Well, I *know* he took it, and you better make him give it back or I'm calling the cops! I'll show 'em what he did to me, and then he can rot in jail!"

"What'd he do to you?"

I yank my jeans down a couple of inches to show her the marks. "All because I didn't want to cook him supper." She looks at my hip, but her face registers nothing. "Goddammit, Momma, are you even listening to me?"

"I hear you! And you stop cussing at me like that, or I'll call the cops myself and have 'em throw you in the loony bin. I'm about sick of your mouth!"

"Good, I hope you do it! Any place is better than here."

I huddle back on my bed, seething with rage and desperation. Now what do I do? That freaking contract's up in a couple of weeks, and Grandma Daisy sure doesn't have the money to pay for a cello. Besides, she trusted me. What if the music store sues her? Aunt Gloria will kill me!

Well, now I can forget about my lessons. Forget about any scholarship. Forget about joining the school orchestra. Hell, without my cello, why bother with school at all? Might as well throw in the towel and drop out now, just like—

Like Anthony.

That's when it hits me: maybe I'm wrong.

Maybe it wasn't Wayne at all.

Because who's the creep who tried to buy it, and then copped an attitude when I told him to go blow? What was he up to today, skulking around in the stairwell? He could've marched right in and helped himself to anything in the house. A locked door wouldn't stop him, that's for sure.

I stare up at one of my Elvises with his massive sideburns and glittering white Las Vegas suit, trying to think of a plan that doesn't involve bloodshed.

Anthony did it. He stole my cello. And I swear to God I'm going to make him pay, but how? How?

Suddenly, I know.

# ••••• **18** •••••

I cut gym the next morning because I'm black and blue, and the last thing I need is for Lopez to notice. I skip music, too, because I can't face Mr. Hopewell. I spend last period in the school library, plotting my revenge.

"Where's your cello?" Jerome asks as we walk home through the cold rain.

I pretend to be fascinated by something across the street so he won't notice my quivering lips. "The contract's up. I had to take it back." I don't dare tell him what really happened. Once I do what I have to do, he might figure it all out.

"Bummer." Jerome pats my shoulder, but all that does is bring me even closer to tears.

I take a deep breath, and decide to launch my attack before I chicken out for good. "Hey, you want to study together? These chapters Finelli gave us are really a bitch."

"Huh?" I hate biology, and he knows it. No wonder he's suspicious. "You want to hit the library?"

"No. I thought we could study in your room."

"Um, we're not supposed to do that, remember?"

"We're *studying*, okay? We can leave the door open. God, Jerome, don't you ever get sick of people pushing you around all the time?"

He considers this, raindrops glinting on his glasses. "Okay."

Aunt Gloria's car isn't there, so I don't bother with the window. I walk right in with Jerome at my side, and Grandma Daisy, full of flour and sweat, greets us in the kitchen. "Fresh cookies! Y'all hungry?" I shake my head, and she tugs the hood of my outermost sweatshirt. "Child, you gonna catch pneumonia runnin' around like that. Tell that momma of yours she needs to go out and buy you a real coat." She pulls the sweatshirt off me so she can throw it in the dryer, and I bite my lip when she gives me an unexpected hug. Wonder how huggy she'll be if she ends up on *Court TV*?

Bubby, trapped in a high chair, chubby cheeks dotted with cookie dough, smells like vanilla when I drop a kiss on his head. He goes back to squishing cookie dough into his tray, and I stumble to Jerome's room through the cluttered hallway, wondering if I'll ever feel like me again.

Jerome has already spread our homework over the grimy floor of his room. While he rambles on about mitochondria and osmosis and everything else I don't care about, I stare at his mattress, wishing I had a better plan, and then I hear myself say, "You know, I'm too hungry to think. Maybe I will take some of those cookies."

Jerome throws the book down in disgust, and I flip up the mattress as soon as he's out of the room. No sign of the gun, but luckily the money's still there. Balancing the mattress on my head, I rapidly peel away some bills. Five hundred, six hundred . . . how much do I need? Should I call and find out? No, no, no, this might be my only chance.

Nine hundred, a thousand . . . eleven hundred, twelve . . .

and then I hear Jerome coming back. The mattress slams down with a muffled plop, and I shove the wad into my jeans and put on an oh-so-innocent face. Twelve hundred bucks—Anthony will *die!* But he can't prove I took it any more than I can prove he took my cello.

So now we're even.

. . .

The next day after school, I blow Jerome off and ride the bus back to Tower City. "Option to purchase"—it says so on the contract. I point this out to that same grumpy lady who blinks at me over the rim of her tiny glasses. "That'll be one thousand and ninety dollars and ninety-five cents." Funny how I don't need an adult around to *buy* the damn thing.

I hand over the clump of bills, take my receipt, and wander back out with a sickening sense of loss. Something important has been ripped out of me now, like an arm or a leg, or maybe something much deeper. Maybe a chunk of my heart. Maybe a sliver of my soul.

Whatever it is, I think it's gone for good.

Days and days pass, and I can't shake this awful feeling. I can't think. I can't eat. I can't even breathe without hurting, and I itch all over like poison ivy. Even heroin withdrawal can't be as bad as this.

When I can't stand it another second, I go crawling to Momma.

Big mistake. She's hasn't been sober one minute since the day she quit her job. "How many times I gotta tell you? Nobody's working! We ain't got the money!"

"But Momma, if I keep playing, I can get a scholarship to Great Lakes." I wave my rumpled brochure. "Mr. Hopewell says I got a real good chance. And look—ninety percent of their graduates end up at Juilliard. Don't you get it? I could—"

Momma laughs, but not like she's amused. "Martha, I hate to bust that bubble of yours, but people like us don't get into no Joo-lee-yard."

"What? What people?" Perfectly frozen, I wait for her to say it.

"Jesus Christ, do I gotta spell it out? Poor people, Martha. Hillbillies. White trash."

"I am not white trash!" I kick the closest chair. "And if we're so damn poor, how come you can buy all that beer?"

"Hey! If you had to put up with all the shit I've had to put up with in my life—"

She launches off on one of her poor-me rants, and I have to shout to be heard. "So what? Just because *your* whole life sucks, why do you have to screw up mine?"

But Momma can outshout me any day of the week. "My life didn't suck till I married that father of yours, and you're just—like—him! Always picking fights, always acting so high and mighty. And both of you with your goddamn music!" Momma kicks that same chair, hurtling it across the floor. "And now I gotta listen to you cryin' about how I'm such a crappy mother. *I don't deserve this!*"

"Well, you're the one who lets *Wa-ayne* slam me around!" Saying his name is like biting into a turd.

"You keep this up, I might let him do it again."

"Good! Then I *will* call the cops and both your asses can sit in jail."

She comes after me finally, but I'm one step ahead of her. "Selfish! That's what you are, a selfish brat. Me, me, me, that's all you think about! Never mind that we ain't got a pot to piss in. Never mind *me*, never mind that *I'm* finally happy!"

"You're not happy!" I scream. "You're drunk all the time!"

"Since when do you care? All you care about is that good-for-nothing cello."

"It's not good for nothing. *You're* good for nothing!"

Stone dead silence. As Momma's face crumbles into blotchy pieces, it hits me what I just said. But before I can think of a way to make it better, she draws herself up and points to the front door. "Well, seeing as you hate me so much," she says quietly, "maybe Wayne's right. Maybe you oughta get the hell out of here."

At first I think she's kidding. Then I realize she's not. "Momma, I'm sorry I said that, I just—"

"Don't you tell me you're sorry! You think you're too good for this family? Go find yourself another one."

Breathing hard, I force my feet into the kitchen. I dial Shavonne's number with a shaky finger, but it's busy . . . busy . . . and then busy again.

"Didn't I tell you to beat it?" Expressionless, Momma cracks open another can of beer and stares at the TV.

"I'm trying, Momma. But I don't know where to go," I croak, fighting back tears.

"That's your problem, missy. You better think of something."

How can I leave with no place to go? Sick to my stomach, I throw some clothes together and climb the fire escape through a torrent of snow. The first thing I hear as I tumble through Jerome's window is: "I told ya, man, I don't know nothin' about no money!"

Jerome's mattress is hanging limply off the bed, and Jerome and Anthony are nose-to-nose. Neither of them pays me a bit of attention.

"Don't you be frontin' me, man. I had it stashed there for weeks. It ain't even mine, and now they be wanting it back, so *stop fucking with me!*" Anthony howls that last part, and I can smell his panicked sweat.

"Well, it ain't me who took it," Jerome snaps. "I didn't even know it was there."

I sit perfectly still, lips cemented shut.

"You lying to me, nigga, you gonna be dead, you hear me?"

"I ain't lying, man. Swear to God, I didn't touch it."

A car horn blasts and Anthony jumps, eyes bulging in horror. With an eruption of F-words, he shoves Jerome out of the way and bolts from the house.

Because it would look too fishy if I said nothing at all, I casually ask, "So what's going on?"

Now that the coast is clear, Mario lugs a squirming Bubby into the room and plunks him in my lap. Bouncing Bubby, I pretend to listen while Jerome explains how Anthony owes money to some big-time dealer. Supposedly he had some of it stashed under the mattress, but gee whiz, now it's gone.

Mario immediately gets defensive. "Well, *I* didn't take none of his money. Whaddaya think, I'm gonna steal from my own brother?"

"Nobody said you took it," Jerome says patiently.

"Well, I don't believe that dawg had no money." Mario scratches his broad belly, deep in thought, then, oddly, throws Jerome a quick hand signal before slouching off to his own room.

"What was that?" I ask faintly.

"What was what?"

"That thing he did with his hand."

He gives me an incredulous look. "You asking me? I got enough on my mind."

I stare out the window over the top of Bubby's curls, afraid my shifty eyes are about to give me away. I feel like a crook, a criminal, the lowest of the low, and not just because I took that damn money. Anthony owed me. It was rightfully mine! I'm just so sorry Jerome got dragged into this whole mess.

Now the extra hundred-and-some bucks stuffed in my pocket are burning my thigh like a red-hot poker. I kiss Bubby to hide my face, and he squeals ecstatically and smacks me in the mouth with his sock monkey. "Ouch, don't do that, silly!"

"Ba-ba-ba-ba-bah!" he replies, digging his nails violently into my chin.

Jerome settles back on the lopsided mattress. "So what's up? You and your old lady fighting again?"

I nod. "She threw me out." Saying it out loud makes it worse, and all the more real.

"How come?"

I jerk my head back as Bubby grabs at my mouth, and I tickle his belly through his Oscar the Grouch shirt. Bubby pushes me away and goes after my glasses instead. "I don't want to talk about it," I mumble, dodging Bubby's happy, flying feet.

*Za-zoom!* Like the Wicked Witch of the West minus the puff of orange smoke, Aunt Gloria materializes out of thin air. She knows I'm here every time no matter how quiet we try to be. "Why y'all trying so hard to aggravate me to death?"

"She can't go home," Jerome says quickly before I can shush him. "She had a bad fight with her mom."

"You think I'm running a homeless shelter here?"

I hear myself begging, "Please! Just for tonight?" Momma might cool off by tomorrow, but what do I do in the meantime? "I promise I'll be out first thing in the morning. Please, please, please?"

She sneers. "And where you think you gonna sleep?"

Maybe she does have a flicker of humanity after all.

"She can have my bed," Jerome offers. "I'll sleep on the floor."

Outraged, she informs him, "Slave days is over, fool. You ain't givin' up your bed to no white girl in this house."

Then again, maybe not.

"Not tonight, not tomorrow night, or any other damn night," Aunt Gloria continues, spinning on her heel back toward the door. "I ain't gonna be raisin' no damn zebra babies!"

Okay, message received, over and out. Swallowing hard, I untangle Bubby and set him gently in the crib.

"Ba-*bah!*" he wails, clawing at my shirt.

"Shush," I whisper. "Go night-night."

Bubby rocks in his crib, tears in his eyes, sock monkey in his mouth, and I stick my feet back through the window without a word to Jerome. If I'm embarrassed, he must be perfectly mortified. Zebra babies? As *if!*

What'll Momma do when she finds out I'm still here? Why, oh why, does she hate me so much? Because I want to go to college? Because I don't want to end up like her? I hunch up on my bed, keeping as quiet as possible as I scribble everything that just happened down in my journal. Beyond my door, I can hear Momma opening beer cans one after another. Well, when she passes out, maybe I can give Shavonne another try.

Slumped against the headboard, I fight to stay awake, but my chin droops lower and lower . . . and next thing I know, I'm watching fireworks on the Fourth of July. I have Bubby on my lap, and both of us laugh and clap at the dazzling explosions. Momma appears, smashed and naked, and stumbles through the crowd, calling "Yoo-hoo! Sugar pie!" Clutching Bubby, I try to worm my way through the throng of laughing people, praying she won't see me—

At first I think it's the fireworks that wake me up: *Pop-pop-pop-pop!* And the sound of exploding glass, the gunning of a motor, shouts from the street, and sirens in the distance. I can hear Grandma Daisy shrieking, "Jesus! Jesus! Jesus!" and it's the most terrifying sound I ever heard.

I throw open my window. More screams from upstairs—Aunt Gloria now, and can that be Jerome? *Whathappenedwhathappenedwhathappened?* Teeth chattering in the frigid wind, I scramble onto the fire escape and make it up maybe two steps before the brilliant beam of a flashlight illuminates the side of the house.

"*Stop right there! Don't move!*"

I freeze.

"*Show your hands!*"

My fingers fly up in the pool of light.

"*Now turn around! Slow-ly!*"

"That's my daughter up there, you dumb son-of-a-bitch!"

Momma? Omigod, what is she trying to do, get 'em to *shoot* me down? Numb with dread, I turn, and something sharp pierces my sock. I hop up with a yelp, losing my balance—and the past fourteen years crawl, not flash, through my brain as I dangle one-handed from the metal rung. *Tick-tock, tick-tock*—and then my fingers slip, and I land in the driveway in a smattering of ice and glass.

Momma grabs my head. "Look what you done," she snarls at the cop.

Stunned by the fall, astonished to be alive, all I can do is watch my own blood ooze into the snow, distantly wondering where all the glass came from. Not *my* window. Jerome's?

The cop wanders closer and tries to make nice in one of those calm, funny voices reserved for mad dogs and mental patients. "Ma'am, the paramedics will look at her as soon as they get a chance."

"She could be dead by then, you son-of-a—"

"Look, lady. We got a dead baby up there. Just get her out of the way, okay?"

Dead baby?

I try to speak, but nothing comes out.

## ••••• **20** •••••

Bright lights, poking hands, and disbelieving whispers.

"... drive-by shooting ..."

"... drug deal gone bad ..."

"... these streets kids, I swear ..."

"... about a year old, I think. Right through the chest, poor thing."

I clap my hands over my ears while people in uniforms finger every inch of my body like they're searching for fleas instead of wounds. Twelve stitches in the foot, seven in the elbow, and five in the thumb. I scream my head off as they pick out the glass, never mind I've already been numbed with needles from head to toe.

Nurses bombard me with questions when they notice Wayne's belt marks, exchanging looks, making hasty notes on their clipboards. Groggy from the pain shot, I pick at the blood around my nails and refuse to answer. All I want is for this hideous dream to end.

Unless, of course, I'm not really asleep. Maybe I'm dead, too, and stuck in my own personal version of hell.

The knock-out drugs finally do the trick. When I open my

eyes, the first thing I see is Momma dozing in the corner of the exam room. I remember where I am, and once I do, I'm sorry I woke up. "Momma?"

Momma's eyelids flutter. "Yeah, sugar pie. I'm here."

"Is Bubby dead?"

"Hush," she says softly. "You rest."

"Is he, Momma?" I have to know.

Momma nods. "Gloria's kid. Some guys came after him and shot up half the house. Lucky thing nobody else got hurt. Lucky thing," she adds, like she knows that's where I went, "you weren't up there when they done it."

Lucky? Lucky thing Aunt Gloria threw me out, you mean.

Hours pass. Momma's obnoxious snores keep me awake as I watch the tiny window get brighter and brighter. I do everything in my power to keep my mind a solid blank. I don't talk to the doctor. I don't talk to the nurses. I won't even talk to the police-woman who pops her head in to find out what I know, or if I saw anything at all.

All I can see is Bubby, and I see him just as clearly as if I'd been there when it happened. I mentally follow the trails of the bullets that blew out Jerome's window and pierced the side of the house. I imagine them ricocheting off the rungs of the fire es-cape, so close to my own window, and so close to me, sound asleep, trapped in that stupid dream.

I picture the bullets in slow motion, sailing through Jerome's room and over his sleeping head, spiraling between the bars of the crib, and burrowing deep into Bubby's chest.

I can see the splatter of blood on the wall next to the crib, a giant red flower with growing petals that drip, drip, drip all the way down to the floor.

I see Bubby's brown curls, long enough to braid, but nobody

bothers to do it, and I've always been glad because I think it's lame to put braids on a little boy, even if he is black, and black people do it all the time. But now these long brown curls are speckled with red.

Red on the sheets. Red on Oscar the Grouch. Red all over his floppy gray sock monkey.

I make this awful, gasping sound just as a bushy-haired doctor in a black crocheted beanie, I mean yarmulke, appears. My tacky blue hospital gown is drenched, my hands slippery as ice.

"Breathe," he tells me, and I jump as he jams a cold stethoscope against my bare back.

I haven't taken a full breath for five minutes. I think I forgot how.

"I can't," I rasp, touching my throat to make sure nothing's choking me there.

"Yes, you can. Deep breath. Good girl."

He smells like coffee, and has jelly smeared on the sleeve of his white coat. After listening to me force air in and out of my lungs, he turns toward Momma and calls her three times before she finally wakes up. I hope she slept off the beer, that he can't smell any on her breath.

Momma stretches, cracking her bones. "Good grief. What time is it?"

"It's after ten, Mrs. Kowalski."

Momma hefts her bulk out of the chair, reaching for her coat. "You feeling okay now, sugar pie? 'Bout ready to go?"

Dr. Yarmulke raises a finger. "Just one minute. If you don't mind, I'd like to keep Martha here for a day or two to make sure she's all right."

"She's fine," Momma argues. "Little banged up is all."

I study the rusty stain on my bandaged hand, amazed at the understatement.

"Martha has been through a terrible trauma. She's obviously distraught, and I think she could benefit from a couple of days in our adolescent ward."

Momma glowers. "Distraught? She's just laying there!"

"Still, I'd like her to be evaluated."

"No," Momma says flatly. "She's coming home with me."

The doctor ignores her. "Martha? Would you like to stay here and talk to somebody about what happened last night?"

A long murderous silence follows while they wait for my answer. I think of all the old movies I've seen about wartime interrogators with their bamboo razors and electrical probes. Man, those guys had nothing on these two. No wonder people break down and confess to crimes they didn't commit.

"I want to go home," I say at last.

"Good. Let's go." Momma throws me my bloody clothes.

But then the doc drops a bomb. "Mrs. Kowalski, I'd reconsider if I were you. We're all aware of the fact that Martha's been abused."

You could hear a feather drop. "What did you say?"

"Abused," Dr. Yarmulke repeats. "Somebody's been hitting her, and we've documented this clearly in her record. Martha, would you like to show your bruises to your mother?"

What for? She already saw them. Oh, why can't he shut up and let me go home?

Momma's face turns eggplant purple. "My daughter tell you that?"

"No. In fact, she wouldn't tell us anything."

"See? That's the problem with you people, you got nothing better to do except stir up trouble, pokin' your noses into poor people's business. Who in the sam-hill do you think you are?" And on and on till I want to crawl into the wall. With my dumb luck, they'll throw *her* in the psych ward. Then I definitely won't have a way out of this rat hole.

"Fine. Take her home. But let me tell you something, ma'am. Somebody *will* follow up on this, and if there's any abuse going on, we'll find out. Understand?"

"Don't you threaten me, buddy. What the hell's wrong with you people? I'm her mother, for Christ's sake. You think I'd sit back and let anybody beat on her?" As she scrawls her name on a piece of paper, I gingerly pull my clothes on over my damp blue gown. That last shot they gave me is re-eally wearing off.

Wayne picks us up in his truck, and aside from a couple of his brainless wisecracks, nobody speaks on the way home. I see a cop in the yard rolling up miles of yellow tape, but other than that, the house looks oddly the same—flapping shingles, peeling gray paint, sagging porch, broken steps. I don't look up at the fire escape, or at Jerome's shattered window. I just walk into the kitchen and stand there, feeling helpless.

"You want me to make you a hot dog or something?" Momma eyes me nervously, like she's waiting for my head to start spinning around.

"Uh-uh."

Normally I don't get headaches—last one I had was my Halloween hangover—but the right side of my brain feels like it's been stun-gunned (bubbybubbybubbybubby) and little golden crinkles dance at the edge of my vision (bubbybubbybubbybubby) so I head to my room and collapse facedown. Trying so hard not to think *bubbybubbybubby* . . . and trying not to remember that it was me who took the money.

Me.

I did it. I took the money. And I'm the one who put Bubby in the crib.

Yep, just dropped him in and told him to "go night-night," and then sprinted the hell out of there before Aunt Gloria could grab another hanger.

*I didn't know, I didn't know, I didn't know what would happen!*

But I took the money.

I put Bubby in that crib.

My journal is on the bed right where I left it. I flip through it briefly, twirl my pen, but I can't write about what happened, not one single word. What do I write besides "Bubby is dead"?

I wham the notebook into the wall, thinking that it's a mistake, that nothing happened at all. Just another twisted, endless dream, like when Momma lumbered naked through the park, hollering my name.

I mean, Bubby could be up there right now, chewing on his sock monkey. Watching the window. Waiting for Martha to come back.

But if he were, I wouldn't be hearing those sounds from upstairs. Spurts of grief. Soft, endless wailing. Grandma Daisy doing her "Jesus, Jesus" thing, only quieter now. Like she's giving up.

So if Bubby doesn't exist, maybe I don't, either. How would I know? How does *anyone* know? I jump up and push my face in front of my dresser mirror. Okay, I have a reflection—that must count for something. Long wild hair, raccoon eyes, a scratch on my chin from Bubby's fingernail, probably.

"Martha," I whisper.

The face stares back, and her empty look tells me the name means nothing to her at all.

I miss four days of school because every time I take a step it's like jamming my foot into a box of barbed wire. Shavonne keeps calling, but I refuse to come to the phone. I can't talk to anyone.

Momma wouldn't let me go to Bubby's funeral, and now she's really laid down the law about me going upstairs. "You are forbidden to stick a single toe in that house. It's too dangerous." And with Jerome's window boarded up, I can't even sneak in.

At first I argue out of general principle. After all, it's the same house. Are we any safer down here?

But do I want to see that empty crib? The bullet holes in the plaster? Grandma Daisy's face?

Fact Number One: I took Anthony's money.

Fact Number Two: If Anthony could've paid up, none of this would've happened.

Fact Number Three: If Jerome finds out, he'll hate me forever.

Poor Jerome. No dad, no mom, and now his baby brother is—gone. I've never seen him cry, not even when Aunt Gloria bashed him with that hanger. But I bet he's crying now. Crying out loud, with his mouth open, the way Bubby used to cry.

Momma doesn't have a clue what I feel like, why I can't stop crying, and how scared I am about ever facing Jerome. Sober today, she corners me in the john. "Martha, please stop this crying. You're gonna make yourself sick."

"I don't care, I don't care!" I'm already sick. I crouch on the bathroom floor, thumping my head against the wall as Momma tries to pull me up. "I want him back. I just want him back!"

"Martha, c'mon. Have something to eat. You'll feel better."

"No!" I may never eat again.

Still, she hovers, and then jolts me to the bone with, "You know what I been thinking? I been thinking about that cello of yours, and . . . well, maybe soon as I find me another job, we can see about gettin' you another one. Think you'd like that?"

She's only being nice because she's afraid I might hang myself in the shower. I know she doesn't really want me to have another cello. And the next time she gets drunk, or pissed off, she'll burn that, too. Like she burned Daddy's violin.

"No," I say into my raggedy towel. "I don't want another cello."

"What?"

"You heard me. I don't want one."

"But why?"

How can I say it out loud, that everything's my fault? And that she's right about me, too, how everything's always about me. Me, me, me! That's why I stole Anthony's money, and why Bubby is dead. All because of that fucking cello of mine!

"I hate it! I'm never gonna play again."

"But why, sugar pie?"

"Stop asking me that! I don't want to, okay? I don't want a freakin' cello, and I don't want any music lessons."

"Well, what *do* you want?" As if anything she could give me could make a difference, could make any of this better.

I can't tell her the truth without hurting her feelings. She already knows how I feel about Wayne, and that I don't want her to drink. Why waste my breath?

What I want is to start over—but not with her. With me.

I want my whole life to rewind and begin again from scratch. I want to be born another person, in a different part of the world, with different parents.

I'm so sick of Martha Kowalski and her big stupid mouth and bigger, stupider dreams, I could rip my own throat out and not feel a thing.

But out loud, all I can say is: "I want you to go away and leave me alone."

## •••••  **22**  •••••

Finally, the next day, I decide to go back to school. I roll out of bed, pull on some clothes, and nibble on a Twinkie, hoping the sugar and chemicals will blast this headache away for good. No such luck, and while I'm scouting around for the Tylenol, I find something else: a whole stash of prescription bottles with other people's names on them.

Damn. Did Momma really quit her job or did she get fired for swiping drugs? No wonder she's been so nice to me lately. All mellowed out on some old fart's Xanax.

I throw the bottles back, my brain thonking against my skull. I have no idea if Jerome's back in school yet, but I leave ten minutes early to avoid him just in case. I trudge along through five inches of new snow, my bandaged foot boiling in pain.

Shavonne catches me outside of homeroom. "You're back! Oh my God, I'm *so sorry* about that baby. You okay? What happened? Hey, how come you didn't call me back?"

She shuts up as a shadow falls across the lockers. I cringe instinctively, expecting Chardonnay, but it's only Miss Fuchs. "Did you bring a note explaining your absence, Martha?"

"I forgot," I say quickly before Shavonne can butt in.

"Ignorant bitch," Shavonne spits out when Miss Fuchs flits away. "Ain't like she don't know why you been gone."

Another shadow falls, this time Mr. Hopewell. Wow, my own personal welcoming committee. "Can I talk to you for a minute, Martha?"

I squeeze my books to my chest. "I got to be in homeroom in a sec."

"I'll write you a pass."

I leave Shavonne stranded in the middle of the crowd, and follow Mr. Hopewell to the music room. "I heard what happened. You doing okay?"

I nod, forcing myself not to glance around. All those instruments, all those music stands, all the empty, waiting chairs . . .

"If you need to talk to someone, I'm sure the counselors will be happy to help. Or you can talk to me, if you want."

I nod again. I must look like a marionette. Speak to me, and an invisible hand jerks my strings.

He gives me a curious glance, then gets down to the nitty-gritty. "I was hoping you'd stop by to tell me why you dropped out of my class."

"I don't have a cello anymore."

"What happened?"

". . . I had to turn it back in. The contract ran out."

"Well, I wish you would've let me know. I have a loaner you can use. Normally I hang on to it in case somebody forgets theirs, but you can use it in the meantime, till we can work something out."

My cheeks flame up. "I don't have the money for a new one, so, like, what's the point?"

Mr. Hopewell's craggy brown face instantly sags. "Martha,

playing an instrument isn't like reading a book. You can't put it down and pick it back up again any old time the mood hits you. You were off to a great start. I hate to see you throw it all away." He marches off and comes back with the cello while I chomp on the nail of my one good thumb. "Oh, it's old, and kinda banged up, but it has a wonderful tone. Here, play something. How about that Schubert piece we were working on?" When I don't move, he lowers the cello in surprise. "Martha, c'mon. What's up?"

My eyes blister as I stare at that instrument, pretending it's nothing but a hunk of steel and wood—but my fingers are throbbing, positively dying to touch it. If I could just play it for one second, if I could just hear a few notes. Touch those cold strings and that warm, smooth wood . . . no, wait, wait, wait!

Reality check: Momma was right. People like me don't go to ritzy music schools, and people like me don't end up at Juilliard.

I am not Jacqueline du Pré, I will never play Elgar, so let him keep his damn cello. I couldn't take care of the last one, and look where it got me.

I edge toward the door, struggling to sound normal. "Nothing's up. I just don't feel like it anymore." I glance at the clock: thirty seconds till science. Will Jerome be there?

"Martha—"

"I'm sorry, okay? But I just can't do it!"

I stumble out blindly without waiting for a pass. Suddenly I can't stand the idea of facing Jerome. *Does he know, does he know, does he know it was me?* Instead, I go to the john where Shavonne and I hang out, sit down on the toilet, and study the graffiti. Left-handed, I add a few comments of my own, mostly about Chardonnay. Then I open a notebook and begin to doodle, and the doodling eventually turns into:

*Dear Daddy—*

The words blur, and I rub my eyes roughly. I chew the end of my pen, thinking and thinking—and then start to write stuff I've never dared to put down in my journal:

*I wish you were alive. I need to talk to someone. I hate my life. I hate everything about it. I wish I could go to sleep and never wake up. Why couldn't it be me instead of Bubby? Why am I alive when I'm always so miserable?*

My hand cramps. I read it over twice. It sounds like a suicide note to me.

*Clank!* A shoe hits the stall. "Hey, why ain't you in English? You got a test to make up."

English? What about biology? How long have I been in here? I rip the letter from the metal spirals, tear it to bits, toss it in the toilet, and flush with my foot.

"So what's your problem?" Shavonne lights up two Marlboros and hands me one as I lurch out of the stall. I stare at it idiotically. "Well?"

I suck on the filter, and retch. "I feel like shit." I throw the cigarette in the sink. "My head hurts. My stitches hurt. I'm in *pain*, okay?" Without a word she hands me a pill out of her purse, breaking rule number one in the Sacred Code of Student Ethics. "What's this?"

"Hell if I know. It's my mom's."

I don't ask for details. I just gulp it with a handful of water.

"Look, I know you strung out about what happened to that baby—"

I fling my hands over my ears. "I don't want to talk about it."

"I know you don't, and that's your problem. You need to deal with this shit, you know what I'm saying?"

"Shut up!" Then I pull myself together, and add more quietly, "Just shut up, okay? I'm dealing with it fine."

"No, you ain't. You just hiding your head, same way you always do."

"I'm not hiding!" I shout, pushing her out of the way so I can get to the door first. "And you're not helping me one bit!"

"Yeah, girl!" she jeers as I take off. "You just keep on running, 'cause that's all you know how to do, ain't it?"

I've got my hoody out of my locker and I'm out the front door before the guard realizes it was a human being, not a rocket-propelled grenade that shot past his face. My ears are numb with cold after less than three blocks. Twelve blocks later, my fingers are icicles, and snot has frozen on my upper lip. By the time I hit my own block, I can't feel my feet at all. I hear Grandma Daisy saying: *Tell that momma of yours she needs to buy you a real coat!* Why bother? I like being numb. Maybe I'll drop dead from hypothermia before I hit the front porch.

Wayne's big green truck with the stupid bumper sticker—I Shot Bambi's Mom and Ate Her, Too!—roars to life in our driveway when I'm two houses away. I slow down and watch it veer into the street, one massive wheel digging a trench in the tree lawn, and then catch of glimpse of Wayne's furious face as he zooms past without noticing me.

I wobble into the house on my cold dead feet, expecting Momma to be all over me for ditching school again. But she's nowhere in sight, and her bedroom door is shut. Whatever she and Wayne were fighting about, it must have been bad.

"Momma? You okay?" When she doesn't answer my knock, I shake the handle, but the door is locked, a very bad sign. This, in the old days, meant she wouldn't be out for ages. "Momma?"

Silence. I think back over what I said to her last night: "I want you to leave me alone." Well, I guess she heard me for once.

Shavonne's crummy pill hasn't kicked in, so I study the

suspicious bottles I dug up this morning. Let's see: Darvon, Valium, Vicodin, Percodan . . . hmm, Percodan sounds good. Maybe it'll perk me up? I pop three, wobble to bed, and pass out cold.

Barely an hour later, someone bangs on the front door. "Go away!" But the banging continues, this time on the back porch, which is like inches from my room. Pleasantly swathed in my narcotic buzz, I float to the kitchen and peer through the curtains. A heavyset black lady, long black coat, bulky satchel, dreads bouncing in the wind. Mary Poppins meets Whoopi Goldberg.

"Martha Kowalski?" She opens the door without an invitation. "I'm Zelda Broussard from the Department of Children's Services. Why aren't you in school?"

Shit, shit, shit.

"I'm sick. I got a migraine." And I am so, so-o-o stoned!

She shoves her card under my nose: Zelda Broussard, with a bunch of initials after her name. Masters degree in what? State-Sanctioned Home Invasion? Still, I feel a sympathetic twinge because "Zelda" is so much worse than "Martha." "I've been asked to follow up on a few things, Martha. Evaluate your home situation, hmm?" She has a funny accent, Jamaican, or whatever. "Where's your mother?"

"Taking a nap."

"Perhaps you'd care to wake her up?"

"I can't. She's got a migraine, too."

"I see." Skeptical gray eyes gleam out of her dark round face, harder and colder than the bottom of an iceberg. I'd never seen gray eyes on a black person before. "I'll wait."

"Yeah, well, you might be waiting a long time."

"Well, then I'll just have to talk to you." I do Shavonne's eye-roll, but it has no effect. "I understand you were in the hospital recently, and the people there seem to think you've been abused.

When they asked you about it, apparently you denied it. Is that true?"

"Is what true?" That I was abused? Or that I denied it? She lost me. Plus my tongue feels bigger than the rest of my mouth, and the flowers on the crappy kitchen wallpaper are dancing in time to her words.

"Has anyone hurt you?" I shake my head. "Is that the truth?" I nod my head. "Would you tell me if they had?"

My head stops moving as I pause to reflect. What am I supposed to say to this lady? That Wayne bashes me around and Momma lets him? Even bashes me herself when the mood happens to hit her? "Can you like, come back some other time? My head really, really hurts."

"Well, I would like to talk to you about that incident the other night. The shooting?"

My thumbnail quivers between my teeth like a windup toy.

"Martha, I know you were friends with the little boy. You must be very upset by all this. I just want you to know I'm a certified counselor, and if your mother agrees, I'd like to talk to you sometime. Hmm?"

I pretend I didn't hear that "little boy" part, and that "hmm" of hers is highly annoying. "I thought you were a social worker."

"I do work for the county, but I also have a private practice."

Well, la-di-da. "My mom doesn't believe in counselors. She says they're all quacks." At least I don't tell her what Momma thinks of social workers.

The lady sighs. I can tell she's a smoker by the way she keeps fumbling with her purse. Yawning enormously so she'll know how bored I am, I fall back into a chair and plunk my head into my arms.

She takes the hint and drops her card on the table. "When

your mother is feeling better, have her give me a call." She says "mudder" instead of "mother," which would crack me up if I were in a better mood. "And you can call me yourself, too, if you need anything."

"Anything like what?"

"Anything at all," she answers with a humanoid smile.

As soon as she leaves, I pitch the card.

. . .

By morning Momma still hasn't risen from the tomb, so I take it upon myself to scribble another note for Miss Fuchs: *Please excuse Martha for all her recent absences. Her injuries are not severe but they hurt like a bitc*—I scratch that out—*but they are extremely painful. She has been very stressed out. I'm sure you know why. Sincerely, Lou Ann Kowalski.* Even a forensic scientist couldn't declare this a fraud. I've been doing it for years.

I can hear Mario and Jerome fighting about something upstairs. They sound so normal that I start to wonder again if this whole gruesome week has been nothing but a nightmare . . .

And when I hear Jerome's knock, I know I'm awake.

"Hey," he greets me, like nothing ever happened.

"Hey." I step outside into a raging wind. "Um, you okay?"

"Yeah. It's tough, but, yeah, I'm okay."

"Sorry I missed the funeral. My mom . . ." I shrug.

"That's okay. Granny passed out, and they had to carry her out. Then Mario punched one of my cousins and knocked out a tooth."

Sorry I missed it. "Is your grandma okay?"

"Yeah. She misses him, though. Man, we all do. I can't get used to him not being around, and Mario, he—"

"Jerome, stop. Don't talk about it, please?"

"Hey, I know you feel bad. We all feel bad. Mario, he cries all the time, and you know he ain't no crybaby." Jerome's voice catches, and he stops walking. "But Granny, she always says you gotta talk out your miseries, 'cause if you don't talk them out, they just eat you up alive."

Talk about him? I can't even think about Bubby. If I think about him now, I'll go crazy for sure.

Jerome surprises me then by reaching for my books. He curls a cold hand around one of mine and says, "Okay, forget it. We gonna be late."

So he doesn't hate me after all, which means he doesn't know about the money. For the first time in days my brain doesn't feel like somebody's mashing it through a meat grinder. Finally I can breathe. Finally I can cry. And I do exactly that as he pulls me along the icy sidewalk.

## 23

Life, more or less, returns to "normal"—but of course that doesn't last. A week before Christmas vacation, I come home from school to find Momma and Wayne huddled together on the couch, drinking as usual, but now toking as well. Looking guilty as hell for one microsecond, Momma struggles to sit up, figures it's too much effort, and falls back into the cushions.

Wayne cocks a jolly brow. Hard to believe this is the same guy who once gave me money for a cello. "Take a hike, little girl."

Seething, I stomp off to the kitchen. My day has already sucked beyond belief. Now *this*?

Shavonne's been absent for a couple of days, and I'm dying to know why. I punch her number into the phone and stretch the raggedy phone cord into my room so I can have some privacy, and not inhale those putrid fumes.

"So what's up?" I ask her. "Where've you been?"

"My mom ain't doin' so hot. She wants me to stay home with her for a while."

"How long is a while?"

"Till my Aunt Bernice gets here, whenever that's gonna be." Shavonne changes the subject before I can bring up the fact that there's a law somewhere that says kids have to go to school. "How's Blubber Butt treating you these days?"

"Shitty as usual. Today she trashed my books. Called me a cu—" I stop, embarrassed. Believe it or not, there are some words in the English language even I can't say out loud. "Then she shoved me into the lockers, and I'd be dead right now if Finelli hadn't come out and kicked her fat ass down the hall."

Shavonne snickers. "Damn, I can't leave you alone for a second."

"And you know what he said? He said they've been trying to get rid of her for years, and that the only way to do it is to, like, document stuff." I pause dramatically. "So now I'm supposed to write down everything she does to me."

"And do what with it?"

"Duh. Turn it in."

"Who to?"

"To Mr. Johnson. The principal?" I remind her, in case she already forgot.

Shavonne blows out a snort. "That freaky old troll? What's *he* gonna do?" My thought exactly. "You're not gonna do it, are you?"

"Hell, yeah! I'm sick of that bitch, and I got two more years to get through."

"Well, hate to say it, sister-girl," Shavonne says sorrowfully, "but you are one dead honky bitch."

She might be right. Ratting out Chardonnay might make things worse, but maybe not. What if it works? If I write everything down, and if Mr. Finelli's on my side, maybe people like Mrs. Bigelow won't be so quick to blow me off.

.  .  .

It starts again the next day, the second I get to homeroom. Miss Fuchs is late, so Chardonnay grabs the chance and tosses my books into the aisle.

Inhaling deeply, I ask politely, "Aren't you sick of this yet?"

"Hell, no!" She blasts me with halitosis.

Calmly I pick up my books, flip open a notebook, and write: *7:47 a.m.—knocked my books on the floor.*

Pure confusion. "What's that, bitch?"

*7:48 a.m.—called me a bitch.*

Chardonnay snatches my notebook. *Thump*-thump-*thump*-thump. Deafened by my heartbeat, I hold my ground. "Give it back, please."

"Fuck's this? You keepin' notes on me?"

*Thump*-thump-*thump*-thump. "Give it back, Char-don-nay."

"Sure." She flings it across the room, then clamps down on my arm, pinching my skin like a pair of pliers. "Look, you. I ain't forgot how you done me at that party, and now you turning into a snitch? You wanna get me kicked out? You want me to do this whole fuckin' year over?"

"That is so not my problem," I squeak, struggling to get my arm back.

She bunches her forehead, her eyes glittery slivers. "Oh, yeah? Maybe I'm gonna make it your problem, you lying sneakin'—" And blah, blah, blah while the rest of the class sits riveted to what might very well turn out to be murder in broad daylight. "So whaddaya say to that?" she ends with delight.

Part of me truly wants to be reasonable. The other part figures she's so out of control, nothing I say can possibly make it worse.

I yank my throbbing arm free, and the second part wins. "I say go fuck yourself."

Faster than a rattlesnake, she jerks the front of my sweater. I can feel her knuckles all knotted in the material, digging into my chest. With all the adrenaline firing through my veins, though, I'm not as afraid as I should be.

"I still got that knife, and I ain't triflin' with you now. Next time I catch you alone? Girl, I'm gonna slice you open like a big fat tomato and stuff your guts up your—"

"Chardonnay! What—are—you—doing?" Miss Fuchs, finally.

Finger by finger, Chardonnay lets go of my sweater and sings, "Nothing, Miz Fee-yooks."

I bite my tongue and go pick up my notebook. One minute ago I was feeling so brave. Now I'm rigid with fear and about to collapse. Shakily I scrawl: *7:50 a.m.—grabbed my sweater, said next time she catches me alone, she will slice me with a knife like a big fat tomato.*

A big fat tomato?

That does it. I smack my notebook shut.

"You go, girl!" Kenyatta hollers as I march out on rubbery legs, ignoring Miss Fuchs's feeble protest. Who cares if the whole school thinks I'm a rat fink? I am not putting up with this shit any longer.

Down in the principal's office, old Mr. Johnson's not impressed with my measly notes. He does send for Chardonnay, though, which was not part of my plan. "She'll just deny it. Why don't you ask somebody else? Ask Kenyatta. She saw the whole thing."

Sweat gleams along the fuzzy rim of Mr. Johnson's ancient brown dome. Bet he's not used to little white girls mouthing off to him in his own domain. "I'm not dragging other students into this, so pipe down now and get back to class."

Pipe down? Does he think I'm making this up? Incensed, I fling myself out of the office.

After lunch, I find this on my locker, scrawled down the length of the door in black magic marker:

NExT
TIME
I SEE U
GET
REDY
TO
DIE
BITCH
!!!

I stare at the message, mouth dry, throat stuffed with cotton. She means it this time. There is no doubt in my mind.

My next class is algebra, and that room is right across from the Life-Skills-for-Dummies Center, which is where Chardonnay goes at this time to learn how to, you know, fry up bologna and stuff. Usually she hangs around in the hall, waiting for poor unsuspecting me. Today, I'm sure, will not be an exception.

Today, however, I bet she does more than call me names. You *can* get a knife past the metal detectors—remember the one I saw in homeroom that first day? Since I can't prove she wrote this, there's no point in running back to the office. Old Mr. Johnson's not about to dust my locker for prints.

Not caring who sees me—and I'm sure that'll be Miss Lopez, jogging down the hall now in her sweaty double-knit shorts—I run out the nearest door and head straight home. Momma's nowhere in sight, and Wayne, mesmerized by a fiery NASCAR wreck on TV, doesn't hear me tiptoe in and snatch a couple of beer cans out of the fridge.

After I finish the second one, I know these won't do the trick. True, I feel buzzed and dizzy, but also bloated and nauseous. Worse, all I can think about is what Chardonnay wrote on my locker, and there's not enough beer in the world to erase those words from my mind.

So, with shaky hands dripping with sweat, I swipe another beer and pop two of those Percodans. Soon my limbs dissolve into puddles of melted wax, and everything bad trickles out of my brain. Chardonnay, Momma, Wayne . . . even Bubby, because Bubby's always in my mind, even when I pretend he isn't.

Well, now I see exactly why people get high! Who *wouldn't* want to feel this wonderful every second of the day?

I hear the phone ringing, far away, like from the bottom of a well. And Wayne's voice, a bit louder: "No, her momma ain't feelin' so good . . . Yep, I'll tell her . . ."

The school, no doubt, ratting me out for bailing. Yeah, he'll tell Momma. If he can wake her up, that is.

· · ·

My own shriek of surprise is what wakes *me* up when Wayne grabs the back of my hoody and drags me out of bed.

"Nap's over!" he yells.

"Get off me!" I fling my hands back to push him away, and accidentally poke him in the eye—*gro-oss!*—but all he does is yank me closer.

"Hey, I got a call from your principal! Cuttin' school, huh?"

"Where's my mom!" I yelp as I twist out of my hoody, leaving it dangling from his fist. He simply drops the hoody, and snatches my ponytail instead. "*Ow!* Let go of me, freak!"

"You wanna talk to your momma? Go right ahead." Hauling me by my hair, he whacks Momma's door with his boot. "Hey Lou Ann, c'mon out! Your little girl here's got something to say to you, honey."

He squashes my face into the door. I scream for Momma, but no, she doesn't answer, she won't help me, and I know I'm alone, just me and Wayne—and if I don't do something now, what's he gonna do to me? So with a Jackie Chan howl, I slam my fist into his nose, blinding us both with a spray of bright blood.

One frozen second of disbelief, and then Wayne lets out a roar and chases me to my room. This time, however, I remember to fight back. I shriek my lungs out, throwing everything I can get my hands on straight at his head till he grabs me, forces me to my knees—and suddenly lets go.

I scramble away, sucking in mouthfuls of oxygen. I swear I'm hallucinating because I see Jerome in the doorway, pointing a gun at Wayne. "Get away from her, asshole."

Face rabid, Wayne warns, "You put that thing down and get the hell outta here, punk!"

"No," Jerome says quietly. "You get out."

I know what Wayne's thinking because I'm thinking the same thing. Geeky little Jerome? This can't be happening.

Stunned, bloodied, Wayne slowly backs off. Then, unbelievably, he strolls out of my room and out of the house.

All those guns in that living room cabinet. Hunting rifles and pistols, World War II relics, even an AK-47, and one with a bayonet. Bet he never once imagined that somebody might use one of them on him.

Tears and snot run down my face as Jerome kneels beside me and hands me my glasses. "Martha, don't move. I'm gonna go call the cops."

"No, don't!" I whimper, clutching at his leg. "All they'll do is arrest *you*."

"What for? For this?" He twirls the gun in disbelief. "It's our word against his." I shake my head fiercely. "Well, at least tell your mom!"

Ha! Tell my mom? Where was Momma ten minutes ago? Why didn't she help me? I know she heard me screaming. "You're so clueless, Jerome. My mom's crazy, okay? I mean ser-i-ous-ly crazy."

Jerome squeezes my hand and holds it a minute till I feel calmer, safer, till the insanity passes. And that's when he does it— he ducks his head and kisses me quickly, a nice normal kiss with no tongues involved. I lean against him, and he leans against me, and I wish we could stay like this all night long.

"Would you really have done it?" I whisper. "Shoot him, I mean?"

"Hell, yeah!" I see a look of sheer fury in his smoky dark eyes as he spins the gun on his finger in that nerve-wracking way. "I'd shoot him in a sec. Him, and those bastards that murdered my little boo. If I ever get a chance . . ." He swallows hard. "Man, I miss Bubby. I miss him so much."

I try to pull my hand away, but he won't let go, so I just stare at the floor, chewing my lip, praying he won't say another word about Bubby.

Jerome's hand tightens over mine. "You gotta talk about him sometime, you know."

"I can't."

"Why not?"

"I mean I don't want to," I finally admit.

"Why you keep acting like he never been born? You ain't the only one hurtin', you know. You think I ain't hurtin'?"

"I don't *care*, Jerome!"

He looks hurt for about one second, and pitches my hand aside. "Yeah? Well, I got a news flash for you—Bubby was my brother, not yours." I kick out at him, but he catches my ankle. "Girl, you so stuck on yourself, sometimes it makes me sick."

Stuck on myself? I open my mouth, never mind that he's right, I *am* a stuck-up bitch, and Momma's been saying that my whole life.

But then I can hear the popping of those bullets again, and the screams, and the sirens, and the shattering glass—and then Jerome pulls me closer and says, very softly, "Granny says it was just Bubby's time."

I'd argue with this—but instead, I start crying. "I miss him so much!" And I keep saying this over and over while Jerome pats my head. Probably the same way Luther Lee Washington patted his dog, Ole Marvin, before somebody ran him over and then nobody would tell Luther Lee . . . and now I see why, because it hurts too much. Maybe it's better to pretend.

"I know. Me, too. I miss him a lot."

I want to tell him about the money, I really do want to confess. But Momma's door swings open with a heavy whack, and there she stands in nothing but her underpants, gigantic breasts slumped down to her belly.

"Sugar pie? That you?" Glistening eyes wander, trying to focus.

"Ho-ly shit," Jerome whispers as we climb to our feet. She must've peed herself because it's all we can smell.

"Where's Wa-ayne? I want Wa-ayne."

She doesn't ask about me. Only Wayne, because that's who she cares about.

"Momma. Go to bed." She reaches out, still whining for Wayne, and I shove her away as hard as I can. "I said *go back to bed!* You make me sick!"

Sobbing, Momma stumbles back to her room. I hear the lock snap behind her, and for once I'm glad.

"Holy shit," Jerome repeats, immobilized by horrid fascination. "What's that all about? Is she psycho or something?"

"Didn't I tell you she's crazy? Maybe now you'll believe me."

The spell is broken, and it's too late for me to confess. And I'm starting to feel sorry I let him kiss me like that. How can we ever go back to being buddies again?

I avoid his gaze. "You better get out of here. I'll be okay."

"What if he comes back? You want me to stay?" I shake my head, so then he tries to force the gun into my hand. "No, for real. Take it!"

I jerk away, sickened by the touch of the cold metal, remembering what I heard that awful night—*right through the chest, poor thing.* Ripping bullets. Exploding glass. Bubby sleeping with his sock monkey, lashes fluttering in his sleep . . . "I can't. I can't shoot it!"

"You ain't gotta shoot it. Just stick it in his face." He pushes it at me again, and this time I take it with quivering fingers. "Remember what you told me a while back? How you'd never let anybody beat up on you?"

Yes. I remember the conversation. And I'm ashamed of it now.

"Be cool." Jerome touches my sleeve and then lets his hand fall away, looking about as embarrassed as I feel. A second later he's gone.

I set the gun on my dresser. How weird it looks, lying there on top of a colorful pile of hair scrunchies, between my copy of *Romeo and Juliet* and my Algebra II workbook. I look at it for a long time, then take a deep breath, reach over, and pick it back up.

This time it's easier, and the longer I hold the gun, the less I'm afraid. I rotate it cautiously around in my hands, then flop back on my bed and rest it on my stomach, enjoying the weight, the certainty of safety.

For the first time in my life, I have power.

I have control.

And not a single drop of fear.

Well, one thing's for sure—forget about Wayne. I have a much better idea what I can do with this gun . . . like take it to school tomorrow, jam it up Chardonnay's nose, and tell her once and for all to stay the fuck out of my life. The idea makes me giggle, but then I'm crying at the same time, making weird, pathetic sounds.

I wish I'd told Jerome he could stay and keep me company. I could tell him I'm sorry, that I know he's sad about Bubby, and that I'm not really as self-centered as he thinks I am.

But now I'm just glad I didn't tell him about the money.

## 24

I have to go to school.

I have to face Chardonnay.

Then I remember the gun.

As soon as I pick it up, the panic disappears and I feel calm, almost high in a supernatural way. I remember her message— *Next time I see you, get ready to die, bitch!*—and I answer her out loud, "Ha! Nice try." You, Blubber Butt, are in for one big honkin' surprise.

I dress fast, stuff the gun into the pocket of my warmest hoody, and screech to a halt by Momma's bedroom door. Still locked, and not a sound to be heard. My hand stops in midair before I can knock. I could be dead right now and she'd never even know it. Instead, I give the bottom of the door a hard kick and slouch out to the kitchen. No sign of Wayne. Could this be my lucky day?

Instead of waiting for Jerome, I head off to school alone. If he knows I'm bringing the gun, he might try to stop me. My mind feels oddly blank as I stare down at my feet in my filthy secondhand Reeboks, putting one in front of the other, then the other, then the other. If I try to form a single thought, my skull might burst into splinters. Keep walking, Martha. Keep walking, keep walking . . .

And then my brain cranks back to life as soon as I hit the school grounds. Hello! Metal detectors? Instant expulsion?

Best-case scenario: a nasty blurb on my high school transcript.

Worst-case scenario: ten to twenty years in maximum security.

Oh, God. It's true. I'm officially insane.

Uneasy, I glance around, pull the gun out of my pocket, and ditch it in a mound of snow piled up high against the building. What the hell was I thinking? Heart whamming against my ribs, I linger outside as long as I can, then slink into homeroom where Chardonnay's jaw drops like a trapdoor. Obviously she figured I'd never show my face here again. How I wish I could've made her day.

Miss Fuchs jumps on me immediately. "You're late, Martha. And Mr. Johnson wants to see you after the bell."

I'll just bet he does, and this time I won't let him bully me. I'll say I'm going to the newspapers, to the TV stations, and I'm getting me a lawyer, and—

But halfway down the hall, Chardonnay's breath flames the back of my head. "Sure hope you kissed your momma good-bye this morning."

Okay, not a problem. There's a gazillion people around, right? But Chardonnay keeps her voice low, growling in my ear that if I don't keep quiet, I'll be picking my kidneys up off the floor. She's not joking, either, because I feel something sharp poking into my backbone. She forces me into a one-eighty toward the nearest stairwell while a gang of tough, sniggering homegirls hem us together. Funny how I never noticed Chardonnay has friends of her own.

Neurons exploding, I drop into a hard crouch. Chardonnay kicks me in the head as she trips over my shoulders, and *bam!* Together we roll down the last couple of steps. Whatever she was holding skids across the tiles, and I snatch it up in a move that'd make James Bond proud. An x-acto knife, huh? Probably swiped it from the art room. Bet old Blubber Butt never took an art class in her life.

The breath oomphs out of her as I jump onto her stomach, noting with satisfaction how her stooges scatter. Still, she manages to gasp, "Get off me, bitch!"

I guess it's the word "bitch" that makes me want to hurt her. First I hold the blade up to make sure she sees it, then I touch it lightly to her zit-ravaged cheek. I'm panting so hard and so fast that my breath fills my ears, along with the *Fight! Fight! Fight!* chants that echo off the walls.

"You ain't gonna do it." But she's swiveling her eyes like a cow in a slaughterhouse. "Girl, get real. I wasn't gonna cut you. What's wrong with you? You can't take a joke no more?"

Ha, some joke. I hold the blade steady, puckering her cheek. She crumples into a blubbering bag of terror, and I can smell her fear—but instead of strength and power, I feel nothing but numbness.

"Why?" It's all I can think of to say.

"Please don't cut me, please don't cut me . . ."

I move the blade one millimeter closer, but it's like watching somebody else's hand, like it doesn't belong to me at all. "Just tell me why you keep *doing* this to me."

"Martha!" Well, well, if it isn't old Mr. Johnson. "Put that thing down! What do you think you're doing?" Huffing and puffing even harder than me.

"Not—until—she—tells—me—why."

"Martha?" Mr. Hopewell. Man, the whole damn faculty must have shown up for this. So where were they two minutes ago when Chardonnay was about to gut me like a fish? "Martha? Come on, baby. You don't want to do this."

"Don't tell me what I want! You have no idea."

I sense him moving, and hope he doesn't grab for the knife. "You got to think about this, baby. Think before you do anything. Please."

Baby, huh? Funny, he'd never dare call me that in class. I shift my weight, remembering how many times I've seen this same scene on TV. Keep 'em talking. Distract 'em. Do anything you can do till the SWAT team shows up.

Chardonnay squeezes her eyes shut and starts sniveling again, only this time she's saying, "Get up, get up! You sittin' on my baby! C'mon, girl, be real. Don't hurt my baby, ple-ease." The palm of her hand taps my thigh. Just taps, taps, taps it, a gentle drum beat—the first time she's ever touched me without causing serious pain.

That's when the numbness lifts and all my feeling surges back. The mind-blowing pain behind my burning eyes. The floor, hard and cold under my knees. The hill of flesh heaving under my butt. The evil, oily sensation of the knife in my hand. And the lightest weight of Mr. Hopewell's fingertips on my shoulder.

"I just want her to stop," I whisper.

"This isn't," Mr. Hopewell says, just as softly, "the way to do it."

Oh, Momma. Momma, where are you?

"She's not worth it, baby. She's not worth it at all."

Chardonnay's eyes fly open, watching in disbelief as Mr. Hopewell snakes a slow hand around my wrist. He must've figured I'd never really hurt her. Otherwise, why would he take that chance?

I let him pry open my fingers and take away the knife.

# 25

*Click, click, click* on the keyboard: *Martha Georgine Kowalski, age fourteen years and nine months, five feet four inches, one hundred and nineteen pounds, brown hair, brown eyes, no distinguishing marks or obvious deformities.*

*Flash!* Mug shot.

*Squish,* roll, *squish,* roll ten times. My fingertips are caked with black ink by the time they finish immortalizing me in their system with all the other "juvenile offenders."

One blue flannel shirt with a missing button, one red T-shirt, bleach stains duly noted, one pair of blue jeans with a ripped knee, one pair of stinky socks, one pair of beat-up nylon Reeboks, a pair of pink flowered underpants minus half the elastic, one plain white bra with a safety pin in the strap. No money, jewelry, keys, trinkets, or anything else that speaks of a real life.

I get to keep my underpants, but not the bra, on the off-chance I might try to do myself in. Ha! As if this whole ordeal isn't humiliating enough, why would I hang myself in a public building with some raggedy, stretched out, hand-me-down bra?

No, I'm not in a cell, just in a very small room, but I feel like a hamster trapped in a shoe box. If only I knew how to chew my way out.

When I hear the jingling of keys and the clank of a lock, I stare at the door in half-relief, half-dread, knowing it *has* to be Momma, ready to bust me out of here—but no, it's that social worker with the ratty dreads, Zelda Broussard.

"Where's my mom?" I demand.

Zelda ignores my question, makes herself at home in an orange plastic chair, and without beating around the bush, asks for my side of the story. So far she's the only one who seems to want to hear it.

"Well," she says when I finish my rant, "as things now stand, there is one thing working in your favor. Your music teacher told the police you were defending yourself, and that the weapon belonged to that other girl—Chantilly?"

"Char-don-nay," I spit out.

"Well, thank God you didn't hurt her."

No, thank God I left that gun outside. One quick bullet versus one dinky little art knife? Yes, it's true. I could've killed old Blubber Butt.

My body shivers as the truth sinks in. "If I tell you something, will you promise not to turn me in?"

"I can't promise you anything, Martha," she answers, crossing her chunky legs.

Not the answer I wanted, but I confess anyway. "I took one of Wayne's guns to school."

"You what?"

"I didn't take it inside, I swear. I left it in the snow."

"Where? Exactly where?"

I tell her where, and she mumbles some not-very-professional words as she whips open her cell and commands one of her minions to get back to Jefferson High and start shoveling through the snow. She listens for a minute before flipping the phone shut, and I brace myself for the worst: somebody already found it, and somebody's dead. What else could make her look at me with that odd, strained expression?

Instead, she says carefully, "Martha. Your mother was taken to the hospital this morning."

I blink. "Why?"

"A drug overdose."

"What?" Oh, God. Why didn't I *check* on her this morning?

"It's okay. She's going to be fine, but—Martha, how long has your mother had a drug problem?"

"She doesn't," I say weakly. "She drinks, that's all. Well, she does take pills sometimes," I add, remembering the stash of brown bottles. "But she's not, like, this crazy drug addict, okay? You know, with needles and stuff." I don't mention the pot.

"Well, she had a lot of narcotics in her system. She will be in the hospital for a while, and hopefully, after that, we can get her into a good rehab center. But what this means is," she continues, "even if the judge does decide in your favor, I'm afraid you will not be able to go back home."

I pick at the hem of my shirt, flinging the word "judge" to the back of my mind. "Can I go see her?"

She gestures widely at the room. "Well, hardly. In case you haven't put two and two together, this is a jail you're in, not the Holiday Inn."

"Hey, this is not my fault! I told them, over and over, that something bad was going to happen, and they all blew me off!"

"Who blew you off?"

"My counselor, the teachers . . . that idiot principal. The whole school, okay? I never would've touched her if I didn't think she was gonna kill me."

"Martha, if you had trouble with this girl in the past, maybe you should have—"

"Don't tell me what I should've done!" I shout. "You don't fucking know anything."

Zelda's cold gray eyes connect with mine like a magnet. "Don't curse at me. Trust me, it will not get you out of here any faster."

Pissed off—and embarrassed—I stomp to the window, a dirty glass square with crisscrossed wires, and cover my face because my head is *pound*-ing and *pound*-ing! "Forget it. You don't know."

"Know what?"

"You don't have a clue what it feels like."

"What *what* feels like, Martha?"

I punch the window with a tight fist. "When somebody wants to kill you!" I scream. I punch it harder a second time, but you can't break this kind of glass. Not like Jerome's window, where one good slam from Aunt Gloria can crack it down the middle. Where a single bullet can make it spray like a billion shards of razor-sharp snowflakes.

"Martha." And then louder, "Martha!"

"What?" My breath fogs the glass.

"You're right," she says, softer now. "I don't know what that feels like. And no, I don't know everything that happened. But I am here for you now, hmm? I can help you now."

The fight drains out of me like air out of a punctured tire. "No, you can't. It's too late."

"No, it's not too late, and this is not the end of the world. I think the most they will charge you with is disorderly conduct."

"That's good, right?" I mumble through my fingers.

"Very good."

"So, like, this judge—when do I get to see him?"

"Monday morning, nine a.m."

"You'll be here, right?" Momma obviously won't.

"I'm not sure," she hedges. "My vacation starts Monday, and I will be flying home to St. Lucia for a couple of weeks."

Ha, so much for helping me. "Huh. That figures."

Zelda reaches toward me and I dodge her hand, and then feel like a retard when she picks her purse up off the floor. I get another one of those "looks" as she rummages for a cigarette and fires it up blatantly under the No Smoking sign. "I wasn't going to hit you."

I touch my warm cheek, almost wishing she would. Hit me hard. Wake me up.

"Let me ask you something. How do you think your mother will feel when she finds out about all this?"

I blink. "How would I know?"

"Think about it, hmm?" she commands through a blast of smoke.

"I don't have to think about it. I don't know—"

My throat clamps shut as I'm struck by a long-ago memory. Momma, cuddled next to me on a big flowered couch, watching *The Wizard of Oz*, and Daddy nearby, tightening the strings of his violin. I didn't get the end of the movie, so Daddy explained, "Dorothy dreamed the whole thing, honey."

Okay, I'm six, and yes, Daddy, I know it's a dream, duh. But how could all those people, those farm guys, that carnival man, be all the same characters who followed her through Oz? That's the part I didn't get.

Momma answered, "Well, sugar pie, it's like this. You can dream you're somebody else, like somebody on TV, right? And you think it's real, and it's real when you're in it. But when you wake up in the morning, you're you again. Now you get it?"

Kind of, but only because of the way she said it, like she *knew* this would make perfect sense to a kid. Then Daddy launched into The Lollipop Kids song, and Momma tickled me and laughed, and I laughed, too, and, well, I don't remember anything else. Except that they were happy. They didn't always hate each other.

And Momma wasn't the Momma I know now.

"I don't know how she'd feel," I finish hoarsely. "It's like, she's not even my real mom anymore, you know?"

Zelda bends over to stub out her cigarette on the floor, the first thing she's done that makes me want to like her a little. "Yes, she is. She will always be your real mom."

I guess that's supposed to make me feel better.

. . .

On Monday morning, at one minute before nine, Zelda flies into the courtroom and runs circles around my own little wiener of a court-appointed lawyer. I huddle on my chair, trying to look remorseful as she blames everything, ha-ha, on that moron, Mr. Johnson. The school administrators, she says, failed to protect me from "an adult student with a history of anti-social behavior who has no business even being in the tenth grade."

She sure came prepared: Statements from witnesses who swear my so-called assault on Chardonnay was strictly self-defense. Notes from my teachers who insist I'm not a certified psycho, only a straight-A student who was pushed beyond the limit of human endurance. The judge agrees, orders counseling and probation, and then, no big surprise, booms out an F-word of his own . . .

Foster home.

•••••• **26** ••••••

The Ten Commandments of the Merriweathers:
  1. Thou shalt worship no other gods except Mr. and Mrs. Merriweather.
  2. Thou shalt not talk back.
  3. Thou shalt hold hands with thy Keepers and say a ten-minute grace before every meal whether or not thou plans to eat.
  4. Thou shalt not shower more than twice a week.
  5. Thou shalt do all assigned chores in a timely manner. This includes the daily dusting of the Goddess's ceramic clown collection *without* referring to them as "creepy little suckers."
  6. Thou shalt not watch TV on school nights.
  7. Thou shalt keep thy eight p.m. curfew.
  8. Thou shalt not use the telephone without permission.
  9. Thou shalt have no expectations of privacy.
  10. Thou shalt keep these commandments, or find thy butt back on the street.

I last four days.
On the fifth day, at lunchtime, I bail out of my (twelfth!) new

school with seven bucks to my name, raided from Mrs. Merriweather's purse, and dump my books in the trash on my way out of the building. Anthony's money is back at Wayne's, and I could kill myself for that. I have no idea what to do, not one single clue, but I am *not* going back to the Merriweathers with all those rules, all that mind control, all those goddamn painted clowns with their beady, satanic eyes. And only two showers a week? I stink! My hair's filthy. My own armpits gross me out.

Nobody asked if I wanted to stay with these freaks. My opinion, as usual, doesn't count for squat.

I don't realize I'm crying till I hear myself doing it. I duck into a phone booth in a gas station parking lot and crouch against the folding door, soaking snot into the sleeve of the itchy nylon parka foisted upon me by the clown gods. I'm mad, but I'm scared, and it's scary how mad I am.

Mad at myself, because yes, I admit it. It's my fault I'm here.

Mad at Zelda for flying off to the tropics instead of hanging around to make sure I survive.

Mad at the Merriweathers for turning out to be assholes instead of the perfect TV family I've dreamed about my whole life.

But most of all, worst of all, I'm so mad at Momma for picking *this* time to end up in the freaking hospital. Now here I am, stuck miles and miles away from my own neighborhood, with nobody at all, and not an idea in my head.

The gas station guy trades me four quarters for a dollar. My frozen finger pokes Shavonne's number into the pay phone, but nobody answers. With a shriek of frustration, I smash the receiver back down.

Now what?

Now nothing. Only place for me to go is back to the detention center. I guess even an eight-by-ten cell with a chicken-wire window beats going four days without a shower. I'll make them find me a better place, or else they can just keep me there. Whatever. I don't care. As long as it's not the clown house.

I'm so exhausted, and so cold, I barely make it to the bus stop. I don't know this neighborhood, but it's close to the airport, with jets thundering overhead like every five minutes. I have to stand for fifteen minutes in my squishy Reeboks, in a sudden flurry of heavy snow, waiting for a bus to take me in the right direction. I press my forehead against the vibrating window, watching brown slush spring up from beneath the wheels, and wish I could curl up on the seat and sleep for two days.

I stumble off at Public Square and then zombie-walk the last twenty or so blocks to the detention center—too stupid to figure out which loop bus I need, but smart enough not to ask that nice policeman over there. Nervously, I hang around close to the door till two older guys stroll out, warming me briefly with a blast of hot air. Megapower attorneys in long coats, carrying briefcases and cappuccinos, obviously talking shop: ". . . kid's got a record a mile long."

Guy number two juggles his coffee to light a cigarette. "I'll get him off."

"Yeah, Dick. You always do."

Hmm, that dude with the cancer stick looks a lit-tle to-o familiar. I inch away, but he notices me, too, and after his friend says good-bye, he takes a step closer. "Do you need some help?"

Do I look that pitiful, or is it against the law to stand here? "Um, no. I'm fine." My mouth waters at the smell of his cappuccino. I think I'd sell one of my body organs right now for a good jolt of caffeine.

The man's cell phone rings out the opening bars to Mozart's

*Eine Kleine Nachtmusik.* Forgetting about me, he pitches the cigarette and drops his briefcase to free up his hands. I peer around him at the door, wondering what I should do—just dart right in and throw myself on the mercy of the first person in uniform?

Something tells me this was a bad, ba-ad idea. Let's see, in the past six hours I've ditched school, ditched the Merriweathers, committed petty theft, and destroyed school property. Four probation violations already and the day's not even over. I go back in there now, I might never see daylight again. What if—?

I jump when Coffee Guy shouts into his phone, "Look! That kid's a victim of circumstance, and I'm *not* going to stand by and let you railroad him into a plea. No jail time, period! I'm not discussing this again."

He smacks his phone shut and shoves it back into his coat, then fires up a second cigarette, puffing furiously. He stares off over my head, looking mad enough to explode, and *bang!* that's when it hits me: I know who he is! Yep, it's that guy who drove me home from Shavonne's on Halloween.

Not just any old guy, either. And not just any old lawyer.

A lawyer who defends kids! Victims of circumstances. Oh, there is so definitely a God, I'll never doubt Him again.

"Wait!" I yell as the man comes to life and swings his briefcase up from the salt-splattered step. "I lied."

"Excuse me?" He does a double take, but I can see he doesn't recognize me. Well, how could he? I was black last time we met.

"I lied when you asked me if I need help. I do need it. Big time!"

"Oka-ay," he says uncertainly, and I can see he thinks I'm about one grape shy of a fruit salad. "Let me give you my card, and—"

"No! I need it now!"

He glances around. "Is somebody with you?"

"No-o . . ."

"Do you have a hearing today?"

"Um, no, but—"

"No? Well, is there a reason you're not in school? Does your mom or dad know you're here?"

Attention, please: Due to a massive brain fart, Martha Kowalski will be unable to answer any further questions. Another one of my stupid ideas! I mean, what did I expect? That somebody like him in his fancy wool coat and his leather briefcase and that clunky gold watch around his wrist would jump at the chance to take on a charity case like me? Lawyers cost money, and I so obviously don't have any.

I will myself to give up and run for my life, but my feet won't listen. Teeth chattering, all I can do is stand there, my long unwashed hair whipping in the wind.

The man moves closer. "I'm sorry. What's your name?"

"Martha," I manage to squeeze out through my numb lips. "You know me, too."

"I do?"

"Yeah. You d-drove me home one night. From the Addamses'."

Triple take this time. "From the *Addamses*'?"

"Yes! Don't you remember? I slimed up your car. I had m-makeup on, and, well, I guess you thought I was black, and then you p-picked up your daughter, and—"

"That was you?" Now, for the first time, he takes a good long look at me. "Oh, Chri—I mean, yes, I remember you. Shavonne's little friend. You fell out of my car," he adds, smiling at last. "And yeah, you slimed it up pretty good." He tosses the cigarette away and holds out a hand for me to shake. "Richard

Brinkman. God, you're cold. Come on, my car's on the street. I'll drive you home."

Home? What home? I pull back, still clutching his warm hand. "No, I just want to t-talk to you, that's all—"

"Well, we can talk in the car."

Dragging my wet feet, I follow him to the long black car. Once I'm inside, the minute he asks, "What's going on?" I blurt everything out because I can't, I *can't* let him take me back to that dog pile.

"And I was gonna turn myself in, but I'm in so much trouble now! And I'm really, really sorry, but I am not going back to that house, and *I don't know what else to do!*" I finish with a pathetic wail, and sink back into the seat, half of me embarrassed and the other half not even caring.

He thinks this over, tapping the steering wheel. "Fine. Let's grab a bite to eat, and we can discuss this like adults." He emphasizes the "adults" part.

This, I think, has got to be a trick. Maybe he plans to roll me out onto the curb as he speeds past the nearest police station.

Instead, he drives me to some fancy east-side deli where my corned beef sandwich and café mocha with double espresso costs twice as much as a week's worth of school lunches. I dig in, trying not to drool as Mr. Brinkman fires questions at me. I can tell he doesn't get it about the Merriweathers. What? No TV on school nights? I have to dust clowns? Everything I say sounds stupid now, even to me.

"Do you have any relatives who can take you in till your mother gets better? Any friends of the family?"

Nobody but Wayne, and forget about staying with him. It's Shavonne I want to live with, but I'm not sure how to bring it up.

"What about your dad?"

"Dead," I whisper, gouging my thumbnail with my teeth.

"How did it happen?"

I don't want to tell him, it's too humiliating—but, well, I bet he's heard worse. "He got murdered. In prison."

Not even a blink. "I'm sorry to hear that, Martha."

Most people say that automatically, but he sounds likes he means it. He gives me a break for a while so I can finish my sandwich in peace, and then I play with a crust of bread while he continues the interrogation. What do I do for fun? Read, watch movies. What kind of books? Elves and magic, science fiction, and yes, even the classics they make me read in school. What kind of movies? Fantasy, horror, almost any dumb comedy. And anything with Elvis, of course.

Then: "So what do you plan to do after you graduate?"

This throws me. "Um, I haven't thought about it much."

"Somehow I find that hard to believe," Mr. Brinkman observes. "I think you've thought about it a lot."

I don't have enough energy to shrug. "Well . . ." Should I say it? Does it sound really, really lame? "I kind of used to want to be a cellist."

"Why?"

Why? Nobody ever asked me this before, not even Mr. Hopewell. I sit there silently, buzzed from the espresso, and think about this long and hard. I have no clear answer, other than the way I felt when I heard *The Four Seasons* that day with Shavonne. But you can't describe that kind of feeling. Words don't exist.

"It sounds stupid," I begin, tearing up the last of my bread crust. "But I touched one once, like for the very first time? And after that, it was the only thing I wanted to do." And before he can fall out of his chair, choking with laughter, I add, "Anyway, I kinda gave it up, so . . ."

He doesn't laugh. He doesn't even smile. "Why on earth would you do that?"

I twitch a shoulder and pretend to study the dessert menu because I'm sorry I opened my mouth, and yes, I'm tired of his questions.

I guess he can tell, because he switches gears. "You know, legally speaking, I could be in a lot of hot water. What I'm doing in a sense is harboring a runaway." He flashes a Hollywood smile, but a cold panic rises inside me, pushing food up to the back of my throat.

I'm not going back to the clown house. I'll kill myself first.

It must show in my face because he lays a hand over mine. "You wait here. I'm going to make a few calls." I jerk in alarm, but he gives my fingers an extra squeeze. "Don't worry. I'm not turning you in."

In total wonder, I watch him whip out his cell phone again and troop out of earshot.

And as hard as I try not to, I feel myself hoping.

## •••••• **27** ••••••

Shaker Heights is one of those la-di-da suburbs on the east side of Cleveland, and the Brinkmans' house is about as la-di-da as you can get. An ivy-covered mansion all decorated for Christmas with white lights, a candle in every window, and a wreath on the front door. Inside, it's immaculate with lots of dark wood and bright chandeliers, a curving staircase, and not one single mouse trap or roach motel in sight.

The lady of the manor steps forward, and Mr. Brinkman announces, "My wife, Claudia."

Blond and gorgeous, like she belongs onstage at the Academy Awards, Mrs. Brinkman touches my shoulder with a warm, "Hi, Martha. Welcome."

"And our daughter, Nicole," Mr. Brinkman continues.

Yes, it's that Nikki chick from the car on Halloween night. I hold my breath, waiting for her next words: *Daddy! Isn't that the little hooker who fell out of your car?*

"Nicolette," she corrects her father, showing off dimples the size of peas. I notice her pale blue eyes and wispy brows, and cheekbones that could've been carved from a hunk of glass. Relaxing my jaw, I force a smile as she eyeballs my smelly sneakers. I must look like a war orphan from the mountains of Afghanistan, which I guess is a step up from looking like a drunken underage hooker.

But wait. I was black, I had braids, and I doubt she saw my face. Did Mr. Brinkman call me by name that night? I don't remember. I barely remember the ride.

Mrs. Brinkman tells Nikki to lend me some clothes and show me where I'll be sleeping tonight. Hoping not to leave dirty footprints on the thick pale carpet, I creep upstairs behind Nikki's shining hair, watching it ripple and swing like a shampoo commercial. Taffy, their silky cocker spaniel, sniffs my grubby shoes for hillbilly contraband as she follows along, tail wagging.

Opening a door to a sunny blue room, Nikki announces, "I'm right next door, through that bathroom, and Mom and Dad are way down at the end of the hall. And that's Daddy's office, next to the music room."

The *music* room? Well, double la-di-da.

"Who's down there?" I ask, pointing toward the other end.

"Nobody. That's Rachel's room."

"Who's Rachel?"

"My sister."

She heaves an armload of clothes at me, and I tuck them into drawers lined with thick, scented paper. I'm glad it's her stuff she's watching me put away, not my own raggedy underpants and stretched-out bras.

"Did my dad tell you I dance?" she asks out of the blue. "I had an audition today, and I'm so excited! I really wanted to try out for Odette, but they wanted a pro, so I got stuck with the ensemble. But I'm glad I got in." At my uncomprehending look, she adds, "It's *Swan Lake*, Martha. Odette's the lead, the principal dancer."

Well, gosh darn it all. I shove the last drawer shut, nicking my pinky as Mrs. Brinkman appears and wraps her arms around Nikki. "I'm so proud of you, honey. You were wonderful today!"

Nikki rolls her eyes over her mother's shoulder. "Thanks, Mom."

Wow, when was the last time Momma said that to me?

"You girls get acquainted, and I'll start supper."

"Want me to help?" I ask, hoping to suck up.

"Thank you, Martha. But you relax, take it easy."

When her mom's out of the room, Nikki winks. "Well, that's one brownie point."

"I'm not looking for brownie points," I lie. "I like to cook."

"Whatever." Nikki shakes away a long strand of hair. "So, like, what grade are you in?"

"Tenth."

"Really? I'm a junior. I thought you were younger."

Well, I am, since I skipped second grade. But maybe if she thinks I'm closer to her age, she won't try to intimidate me so much.

"How old is your sister?" I ask, hoping she'll forget about me for a sec.

"Rachel? She died."

"Oh. When?"

"A couple of years ago."

"Oh," I repeat lamely, then, "Sorry."

"Yeah, well, it's not like we were close or anything, but . . . well, thanks."

That's kind of a weird thing to say, and I wait for her to throw in some more details, but she does no such thing. She just looks at me, and I look back, seeing nothing in her face that says she knows who I am.

"Think I can take a bath?" I ask, since obviously I won't be hearing any more about Rachel.

"Knock yourself out. There's extra towels in the hall."

On my way back from the linen closet, I hear my name through the door of Mr. Brinkman's office. I trip to a halt, ears standing straight out. "Tim, I don't care how long those people have been at this. That kid looks like she hasn't had a bath in a week."

Great. Tell the whole world, why don't you?

"Yes, I know the mom's a head case. That's beside the point. I want these people investigated, and, no, I'm not sending her back . . . Yes, it's fine with them, too. You'll make the calls? . . . Thanks, Tim."

Flying to the john, I rip off my clothes. Not a single speck of green mold caked around the faucets, and the tub is so clean, so sparkly, it's a shame to grub it up. Water shoots out in jet spurts from every side as I sink down into the warm bubbles, scrub my skin raw, lather my hair, and then bob in the suds with my heels anchored to the rim.

Normally I don't believe in fate or destiny. But what happened today is too eerie to be a coincidence. I feel so out of place in these fancy rooms, and yet—even weirder—it's like another part of me feels completely at home.

Ha! My heels slip off the edge and I spit out suds. The only reason I'm here is because Mr. Brinkman knows I'm friends with Shavonne. Well, he's the lawyer. There must be some way for him to fix it so I can go stay with the Addamses.

. . .

Dinner is awesome. For once I eat at a table with a real tablecloth instead of out of my lap in front of a parade of reruns. The silverware matches, the china matches, and I sip bottled water out of a crystal goblet with crushed ice and lemon. Thanks to Nikki, nobody bombards me with questions because they're too busy listening to her blab about her audition. I squint up at the chandelier, marveling at how *totally fantastic* I feel . . . and then I realize why: for the first time since Bubby died, I don't have a single twinge of a headache.

Later, Mrs. Brinkman hands me an extra blanket at the door of "my" new room. "It gets chilly in here at night, so bundle up. And if you need anything, just give a knock on Nikki's door."

"I won't need anything." I hug the soft blanket, and she waits, watching me with a half-smile, like she knows I have something to say. "Um, thanks. A lot. You know, for—" *Saving me* sounds goofy, but what else can you call it?

She touches the side of my head. "Sleep tight, hon."

I sleep tighter than tight.

No dreams. Nothing. The best sleep I ever had.

## 28

The dog wakes me in the morning, shoving its wet nose into mine. Amazed, I stare at the sky-blue walls striped with sunshine, at the leaded-glass windows and lacy drapes. Big TV in one corner, with a built-in DVD player, no less. Artwork on the wall—Degas, Monet, obviously not originals, but not those cheap drugstore prints, either—and the kind of gleaming wood furniture that comes as a set.

Wow, I'm still here. Nothing changed overnight.

Nikki pokes her head into the bathroom as I'm brushing my teeth with a brand new toothbrush, and toothpaste that doesn't taste like it came from a dollar store. "Hey."

I spit into the sink. "Hey."

"You want to go riding with me this morning?"

"Riding? You mean horses?"

"Yeah, I have two of my own, and one's really sweet. A baby could ride her. C'mon, it'll be fun."

I picture razor-sharp hooves trampling me into a bloody puddle. "Um, no thanks." I don't need to be spending hours alone with this Nikki chick anyway. What if she starts asking about me?

Unless she already knows. Maybe her dad already told her the whole story.

Instead, Nikki knocks me away from the sink and goes off on like six different tangents as she layers on lipstick. Not only do I have to hear about Justin, her ultracool boyfriend, but about all her friends at Waverly, a totally exclusive school probably reserved for female descendants of the Mayflower pilgrims. Oh, and her cousin Danny "who's like my best, best friend!" and who'd be "perfect for you!" if he wasn't already attached.

If she wants to blab about something, why doesn't she blab about her sister? Like, how did she die? Or maybe it's none of my business.

Then: "Don't you have a nickname or something? I mean, honestly—*Mar-tha*?"

No shit. Same thing I've been saying these past fourteen years.

"I hate my name," she goes on. "There are like three other Nicoles in my drama club, so as soon as I'm old enough, I'm changing it to Nicolette. What's your middle name?" She makes a face when I tell her. "Georgine? Eew, that's just as bad. Wait, wait! I got it—Gina! It's perfect."

Gina? Gina . . . Gina. The more I say it to myself, the more I like it. Gina Kowalski? Yeah! Gina Kowalski.

Over breakfast, Mr. Brinkman asks Nikki, "So are you ready to go pick out a Christmas tree this morning?"

Nikki makes a face. "Oh, Daddy. I'm too old for that stuff. Anyway, I'm going riding." She jabs a spoon in my direction. "Take Gina, why don't you?"

"Gina?"

"That's her nickname," Nikki informs him, sparing me from explaining.

The idea of tramping around in the snow in search of the perfect tree doesn't exactly thrill me, but I go, because it gives me a chance to be alone with Mr. Brinkman. After picking out a huge, fragrant green pine tree—nothing at all like the metal pole with the tin foil branches Momma hauls out every year—we stop for lunch, and that's when I ask him flat out how long he's gonna let me hang around.

"I don't know, Gina. Your mom needs to go back to rehab, and that'll take a few weeks, so you're certainly welcome to stay here until other arrangements can be made. Of course," he adds, half to himself, "there's the matter of your social worker. And we'll have to get you registered for school."

Other arrangements? "Well, I was kinda hoping I could move in with Shavonne."

"That's not very likely. They have enough going on right now."

I chew hard on my straw. This is so not what I wanted to hear.

"Oh, I almost forgot. I have something for you." Mr. Brinkman digs into a coat pocket, and drops Shavonne's mood ring into my hand. "Must have fallen off in my car."

"Wow, thanks."

"I haven't seen one of those in years," Mr. Brinkman says, watching me stuff the ring into the pocket of my jeans.

"It doesn't work," I confess. "It stays black all the time." I take a deep gulp of my Coke, wondering how to bring it up, and then finally ask point-blank, "So, does Nikki know about me?"

"She knows you need a place to stay because your mother is ill. I didn't tell her about the trouble at school if that's what you mean."

"I mean, does she know who I am?"

"What? Oh, because you were in the car that night? I don't think so. Why?"

"So she doesn't know where I live, or about my dad, or—" Or the fact that I just got sprung from jail and I'm on probation for a year.

"Gina, I promise you, I haven't said a word. I haven't told anyone except my wife."

"But what if people start asking?" I hear sheer desperation creep into my voice.

"What would you like me to tell them?"

I already have this part figured out. "Can't you say I'm a friend of the family? Like somebody from out of town?" Like from Tahiti, or Hong Kong? Just not from the ghetto.

Mr. Brinkman shakes his head, but he's smiling. "Well, one of my associates moved to Columbus recently. How would you like to belong to him?"

"Yes! And I can say that my mom's sick. That wouldn't be a lie." Boy, I'm really getting into this. "And that my dad's really busy, and that's why they sent me up here." This sounds perfect until I remember Shavonne's mom and how the Brinkmans happen to know her in the first place.

Glumly, I add, "Never mind. It won't work. Mrs. Addams knows who I am." What am I supposed to do, hide in a closet when she shows up to clean?

"I don't think you have to worry about Mrs. Addams right now. She's been out sick for quite a while. My wife already hired another housekeeper." He doesn't mention the HIV, and I wonder if he knows. "When you talk to Shavonne," he adds, "please let her know we're all thinking about her."

That's when it hits me: Shavonne has no idea I'm staying with these people. How can I be Gina, this mystery girl from out of town, and still be friends with the daughter of the Brinkmans' housekeeper?

"Um, I don't think I'll be talking to her. Maybe I better not tell her where I am. If this is gonna work, I mean."

"And what about your mom? Do you want to go visit?"

I fidget. "Not really." What if she's zipped into a straitjacket and doesn't even know me? Drugged, diapered, drool dripping from her chin. No, no, no! I can't even think about Momma, or the fact that she just tried to freaking die on me. I want to be happy for a change. Is that such a crime?

. . .

Later on, I'm in trouble. I hang out with Nikki as she gets ready for a double date with Justin and Danny and Danny's girlfriend, Caitlin. Without warning, she asks, "Is your mom gonna get better? I heard Daddy say she has some kind of mental disorder." She jabbers on before I can invent an answer. "It's not schizophrenia, is it? That's incurable, you know."

"No! That's not what she has."

"Schizophrenia's hereditary. I did a report on it once. Sometimes it's passed on from generation to generation. You could have it yourself and not even know it."

I don't mean to shout, but it happens anyway. "I don't have schizophrenia! You don't know what you're talking about."

Nikki practically keels over. "God, Gina. I didn't mean *you're* schizophrenic. I only meant that people can have it and not even know till they have like some kind of breakdown."

"Well, I don't have it, okay? And neither does my mom."

"Okay, okay." But clearly I haven't convinced her, because she kind of slithers away. Then, "Sorry. I'm not trying to be nosy. Let's just, you know—be friends. Okay?"

Trying not to flinch, I meet her eyes. She's so beautiful with all that long, blond hair, those cover-girl cheekbones. Even the way she carries herself, like absolute royalty. Friends? How? We have nothing in common. It's a holy miracle we're even breathing the same air.

But I nod anyway, and she leaves for her date, and then it's up to me to help her parents decorate the new tree. When the Carpenters start singing "Merry Christmas, Darling" on the radio, I remember how this is Momma's favorite Christmas song and think: I shouldn't be here. I should be home with Momma, listening to the Carpenters, trimming our own mangy metal tree, and . . . and what? Watch her get drunk and start blubbering, and call up her old boyfriends and beg them to come over, and then get mad at *me* because nobody'll give her the time of day, and because the tree looks like shit, and she's low on booze and none of the liquor stores are open, and then we can start screaming at each other, and . . .

No. This is much, much better. And now that Nikki's gone, that crazy feeling is back, that sense of belonging to a place where I've never belonged. I think I know these people, but I'm not exactly sure how. Like when Dorothy wakes up, thinking she left her best friends back in Oz, but—surprise!—there they are, hanging around her window, happy to see her.

Sitting cross-legged on the carpet, I sip hot apple cider and watch Mr. Brinkman adjust a string of lights while he sings along with the music . . . Mrs. Brinkman, too, joking with him, picking stray bits of tinsel out of his hair. I feel the heat from their bodies. I hear how they breathe. Every movement, every glance, every word they say makes me ache inside with a weird, familiar longing . . . like maybe, fourteen years ago, God majorly screwed up.

He passed up the Brinkmans, and dumped me on Momma instead.

## 29

Mrs. Brinkman informs me, delicately, that I could use a new wardrobe. Wisely, I don't respond with "Gee, ya think?" She drives me to Beachwood Place, the ritziest mall I've ever been in—Shavonne would go insane!—and sweeps me through store after store, whipping out her charge card again and again.

"Nikki and I used to come here all the time," she says with a small sigh. "Now she acts like she doesn't want to be seen in public with me."

Speechless, I follow this crazed fairy godmother as she snatches up shirts and pants, skirts and sweaters, and points me to the dressing rooms. Then shoes, then purses, a couple of very dressy dresses, and enough new underwear to last me forever.

By the time we get to the coat department at Saks, I'm numb with exhaustion. "Let me know if anything catches your eye," Mrs. Brinkman commands, holding my coat from the clown house far away from her body. Well, the first thing I notice is the same black coat I saw in the window at Tower City that day with Shavonne. "Do you want to try it on?"

I gawk. Okay, it's marked down—but I bet you can get cars cheaper than this.

"Good grief, Gina. Stop memorizing the price tags." She paws through the rack to find my size. "Here. Oh, this is beautiful."

It is! Long and heavy with a satiny lining, it's simple and elegant and positively perfect. The clerk snips off the tags so I can wear it out of the store along with my warm, shaggy new boots with the wrap-around laces. Leaving the clown coat behind, I practically skip out to the car.

.  .  .

That evening, Nikki's uncle Ted and aunt Elise stop by, along with Nikki's cousins, Danny and Natalie. Natalie's fifteen, arrogant, and undoubtedly a puker. She barely grunts "hi" with a faint anorexic smile, and Nikki flashes me a thumbs-up before the two of them vanish upstairs.

This leaves me with Danny. Was this Nikki's plan?

"You want to go down and listen to some music?" he asks.

"Down" means to the family room in the basement with its big-screen TV, leather furniture, pool table, and bar. Danny pours himself a 7Up and adds a hefty splash of whisky. "Do you want anything, Gina?"

Well! Mr. Brinkman already told me the bar down here is strictly off-limits. At the time I tried to look highly insulted, even though I'm the one who got drunk and fell out of his car last Halloween. So maybe that rule only applies to me.

"I'll take a 7Up. Plain," I add.

He is *such* a babe! Shockingly white smile, tousled boy-band hair, the same frosty blue eyes as the rest of the Brinkmans. We sit on opposite ends of the couch after he hands me my drink, and at first he comes off a bigger geek than Jerome. President of his senior class at Gilmour Academy, chess club, debate club, and editor of the school paper. But he also plays racquetball and belongs to a ski club, and his biceps, I notice, are about as big as my thighs. So much for geekdom.

"What kind of music do you like?" he asks, flipping through a rack of CDs. "Who do you listen to the most?"

"Beethoven," I say automatically.

He glances over with a funny look, and I wonder, Was that the right answer? Wrong answer? But no, he looks pleased. "Wow, you like classical music?"

"I love it," I say, relieved.

"I play the piano, and I do some of my own composing. Actually, I've been working on something for weeks. You want to hear it?"

"Sure."

We grab our drinks and head upstairs to the music room. It's not as cozy as the family room, but infinitely classier with its wall of French doors, and the big Persian rug covered with red and gold designs. Checking the tone of the grand piano with expert fingers, Danny says over his shoulder, "So now you know all about me. What about you?"

I chomp hard on a piece of ice, and nearly knock out a filling. "Not much to tell."

"Ah, a woman of mystery." Why does that smile of his do such weird things to my stomach? "How long are you staying with my uncle?"

"Um, I'm not sure."

"You miss your folks?"

I cross my fingers. "Yeah, I do. My mom's kind of sick, though. She'll be in the hospital for a while, so that's why I'm staying here."

"Bummer. Nothing serious, I hope."

I think fast. "No, it's just this . . . I don't know, this nerve disease thingy."

"Wow, sorry. So, what about your dad?"

I do one of those blasé Nikki head-tosses, which probably makes me look like I have a nerve thingy of my own. "I don't see him all that much anyway." At least that's not a lie.

"That's tough." Danny waits a beat, and I pray he doesn't ask me anything about Columbus, Ohio. Instead, he takes my wrist and pulls me down so we're shoulder-to-shoulder on the narrow padded bench. "It's not finished yet, but—well, I think you'll like it."

I do. It's jazzy and soft, and very beautiful. Yet all I can think about is how his arm is touching mine, how I can smell his shampoo and the fabric softener on his shirt. I watch his fingers as he skims the keys, and imagine those same fingers touching me . . .

"Do you play?" Danny asks, jerking me out of my fantasy. "Piano? Anything?"

The words fall out before I get a chance to stuff them back. "I played the cello for a while."

"Cool! Did Uncle Dick show you his?" And he jumps off the bench, ducks into a closet, and with his back still to me, says, "It's over a hundred years old. It belonged to my great-great-grandmother."

As I stare hard at the cello case he's just pulled out of the closet, trying to exhale around the spongy wad in my throat, Danny's dad hollers up that it's time to go. Fighting the magnetic pull of the ancient instrument, I pick up my dreary feet and follow Danny downstairs.

"Well . . . see ya," we say at kind of the same time.

He leaves with his family, and I watch the red taillights disappear down the street. Boy, if mental illness *is* hereditary, then I must have it for sure. This guy is wa-ay out of my league, plus he already has a steady girlfriend . . . although, come to think of it, he never did bring up her name.

I wander back up to the music room, still smelling his scent, still feeling his shoulder—and trying like crazy to pretend I don't care that he didn't kiss me. I clumsily pick out the first bar to "Love Me Tender," and then catch the spark of the cello out of the corner of my eye.

The whole time my feet are moving, the whole time I'm un-latching the case, I'm telling myself I do *not* want to play it. Then that wonderful smell surrounds me again: old varnished wood and rosin, oil, and metal. The smell of the hands of all the people who played it in the past.

I don't take it out. I don't even pick up the bow. In fact, I'm only kneeling over it when I hear voices in the hall as Mr. and Mrs. Brinkman mosey past the door.

". . . a little rough around the edges, Richard, don't you think? And why on earth didn't you tell Ted the truth?"

"Shh, I already explained. It's not a big deal, all right?"

Abandoning the cello, I linger by the door till they disappear, then slink after them on tiptoe. The double doors to the master bedroom stand slightly open, and, shame on me, I hear every word.

"She doesn't want anyone to know about her, Claudia."

"Who'd figure it out?"

"Well, Nikki for one. And if I tell Ted, he'll blab it to Elise. My God, Claudia, I wish you could've seen the look on that poor kid's face. She literally begged me."

"Well." Mrs. Brinkman sounds doubtful. "I don't think Ted bought that story about some old business partner and his sick wife, and how they can't even take care of their own child!"

"We have to give her a chance. Don't you think she deserves her privacy?"

"I don't like lying to Nikki, that's all."

"No. If I can pull a few strings and get Gina into Waverly, then she's going to need to start off with a fresh slate. You know as well as I do, Nikki's got a big mouth."

Excuse me? Did he say Waverly?

"Wouldn't it be simpler," Claudia asks, "to just send her to public school?"

"She was in a public school, and you know how that turned out. She deserves better."

"What makes you think we can get her into Waverly?"

"Claudia, she's smart, she makes excellent grades, and until that one single incident, her record was nearly flawless. Besides," Mr. Brinkman adds slyly, "the dean owes me a favor. His youngest son was charged with possession a while back. Second offense, too."

"And you got him off with—?"

"Community service and rehab."

"Richard," Claudia says slowly, "where are you going with this?"

"What do you mean, where am I going?"

"Think about it for a minute . . ."

Mr. Brinkman lowers his voice, and I can't hear his answer. Think about what? Does she not want me here or something?

Then I hear him say, more clearly, "Well, I'm heading out for a while."

"So late?"

"I won't be long."

"Richard—"

It sounds like a warning, and then Mr. Brinkman replies in the tight, testy voice I haven't heard since the night he drove me home from Shavonne's. "Don't flip out on me, Claudia. I'm not

Ted, okay? I'm out of cigarettes, and I just need to get some air. I'll be right back."

That's my clue to get the hell away from their door. I dart back to the music room to put away the cello, my insides churning like a cement mixer. When Mr. Brinkman tromps in, as I figured he might, he holds up a hand at the look on my face. "Hey, it's okay. You don't have to be afraid to touch things around here." He nods at the cello. "I wondered when you'd find that. Incredible, isn't it? Feel free to play it any time you want."

"Thanks, but—" *I really don't want to!* Cheeks on fire, I murmur, "Excuse me" like the polite little girl I'd like him to think I am, and rush back to my room where I can be alone with my thoughts.

But it's not "my" room. It's only the guest room, because that's all I am—a guest in this house. Some "poor kid" according to Mr. Brinkman. Somebody "rough around the edges." All these lies and stories and even my made-up name can't change the fact that this is not my home.

I'm a visitor, that's all. A temporary intruder.

# ••••• 30 •••••

Over the next few days, I try to "memorize" the Brinkmans—how they talk, how they eat, how they answer the phone. Even the way they shake hands or get up from their chairs. I memorize everything, and make myself do it exactly the same way. No "ain'ts" or "can't hardlys" or other hillbilly expressions. Most of all, no cuss words, not even in front of the dog.

Nikki donated one of her notebooks so I can start a new journal, but I'm barely a page into it when the doorbell rings. Well, well, well, Ms. Zelda Broussard—the one person on earth who knows all my dirty secrets. Holding my breath, I hang over the banister and listen to her complain about how I ran away from the Merriweathers, and how she's even more pissed off because the Brinkmans butted in. Mr. Brinkman informs her that she doesn't have all the facts, and anyway, there's some kind of hearing tomorrow. Smugly he adds, "Possession is nine-tenths of the law," and whatever that means, it makes her blood boil.

I beat it back to my room as she marches upstairs, but don't quite get the chance to slam the door in her face. "Well, Martha. You certainly picked the winning ticket this time."

"I didn't pick anything. They picked me." As she strolls around, looking at this and that, I ask, "What're you doing here anyway?"

"I am *trying* to do my job." A brilliant gold scarf wraps her dreads in a bunch, and dangly gold bracelets drip from her pudgy wrists. Souvenirs, no doubt, from her fabulous vacation. "Well, well, so tell me. What was so bad about the Merriweathers?"

"They're jerks," I spit out, wondering where Nikki is, praying she doesn't overhear.

"Jerks? In what way?"

"I don't want to discuss it."

"You know, they've been caring for kids for almost twenty years."

"So? They're still jerks."

Zelda picks up my journal, studying the cover. "The Brinkmans seem to be quite taken with you, hmm? 'Charming and intelligent' were their words, as a matter of fact."

I grab my notebook out of her paw. "I am intelligent."

"And charming," she adds.

"I can be charming," I agree with a charmless sneer. "What are you so mad about?"

"Who says I'm mad?"

"Well, you're acting mad. Look, he picked me up off the freaking street, okay? I didn't ask to come here. What do you think, I go around town begging rich people to take me home?"

Zelda heaves a sigh. "Martha, this is fine. I have no problem with it at all, just as long as you remember this is only temporary. You won't be spending the rest of your life here, you know."

Whose side is she on? "You think I'm stupid? Oh, and my name is Gina now, by the way."

This throws her for a second. "Gina?"

"G-i-n-a. Gina."

Zelda flips up her eyebrows. "Well, *Gina*. I know you are not stupid. I just want you to keep in mind that your mother does want to get better. And that as soon as she does, she is going to want you back."

Icy fingers tickle my backbone. "Maybe not."

"You're not very happy about that, are you?" Zelda observes.

"I never said that. Anyway, you don't know how I feel."

"Then why don't you tell me, hmm?"

I wish I could. I wish I could say to her face that even if Momma does get better, I'd still like to hang around here. Not because the Brinkmans are rich, but because they're so normal, and yeah, it's nice to be around normal people for a change. People who don't get drunk or stoned or goof around with guns. People who don't get fired from their jobs or slam me into doors, or, in general, act like pathological freaks.

*This* is how people should live, how *I'm* supposed to live. How can she not see this? How can she not understand?

"Nobody knows about me here. They don't know about Chardonnay and they don't know I got expelled. They don't even know where I live. I'm supposed to be from Columbus."

"Columbus?"

"Yes! And I want to keep it that way, so don't blow it for me, okay?"

I can tell she's getting ready to say something profoundly un-nice, but I don't give her the chance. Instead, I ask about the gun and she says yes, they found it. "What in the name of God were you doing with a gun?"

"I thought Wayne was gonna kill me, okay? He beat me up the day before."

Okay. I said it. It's out. Now deal with it.

"Well, it wouldn't have helped you much. The thing wasn't even loaded."

What? Did Jerome know that? Why would he give me an empty gun?

I throw myself on the bed and pull the pillow over my head. "I'm tired of talking. So why don't you just go?" An empty gun? A freaking empty gun?

"Excuse me?" Her note of astonishment gives me a twinge of satisfaction.

"I said why—don't—you—*go*? Did you hear me that time?"

Zelda's fierce stare singes me through the pillow. "Yes, Martha. Loud and clear."

"I already told you. There's nobody here by that name."

"Oh, I think there is." And out she glides, leaving me to slow-bake alone in my fairy-tale room.

.  .  .

Our court hearing the next day isn't even in a real court, just some stuffy old office, and Judge Timothy Monaghan—yes, the Tim from the phone call—turns out to be Mr. Brinkman's old college roommate, of all things.

"I spoke with your guardian ad litum," he tells me, "and—"

"Who?" I butt in, like totally against protocol.

"Mr. Lipschmidtz. He was appointed by the court to see to your best interests, and he has no objection to your staying with the Brinkmans."

Not that I'm thrilled that some guy with a name like Lipschmidtz gets to make my decisions, but, hey, this means I win! On top of it, with a bit of coercing from Mr. Brinkman, the judge zaps away my probation with a wave of his magic wand.

"Don't let me down, now," he warns, shaking my hand. "You stay out of trouble."

"I will. I promise." I do everything but curtsy. Ha, so much for Zelda. I bet she blows a gasket over this one.

. . .

Christmas morning I dread the idea of watching Nikki open up her presents. I stay in bed as long as I can, wondering how Momma will be spending the day. Roped to a wheelchair in front of TV cartoons while some grim, muscular nurse forces tranquilizers through her teeth?

But Nikki drags me downstairs, and I find *Gina* written on an enormous box under the glowing tree. "Omigod!" My trunk! I thought it was gone for good. I tear the extra key away from the bottom, and when I fling open the lid, all my stuff is still there. My Elvis posters, too, all neatly rolled up on top, and Anthony's money and my Percodan tucked safely out of sight.

I have no idea how Mr. Brinkman got this out of Wayne's house, and with Nikki in the same room, I'm not about to ask. I shoot him a pleading look, and he winks reassuringly. "I just thought you might appreciate having a few of your own things."

"I do! Thank you, thank you!"

And that's not all. Taped under the lid is a gift certificate for a year's worth of cello lessons with somebody named Leopold Moscowitz on Shaker Square.

"I said you could play the one upstairs," Mr. Brinkman reminds me. "I wasn't kidding."

I clench my fingers, crumpling the envelope as sweat gathers in my armpits and my chest begins to buzz. I never said I wanted to play it. Does this mean he plans to make me?

"Well?" Nikki bounces a scrunched-up ball of paper off my head, determined to snag back center stage. "Say thank you, dummy, and let me open my stuff."

"Thank you," I whisper, the envelope shivering in my hand.

While Nikki screams with ecstasy over a stunning bracelet, I sneak off to the music room, shut the door, and open the cello case without touching the instrument.

I don't want to play anymore. I remember telling him that, too, but I never told him about Bubby, or why I quit the cello in the first place. Maybe if he knew, he wouldn't be so quick to try to change my mind.

I touch the dull wood of the instrument, leaving an invisible imprint, and run my fingers down the length of the strings. It's old, very old, like nothing I've ever seen. A priceless family heirloom that I can play whenever I want.

*If* I want.

## 31

Tonight is the Brinkmans' New Year's Eve bash, and guess who calls me? Danny, Danny, *Danny*! "You gonna be home tonight, or do you have other plans?"

Me? Other plans? Clearly he has me confused with somebody else. "No, I'll be here."

"Great. See you then."

So, like, is this a "date"?

What if I screw up? Blab out a four-letter word?

What if he gets personal, starts asking questions and stuff?

What if I totally spaz out before he even rings the doorbell?

Nikki and Justin are hitting a different party tonight, and Nikki drops me a zinger before she leaves. "Danny thinks you're hot."

Ha, ha. "No way."

"Way. He says you two are like soul mates or something." She twists and turns in front of the full-length mirror on the back of my door, critically surveying her slinky strapless dress, oblivious to the fact that it's pushing zero degrees outside. "Ugh, I'm obese! I so-o need to lose like ten pounds."

I'm too busy thinking "soul mates" to helpfully point out that she's what, a size zero? Finally I ask casually, "Well, what about his girlfriend?"

"Who, Caitlin?" Nikki flaps a freshly manicured hand. "Oh, she's history. She threw his ring at him last night and almost took out an eye."

"Ring? Were they engaged?"

"No, dummy, his class ring. He told her she's too clingy— which she is!—and that maybe he wants to see other girls, so she told him to eff off. And since Danny told me all this himself, he must want *you* to know, too, so . . ." She winks at me like we're the best of friends. "Good luck!"

If she's lying, I'll kill her.

. . .

Danny shows up at ten, and the first words out of his mouth are, "Wow, you look great."

"Thanks." I spent the past four hours preparing for this night, half that time plucking my virgin eyebrows. I'm wearing a new dark green sweater, and, thanks to a ten-dollar bottle of name-brand conditioner, my hair hangs in glossy spirals instead of a mess of frizz. "So do you."

Man, does he ever, in his jeans, a silky shirt, and that sexy stubble on his jaw. Hoping my legs don't melt, I follow him down to the family room, wondering what I can eat that won't poison my breath. Not that I plan to get that close to him, of course.

We crank up the music and shoot some pool, which is all I did during my delightful stay last summer at that lunatic asylum that passed for a group home. I purposely flop a ball so he won't think I'm a show-off, and he gives me this look, like, how dumb do you think I am?

"Sorry," I murmur. "Wasn't paying attention." I smack the next three balls right into the pockets, never mind that I'm so distracted by his impossibly perfect body that I can't hardly—I mean *can* hardly—tell which ball is which.

Sufficiently beaten, Danny flips on another CD, and it's Celine Dion's version of "At Last." Without even asking, he takes the pool cue out of my hand and slides his arms around me to dance. I promptly step on his toe—nice!—but he only pulls me closer. He's a perfect gentleman, too, unlike that maggot Maurice.

"All we need now is some Elvis," he says when the song ends.

I nearly stomp on another toe. "You like Elvis? I love Elvis!"

I feel him smile into my hair. "I kind of figured you would."

What *I* need now is something to drink because my throat feels like gravel, I'm still obsessing about my breath, and the fact that he loves Elvis totally blows me away. I untwist the cap on a bottle of Evian as he moves over to the stereo, and nearly spit out a mouthful of water when I hear the first line to the most romantic Elvis song ever—"Wise men say . . . only fools rush in . . ."

Danny takes my hand again, and we stand there, scarcely moving to the music. Every detail of this dance feels seared into my brain: the warm muscles of his back, the way his cheek rests on my head, the pulse in his throat . . . then he kisses my hair, my forehead, my cheek, and finally my mouth. A *very* long kiss, with a very fresh tongue.

"You're so beautiful, Gina." His blue eyes shine down, and I feel faint and giddy because nobody has ever looked into my face like this. And nobody ever ran their fingers through my hair unless they were trying to yank some of it out. "You look like . . . I don't know, like autumn or something, all green and brown." He pulls off my glasses and leans closer. "I can't even tell what color your eyes are. Sometimes they look brown. Sometimes kind of golden."

My tongue has disintegrated.

"Amber, maybe. Like falling leaves." He kisses me again and again, and before I know it I'm down on the couch with his long fingers sneaking under my sweater. My mind quakes with an image of the Brinkmans popping in to find their darling nephew with his hands on my boobs—but even that's not enough to make me push him away.

Over and over, he whispers how beautiful I am while his hand stretches the waistband of my brand-new, skintight, low-cut Sevens, creeping like a tarantula toward my new silk bikinis. Oh-h, God! And now his crotch, hard as a rock and about as big as a cucumber, is pushing into my thigh as he takes hold of my hand, drags it downward, and *whoa!* Stop—the—music! I'm seized by rigor mortis.

With one last kiss, Danny straightens up with an explosive, "Wow!"

Omigod, one more minute and that would've been *it.* Sex right under the noses of the nice people who literally saved me from the gutter. Sex with somebody I've only laid eyes on once before. Funny, I can't decide if I'm glad, or highly bummed out that one of us, namely me, came to our senses.

On the big-screen TV, the New Year's Eve ball takes the plunge. Smiling, and kind of avoiding each other's eyes, we toast to the New Year and then cuddle on the couch. I feel so-o strange, both hot and cold, both excited and exhausted, and—well, could "horny" be the right word?

When the New Year's Eve show is over, he takes his time kissing me goodnight. "I had fun, Gina."

"Me, too."

"I'll call you soon. I promise."

. . .

For the next two days, he's all I can think about. Danny Brinkman, Danny Brinkman. How he touched me, how he kissed me, the way he smelled, the way he smiled. The phone, though, stays silent. Sadly I figure, promise or no promise, I probably pissed him off when I wouldn't let him go all the way. Still, did he honestly think I'd want to have sex there on the couch with a hundred people upstairs sipping cocktails and blowing horns?

But now it's time to go back to school, and I'm trying to keep my mind on what's *really* important. Yes, I'm going to Waverly, and this is how it happens: First I take an entrance exam, and I totally ace it. Next, I have to be interviewed by the school dean with the druggie son. After promising me everything will be kept strictly confidential, he asks about the "incident" with Chardonnay. Nothing for me to do but tell him the truth.

Tipping back in his chair, he takes in every sweet detail of my ingénue get-up. "I can't even imagine that. You hardly seem the type."

I smooth my skirt with a demure smile. "I'm not. I promise. It just, um, got out of hand, and I was scared, and I didn't know what else to do, and—" I shut my mouth before I get too carried away.

The dean says he understands, and gives me one warning: I have to abide by the rules one hundred and ten percent. If I don't, I'm outta there, adios, end of story. "I hope you'll be happy here, Gina."

I offer him my newly acquired classic Brinkman handshake. "Thank you, sir. I'm honored to be here." Dude, you have *no-o-o* freaking idea!

## 32

Next to Jefferson, Waverly Academy isn't even on the same planet. No guards, no boys, no weapons in sight. No ear-splitting rap, no gum in my hair, and not one single shadow of another Chardonnay. How did I survive that hellhole?

Oh, wait. I didn't.

On the official forms I write "Martha Kowalski" but I tell them right off the bat I only answer to Gina. *Gina, Gina, Gina* . . . I write it over and over in my neat loopy handwriting, dotting each *i* with a teeny circle. I look like a Gina in my long cello-friendly skirt, pointy, high-heeled boots, and the toxic layers of mascara it took me an hour to apply.

But best of all, I *feel* like a Gina. I blend in, safe and anonymous, with this trendy crowd of rich white-bread chicks with their camera phones and palm pilots, and hideously expensive haircuts. Maybe I don't have the toys, but I do have the hair now—gold highlights and a celebrity hack job, courtesy of Jean-Philippe, Mrs. Brinkman's stylist, who jabbers with her in French.

God, I wish Momma could see me now. Mr. Brinkman's been asking me if I want to go see her, and I finally broke down and said yes. I just want to make sure she's not as bad off as I imagine.

The only glitch at school is my last-period study hall. Three rows away and one desk up sits Danny's old girlfriend, Caitlin Mackenzie. Well, doesn't *this* bite the big one? Very small, very cute, with big, brown cow eyes and spiky black hair streaked with maroon. A microscopic diamond glitters in her nose, making my own unadorned nostril quiver in sympathy. Damn, she looks happy. Is she back with Danny? It's been three full days now, and he hasn't called.

Munching my nails, I try to force my attention back to my homework. But I hear Danny telling me how beautiful I am, how I remind him of autumn—and I waste the whole study hall day-dreaming about his kiss.

Back home I get a very nasty surprise. Mrs. Brinkman shows me a letter from Momma's social worker: *Mrs. Kowalski is doing well in rehab and will soon be transferred to a community facility. Regrettably, because she feels she needs to deal with some personal issues, she has requested that her daughter, Martha, not visit at this time.*

I'm majorly pissed off. Plus, my feelings are hurt, and Mrs. Brinkman can tell. "Well, wait a couple of weeks, and maybe we can try again."

What-*ever*. I nod airily, like I couldn't care less, wishing I could talk to someone about this, like maybe Shavonne. I really miss her, especially since I started school, but do I dare tell her where I am? What do I say? "Hey, I'm staying with the Brinkmans, but don't ever, ever call me because I don't want Nikki to know I'm not from Columbus"? Same with Jerome, because he might just give me away.

Already this fantasy is getting complicated.

.  .  .

After dinner, it happens. The phone rings, and, yes, it's Danny, and, yes, he wants to go out, and, yes, he's picking me up in thirty minutes! I shower fast, then prance around in my walk-in closet in a state of naked panic. Dress or skirt? Pants or jeans? White lace bikini or cream-colored French-cut?

Gina's reflection replies: "You are *such* a *slut*. You think he's gonna see 'em?"

I don't know. Maybe? No! God, I hope so.

Mrs. Brinkman's not thrilled about me going out on a school night, but Danny promises to have me home by ten. We hang out at a coffee shop near Shaker Square, and lucky for me Danny does most of the talking while I sit there happily, holding his hand under the table. *Thump-thump, thump-thump.* Move out of the way, ribs, my heart's gonna explode!

Even though I don't ask him, he eventually brings up Caitlin. "We broke up a few days ago. She kind of gets on my nerves." Why? What does she do? Tell me, tell me, so I don't do the same thing! "I see her around at the ski club, but that's about it."

"She skis, too, huh?" Okay. I can learn.

"Well, that's all we have in common. I guess her dad told her musicians don't make any kind of money, so she started giving me grief about going to Juilliard—"

Wait. Stop the clock! "You're going to Juilliard?"

"Oh, yeah. Music composition. I passed my audition and everything."

Oh, if I wasn't so hot for him, I'd rip him to pieces.

Danny looks off into the distance. "Cait couldn't care less about my music. She's clueless, you know? I mean, music to a musician is like what, art to an artist? Writing to a writer? It's all you can think about, it's like—"

Yes, yes! I know exactly what he means. How dare that diamond-nosed midget expect him to give it up!

"A passion," I blurt out, finishing his sentence. "I know! I know what that feels like." At least I did, at one time. And now my mind wanders to Mr. Brinkman's cello, just sitting there in its dusty case, alone and unused . . .

Danny watches me intently for a second, then tosses some bills on the table. "Come on back with me, Gina. I've got a surprise for you."

He lives a few blocks from the Brinkmans, in a house twice as big but not nearly as homey. And, at this moment, definitely unoccupied. Trying to squelch the ding-ding-dinging in my brain, I ask innocently, "So, like where are your folks?"

"Out," is all he says as he tows me over to his piano. "I finished that piece I was working on, and I wanted you to be the first one to hear it." His gold class ring glitters as his fingers sweep over the keys, and after he finishes the jazzy, romantic tune, he asks, "Can you guess the title? I kind of named it after you."

Martha? I think stupidly. And then he shows me what he wrote at the top of the page:

*"Autumn" by Daniel Brinkman*
*For Gina*

"Wow." That's me, I remember. Me, Gina. "That's so cool! Thanks."

Pleased, he leans over to kiss my cheek. "So, you want something to drink?"

"Sure." I follow him to the bar where he pours two Cokes,

adding a smidgen of rum to both. "Yikes, what're you trying to do, get me drunk?"

"No way. Uncle Dick'll kill me if I bring you back drunk."

"Oh, he's already seen me—" I stop as his eyebrows shoot up. Straight, black, impossibly thick eyebrows, like those dark, sexy guys in foreign films. "Never mind. It's a long story."

Smiling, Danny brushes his knuckles along the side of my face. "So when are you gonna start telling me some of these long stories of yours?"

I take a gulp of my Coke, tasting the rum. Gina, I know, is treading on ver-ry dangerous ground here. "Oh, one of these days I'll tell you all my secrets."

"Promise?"

"Promise." Another big fat lie.

He shows me around his Taj Mahal house and then leads me, kind of bashfully, into his bedroom. My brain alarm dings even louder, but my feet keep moving. I case the photos on his dresser, jealously searching for Caitlin, as he flips a CD into the player. Once again, Elvis starts singing, "Wise men say . . ." and Danny, without a word, yanks his sweater over his head, holds out a hand, and smiles that dark, sexy smile of his—and that's when it hits me.

Tonight's the night.

Setting my Coke aside, he pulls me down beside him onto the fluffy plaid comforter. "Gina. Have you ever been with a guy?"

Dazed, I shake my head. What, he can't tell?

"I promise I won't do anything you don't want me to do. It's just that—it's like I've known you my whole life, and I don't even know the first thing about you. Just that you're so, so beautiful." He brushes my hair back and starts kissing me everywhere.

Okay, okay. There's gotta be a thousand reasons why I better come to my senses again. Like, what about those incurable diseases they warn you about in school? Oh, and don't forget Momma's you-let-a-boy-into-your-pants-once-you-ain't-never-gonna-see-him-again speech?

"Don't be nervous," he says softly into my ear, his hands already under my yellow cashmere sweater, unhooking my bra, pulling it free. He tries to slide my sweater over my head, but, horribly shy, I push him feebly away. So he fastens his lips to my throat, then moves them lower . . . and lower. "I'd never do anything to hurt you, Gina," he says between pants. "If you want me to stop, then tell me, okay? Trust me."

I soak up every word, wondering what the old Martha would say—but no, I won't think about Martha. I'm Gina now, and I'm with Danny, Danny, Danny . . .

So I do it. I trust him, and I let him go all the way, trying not to pay attention as he fumbles, one-handed, with what I guess is a condom wrapper. I've seen R-rated movies with Shavonne, so I figured I'd know what to do, or at least be able to fake my way through it. But it kind of hurts, and it's faster than I expected, too fast for me to do anything back.

Then he holds me so tight, I can feel my bones crack. "I love you, Gina."

And Gina whispers back, "I love you, too."

## 33

Professor Leopold Moscowitz: short and stocky, with a flowing gray mane, thick overgrown eyebrows, and clacking dentures. First thing out of his mouth at the start of my lesson is that he doesn't, under any circumstances, "poot up vit boo-shit." "Boo-shit" meaning not practicing, not paying attention, tardiness, skipping lessons, or not progressing as fast as *he* thinks I should. He doesn't waste his time, he adds, with no-talent nobodies. At least that's what I think he said. His English sucks, and those clacking teeth drive me nuts.

"Play," he says, thrusting a pile of music at me.

"Can I look it over first?"

"Vat's to look over?" *Clack, clack.* "You can either play it or you cannot play it. And vee only have an hour, so do not vaste any more of my time."

Sheesh! Slowly I open the case, and the professor stares at the cello like I just unveiled the Holy Grail.

"Magnificent," he murmurs, touching the scroll. "Treat it with kindness, with respect. It vill be your best friend."

I lift the cello out with cold, cold hands. I haven't played for so long, how can I possibly play now? I couldn't even bring myself to tune it, and had Danny do it for me. Until now, this very moment, I've hardly touched the thing at all.

But the cello climbs into my arms with a will of its own, the bow fitting into my fingers as naturally as a pencil. I fill my lungs, straighten my shoulders, and concentrate only on the music in front of me. When the notes come out frazzled, I wonder if it's too late. Maybe it's already gone, everything I learned.

"Stop, stop!" Covering his ears. "Oy, I can't bear it!"

"Um, I haven't played for a while—"

His beady eyes gleam. "Hmph!" *Clack, clack.* "That is perfectly obvious."

"—and I'm trying to focus, and—"

"Do not focus! Just look at the notes and play."

I suck air in, whoosh it out slowly, and raise my bow again. Okay, don't focus, don't concentrate, just look—at—the—notes—and—play! I touch the bow to the strings, and after another wobbly start, I'm back—my eyes see the notes, and the music flows from my brain, down to my fingers, and out through the cello. I don't even know what I'm playing, but it's very heavy on the vibrato, which is when you make your fingers quiver on the strings. Mine quiver so hard, my left wrist almost cracks in two.

I finish with a dramatic screech and then sit there, panting. The roof doesn't cave in. In fact, nothing happens at all. Is he the least bit impressed? Who can tell? That homicidal look on his face seems to be his normal expression.

Silence, heavy shrug, and one final *clack*. "Okay, you need vork. But ve'll see vat you can do."

· · ·

From then on, I spend every spare moment with either my cello or with Danny. Movies, dinners, playing our instruments together, and concerts, lots of concerts! The ones at Severance Hall are my favorite. Every time we go, I sit there in a trance, soaking up the music, and picturing me up there in the middle of that orchestra. I want to see the conductor's face for a change. I want to feel the hot lights on my skin, feel the music from every side, feel that thundering applause—and know, without a doubt, that people are clapping for me.

Danny's the only one who even remotely understands. Now he's teaching me how to write music, and it's hard, but a lot of fun. I hate when we're not together, and I think about him every second. I even sleep with the yellow sweater I wore that first night, just so I can smell him all night long.

Tonight Nikki catches me floating upstairs after he drops me off. "Nice hickey," she comments with a vicious grin.

I slap my hand over my neck. "Um, so how was rehearsal?"

Nikki tugs at her leotard. "Awesome! One of the girls ripped up her knee, so they gave me her part. Now I'll be onstage even longer, and I get my name and bio in the program." She pirouettes alongside me as I make a beeline to the john. "Did Danny tell you about the party?"

"What party?"

"Natalie's birthday party tomorrow."

"He didn't say anything about a party."

"Oh, he probably just forgot."

When Danny calls me a while later for our usual bedtime chat, I lie there with Taffy's chin on my ankle, waiting for a chance to ask about Natalie's party—but he goes on and on about his "Autumn" composition and how he just now decided to enter it in a competition, and, well, it'd be rude to change the subject.

Then his dad, sounding unnervingly like Momma, hollers at him to "get off the goddamn phone!" So he finishes with, "Love you, babe. God, I can't wait to see you!"

"Me, too." His father's bitching grows louder, and I quickly add, "So I guess I'll see you tomorrow at—" But the phone goes dead. "Asshole!" I snap, meaning his dad, of course, and Taffy's head perks up, like, Hey, what's with you?

Poor Danny. Maybe music's not the only thing we have in common.

## 34

It's weird that Danny doesn't call me before Natalie's party, but I'm so busy figuring out what to wear, I hardly give it a thought. I wiggle into a short ruffled skirt and tights and an autumny-colored turtleneck sweater, then blow dry my hair while Nikki hands out pointers.

Then, as I'm twirling in front of the mirror, I hear, "Hey, who's this?"

In her hand is Jerome's class picture. She took it out of my trunk!

Out loud I say calmly, "Oh, him? He's just a friend," but inside I'm screaming: *Get out of my shit and mind your own beeswax!*

"So who is he, like your boyfriend or something?" she asks, staring at the *X*'s and *O*'s Shavonne drew on the back.

I force a laugh. "My boyfriend? No, he's just somebody I used to know." From where? From school? From the neighborhood? Jesus, no, not the neighborhood. Whatever possessed me to leave that picture right on top? Am I subconsciously trying to screw up?

With a sunny smile, I pry it away, bury it, and snap the latch of my trunk. Nikki doesn't mention it again, but on the way to the party she sends me odd searching looks, like she's trying to figure something out.

Except for the other Brinkmans and a couple of girls from school, I don't know anyone at Natalie's party. Most of the kids are Natalie's pals, and Nikki introduces me as "a friend of the family." They all say hi and then promptly ignore me. Danny, too bad for me, doesn't seem to be around.

My unspoken question gets an answer when I hear Natalie complain, "That brother of mine is so totally dead! I can't *believe* he went to New York. My mom's ready to kill him."

"Typical," Nikki says with her usual flick of a hand. "So when does he get back?"

"Tomorrow night, I guess. If they don't get snowed in."

New York? Danny never said a word about New York. "What's he doing there?"

They both look at me like they forgot I'm in the room, and Natalie nudges Nikki with her bony elbow. "Skiing, what else? You mean he didn't tell you?"

Nikki sends me a semiapologetic smile. "I told you he forgot. His memory's awful. Nat, you remember last year, when he took Caitlin to homecoming and forgot to hire the limo? God, she was mad! Oh, and I remember—"

Blah, blah, blah. I move away, sick and unsteady. So does this mean Danny went skiing with Caitlin? And purposely didn't tell me because he knew I wouldn't like it?

I wish like hell I'd never come to this stupid party. Nobody's talking to me, I didn't think to bring a gift, and the music they're listening to sucks beyond belief. I hide out in the kitchen for a while, stuffing my face with Fritos and listening to Danny's dad howling uproariously in the next room. He's had a few too many. God, I wish I could join him!

When I get back to the family room, Nikki and Natalie are gone. Completely invisible to everyone else, I fetch my coat and slink out the back door into the garage. My heart pings at the sight of Danny's red Corvette. Do I consider myself dumped, or do I have to wait till it's announced?

Swallowing hard, I rub the hickey under my turtleneck. Voices hum just beyond the door at the other end of the garage. I move closer in time to hear Natalie say, ". . . with my dad acting like an obnoxious asshole as usual. It's so embarrassing."

"Yeah, I know," Nikki answers. "Been there, done that."

"At least your dad's sober now."

"Yeah, well. Who knows for how long?"

"At least he goes to meetings. Mine won't."

"Well, mine has no choice if he wants to stay married to my mom."

Meetings? As in AA meetings? *Mr. Brinkman?*

Edging closer, I sneak a peek through the window. Natalie, huddled in the crushed snow against the side of the garage, puffs on a cigarette before passing it to Nikki. Trust me on this one: it's not tobacco they're smoking.

"They still doing okay?" Natalie's foggy breath clouds her semiskeletal face.

"Far as I can tell."

"They talking about it yet?"

"About Rachel? Nah. Not a single friggin' word."

"Well, you're just as bad," Natalie points out.

"What's to talk about? I mean, it's been almost two years."

"You miss her?"

"Duh! What do you think?"

"Well, you always said she got on your nerves," Natalie reminds her.

"I did not!"

"No big deal, Nik. Sisters get on each other's nerves all the time. Brothers, too," she adds darkly.

"Yeah, whatever. Let's not talk about this anymore."

Damn. Why not? I found out more about this family in the past five minutes than I've been able to learn over the past few weeks.

"Pretty good." Nikki, mellowing out, watches a puff of pot smoke curl away from her lips and vanish into the air. "Way better than the crap I got from Justin last week."

I swear I don't know what blows me away more, finding out that Mr. Brinkman's in AA or watching Nikki smoke a joint.

"So what's the story with what's-her-face?" Natalie asks abruptly. "Is she banging my brother? C'mon, Nik. I know he tells you everything."

"Hey, why don't you ask him yourself?"

"I'm not asking him anything. He couldn't even hang around for my party."

"Yeah, that was harsh. Anyway," Nikki adds, lowering her voice, "I'm not a hundred percent sure, but I think she prefers her guys a *lit*-tle bit darker."

"Huh?"

"We're getting ready to come over here, right? And she's got this box or something that she keeps all her junk in, and there's this picture of some black guy, with hugs *and* kisses all over the back!"

Natalie nearly strangles on her next toke. "Shut *up*!"

"Swear to God, Nat, I almost peed my pants. Oh, and then she like grabs it right out of my hand. It was funny as hell. You should've seen her face."

"Well, you know what they say about men of color." Giggling,

Natalie whispers something to Nikki, something that sends them both into a spluttering fit. And I know what she said, because Shavonne told me it's true.

Spinning around, I rush back toward the house, whacking my leg against the bumper of the car. This is just—too—much! First Danny sneaking off to New York like that. What did he think? I wouldn't come to this party, wouldn't figure it out? Then I find out Mr. Brinkman goes to AA. How is that even possible? He's the most perfect person I know! And now his treacherous daughter is starting rumors about me?

Somehow I endure the rest of this suck-fest, only because Mr. and Mrs. Brinkman hang around till the very end. I hit my bed the instant I get home, but sleep doesn't come. Instead, I keep imagining a ski lodge and two shadowy figures in front of a fire, sipping spiked hot chocolate, laughing and whispering, then sneaking off to have mad, passionate sex. Because even though it'd been my first time, no way can I say the same for Danny. That one-handed rubber trick of his gave him away.

Huh. I bet Caitlin isn't afraid to take off her clothes. I bet she prances around naked with hardware through her nipples. I twist and flop, knotting the sheets around my throat. What if he gives her his ring again? What if I lose him forever?

Finally I sleep, and then I don't want to wake up. I spend the next day in bed with only Taffy for company, wondering if this is how Momma feels when she locks herself up in her room.

Finally Nikki pounces in and tosses me the phone. My pulse quadruples its speed when I hear Danny say, "Nat told me you were at the party yesterday. God, Gina. I'm so stupid! I can't believe I forgot to tell you I wouldn't be there. We've been planning this trip for weeks and there was like no way out of it. Honestly, Gina. I'm really sorry."

Oh—my—God. He didn't dump me at all. He did forget! A totally honest mistake that anybody could make. Why do I always jump to the wrong conclusions? Do I enjoy making myself miserable?

"You want to get something to eat?" he asks hopefully.

"Oh, I guess." A pathetic attempt to sound relaxed. "Give me an hour, okay?"

One hour later he sweeps me into his arms. Once again he begs me to forgive him. Well, of course I do. How could I not? And I'm proud of myself for not asking about Caitlin. Maybe she was with him . . . but then again, maybe not.

Maybe I'd rather not know.

"Come home with me, okay?" he says, mouth warm against my ear.

I don't even think of saying no. His house is dark, and he lets us in with his key, and five seconds later we're back in his room. This time I let him pull off my clothes, one piece at a time, and drop them to the floor. He dumps me on the bed, still whispering in my ear. I soak up each magical word as the mattress bounces beneath us, waiting for that "feeling" I hear so much about, the one that'll make me gasp and shriek like Meg Ryan in *When Harry Met Sally*.

No such luck.

"I love you." Danny, when he can talk again, pants this through a mouthful of my hair.

I wrap my arms around his neck, feeling his stubble on my collarbone, his breath on my neck. "I love you, too."

No, he *couldn't* have been with Caitlin. There is just no way.

. . .

Nikki pokes her head out of her door when I make it back home two minutes before curfew. "See? You were all freaked out for nothing."

"Who said I was freaked out?"

"Well, nobody saw you all day. I thought maybe you slit your wrists or something. You know, since Danny went to New York and all."

Am I imagining it, or does she seem pleased at this idea? Feeling my secret inner bitch begin to rear her ugly head, I toss Nikki one of her own go-to-hell hand flips and sashay into my room. If I say one word, we'll both be sorry.

Too dense to take a hint, Nikki follows me in. "Um, are you mad at me or something?"

"Why?" I kick off my clothes and pull on my pj's. "Oh! You mean because you told Natalie I already have a boyfriend even though you *know* it's a total lie?"

"What? No, wait, no, I didn't, I mean, I—"

And she's a liar on top of it.

"I'm not deaf," I remind her. "I heard every word you said."

Nikki recovers faster than I expected. "Well, even if he is, it's kind of cool, I think, hooking up with a black guy. Not that *I'd* have the guts to do it. But you're so earthy, Gina. You kind of do what you want, and don't even care what people think. Right?"

Wrong. I care a lot. That's my whole problem.

"Do you mind?" I ask, because she's blocking the bathroom door. "I'd like to brush my teeth."

Eyeing me nervously, she steps aside. "So what else did you hear?" Translation: Are you gonna rat me out for toking behind the garage?

Ha! Now it's Nikki's turn to worry and sweat, and hope nobody finds out her embarrassing secrets.

" 'Night, Nikki," I say sweetly as I close the door in her face.

How did I ever think we could possibly be friends?

## 35

Question to myself: How would I feel if Shavonne disappeared from the face of the planet?

Answer to myself: Exceedingly shitty.

I mean, it's not like I have to tell her where I am. All I have to do is let her know I'm alive. And since Mr. Brinkman just gave me a cool little cell phone of my own, I don't have to worry about "Brinkman" popping up on any caller ID.

But when I dial her number, her phone is out of service, so now there's only one thing left for me to do. After finishing up with my cello lesson one day, I take the rapid transit to Public Square, then grab a bus to the projects. At school I told Nikki that I'd be stopping at a friend's, and she asked, What friend? like I have no friends of my own. I gaze out the grimy bus window at a neighborhood that's ten times worse than I remember, right down to the squished cat on the curb and some dude peeing on a dumpster.

Swinging my cello case, I leap off the bus and race to Shavonne's. "Hi. Remember me?"

Shavonne's mouth hangs open. "Wow. What the fuck?"

I haven't heard that word for so long, it makes me break into a grin. "I called you a couple of times, but your phone's been disconnected."

"Well, that's what happens ain't nobody payin' the bill."

I breeze in and proudly model my exquisite black coat, but she looks me up and down without any oohs or ahhs. Her unbraided hair fans out in a dark cloud, and she's skinnier than ever. "You sick or something?"

"Why?" she asks snarkily. " 'Fraid you'll catch something?"

"Don't be stupid. You just look . . ." Sick, I finish silently.

"My mom's in the hospital. And Aunt Bernice moved in with us, and she's on my last livin' nerve! Bitch even let my cat out and I ain't seen her since. Yeah, I'm sick!"

I remember, but don't mention, the dead cat on the curb. "Sorry about your mom."

Shavonne shrugs this off. "So where you been, anyway?"

I think each word carefully before I say it out loud. "My mom's in rehab again, so I'm in a foster home now."

"Get out! Where at?"

"Um, not far. It's a nice place. Nice people, too." I rush on before she can ask any questions about my new "family." "And guess what? I got a boyfriend. And guess what else? We did it!"

"Did what?"

"You know—it!" Exasperated, I spell it out. "I had sex, Shavonne! Oh Go-od. I am so in love."

"You liar. You did not."

"Oh, yes I did. Shavonne, he's awesome! We have so much in common, and he's so-o-o good-looking, like a movie star or something, and he's rich, and he's got these amazing blue eyes, and—"

Shavonne fakes a gag. "He that good-lookin', he gotta be gay."

"What? He is not!"

"Well, if he ain't, then he gotta have some kinda anterior mo-tive to be hangin' 'round you. You might be lookin' pretty slick these days, but sister-girl? You ain't nothin' but a hound dog."

I can't believe she'd try to use Elvis against me. "It's ulterior motive. Ulterior! God, don't even try to insult me if you don't know how to speak English."

"Okay, okay. Ul-ter-i-or motive."

"You don't even know what that means."

"You just come over here to piss me off?" she demands.

"You're pissing *me* off," I shoot back. "Why are you being so nasty to me?"

Shavonne leans forward to scream in my face. " 'Cause I don't give a shit about your faggot boyfriend! My mom is sick! She could die any day."

"Well, mine's sick, too. She almost died herself. She OD'd on pills, okay? Why do you think I can't go home?"

"It ain't like she got AIDS. And everybody knows about it, too, thanks to Aunt Bernice's big mouth. I got people at school who don't even want to sit down next to me. You think that's fun? Gimme your crazy old lady any day of the week."

This is the stupidest argument I've ever been in.

"You got something to drink?" I ask abruptly.

"Help your own damn self. I ain't no freakin' waiter."

I find an Orange Crush in the back of the fridge, and then rack my brain to come up with a neutral topic. "You still painting and stuff?"

"Not much. No money for supplies, ob-vi-ous-ly," she adds with a resentful glance at my coat.

This is so not working out. "Um, is Chardonnay still around?"

Shavonne relaxes a fraction. "Nope. After you sliced her up that day, they canned her triflin' ass."

Canned mine, too, but no point in reminding her. "I didn't slice her up. I didn't even nick her."

"Ain't what I heard." Shavonne's lips twitch in an almost-smile. "Hey, did ya hear she finally squeezed out that two-headed fetus of hers? Girl, that thing's uglier than a busted boil. Kenyatta saw 'em at Eagle Mart, and Blubber Butt was stuffin' rubbers in the stroller."

Well, thank God for that.

"And Jerome's been by. He keeps asking about you, wondering why you ain't called him. Why don't you give me your number and I'll give it to him?"

Just what I need. My nonexistent black boyfriend calling the Brinkman house.

I squint nervously at the clock. "I can't stay too long."

"You just got here," Shavonne points out.

"I know, but I've got to get back before dark."

"Aw, Aunt Bernice can take you home when she gets back from the hospital." Shavonne's already scrambling for paper and a pencil.

"Seriously, I gotta go—" I stop. "Where's my purse?" Where's my obscenely overpriced one-hundred-percent-calfskin, Juicy-freaking-Couture handbag? Did I leave it on the bus?

"Got any money?" I ask, feeling horribly faint.

Shavonne scoffs. "Yeah, millions, if I can dig up the combo to my safe."

I'm dead meat without any bus fare, and I thank God over and over that my ritzy new cell phone is still safe in my coat pocket. I dial the number with dread, praying Nikki doesn't pick up. All I can do is tell Mrs. Brinkman the truth, that I'm stuck in the ghetto without a way home.

Shavonne fixes me with a laser stare. "You didn't give her the address."

"I didn't?"

"No. All you said was, 'I'm at Shavonne's.' "

I try to think of a way out of this. Like, duh, of *course* I gave her the address before I even came over here. That would be perfectly reasonable, perfectly believable. But it won't keep Shavonne from finding out where I live now that Mrs. Brinkman herself is already on her way.

I have no choice but to confess, and Shavonne blinks in astonishment. "The Brinkmans?"

"Yeah."

"My mom's Brinkmans? With the yappy little dog and the snotty daughter?"

"Yeah." I give her the CliffsNotes version. "And I didn't tell you at first because it's just so weird." And I didn't want you calling me! But how can I say that?

"The Brinkmans," she repeats. "Wow. I mean . . . wow."

"Yeah. And did you know they had another kid who died?"

"I heard that once," she says absently, still stuck on the idea of me at the Brinkmans.

"So what happened to her?"

"Ma never said. Probably she got her head sucked into that fancy bathtub of theirs." Shavonne giggles. "Or maybe Nikki slipped her a poisoned apple."

"Not helpful, Shavonne."

"So ask them, why don't you? I don't know, and I don't care."

The conversation dwindles, so Shavonne digs up a battered drawing pad and a tiny piece of charcoal. She sketches in silence, forcing me to stare at the wall—her cable TV has also been cut off—till Mrs. Brinkman shows up and toots the horn.

Shavonne sneers through the window. "Oooh, a Jag-you-ah-h? What she do, make you ride in the trunk?"

Ignoring this, I throw an arm around her neck. "I'm really, really sorry about your mom."

She hugs me back tightly, hanging on a couple seconds longer than necessary. "I know. And I'm sorry I'm such a bitch." She bops me in the head as I duck out the door.

Mrs. Brinkman attacks me before I get a single foot in the car. "You better have a good explanation for this, Gina."

"I lost my purse. I said I was sorry."

"I don't mean that. I mean, what were you thinking? Riding a bus through a neighborhood like this."

A neighborhood like this? This used to be my neighborhood in case she forgot.

"If you wanted to visit Shavonne, why didn't you ask me? I could have driven you myself. My God, don't you read the news-papers? Where's your common sense?"

"I couldn't!" I burst out. "I was afraid—" I bite my lip.

"Afraid of what?" She looks genuinely flabbergasted. "That I wouldn't let you come?"

"It's not that, I just—" Dammit, Gina, say it already! "I didn't want Nikki to know where I was." Then, in a teeny voice, "You didn't tell her, did you?"

Mrs. Brinkman sighs. "Of course I didn't." I fall limp with relief, till she adds, "Let me ask you something. Don't you find it tiresome, this cloak-and-dagger routine of yours?"

"Huh?"

"Pretending to be someone else. I mean, really, why bother? You're smart, you're funny, and you've got a very good heart. You shouldn't have to lie to feel . . . accepted." She says it as an after-thought, like it's not important at all.

"I don't lie," I lie.

"No? Well, have you gotten around to telling Danny you're not from Columbus?"

Hell, I haven't even told Danny I'm only fourteen. Like Nikki, he must think I'm fifteen because I'm already a sopho-more. Going on sixteen, too, since I have a birthday coming up in March.

"Well?" She waits, and I can hear the humming of her bull-shit detector.

"Not yet," I finally admit. "You didn't say anything, did you? To his folks or anything?"

Mrs. Brinkman tugs on her leather-gloved fingers. "No. But only because, to be perfectly honest, I didn't think you'd be with us this long. Now don't get me wrong," she adds quickly. "I'm glad you're here, and you're welcome to stay as long as you like. But if you're going to be part of our family, you need to be hon-est. And the longer you wait, the harder it's going to be."

I twist a button on my coat.

"Gina?"

"I heard you!" It comes out kind of snarky, so I quickly add, "Okay. I'll do it. I just have to, um, figure out what to say."

Mrs. Brinkman nods, satisfied. "And I think now might be a good time for us to have a talk about you and Danny. I know you really like him, and he certainly seems to like you. But he's what, three years older? And boys, if you don't already know it, can be, *mmm*, a bit pushy at times. I'm not saying Danny is, but—well, I'd hate to see you in a situation you don't feel you can get out of."

I nod with the seriousness of any fourteen-year-old virgin. "I'll be careful. I promise."

"I know, and I trust you. I just wouldn't be doing my job if I didn't get on your back about this."

Okay, I believe her, but I'm getting sick of the lecture. "Shavonne's phone got disconnected. She says they can't pay the bill."

Mrs. Brinkman throws me a look. "Are you changing the subject?"

"No! But doesn't that suck?"

She thinks for a moment. "Yes. I'm sorry. I'll take care of it tomorrow."

"You will?"

"Of course I will. It's the least I can do. Mrs. Addams was with us for five years and, well, I feel terrible I didn't think of helping them out before this. Anything else you think they need?"

"Everything," I say, elated that Mrs. Brinkman's not going to kill me after all, and on top of that she really wants to help Shavonne!

"I'll talk to my husband," she promises, smiling now, which makes me smile, too. "We'll do whatever we can."

"Thanks! And I really am sorry, you know. For sneaking off, and—" Being my usual snotty self. I really do have to watch that.

She reaches over and squeezes my hand. "I know. Just please, please, Gina—"

"I know. Be honest." I make a face. "Okay, I'll tell Danny."

She squeezes harder, with an edgy glance in my direction. "This isn't just about Danny, Gina. You need to start being honest with yourself."

## • • • • • 36 • • • • •

On Valentine's Day, I have my first counseling session with Zelda because that's the one thing Judge Monaghan refused to throw out. First she bulldozes me with what she considers good news: Momma finally made it to a halfway house, so it's just a matter of time before they dump her back into society—after she finds a job, of course, and some place to live. Not with Wayne, Zelda assures me. Momma decided that for herself.

That's about the only good thing I've heard so far. "Well, if she's so much better, then how come I can't see her?"

"She's recovering, Martha. She needs to concentrate on herself."

"Well, maybe *I* don't want to see *her*. Anybody think of that?"

"I understand," she says.

Understand? Ha! It wasn't her mom who OD'd under her nose, never mind that I would've been the one to find her cold dead body.

"So," she continues, "how are you doing, hmm?"

"Well, I'm playing the cello again. I'm in the school orchestra now, and I'm taking private lessons. And—!" I pause for effect, saving the best for last. "I'm auditioning for the Great Lakes Academy of Music."

Yes, it's true. I'm officially signed up, and my audition's in April. Mr. Brinkman was thrilled when I told him I want to do this, got me the paperwork and stuff, and made a big deal out of the whole thing. Even Professor Moscowitz says I should give it a shot. Funny, since he's the one who's been telling me I'm about as coordinated as a gorilla.

Zelda seems pleased, too. "Well! Congratulations."

"Yeah, isn't it cool? I'm even composing my own piece." Not from scratch, exactly—I've based it on some old seventeenth-century tune Danny dug up—but still, it counts.

"Wonderful, Martha. I'm sure your mother will be very proud of you."

"Man, I can't believe you said that with a straight face."

"You don't agree?"

I ignore this. "Look. The Brinkmans think it's cool I play, and they're, like, spending all this money on my lessons, and—well, they *expect* me into get into that school. It's just different here, you know?"

"So how do you think you will feel," she asks slowly, "when the time comes for you to go home?"

What is she talking about? I am home.

That's when I realize the truth for the first time.

Yes, I love my mom, because she's my mom, okay? Yes, I do want her to get better, and, yes, I want her to be happy. But even if that happens, I don't want to leave the Brinkmans. Whether Momma gets better or not, whether she stays sober or not, I am so not leaving this house alive.

Once again, Zelda zeros in on my exact thoughts. "Ma-artha . . ."

"Gina," I remind her through clenched teeth.

"You remember this is temporary?" She watches me wind a strand of hair around my finger, examining it for split ends, and takes the hint. "Well, keep up the good work. I'll see you in a couple weeks."

Well, at least she didn't make me talk about Bubby. And now, thinking about Bubby makes me think about Rachel. I've been here two months, and except for Nikki that first day, and at Natalie's party, not one single person has mentioned her name.

I know she existed—there are hundreds of photos of her around, from baby pictures up to, well, almost my age, I guess. Dark hair like Mr. Brinkman's, not blond like Nikki's, but with the same arctic blue Brinkman eyes, same dimples, same dazzling red-carpet smile. I even peeked in her room once, but it didn't tell me much. Most of her stuff is gone. It kind of made me sad in a way.

Do they feel about Rachel the way I feel about Bubby? Like, if I do think about him, it's like picking open a scab. I start to remember little things, like that Labor Day barbecue, how Bubby smelled like barbecue sauce and sweet baby sweat, how he fell asleep in my arms . . .

The memory threatens to choke me like a massive hairball. God! If thinking about Bubby can make me so suddenly depressed, what'll happen if Zelda starts making me say this stuff out loud?

Back home, I swallow one Percodan to ward off a migraine. Danny's taking me out to dinner, and I want to enjoy myself and not be in pain. And I think I'll ask him about Rachel, too. He never brings her up either, but maybe I can work her into the conversation. Too bad I didn't think of this before.

. . .

The restaurant Danny picks is so incredibly fancy, I spend the first two courses gawking at the tuxes on the waiters, and wondering why nobody thought to stick the prices on the menu. By the third course, I make more of a point to pay attention to Danny and unfortunately don't think of Rachel till it's time for dessert.

But when my cheesecake and coffee arrive, Danny sidetracks me with, "Hey, did you decide what you're playing for your audition yet?"

"Yes! *Sleepers, Awake.*"

"Solo?"

"Well, um, I could use an accompanist," I hint, licking cream cheese and crumbs from my cold fork.

"Me? Hey, I'd love to."

"Really?"

"Absolutely."

"Thank you, thank you! Oh, I just gotta get into that school!"

"You will," he promises. "It's the best school around. That's where I wanted to go, too, except my dad wouldn't let me."

"How come?"

Danny shrugs. "Well, it's not exactly college prep, you know. My dad's got this thing about me going to medical school. You know, take people's gall bladders out for the rest of my life, like he does."

"But you're going to Juilliard, right?"

"Yeah, but—well, that wasn't easy." Face clouding over, he drops his voice, like he's afraid the wrong person might be listening. "In case you haven't heard, my dad's got a drinking problem.

He's not the easiest guy to talk to. Um, Nat told me how he got blitzed at her party and made a real ass out of himself."

"He wasn't so bad," I fib. "A little loud, maybe."

"We don't get along," he says bluntly. "He can be a real jerk when he's drinking, and my mom blows it all off. I mean, wait till he cuts into the wrong person one of these days and gets sued for malpractice. Maybe then she'll start paying attention."

Okay, forget Rachel—now is my perfect chance to tell him about Momma! The perfect time to let him know he's not alone, that I know exactly what he puts up with day in and day out. I can totally spill my guts and tell him everything, everything . . .

But, very quickly, like he's anxious to change the subject, he reaches into his pants pocket and holds out a tiny box. "Hey, happy Valentine's Day."

Inside the box, I find a sparkly, floating heart on a delicate silver chain. "Oh, my God. It's beautiful!" And the first real piece of jewelry I've ever owned. "Thank you," I add in a whisper, touching the tiny heart.

He takes it from me, and fastens it gently around my neck. "Come on. Let's get out of here."

His folks are home for a change, but he sneaks me in anyway, and as we're rolling around under the covers, I hear a distinct snap. "Oh, shit." Yep, my glasses, busted beyond repair.

Danny grins. "I think that's the first time I've ever heard you swear." I'm ready to die of embarrassment, but he laughs and kisses me hard as I stammer an apology. "Hey, why don't you try contacts this time? Show off your eyes!"

Thankfully, Mrs. Brinkman thinks this is a great idea, so the next day I get contacts, plus a trendy new pair of glasses. I stare dumbly at my reflection in every shiny surface, shocked at the sight of my own face without a hunk of plastic on my nose.

I thank her over and over again, and say "Mrs. Brinkman" so many times, she finally laughs. "Oh, don't be formal! You're part of the family now. We don't mind if you use our first names." So now it's Richard and Claudia, and see? I was right . . .

I *am* part of this family. Claudia said so herself.

I hate to say it, but lately Shavonne hardly crosses my mind. I'm so busy with Danny and school and my twice-a-week cello lessons, to say nothing of getting ready for my Great Lakes audition. Plus I made two friends in the orchestra, Faith Kwan and Chloe Eisenberg, and thanks to them—and a generous allowance—I've discovered the joy of becoming a mall rat.

I'm not avoiding Shavonne, exactly. I just haven't figured out a way to tell the rest of the world that I'm not really "Gina." Once I do that, I can get back together with Shavonne. Jerome, too. I really do miss them, now that I think about it.

So what does Shavonne do? She calls *me*. Luckily, I make it to the phone before Nikki. "Yo, Mar-tha!"

"Oh, hi," I say softly, glancing around just in case.

"Hey, I got my phone turned back on! Boss Man sent us some money. You didn't put him up to it, did you?" she adds suspiciously.

"Not me," I fib, unsure if this would be a bad thing or a good thing.

"Why you whispering?" she blasts in my ear.

Claudia's right. This stuff is re-eally getting old.

"So, did you call Jerome yet? Girl, he been buggin' me to death—"

"I told you, I've been—"

"Busy. Yeah, I know. Busy with what?"

"Duh. My audition?" I quickly fill her in on Great Lakes, how Danny's going to accompany me on the piano, and how I'm composing my own piece. Without comment, she lets me ramble till I run out of breath. "You still there?"

"Yeah," she says shortly, ignoring everything I said. "Well, I gave him your number, so I guess he'll be calling you."

"You *what?*" And it comes out sounding awful.

Long silence. "Okay. I get it now, bitch." She hangs up on me flat.

Crap, crap, crap! I dial her back. "Look, I'm sorry. But I gotta talk to you about something—" How, how do I explain it?

"Talk to me about what? Your wonderful, perfect life? You and that piece of shit cello of yours?" Stunned, I can't speak, and then she blurts out, "Sorry! I'm sorry. Don't hang up on me, okay?"

"I wasn't going to." Even though I almost did.

She's crying now, and Shavonne never cries. "I just want things to be like they used to be. I just want us to be friends—"

"We are!"

"—and I want my mom to get better, okay? I can't stand this no more, all this in-between shit. Either let her die, or don't let her die. You know what I'm sayin'?"

"Maybe she won't die, Shavonne. People can have AIDS and live a really long time."

She sniffs once, and her voice is steady again. Too steady. "Uh-huh, that's right. You the expert on everything. Anyway," she yammers over my feeble protest, "have a great life. Let me know when you can work me into your busy-ass schedule." Bam!

If I were any kind of a friend, I'd call her back again, but now *my* feelings are hurt. Hey, it's not my fault her mom is sick, and it's not my fault she's so jealous of me. For the first time in my life, I like my life. Why apologize for that?

. . .

That night I dream about money falling from the sky, and a sock monkey dancing through piles of green bills. By morning I'm exhausted, and the day lasts forever. When study hall rolls around, I finish up my science homework in eight minutes flat and then hunch over my notebook, writing *Danny Brinkman* in perfectly aligned columns. Brinkman, Brinkman, what a beautiful name!

I write my own name, too, and then somehow *Gina Kowalski* turns into *Gina Brinkman*. I scribble and scribble, forgetting all about Shavonne as I find myself sucked into a brand-new fantasy:

*Gina Brinkman, the newly adopted daughter of prominent Shaker Heights attorney Richard Brinkman, invites you to her debut at Severance Hall.*

*Renowned cellist Gina Brinkman, appearing in person at Carnegie Hall.*

*Gina Brinkman, principal cellist for the Cleveland Symphony Orchestra and wife of renowned composer Daniel Brinkman, is considered by many to be . . .*

My pen stops dead as a shadow hits the page.

"Gina, right?" It's Caitlin Mackenzie, who knows perfectly well who I am. "Is it true you're still going with Danny Brinkman?"

I flip my notebook over. "Maybe. Why?"

"Well, I'm not sure if you know this. But Danny and me, we're practically engaged?"

Um, excuse me, Caitlin. What galaxy are you from? "Well, that's news to me. I don't see a ring on your finger."

"Oh, we go through this all the time. Typical guy stuff. They get on these kicks about going out with other girls, and once they get it out of their system, they always come back. At least Danny does," she adds with a confident smirk.

I'm sweating like a pig, and not only that, I can't seem to tear my eyes away from her jeweled nostril. "So, like, is this something I should care about?"

Broad smile. "I just thought I'd tell you before you get too serious about him. I mean honestly, Gina. You're a sophomore, right? Danny and I, we're both graduating this year. What do you think he's gonna do with some high school kid?"

I can't say a word. I just wish to hell I'd cut study hall today.

"We had a really long talk, on that ski trip we took?" None of her questions are really questions, and it bugs me to no end. "And we'll be back together before you know it. Anyway, I thought I should tell you."

That freaking ski trip!

"Well, thanks for the warning," I manage to reply. "But don't bet on it, okay?"

"Oh, it's a pretty safe bet. Why don't you ask him yourself?" Exceedingly smug, she saunters back to her own desk, and I can see her lacy underpants peeking out of her jeans as she bends over toward her snickering friends.

Well, what—a—bitch! Do I tell Danny about this? If I bring up that ski trip, he might think I don't trust him. I crunch my knuckles and take a few deep breaths. Oh, forget it! That nose-studded midget-freak is obviously delusional. Danny loves me and she knows it. No wonder she's flipping out.

. . .

The house is deserted when I get home, and I love having it to myself. This is exactly the kind of house I'll live in when I'm famous.

Huge, quiet, and peaceful, with everything perfectly in its place. Nobody complaining or screaming, no rude interruptions—

The front doorbell chimes, and I hear "Martha! Yo, Martha!" and spy Jerome waving wildly through the window.

What the—? I tackle the hysterical Taffy and shut her up in the basement. No point in asking him how he got my address. Shavonne's revenge, no doubt.

He trudges in and gazes around, awestruck. "Damn. Ain't this nothin'?"

We stare at each other in bare recognition. Taller now, he looks different with his hair twisted into braids, and I sure don't remember his shoulders being this big.

"You look cool," he says. "Nice hair. Where's your glasses?"

"Contacts. Hey, you look really good, too."

That said, we stand there like dummies. I think about hugging him, but it might embarrass us more. I bring him some leftover cherry pie, and as he shovels it in, I notice the way he slouches, how he seems older and tougher, and—well, a lot like Anthony.

"Shavonne sent you, right?"

"Naw, it was my idea."

"Everybody okay? Your grandma and them?"

"Yeah, we're all fine." He catches me up on some stuff at school, and on Mario's latest antics and Aunt Gloria's latest meltdown, and how Wayne's crankier than ever since he broke down and got a job, and how he's threatening to evict the Lindseys now that Anthony's lowlife homies seem to have taken up permanent residence. He chews quietly for a moment before adding, "Guess what? My mom's back."

"What?"

"Yeah, she got a place in the projects and, well, she wants me to come live with her now."

"Live with her? Really?" He nods, so I ask, sounding a bit too much like Zelda, "Um, are you happy about that?"

"What do *you* think?"

"I don't know. That's why I'm asking."

Jerome studies Claudia's row of suspended copper pots, like one of them will magically come to life and tell him how he should feel. "I guess. I don't know. She sure ain't changed much."

Biting my tongue, I wait for the details and when he doesn't offer any, I switch back to Shavonne. "When you talk to her, tell her I'm sorry, okay? About not calling her and stuff."

"She thinks you're mad at her 'cause you never want to hang out."

"I'm not mad, and I just saw her—" When? Oh yeah. Weeks ago, the day I lost my purse.

My head swivels in the direction of the ticking clock. Jerome notices. "Well, I gotta take off. Where's the john around this place?"

I show him around upstairs, and turn him loose in my bathroom. Downstairs, I'm scampering back and forth, cleaning up evidence, when a long, ragged shriek splits the air. Nikki, bug-eyed, stands frozen in the hall, watching Jerome hip-hop his way down the sweeping staircase.

Babbling, I rush over. "Um, Nikki, this is Jerome. Jerome, this is Nikki—I mean, Nicolette."

Jerome sticks out his hand. "Yo, Nik-oh-lette. 'Sup?"

Nikki recoils, and I shuffle her aside. "Hey, I thought you had a rehearsal."

"I did." Nikki's steely eyes stay glued to Jerome. "It was canceled."

Graveyard silence. Jerome takes the hint. "Wow, man. Gotta roll." He waves me away as I tag on his heels. "Naw, it's cool.

Gimme a call sometime." He swaggers off down the driveway, hands deep in his pockets.

Nikki's all over me in an instant. "Is that the guy from the picture? What's he doing here?"

"He just stopped by to say hi. I told you we were friends," I remind her defensively.

"Well, how'd he get here? He didn't come in a car."

"How would I know? Maybe he took the bus."

"From Columbus?" At my vacant look, Nikki adds impatiently, "Columbus, Gina. Isn't that where you're from?"

Trapped and confused, I blurt, "Yes! I mean, I think he took a Greyhound."

"So what was he doing upstairs?"

"Using the john!"

She points to the back hall as she frees poor Taffy from her prison. "Well, there's one right here in case you never noticed."

"Jeez, Nikki. I showed him around, okay? If there's something you want to say, then why don't you say it?"

"Say what? Boy, are you paranoid." Nikki flips back her mane and heads upstairs. "I'm taking a nap. And don't wake me for dinner. I'm on a diet."

I hug my chest, trying to slow my thudding heart. Well, one thing's for sure: things can't possibly get shittier.

# ••••• **38** •••••

Later, as I help Claudia clear the table after dinner, I try to think of a nonchalant way to bring up Jerome. I'm sure Nikki's holding out for exactly the right moment to spring it on her folks that I had a guy in the house—*plus* it was a black guy, *plus* nobody else was home. I need to give them my version before Nikki poisons their minds.

But we're singing along with The Beach Boys: "Aruba, Jamaica—ooh, I wanna take ya!" as we put dishes away, and the next thing I know, Nikki's screaming in the doorway. "Mo-om! I've been calling you forever!"

Claudia snaps off the radio. "What's wrong? You look flushed."

"My head hurts. I need a Motrin." As Claudia gets it from the cupboard, Nikki's fiery stare never leaves my face. Huh? What did I do? I was just goofing around with her mom.

"Maybe it's a good thing you skipped your rehearsal." Claudia touches Nikki's forehead. "You do feel a little warm, honey."

Nikki jerks away. "I didn't *skip* my rehearsal! I don't skip rehearsals. It was called off, okay?" She grabs the pill, gulps it, and slams the glass on the sink. "Where's Daddy?"

"He went"—Claudia sends me a sideways look—"to a meeting."

Funny how she has no idea I already know that Richard goes to AA. It's even funnier to find out that she wants to keep it a secret from me. Weird, but I can't picture it—Richard drunk? What's he like when he's loaded? Does he get goofy like me? Vicious like Wayne? Obnoxious like his brother? Or maybe he's more like Momma with her bizarre combo of maudlin, slobbery-affectionate, and mean, mean, mean.

"Well, I gotta use his computer," Nikki announces, spinning on her heel. "My laptop's messed up."

"Oh, Nikki. You know your father doesn't like you going into his office."

"It's a paper for school! It's due tomorrow! Would you like me to flunk English, Mother? Would that make you happy?" Without waiting for an answer, she whirls out and goes straight upstairs to Richard's office, slamming the door hard enough to rattle the pots and pans.

Claudia sighs. "She's been so moody since she started those rehearsals. I honestly don't think she's getting enough sleep. And I know she's not eating enough."

Yeah, poor Nikki's overworked. Poor Nikki's under pressure. Is that any reason to act like a colossal bitch? Pressure, my ass. Try living with Momma for a week.

. . .

Danny pops in later to help with my cello composition, and just seeing him, being with him, perks me back up. True, thanks to Caitlin, I keep obsessing about that ski trip. Did he know he wouldn't be at Natalie's party, and purposely not tell me? Probably so, and I know why—because he knew I'd think the worst, which is exactly what I did.

Okay, I don't like the idea of him keeping secrets from me—and yet, who am *I* to talk about secrets? Look at my parents. Look how I was living. White trash, Momma calls us, and it doesn't even bother her to say it. Would Danny feel the same way about me if he knew who "Gina" really is?

Yes, yes, he would! He's not a shallow fake like his dad who only wants him to be a surgeon instead of helping him do what he loves best, playing and composing music. I know what his music means to him, and Danny knows the same about me. He won't care where I come from, once I get the chance to break the news. I told Claudia I'd do that, and I will, I promise.

Just not right now.

When we finish with the music, and Danny starts kissing me again, all those nasty doubts fizzle out of my head along with any thoughts of Caitlin and her inane, twisted ramblings. We make out like crazy, then come up with a plan for Saturday night: movie, maybe dinner, and then back to his house since his parents will be out of town all weekend.

"Okay, see you Saturday," he says, kissing me good-bye. "Wear something sexy."

Ha, poor Caitlin. She doesn't have a clue.

## ●●●●● **39** ●●●●●

When Saturday night rolls around, Danny is late picking me up. On top of that, he doesn't bother to come to the door. He toots the horn from the driveway, something he's never done.

"Hi," I greet him as I climb into the car, fighting to keep my extremely short skirt from hiking up around my hips. It's way too cold to be wearing anything this skimpy—already my thighs are numb—but I wanted to look sexy as hell. I succeeded, too.

"Hi," he answers without even glancing at my legs.

I lean over to kiss him. He kisses me back, but I can tell something is wrong. His lips barely move. "Hey, are you okay?"

"I'm fine," he says shortly, nearly giving me whiplash as he shoots the car into the street. "Tired tonight."

This is so not like him, and I wonder if Uncle Ted's been giving him a harder time than usual. But no, his folks are out of town. Wasn't that the whole point of tonight?

"What're we going to see?" I ask brightly. We take turns picking out movies, and it's Danny's choice tonight.

He names some movie I never even heard of, and then doesn't say another word the whole way to the theater. It turns out to be some artsy Swedish film, in black-and-white no less, and it is b-o-r-i-n-g! A comedy would've been better, or maybe a good slasher flick.

Twice I reach over and take his hand. Twice he lets go and folds his hands in his lap. I wonder if Nikki dropped a bug in his ear about Jerome. Pretending he doesn't see me trying to catch his eye, he studies the fuzzy English subtitles like he's really into this dumb movie. Maybe he dragged me here on purpose to torture me into confessing.

I suffer through the whole two-and-a-half hours in absolute despair, hoping to think of a way to bring the subject up over dinner. Am I not allowed to have friends who happen to be boys? I did nothing wrong! It's not my fault Nikki's got such a dirty mind.

I know I'm doomed when, after the show, Danny decides to take me straight home. "I've got a racquetball game tomorrow, so I can't stay out too late."

How could he pass up this chance for us to be together? Hurt beyond belief, I slump down in the seat till we roll into my driveway. When he shoves the car into park and moves closer to me, I'm ready to kick myself for being so typically paranoid—

"So, Gina. How's your mom?"

"My mom?"

"Yeah. Your mom."

"She's fine. I mean, she's getting better every day."

"So what exactly is that disease she has? Some kind of nervous disorder, you said?" I stare in horror as he throws me a few prompts: "MS? Epilepsy? Some kind of brain cancer?"

"*Cancer?* No, it's nothing like that. More like—" My mind spins madly as I try to figure out two things: where this conversation is going, and can I get away with another lie? "Um, why do you want to know?"

"I've been hearing a few things," he admits, moving back a bit. Dread creeps into my bones. "What things?"

"I heard your mom was in the hospital, and not because of some nervous disorder."

Go ahead, Gina. This is your chance. You can tell him about Momma and the drinking and the drugs. Tell him about Daddy and what happened to him in prison. Tell him how they kicked you out of school for jumping a pregnant girl and sticking a knife in her face in front of a hundred witnesses.

Tell him how the drug gang drove by and shot up your house, and how they murdered the baby sleeping right over your room.

*Tellhimtellhimtellhim!* Why can't you open your big mouth?

But all that comes out is: "She's depressed a lot. She's being treated for depression."

"Then why aren't you with your dad?"

Now it's perfectly clear what's happening, and still I blather on. "I already told you. He's busy with his job."

"Which is—?"

"He's a lawyer, okay? He used to work with your uncle." I search Danny's face, but it's too dark to see much. "So what's with the third degree? Who's been telling you this stuff?"

Danny sighs hugely. "Shit, Gina."

"What? What?"

"Will you quit playing this stupid game? I know about your mom."

I swallow hard. "What do you know?"

"I know she's an alcoholic and a drug addict, and she's not even in the hospital, it's some kind of homeless shelter—"

"Halfway house," I argue, making things worse.

"—and that your dad died in prison. Years ago, right?"

I could end this right now if my brain could only find the

right words, and if my out-of-control mouth would let me say them. This is my one last chance to get it all out in the open, so what do I do?

I blow it.

"I don't know what you're talking about. Is this, like, some kind of joke?"

"Do I look like I'm laughing?" He slams a hand on the steering wheel, and I jump two feet. "And you know what really pisses me off? I told you everything about me, all that stuff about my dad, about my music. Everything that's important to me, everything I want to do with my life. And you did nothing but lie to me from day one."

"What did I lie about? I told you my mom was sick."

"You didn't tell me you live in Cleveland, you didn't tell me you got expelled from school—and you sure as hell didn't bother to tell me you're only fourteen! Jesus Christ, are you trying to get me arrested for rape?"

"You're not eighteen yet," I say with unearthly stupidity, "so why would they arrest you?"

"You're not listening, Gina!"

"You're not listening to me either. Just stop yelling, okay?"

"Okay, fine. Let's hear it." He waits in dead silence while I nibble intently on a thumbnail. "Go ahead, tell me everything. Tell me it's all a bunch of lies, that everything I heard about you is bullshit."

It happens again. My throat clamps shut, strangling me. Maybe I've told so many lies, it's impossible to tell the truth.

"That's what I thought," Danny says quietly. He reaches past me to push open my door, and his arm brushes my chest in a way that makes me want to grab him and hold him. But in the glow of the dome light, his pale Brinkman eyes are flat and cold. I realize now, nothing matters to him anymore. All those things he used to say, all those ways he touched me—he's forgotten everything, like none of it ever happened.

Like a decomposed corpse arisen from the grave, I climb out of the car and stagger into the house. Stupid, stupid! I should've known this would happen. I should've known I didn't deserve to be this happy, that nobody would ever really love me that way.

Why would they? Why?

I cry in bed for hours and hours till I practically smother in all the snot, and the pain in my chest grows to unimaginable proportions. Over and over I say his name into my soggy pillow, praying he'll call me, that he's already had second thoughts. Maybe he realizes how badly he hurt me, and he's trying to call me right now! Taffy whines sympathetically as I cuddle the phone, waiting for it to ring. Just waiting and waiting, listening and listening.

It never happens.

Finally I get up because I can't take it anymore. I need to sleep.

I need to stop thinking.

I tiptoe through the house like a burglar and fumble around behind the bar. Three bottles of beer, cold and delicious. The first is gone in less than a minute, and the second one makes me dizzy but doesn't knock me out. So then I dig out my Percodans—I have four of them left—and wash down two with a swig of the third beer.

All I can think about are the things Danny once told me.

How he loved me, how he adored me.

How beautiful I am.

How he'd never, never hurt me no matter what.

Trembling violently, I pop the last two pills and polish off the beer. Then I rinse out the bottles, wrap them up in the yellow sweater that still smells like Danny, and savagely stuff the whole thing into a far corner of my closet.

Oh, why did I lie in the first place? Why couldn't I just be honest?

Because I wanted to be Gina. And Gina has too many secrets.

After wallowing in misery for the rest of the weekend, I force myself to get up Monday morning and move. My insides feel shredded into a billion bloody pieces, and I can hardly pop my contacts into my grainy, swollen eyes. I sleepwalk through school, cutting last-period study hall so I don't have to face Caitlin Mackenzie.

Dinnertime, Nikki picks at her broccoli, mentally adding up the carbs. "So, Gina, too bad about Danny, huh?"

I don't know why she suddenly hates me. What did I ever do to her?

"What's this about Danny?" Richard asks.

"He broke up with her," Nikki says casually, keeping her eyes on her fork.

Richard and Claudia glance at me in shock, and I throw down my napkin and shoot out of the room. Only one minute later, Claudia pushes open my door. "Gina, talk to me."

I shake my head under the pillow. I'll never get over this, never, never, never! I will go to my grave still bawling about Danny.

"You want to tell me what happened?"

"You know what happened," I mumble into my mattress.

"Somebody told him about me and now he won't even talk to me." What really sucks is that I don't even know who to blame. Nobody *knows* anything except for Richard and Claudia, and no way in hell would they ever do this to me.

I wait for Claudia to say I told you so, but she just pats my back and says she's sorry, and then leaves me alone to stare hopelessly at the phone. But I'm not even allowed to be miserable in peace because Nikki comes up and starts blasting Tchaikovsky. Nobody tells her to turn it down because nobody tells Nikki what to do. She treats her whole family like shit, and yet they think she walks on water.

Exasperated, I pound on the door and when nobody answers, I kick it open. Empty! Guess she only did this to annoy me, and boy, did it work. I whack off her stereo, and that's when I see it: one single black capsule, out in plain sight.

Okay, I'm no expert. But golly-gee-whiz, it looks like one of those old diet pills Momma used to pop, and not for the sole purpose of knocking off a few pounds. No wonder Nikki's been acting so psycho. Stress, huh?

Keeping one eye nailed to the door, I find a few more of the same pills wrapped up in a Kleenex, tucked neatly under a batch of Victoria's Secret butt-floss thongs. Personally I couldn't care less if Nikki annihilates her brain cells. But if Richard and Claudia find out—

Why is this family wasted on Nikki? She doesn't appreciate them. She doesn't deserve them. I stomp out in disgust, leaving the black capsules behind. Fine! I admit it. I did take those Percodans, but not to get high or anything. I only wanted to sleep so I could stop thinking about Danny—and that doesn't count.

· · ·

With my audition coming up, as much as I'd like to, I can't afford to stay in bed and turn into a fossil. Day after day I work on my composition, scribbling at school, in bed, and even on the toilet. Night after night I'm up till all hours, playing *Sleepers, Awake* without an accompanist. No straight A's for me this semester, thank you very much. But who cares about Nathaniel Hawthorne, or why $X$ equals $Y$ when your whole future, your whole existence is majorly at stake?

When my big day comes, I'm screwed from the start because I have nobody to go with me. Richard has an emergency court hearing, and Nikki drags Claudia to *her* dress rehearsal "for emotional support." Jittery and depressed, I take a cab to University Circle alone. After all our plans, after all his help, Danny's not with me on the most important day of my life. It feels so wrong.

When I first see the school, I'm kind of disappointed. Just an old granite building with a crummy little sign: Great Lakes Academy of Music. Inside, though, it's cool and pleasant with glossy wood floors and huge arched doorways. I huddle on a bench in the hall, waiting my turn, trying hard not to listen to the kids ahead of me. Compared to these pros, I suck, suck, suck!

I've already tuned my cello fifteen times today, but I do it again to keep my mind off the competition. The C string seems off, and now I could smack myself for not bothering to spring for an electronic tuner, for thinking I'm so smart and so cool to be able to tune the strings by ear. I guess I could borrow one, but then I'd look amateurish, unprepared . . .

"Gina Kowalski?"

Numb with dread, I pry myself up, meander into the main room, and sit down in front of the panel of unsmiling strangers.

"*Wachet auf,*" the head honcho announces. "*Sleepers, Awake* by J. S. Bach."

My right eyelid twitches. "Um, my accompanist couldn't

make it, so . . ." But he just beckons to some kid who jumps up, spits out his gum, and stakes claim to the piano bench.

Okay, that was easy. I breathe deeply, blank out my brain, raise my bow, and start to play. My eyeball spasms the whole time, and my armpits are drenched, but except for a couple of itty-bitty mistakes, I play it through perfectly.

"I believe you have a composition to show us?"

By now I'm having one of those out-of-body experiences. My spirit, high up in a corner, watches me saw through the music, the notes strained and foreign in this huge echoing room. They Xerox a copy and scribble across the top: *Gina Kowalski/ Variation on a Theme by Rupert Campbell*. Rupert Campbell, they're thinking. Who the hell is he?

Then: "Very nice. Thank you. We'll be in touch."

## ..... **41** .....

As my own dumb luck would have it, my birthday, March twenty-second, falls on the same day as opening night of *Swan Lake*. Richard and Claudia want to take me to dinner, but Nikki's pitching a fit. Because it's *her* special night, she wants to hog the whole day. No sharing the glory, and especially not with me.

Claudia says, reasonably, "Nikki, the show isn't until eight. We have plenty of time to go out."

"I don't feel like it. I'm too stressed out. Why can't you guys pick a different night?"

All eyes fall on me, and boy, talk about stress. But really, who cares if we go now or a month from now? Heck, even Momma couldn't be bothered with my birthday this year. No card, nothing.

"Okay with me." But my jawbone is throbbing.

"Well, it's not okay with me," Richard tells Nikki. "I don't recall ever skipping *your* birthday, so if you're that stressed out, you can just stay home."

Claudia tries to smooth that one over. "If we leave now, we'll be out of there by six. You'll still have a couple hours before the curtain goes up."

"Mom, it takes me that long just to put on my damn makeup!"

Richard holds up a hand. "Either come with us now, or stay home and sulk. This conversation has gone on entirely too long."

"Fine!" Nikki shouts. "Go without me. Who cares?"

"Wait," I butt in. "It's no big deal. We can go some other time." Anything, anything to stop the arguing.

But Nikki only scoffs. "Gee, thanks, Gina. Now you're everyone's little darling."

"Nikki!" Richard's voice hits us like a thunderbolt.

"Well, it's true! She's just like Rachel, always sucking up to you guys. Gina this and Gina that! Well, I'm sick of it, okay? You all make me si—"

Richard's hand shoots out, landing smartly on Nikki's left cheek. "And I'm sick of your mouth," he says, deadly calm.

Nikki flees, clutching her face in shock. Me? All I can do is stand there, unable to believe what I saw with my own eyes. A livid Claudia pulls Richard aside, and for once in my life I have no desire to eavesdrop. I fly upstairs, hating the fact that it's my own birthday that started this mess.

Nikki strolls in as I'm wrestling with a pair of pantyhose. One big red handprint covers her left cheek, so now I guess her makeup will take her twice as long.

"Sorry, Gina." She doesn't sound sorry in the least. "I'm such a bitch sometimes."

I hoist up my pantyhose and yank down my dress. Does she expect me to dispute this?

"It's just that I'm so stressed out, I don't know what I'm saying half the time."

If I hear the word "stressed" one more time, there's gonna be one less swan dancing around that lake.

"So, anyway. Have a good time, and I hope you like the ballet. And I hope everything goes okay between you and Danny tonight."

Now *this* gets my attention. "Danny?"

"Yeah, didn't you know? He'll be there with his folks, and . . ." She fiddles with her pink leg warmers, and I detect a hint of a sly smile. "Well, he's bringing Caitlin. You're all gonna be in the same box together, so I thought I'd give you the heads up." She breezes back out with a strangled "Toodle-oo!" over her shoulder.

Danny and Caitlin. Why didn't anyone tell me? Do they honestly think my idea of a fun time is being trapped in a confined space with Danny and his ski-skank?

I whip off my clothes, throw on my pj's, and stagger downstairs to tell Richard and Claudia that I've unexpectedly been stricken down by a gory virus. After a brief and somewhat suspicious interrogation, they give me my birthday present, a complete CD set of Bach's *Brandenburg Concertos*. Lulled into mindless oblivion by flutes, violins, and harpsichords, I burrow under my warm quilted spread and do nothing but vegetate.

By midnight everyone's back, and man, you'd think it was opening night on Broadway. The Brinkmans gush on and on about Nikki's "stage presence" and how it's only a matter of time before she snags a major role, blah-de-blah. I nod politely as I try not to imagine Danny and Caitlin holding hands, sneaking adoring looks . . .

Nikki's radiant, and wired as hell. "Oh, Gina! I'm so sorry you missed it."

Yeah, I bet you are.

She flits up to bed and Richard follows, ruffling my hair as he passes by. Claudia makes me some hot cocoa and asks how I feel.

Poking at the marshmallows floating in my mug, I finally admit I wasn't sick, I just didn't want to go.

Her perfectly mowed eyebrows fly up in an arch. "Gina, why?"

"I didn't want to have to sit with Caitlin, that's all."

"With Caitlin? Honey, Caitlin wasn't there."

Did I hear her right? "Danny didn't bring her?"

"No, Danny didn't bring anyone. Why would he bring Caitlin, for goodness sake?"

Because that's what that lying, conniving, despicable daughter of yours told me. Shit! This means that if I'd been there, he'd have been stuck with me all night. He would've *had* to talk to me. There'd be no graceful way out of it.

I've lost my taste for hot chocolate. "Guess I'll go back to bed." And hopefully lapse into a year-long coma. Anything to keep me from murdering Nikki.

"Gina, wait. Are you doing okay? Are you happy here?"

"Sure I'm happy." Well, maybe not at this moment, but, yes, I'm basically happy. Can't she tell?

"Well, I want you to know, we're glad you're with us. Nikki too, although she doesn't always show it." Claudia's smile wavers. "I'm not sure if you know this, but we lost our other daughter a while back."

Omigod. Somebody finally said it.

"Her name was Rachel. She was a year younger than Nikki, and—well, it's been hard on all of us, but especially hard on Richard. He and Rachel were very close . . ." She trails off, losing focus for a second. "You're a lot like her, Gina."

That last sip of cocoa curdles in my stomach. Is this why he took me in? Because I remind him of his dead daughter?

Claudia pats my shoulder, her smile a shade too bright. "Well, it's getting late. Remember to turn off the light, okay?"

I nod woodenly. And then as she starts through the kitchen door, I ask her what I've wanted to know since the day I moved in here. "How'd she die?"

Claudia stops, but doesn't turn. "She was hit by a car."

My scalp prickles, but at the same time I'm thinking that people get run over all the time, so what's the deep, dark secret? "I didn't know. I'm sorry."

"So am I," Claudia says quietly, and walks out the door.

## ●●●●● **42** ●●●●●

Another appointment with Zelda, and I am so not in the mood. I'm still mad at Nikki, and even madder at myself for letting her trick me into missing that ballet. And all Zelda wants to talk about is Momma, Momma, Momma.

"I spoke to her social worker at the halfway house. She's had a few job interviews, and she's taking good care of herself. And yes, she's still sober and doing very well on her medication."

"What medication?" I ask narrowly.

"Antidepressants, I believe. To help level out her moods. And," she adds, "she's very anxious to see you."

"Wow. That's a switch."

"Martha," Zelda begins in her sing-song accent, "why do you always have to be so sarcastic? Is this a defense mechanism with you? Is it so difficult to be pleasant? Are you always so angry at the whole world?"

Shocked by the attack, I can only stare for a second. "I'm not angry!"

"Yes, you are. You're angry, and you're scared." I try to speak, but she steamrolls right over me. "And you know what? You have every right to be, but you need to acknowledge it. Don't let it eat away at you, hmm?"

"I'm not angry," I repeat loudly. "Why should I be angry?"

"Why indeed? You are exactly where you want to be right now, aren't you? And even though it's only temporary"—God, I wish she'd quit saying that—"you've seen exactly what your life could be like, what *you* could be like if you put your mind to it. You are safe, you are happy—but you still have so much anger, and so much pain, and you have to deal with that, Martha. Yell at me all you want, say whatever you want to say to me. I don't care, this is my job, and it doesn't bother me in the least. But don't lie to yourself and pretend everything is rosy, because it's not."

"Okay," I say, just to shut her up.

"Okay what?"

". . . I'm angry."

"What about?"

Ha! Like I even know where to start. "Okay. First of all, my boyfriend dumped me. And Nikki hates my guts, and I did nothing to her, nothing!" I tick off each item, one by one. "Oh, and I just found out that the reason I'm with the Brink-mans is because they think I'm a lot like their dead freaking daughter."

Zelda soaks this all in. "Well, first tell me about your boyfriend. Why did he dump you?"

Aside from the Brinkmans, I've only told Chloe and Faith about Danny. But even then I had to use some lame, made-up excuse—*oh, we just decided to see other people for a while*—because how can I tell them the truth? With Zelda at least, I don't have to dance around the real story.

" 'Cause he found out about me," I admit.

"Found out what?"

"Everything. My mom. Getting expelled. How I'm really not from Columbus."

"You mean you never told him?"

I kick the leg of her fancy desk. Why can't she just give me the lecture and be done with it?

"How did he find out?"

"I have no clue."

"How old is this boy?"

"Um, almost eighteen," I admit in a tiny voice.

"I see. Were you sleeping with him by any chance?" I splutter all over myself, amazed at her nerve. That's all the answer she needs. "Well, you're a smart girl. I assume you used some kind of protection, hmm?"

"God!" My face feels like somebody shoved it into a gas grill. "Do you, like, even know what the word 'privacy' means?"

"I am not here to judge you, Martha. But you are the one who brought it up, so maybe it's something we should discuss." She watches me pick at a nail, tearing off a bloody shred. "It's very painful to lose someone you love, but . . . well, it hurts even more when you blame yourself. It makes it harder to let go."

Man, this lady can flip back into shrink mode at the drop of a hat.

"Who cares? It's over. I don't want to think about it anymore."

"That seems to be the way you deal with everything. Your boyfriend. Your mom. That shooting incident last fall." I yank the bulky collar of my sweater over my face, but Zelda only waits till I run out of air. "Why didn't you tell the young man *why* you ended up with the Brinkmans? I mean, if you thought he was serious about you, and you obviously did, why did you feel you couldn't tell him the truth?"

I finger Danny's necklace, my Valentine's Day gift, my one last link. "Um, I don't know. Because I'm basically a coward?"

"A coward." Mild surprise. "Why do you think you're a coward?"

"Well, you're the one who keeps saying I'm scared."

"Being scared and being a coward are two different things."

That's news to me. "So what's the difference?"

Instead of answering, she asks, "Martha, what were you thinking about that night on the fire escape?" I never told her about the fire escape, or anything else about that night. I wonder how she knows. "What made you go out there?"

I haul my feet up into the chair. "I don't remember."

"Oh, I think you do."

"You don't know anything about it!"

Zelda tilts back in her chair and plays with her rings, watching me closely, waiting for me to explain. I stare at my hands, tracing the calluses on my fingers, the scar on my thumb.

"I knew something was wrong," I hear myself say. "I heard all these sirens."

"Did you hear the shots?"

"No. I heard fireworks."

"You heard gunshots, Martha. Those boys were shooting up your house. It was a dangerous situation, and it was dark, and it was snowing—"

"And I heard everyone screaming," I whisper back.

"Were you scared?"

"Yeah," I admit.

"Why?"

"I knew . . . I just kind of knew something bad was happening . . ."

"And?"

"I wanted to go see. I wanted to help."

"You wanted to help," Zelda repeats quietly. "You were scared to death, and still you climbed up a fire escape in the middle of the night with no coat on, no shoes, in below-freezing weather, with sirens and police cars and people screaming?" I nod, and ridiculously burst into tears. "Well. That really doesn't sound very cowardly to me."

I can't answer because I'm crying too hard. And when she adds, "You must have loved him a lot," it only makes me blubber a thousand times worse.

## 43

I need some time by myself to take this all in. Richard has hundreds of classical music CDs, and I play one after another, huddled for hours in the music room with only Taffy beside me. I remember when Jerome told me what Grandma Daisy likes to say, how if you don't talk out your miseries, they eat you alive.

I do feel better, and I only wish I could've told Zelda more. Like, would she still think I'm so brave if she knew about the money, if she knew the real reason Bubby is dead?

Probably not.

The last CD ends, a piano sonata by Chopin. I pick through the shelf again and whip in my breath when I find Jacqueline du Pré and Elgar's *Cello Concerto in E Minor*. I wiggle it briefly in my hand, trying to decide—do I really want to hear this again, or will it make me remember other things I don't want to remember?—and jump when I notice Nikki standing behind me.

"I saw a movie about her," she says, nodding at the CD. "That girl was so-o off the wall, and she died a horrible, horrible death. I cried at the end, even though it kind of grossed me out."

Well, thanks. This is not what I needed to know. "Did you want me for something?"

"Oh, yeah." With a wicked gleam, she pulls her hand out from behind her back and holds out the phone. "For you."

I snatch it away, figuring it's either Faith or Chloe—but no, it's Shavonne. And here I thought she'd never speak to me again. "Hi, what's up?"

"Girl, same old shit. What's up with you?"

"Not much," I fib airily, then cover the mouthpiece as Nikki hovers at my shoulder. Damn, why didn't I give Shavonne my cell phone number? "Do you mind?"

"Oh, gosh, not at all." With a sunny smile, Nikki flits out.

Silence. Should I ask about Shavonne's mom, or wait for Shavonne to bring it up? I never know if she's going to spaz out on me.

"You still seeing that guy?" Shavonne asks, radar zooming in.

"No. He dumped me." My voice cracks and I have to lean into the wall.

"No way! That dickhead. What happened?"

"It didn't work out," is all I can say.

"Well, forget it, sister-girl. You way better off without his sorry white ass. That faggoty rich boy don't deserve you no way."

And this, I know, is why I truly love Shavonne. She knows what I need to hear and she always says it. Not "I hope you made him use a rubber, you moron," or whatever Zelda meant by that protection remark.

But then she asks, "Can I come over?"

"You mean like over here?"

"Girl, I am serious. If I don't get out of this house now and away from Aunt Bernice, I swear to God I'm gonna lose my fuckin' mind."

Right, and exactly how would I explain her to Nikki? Danny, as far as I know, hasn't blown my cover because if Nikki knew, the whole school would be buzzing.

"Shavonne, I don't know. I got a paper due tomorrow, and a science test, and—"

Call-waiting beeps, I put her on hold, and—omigod!—it's Danny. Like somebody kicked me in the gut, I can't draw a single breath.

"Hi." He sounds surprised, like what, he forgot I live here? "Can I talk to Nik?"

Not me. Nikki.

"Hold on," I croak, and switch back to Shavonne. "I have to hang up. I got another call."

"Screw that," Shavonne snarls. "You're talking to me!"

Yes, but it's Danny! This might be my last chance.

"You there?" Shavonne booms in my ear. " 'Cause I really, *really* gotta talk to you about something—"

*Tick-tock-tick-tock.* "Look," I plead. "This is really important. I swear I'll call you right back."

"Aw, don't waste your precious time." *Slam!* She does it to me again.

I click the button, but by now Danny's gone. I wait for him to call back . . . and wait and wait . . . and when he finally does, Nikki manages to grab the phone first. From her one-sided conversation, I know there's a party tonight, and I seethe with such jealousy, I start to see double.

If Shavonne hadn't held me up, would Danny have talked to me? Given me a chance to explain?

Now I'll never know.

. . .

Instead of calling Shavonne back, I tackle my homework, figuring I'll give her a call as soon as I wrap it up. Compared to Waverly, Jefferson was a piece of cake, and now, for the first time in a long time, I actually have to study. I can't find my science notebook, so forget about tomorrow's quiz, and I haven't even started my paper for English. *The Scarlet Letter*? Puh-lease. Some classic! This book is unreadable.

So unreadable, in fact, that I fall asleep with my face in page fifty-seven—and then I'm jerked back into consciousness by the *Swan Lake* overture, booming at top volume from Nikki's room. Twelve-fifteen? Is she insane?

Outraged, I jump up, rush into the bathroom, and hammer on her door. "Ex-cu-use me, but do you mind turning that down?"

"Hey, Gina-Gina." I hold my breath as she blows booze fumes up my nostrils. "Chill out, already." She hangs onto the door till I manage to slam it. Her answer to this? Crank up the music even louder.

I perch on my bed with my fists smashed over my ears, trying to grasp the fact that Nikki, perfect Nikki, Miss Walk-on-Water Nikki, is smashed out of her skull. When I can't stand the racket any longer, I hop back up and plow into her room. "You either shut that thing off or I'm gonna throw it out the window. I'm tired, Nikki!"

"Jesus!" She slaps off the stereo and roughly shoves me back into the bathroom. "Anybody ever tell you what a pain you are? Go back to bed then, you whiny little baby. Nighty-night!"

Maybe it's because I'm still half-asleep. Or maybe it's a flash of my hereditary insanity. Or maybe I'm so pissed off that she had enough nerve to put her *hands* on me, I have to say something to keeping from ramming her ass right back.

Whatever the reason, I give a pretty clear-cut reply: "Fuck you."

Wow! Instant rampage. "What? What? How dare you say that to me? Who do you think I am, one of your slimy ghetto pals?"

Ghetto pals?

"I know who you were talking to on the phone tonight," she rages on. "You think you're so smart, don't you, *Martha*? Well, guess what? I know all about you, how you're nothing but a slum rat with a criminal record, and how they, like, threw you out of school for stabbing some girl—"

The earth screeches to a halt. "I didn't stab anyone!"

Nikki's face splits into a grin. "Oh, and I guess your mom's not some kind of crazy drug addict, either. And your dad, what'd he do? Didn't he like die in prison or something?" My neck cracks with the effort of shaking my head back and forth, hair flying, denying it all. "Oh, you should've seen Danny's face when he heard *that* little tidbit," she finishes happily.

My head stops moving. I think I've been electrocuted.

Nikki leans an elbow on the bathroom wall. "Not so tough anymore, huh?"

"I never said I was tough."

"You never said a lot of things. But Daddy told me the whole story."

Oh, right! No way. "You're such a liar."

Nikki snorts. "You're calling *me* a liar?"

"He never told you anything. You're making that up."

"Hey, he's my dad, not yours. He doesn't care about you.

He feels sorry for you, okay? So go ahead, suck up to him all you want. You're wasting your time." She darts away and comes back, waving my science notebook. " 'Gina Brinkman, Gina Brinkman.' Ha, wait'll he sees this—he's gonna have you committed!"

"Nikki, don't." I lunge crazily and hit the bathroom door, and Nikki snaps the lock while I'm blinking away stars.

Everything's in that notebook: all my fantasies about Danny, about being adopted by the Brinkmans. Rows and rows of *Gina Brinkman*, page after page.

Thinking that it's a good thing her parents' room is on the other side of the house, I throw myself into the door. "Give it back, Nikki! I swear, I'm not kidding."

"Go to hell, Gina Brinkman!" Maniacal giggling.

"Goddammit! Give it back, or I'll—" What? I'll what? "I'm gonna tell 'em about those pills."

Touché! Silence, and when she creaks open the door, I notice her eyes for the first time: huge black pools surrounded by tiny rims of pale blue. "What pills?"

"You know what pills. The ones I found in your room."

Lucky for me she doesn't go for my throat. "You went in my room?"

"Give it back! Or I'm going straight to your dad."

"Knock yourself out. It's your word against mine, right?"

Right, but if I can get them to search her room . . . "Fine. Let's go."

I grab her sleeve, but she wrenches away. "Wait!" So I wait. "Don't say anything. They'll flip out on me, okay?"

"Then give—me—back—my—notebook."

A second later, the notebook ricochets off my head. "They're only uppers! And I need them, okay? How'm I supposed to keep up with my classes? How'm I supposed to keep my weight down? I have to dance, remember?" She stops me with an iron arm as I try to slink off. "Everybody I know uses that stuff. I bet you'd take it yourself if you weren't such a pathetic little suck-up. Ri-ight, Mar-tha?"

When she calls me Martha again, I lose it. "Hey, you can take fucking cyanide for all I care, so go ahead! Do it!"

"I hate you!" she screams, and savagely slams the door.

"I hate you, too," I say to the shivering wood.

Flipping through my notebook, I check each page for my stupid, immature babblings, and rip out and flush every incriminating sheet. Then, as long as I'm destroying evidence, I hit my closet as well. I dig out my yellow sweater and the three empty beer bottles, and tiptoe through the dark to carry it all out to the trash. Taffy follows, squats, and then dances beside me as I squeeze my eyes shut and yank down on Danny's necklace. The chain snaps as I rip it from my neck, and the silver heart skitters into the trash can with a soft metallic chime. Then I kneel in the grass, in the moonlight, in the cool night air, and hide my face in Taffy's silky fur.

I know Richard didn't tell her. I know it in my heart.

. . .

When I get downstairs in the morning, Nikki's finishing up her so-called breakfast—a half of a piece of toast and some watered-down OJ. The second she sees me, she pops up and leaves the room.

Claudia fills my juice glass. "I take it you two aren't getting along."

Brilliant observation.

"Well, it'll blow over. She's been working herself so hard, and now she tells me she wants to audition for *Sleeping Beauty*. I have no idea where she gets all her energy."

Ha. I do.

Finally she notices I haven't said a word. "Gina? What's the matter?"

Before I can open my mouth, Nikki flies back into the room. "My bracelet's gone!"

"What bracelet, sweetie?"

"The one Daddy got me for Christmas. It's not in my jewelry box."

I hate the way she's looking at me. Like, hello! She thinks *I* took it?

"Are you sure?" Claudia asks. "Why don't you look again?"

"I'm telling you, it's gone. Somebody stole it." A theatrical pause. "And I'll bet you anything it was that friend of Gina's. That black guy."

Claudia's coffee cup clatters. "What are you talking about?"

"Oooh, gosh. I guess Gina never mentioned it." Nikki's glacial eyes meet mine, a declaration of civil war.

I hoot. "Are you nuts? Jerome wouldn't touch your bracelet."

"Well, who else then?"

"Nikki," Claudia begins, but she's looking at me kind of funny. "Please don't accuse anyone till we have all the facts. Gina, who's Jerome?"

"A friend of mine. He stopped over one day. And he didn't take it," I repeat to Nikki. "Jerome doesn't steal. You don't even know him."

Nikki ignores this. "Mom, she even let him upstairs. And then when *I* showed up, he couldn't wait to get out of here. It's true, I swear it. Go on, ask her."

"Gina?" Claudia seems to be choosing her words ver-ry carefully. "Is there any special reason you didn't mention this to me before?"

I can only sit there, utterly speechless. I did try to tell her that night in the kitchen, but then Nikki came in and, well, I hardly thought about it again. But so what? It wasn't Jerome!

Claudia turns back to Nikki. "Well, look around again and if it doesn't turn up, your father'll just have to replace it for you. Thank God it's insured."

Nikki tilts her chin. "Well, all I can say is, Daddy'll have a fit—Oh, here he is now."

Richard's not smiling as he walks into the room. At first I think he overheard our conversation, and I fight a primitive urge to bury a fork in Nikki's skull. I hate her! And I hate the way I'm feeling, like I did something horribly wrong.

Nikki springs up. "Daddy, I have to tell you—"

"Not now, Nik. I have something to say."

A cold iceberg of terror crunches my chest. Maybe Nikki already told him about my notebook, and now he'll demand an explanation. *Adopt you? Are you nuts? Whatever gave you that bogus idea?*

Unless, of course, it's something even worse. Like something about Momma, about her wanting me back?

No! I won't go.

I'll do anything they want. I'll be nice to Nikki. I'll pretend last night never happened. Hell, I'll even say *I* swiped her crappy bracelet. But I'm not going back to Momma, and nobody can make me.

Mr. Brinkman's big hand rests heavily on my shoulder. "There's no easy way to say this. But Mrs. Addams just passed away."

## 44

Why didn't I bother to call Shavonne back?

Why didn't I say, "Yeah, come on over!"

Why did I blow her off?

Because I was too busy freaking out about Danny, and now it's too late. What kind of friend do you call that? Shitty, that's what I call it. I was even happy Mrs. Addams was sick, just so she couldn't come back to the Brinkmans and expose me as a fake. Come on, Gina, admit it. Weren't you jumping for joy?

Her mom can't be dead.

Oh, yes she can be. And, yes, she is.

Tonight I'm going to the wake with Richard and Claudia, and it doesn't even matter that Nikki knows. She knows who I am, that I'm friends with Shavonne. Soon she'll announce to planet Earth that Gina's a lying loser with a lunatic mom and a dead jailbird dad.

I wish I could disappear.

"Nikki, are you sure you don't want to come?" Richard asks before we leave. He hasn't said a word all day. Neither has Claudia, come to think of it.

Nikki, who hasn't spoken to me, period, since that bracelet thing, is too busy counting out celery sticks and raisins to even glance up. Her shoulder blades poke through the back of her sweater, and I wonder if that's the reason for Claudia's suddenly pained expression.

"What for?" Nikki takes away a celery stick and adds another raisin.

"Because I think her *daughter* would appreciate it," Richard says sarcastically, ignoring Claudia's warning touch to his arm.

*Whap!* Celery and raisins go flying off the table. "I'm not going to another funeral!" Nikki screams, and clatters out of the kitchen.

Another funeral.

Rachel.

That's what this is about. Another funeral for the Brinkmans, probably the last thing they need.

"You spoil her," Richard growls at Claudia.

"You had your chance," she shoots back in a brittle voice I've never heard.

"What's that remark supposed to mean?"

"You know exactly what it means."

I stare at the strange expression on Richard's face—half agony, half fury—with no idea what it means. What's going on? It can't just be the funeral. He storms out ahead of us, and next thing I know, Claudia's eyes spill over with tears. I reach for her limp hand, and she lets me take it, and together we follow Richard out to the car even though this, I know, is the last thing I need, too.

. . .

The chapel is packed with flowers and people, everyone bawling and praying and carrying on. Kenyatta and Monique hug me like

some long-lost sister, and I finally meet the infamous Rodney/
Rashonda—dark-skin, slanted eyes, and astonishingly beautiful.
In fact, he looks an awful lot like Shavonne.

Hunched between the grim, red-eyed Brinkmans, I endure
the sermon, leaping out of my skin with every "Amen!" or "Praise
Jesus!" All those endless eulogies about how wonderful Mrs. Addams was, how tragic this seems, and how God needed her more
because God has a pla-a-an . . . oh, gimme a break! God doesn't
need Shavonne's mom. Shavonne needs her mom.

Rocking like a metronome, I mentally zone out till the final
"Amen!" The room explodes into ear-splitting grief, everyone
wailing and sobbing and, in general, making a bigger commotion
than the sinking of the *Titanic*. I can't look at the coffin because
it's too hideous, too unreal. Instead, I flee to the back of the
chapel while Richard and Claudia pay their respects.

Shavonne looks small and strangely nunnish in a black dress,
probably the only one she owns that doesn't show off her boobs.
I touch her wrist. "Hey, you okay?"

She rips me apart with burning, glassy eyes. "Like you care?"

Everyone hears, and my face grows hot. "I-I'm sorry about
the other night. I wish we could've gotten together, but—"

"Fuck off." Shavonne turns away. "I'm through with you."

Kenyatta puts an arm around her, but Shavonne flings it away
and storms off. I rush after her, snatching at the back of her dress.
"Shavonne, please!"

She pushes me hard. "You come cryin' to me 'cause Chardonnay's after your ass. You come cryin' to me 'cause somebody
throws you off a porch. You come cryin' to me 'cause nobody'll
buy you a damn cello. Now what? Your life is so perfect, so who
needs me, huh? Why don't you just go back home and shove your
own self up your ass?"

Kenyatta and Monique cluster around, trying to drag her back toward the chapel. Stunned and silent, I watch her elaborate braids bob away, and then finally scream after her, "My *life* is not *perfect!*"

"So what?" she screams back.

I sneak outside and cry under the dark shadow of a brick wall, and this is exactly how Jerome finds me. Seeing him now is like seeing a flash of Bubby, and I think about how he's dead, and why he's dead, and I start bawling even harder. I don't think I can ever stop.

Jerome pats me awkwardly. "Aw, c'mon, Martha. You know she didn't mean it."

"Yes, she did, and I don't blame her! Her mom was dying and I just ignored her."

"Ain't nothing you could've done."

"I could've been there, at least. She would've done it for me."

"You heard what the preacher said. It was just her time. Shavonne, she knows that."

I wrench away. "Yeah, like it was Bubby's time, you mean?" *Bubby, Bubby!* And out it pours, the avalanche of truth. "If I hadn't taken that money, he'd still be alive."

Jerome grows rigid. "What money you talkin' about?"

Who cares? Let him hate me. I so totally deserve it.

"Anthony's money. He stole my cello, so I stole his stupid money, and then those guys came after him when he couldn't pay up. It was all my fault! And I wanted to tell you so bad."

"Girl, you crazy." His voice is a hunk of steel. "You didn't take no damn money."

"Oh, yes I did!"

"Not all of it," he argues, and I wonder how he knows. "How much you take?"

"I don't remember. Maybe a thousand bucks? I don't know what was left."

Jerome picks at a shoelace, shaking his head. "Anthony, he had like twelve grand under that mattress."

"What? No way! I never took twelve thousand bucks, Jerome."

"I know you didn't. I did." At my disbelieving look, he shouts in my face: "I took the money! Man, you retarded or what? He never even missed what you took, 'cause I took most of it first. And that's why Bubby's dead, okay? Not because of you."

"But why? Why'd you take it?"

He drops to the grass and rests his elbows on his knees, his forehead buried in the heels of his hands. "I wanted my mom back, that's why. I wrote her a letter and told her about the money. Didn't say where I got it from, I just told her I had it. I figured if she thought I had money, she'd want to come back, so . . ." Jerome gulps. "Well, it worked. She's back."

"You gave her Anthony's money?"

"I—"

I shake him with both fists. "And you know what she'll do with it? She's gonna blow it on drugs. She's a junkie, Jerome! Why do you want her back?"

In the glow of the dirty streetlight I see tears stream down his cheeks, feel his shoulders shudder under my hands. "I don't know, I don't know. Girl, you *got* a mom. And maybe she's crazy and maybe she treats you like shit, but at least you got one. You don't know what it's like." He buries his head deeper, and I have to strain to hear his words: "So it was me, okay? Me, not you."

We sit there for a long time, both of us crying, till Claudia and Richard come looking for me. When they see our faces, I know what they're thinking, that we're just two old friends crying over poor Shavonne.

If only they knew.

## 45

March creeps into a gray, rainy April. I keep thinking about Mrs. Addams. I keep thinking about Bubby. All of it makes me wonder, Who's gonna be next? Whose name is next on God's needed-more-up-here list?

Momma?

No! Zelda swears she's fine.

The fact that Nikki knows my dirty secrets makes life ten times worse, and each day I wake up to a putrid smog of doom. I can't think. I can't concentrate. By the end of the month I've lost five pounds and three-tenths of a point on my GPA, and I'm harvesting a zit the size of Pluto in the middle of my chin.

Because Nikki's a grade ahead, I rarely run into her at school, but lately she seems to be lurking every time I turn around. Behind me in the lunch line, and we don't even have lunch at the same time. At the end of the hall, hovering near my locker. Wandering out of a lavatory as I'm jiggling my way in. It's like she knows where I'm going to be and makes it a point to be there. Maybe it's a game, but it spooks the hell out of me just the same.

Chloe and Faith meet me for lunch today as usual, blabbing

about the school concert, their horny boyfriends, a possible cruise to the mall. Would they be acting this normal if Nikki had already ratted me out? Of course not. Still, whenever somebody glances my way, I wonder if they know, what they're thinking, what they're whispering behind my back. Stuff about white trash? X-ACTO knives? Oh, yeah, don't forget "slum rats."

As the lunch bell rings, Nikki strolls into sight with her drama-geek pals. Chardonnay-style, she smiles, holds up a pen, and jabs the air a few times.

Faith sends me a funny look. "What's that all about?"

I'm not sure, but I think the so-called jig may be up.

Too freaking paranoid to go to my next class, I tell the nurse I have cramps, call Claudia to bring me home, and then hole up in my room, consumed by a blistering red fury. Why, why does Nikki hate me so much? Because she thinks I'm a suck-up? Because I remind them of Rachel? Well, thanks to Miss Nicolette Brinkman and her big honkin' mouth, my whole existence is spinning back into shit mode.

Fine! If Nikki wants to fight dirty, I can fight dirty, too. Wait till Richard finds out his darling baby's a crank queen.

By now, of course, those capsules are long gone. I hunt through her closets and every single drawer, and check under the mattress and even in the toes of her shoes. I find birth control pills—wow!—and some X-rated e-mails, but nothing stronger than a jar of chocolate-covered espresso beans.

But I do find one thing: that freaking bracelet! And that's how I figure out she lied about losing it, that she only did it to get me into trouble.

I study the sparkling stones through a dull red haze. No way will I let her get away with this.

Minutes tick by, then an hour. Finally I hear Nikki come

home from school and start fighting with Claudia about some party she wants to go to with Justin tonight. Thundering up the stairs, she stops dead when she sees me.

"What are you doing in here?" she yelps when she notices her drawers open, her clothes flung around, and all her sheets on the floor. "You trashed my room?"

Claudia's there in a flash, and smacks a hand over her mouth. "Gina! What happened here?"

Considering everything, I sound pretty calm. "I was looking for drugs."

"Drugs!" Nikki squeals. "Are you out of your mind?"

"She is doing drugs. She even admitted it. She says everyone takes them, and it's the only way she can keep up."

Claudia whirls on Nikki, and Nikki jumps back in alarm. "Mommy! You don't believe her, do you?"

"And look what I found." I dangle the bracelet under Nikki's nose. "It was right in your jewelry box. Nobody stole it. You made that up."

"Yeah, right. If that bracelet was there, you put it there yourself. Mom, can't you see what she's trying to do? You know I don't do drugs, and you know I don't lie. Why would I lie about my bracelet? I mean, what's the point?"

"It would get me in trouble," I snarl. "That's the point."

"I never said you took it. I thought it was that friend of yours."

"Yeah, well. You lied about that, just like you're lying about those pills."

"What pills?" she shrieks. "Did you find any damn pills? No!"

"Stop it, both of you!" Claudia grips Nikki's arm. "Nicole, I want the truth. Are you using drugs?"

Nikki giggles. "Come on, Mom. Why don't you ask *Gina* if

she's on drugs? She's the one making up fairy tales about my bracelet."

"I—am—not—making—it—up."

"She probably took it herself," Nikki continues, "so why doesn't she admit it?"

"Bullshit!" I shout in a very un-Brinkman-like way. "I never touched it!"

Nikki, cool and unperturbed, folds her arms with a sweet smile. "Mom, I promise you that bracelet was not in my jewelry box. I have no clue where it's been. And I don't do drugs. I swear, I've never even tried them."

Gotta hand it to her, she's a better liar than Gina. Both of them stare at me: Nikki with pity and contempt, like she already knows she's won. Claudia with—disgust? Is that what I see?

Opening my fingers, I let the bracelet plunk to the floor. Nikki scoops it up like an abandoned baby. My face is numb, my fingers are numb, and I wish to God I could drop over dead because I can't stand that look on Claudia's face.

"We'll talk about this later, when Nikki's father gets home." Nikki's father, she says. Like she has to remind me who he is.

Nikki waits a beat after her mom leaves the room. "Justin's picking me up at five. I've got to get ready." Another unpleasant pause. "So, like, that means you can get out of my room now, Gina . . . Martha. Whatever your name is this week."

I edge toward the john. "One of these days they're gonna catch onto you, Nikki."

"Yeah. You wish." I'm halfway through the door when she adds softly, "By the way, slum rat, thanks for trashing my room."

Poor Nikki doesn't even see it coming. I turn and charge, slamming her into the dresser. "Ow!" she screams. "Get out of here, you asshole!"

That's exactly what I do. Out of her room, down the steps, and right past Claudia. I rush out the door and run till I reach the end of the tree-lined street.

I never, never should've mentioned those pills. Why would Claudia believe me without any proof? I'm not part of that family no matter how hard I pretend to be. And now that I've assaulted their precious daughter, they won't wait around for Momma to nab me. I bet they kick me out tonight. They'll toss my stuff faster than they tossed out Rachel's. Toodle-oo, slum rat!

Rain drizzles down, damp and cold, and I feel my designer haircut shrivel and frizz. With no jacket and no idea where to go, I just trudge along the sidewalk till a horn honks beside me.

"Gina, wait!" I point my nose to the gray sky as Nikki's shiny yellow car follows haltingly along the curb. "I'm sorry."

Yeah, like I'm gonna fall for that.

"Gina, I said I'm sorry! Come on. Let's be friends again."

I stab my middle finger in the air and keep on walking.

"Gina!" she shrieks through the car window. "My mother will not let me try out for *Sleeping Beauty* unless you let me apologize for calling you an asshole!"

I pick up some speed, but the rain pours down harder, and eventually I realize I don't have much of a choice. Sloshing across the tree lawn, I climb into the car, shaking my hair out like a golden retriever. "Just so you know? I don't give a shit about your ballet."

"Obviously," she says, just as sarcastically.

"And no, I don't want to be friends. I don't want you to come near me."

It amazes me how offended she looks. "What did I ever do to you?"

"You ruined everything for me and Danny."

"I didn't ruin a thing. I just told him the truth about you."

"You don't even know me! How could you know the truth?"

"All I know is what Daddy told me."

I flinch. "He wouldn't do that to me. Why do you keep lying about that?"

"So take it up with him, why don't you? You think you know him so well, you think he's so perfect? Ha! You have no clue *what-so-ever.*"

"I know him fine. And I know what he's gonna say when he finds out you're doing drugs."

She sends me a sizzling look of contempt. "Popping a few diet pills isn't doing drugs. Smoking a joint every now and then isn't—doing—drugs! God, what are you, the local DARE rep around here? You never get high, you never get drunk? You never feel like you want to, to just get away from yourself for a while?" Before I can answer, she aims a finger between my eyes. "If you say no to me, Gina, then you're a bigger liar than I thought."

No way am I going to brazen this out. Instead I say, "People die from taking that stuff. How can you do this to your folks? I mean, you're so lucky, Nikki. You have no idea."

Chin set like stone, Nikki slams the car into gear. "Don't tell me how lucky I am! And quit whining about my poor parents and how sa-a-d they're gonna be, 'cause you know what? They're mine! And they're still gonna be mine after you're gone."

The words cut into my heart because I know she's right.

We say nothing else till Nikki turns into the winding driveway, rain thudding noisily on the convertible roof. We wait for a few minutes, the windows fogging over with steam and our silent fury, but the torrent hammers on.

"Race you!" Nikki shouts, and leaps from the car.

We skid across the wet grass, both of us soaked by the time

we make it to the back porch. Nikki touches the doorknob, then draws away and huddles there for a second, hair plastered down in ropes of dripping gold.

"Deal," she offers. "You shut up about those pills and stop trying to nail me, and I won't say another word about . . . you know, what we talked about."

"Yeah, right. You already blabbed it to the universe."

"I did not! I only told Danny."

"Ooh, I only told Danny!" I repeat, mimicking her hurt, innocent voice. "Yeah, the worst person you could've told. God, Nikki, why do you hate me so much? Are you pissed off 'cause I'm here? Are you, like, jealous of me or something?"

"Jealous!" Nikki screeches. "Oh, do *not* make me laugh! Why would I ever, ever be jealous of you?"

"Then why did you do it?"

She scooches closer to the brick wall, like she's afraid I'll attack her again. "I swear, I don't know. It just came out. But he's the only one who knows, and I made him promise not to tell anyone. Daddy swore me to silence."

"I bet Natalie knows. Or Caitlin."

"No, they don't. I would've heard about it by now." At my disbelieving look, Nikki throws up her hands. "Fine. Don't believe me."

Is she yanking my chain? How would I ever know?

"Gina, you didn't admit anything, did you?"

"No-o, not exactly." Except for that halfway house remark.

Nikki smiles knowingly. "So I can take it all back, right? Just say I was jealous, that I made it all up. He really liked you, Gina, honest. Maybe it's not too late."

Fat chance. Now that he knows I was only fourteen, he'll never come near me again.

"Why would you do that?" I ask warily. "What's in it for you?"

"Just quit trying to tell my mom I'm some kind of addict, okay?"

"She doesn't believe me anyway," I remind her. "She thinks I'm a lunatic."

"No, she doesn't." Nikki turns away, but not before I notice the faraway look in her eyes. "But if she knows about the pills, she won't let me dance. She's always warning me about how ballerinas get so obsessed, and take uppers, and puke after meals—I don't do that," she adds, almost too quickly. "But I have to dance! It's like my life, okay? How would you feel if somebody took your cello away?"

I already know how I'd feel. Nikki's the one without a clue.

"I'll take care of Danny," she promises. "But you have to swear you won't say a word to my folks. Not one—single—word, Gina, no matter what."

God, I want him back so much! I wish I didn't, but I do.

"Okay," I agree, and hold out my hand. "I swear."

After a second of hesitation, Nikki touches my fingertips, then drops her hand to her side without looking me in the eye.

## 46

So Nikki goes off to her party with Justin, never mind that it's a school night or that it's on the other side of town, or that she can't name a single other person who'll be there. Claudia throws up her hands and simply gives up, and once again Princess Nikki gets her way.

The house is mine, with Richard and Claudia out celebrating their twentieth anniversary. I shake off Chloe and Faith, who try to drag me into a three-way gossip-fest, and curl up with my homework and my buddy Taffy instead.

Shortly after ten, I hear the back door fly open, and the almighty F-word spew forth from Nikki's golden lips. She stumbles downstairs to the family room and throws her arms around my neck. "Hey, Gina-Gina! I'm so glad to see you!"

I gape over at Justin who's waiting on the steps, obviously wishing he were anywhere but here. "What's with her?"

"Don't talk to him!" Nikki yells. "He hates me. He ruined my whole night."

"I don't hate you, Nik." Justin runs his fingers through his choppy, bleached-blond, wannabe surfer-boy haircut, and leans into the wall. "I thought she was gonna get hurt, so I brought her home."

"I was having fun!" Nikki roars.

"Fun?" Justin barks out a half-laugh. "Jumping on guys you don't even know?"

Nikki hugs me harder. I nearly choke on the stench of liquor. "Geee-na loves me. Geee-na's my sister! Aren't you, Gina-Gina? My adopted little sister."

I peel her off. Her skin is desert hot, pink and glowing, her glassy eyes positively demented. I stare up at Justin, wishing I could smack him. "What'd she take?"

Justin shrugs, like he doesn't know, or doesn't care. But his eyes are watery, his jaw clenched, and he won't look at me, so the shrug means nothing. "There was X at the party. I told her not to take it."

"Happy pills," Nikki sings out. "I took happy pills, see?" And then she giggles hysterically to show me how happy she is.

X. Ecstasy. A big party drug, the stuff that makes people croak on the dance floor. I saw it on the news—you can literally drop dead. I snatch Nikki's arm, but she yanks it away and spins around the room, long hair whirling and slapping her face.

"We gotta call someone," Justin insists, shuffling nervously, swiping at his nose. "I mean, she's like out of control, man. She tried to jump outta the car. She even had the goddamn door open!"

"Shut up! You ruin everything!" Nikki throws herself on the couch, squashing my homework, and starts stroking her arms, like she just can't bear not to be touching her own skin. It's so bizarre! It scares the living shit out of me, too.

"I'm calling her dad," I tell Justin, who gladly leaps out of my way. But before I can reach the first step, Nikki's up from the couch and swinging from my back.

"You promised! You swore! You said you wouldn't tell, re-member? Remember what you promised?"

I buck her off, and then stand there, helpless. I did promise her that, yes, because she said she'd fix things with Danny. But what if she drops dead in front of my eyes?

She's right. I *am* her sister. I can't let her die.

Justin slithers up a couple of steps. "I'm out of here, man. I've had enough of this shit. All she ever wants to do is get high."

"Wait!" I scamper after him. "You can't just leave. This is your fault, too! You're the one who gives her the pot." And prob-ably everything else she takes, too.

He whacks an angry fist on the railing. "This—isn't—pot! I didn't even want to go to this stupid party 'cause I know these people, and they're, like, hard core, okay? I'm not getting busted just because *she* likes to get wasted!"

Below us, Nikki snickers and dives back onto the leather cushions. "So leave then, you prick. You don't care about me. No-body cares! Only Gina," she adds with a demonic giggle.

Justin jerks me closer, voice low and urgent, sweat shining on his lip. "Just make her drink something, okay? She's burning up. And tell her folks to come home, 'cause I'm not sure what all she took. She's done this before and, well, it could get really bad."

Nikki bounces up. "What're you whispering about? Why are you holding her hand?"

I drop Justin's hand and wipe the sweat off my palm. "Um, Nikki, you want a Coke? Or maybe some water?"

"No! I want to know what you're whispering about. Are you two doing each other? Huh? What's the matter, Gina, screwing Danny's not enough? You have to screw my boyfriend, too?" Crazy, irrational, on and on. Like dealing with Momma, only worse, because it's Nikki.

Danny or no Danny, this is so not worth it. Knocking Justin aside, I race upstairs and dial Richard's cell. "You gotta come home, it's Nikki, she did something, took something—" He hangs up before I can finish.

When the door slams again, I know Justin is gone for good. Nikki's right, he definitely is a prick. Back in the basement, Nikki's happy again, and this time it's Taffy who's the target of her affection. She sweeps the dog up and dances around, swinging the terrified thing from side to side. Taffy yaps frantically, desperate to escape.

"My little Taffy," Nikki coos, kissing the dog's silky face. "My little Taffy loves me, don't you, baby? Don't you lo-ove your little Nikki? Don't you just lo—"

*Chomp!* Taffy's teeth snap down on Nikki's bottom lip. Blood squirts, Nikki dumps the dog, and stares, confused, at the red splotches on the front of her tank top. When she figures out what happened, it's like a scene from Stephen King, and I have to tackle her as she makes a murderous dive for the dog.

"Stop!" We struggle until I give her hair a rough yank because that's the one thing that always gets *my* attention.

Works for Nikki, too. She falls to her knees, sobbing, "Don't call my mom, please don't call my mom!" I hug her and rock her and pat her on the back, thinking: Pleasecomehomepleasecome-homepleasecomehome!

When Richard and Claudia finally do burst in, Nikki knows I betrayed her. She launches another attack, leaving a few claw marks on my neck, and Richard grabs her while Claudia punches 911. Nikki then turns on her dad, screaming, "I'm not going to any damn hospital! Why don't you just kill me instead? You're so good at it, Daddy, so c'mon, do it! Just like you killed Rachel when you fucking ran her over!"

A deadly chill sweeps through the air as Richard lets go of Nikki's flailing arms. Nikki topples over and beams up at me from the floor, blood leaking from her ravaged lip. "You didn't know that, did you? You think he's so wonderful? He ran her over in the driveway 'cause he was too drunk to see straight! Just rolled right over, and went and parked the damn car. He murdered my sister! He didn't even know it till my mom went looking for her."

"Nikki." Richard's face is ghostly white.

"You should've gone to jail, but no-o! You know all the right people, don't you, Daddy? Every cop around. All those lawyers and judges." She drops her voice. "He killed Rachel. And he should've gone to jail." She whispers it again and again, rocking mindlessly on the carpet.

Without another word, Richard walks out. I squat next to Nikki, shaking so hard I can barely keep my balance. "I hate you, Nikki. You hear me? I hate you!"

Nikki laughs, a sad, tired laugh. "You don't hate me, you love me. That's why you want to *be* me so much. That's all you've wanted since the first day you got here."

"I never wanted to be you. You couldn't pay me to be you."

"You're lying, Gina. That's all you know how to do."

She rolls over and hides her bloody face, and by the time Claudia gets back, she's either asleep or passed out. I can't find Richard anywhere in the house, and I finally spot him on the deck, standing alone in the dark. The red glow of his cigarette moves upward, then sweeps back down as he flicks away ashes. He doesn't know I'm there till I open my mouth.

"I'm sorry." I sound funny and hoarse, like I'm the one who's been screaming. What's strange is that I don't even know what I'm sorry about. For not trying harder to make Claudia believe me? For not going to him in the first place when I found out about the pills?

Or maybe for just being here, for hearing the truth about Rachel. For knowing all his secrets the same way he knows mine.

"She was putting her bike away." Richard's voice is husky, but perfectly clear over the rustling trees. "I lost a case, a case I would've won if I hadn't been drinking all afternoon, so I went out afterward and drank some more. It was dark, and I didn't even have my damn lights on, and I ran over her in the garage. And, yes, Nikki's right, I didn't even know it." Pause. "You've heard the term, 'beating the system'?"

I nod, swallowing hard, but he doesn't say anything else because, at that exact moment, the rescue squad and the cop cars roar up, as out of place in this neighborhood as the starship *Enterprise*. Richard draws me close, holds me for a second, and then throws his cigarette in the bushes and hurries back inside. I stay where I am, the chilly night wind fanning my face. I see the shadow of the garage looming in the moonlight and hug my arms to my chest.

But it's Nikki I'm thinking about. Not Rachel at all.

## 47

The house is a morgue with Nikki gone, shipped off to a treatment center, four weeks under lock and key. Richard hardly speaks. Claudia's always in tears. Neither of them says a word about what happened that night. For all anyone knows, Nikki could be off on a Disney cruise.

Zelda calls this "denial." Alcoholic families are notorious for this, she says. Not only do they act like there's no problem with addiction, but they don't like to talk about other problems, either. Just keep your mouth shut, pretend everything's fine. In other words, exactly what Momma and I do.

Bad thing is, Zelda wants me to live somewhere else. She thinks this "situation" is too stressful for me, and that the Brinkmans have enough to worry about without me hanging around. "I spoke to Mr. Lipschmidtz, and he is already looking into other places—"

"Who?"

"Your guardian ad litum, remember? And he said—"

"I can't leave now. They need me."

"They need each other, Martha."

"They need *me!*" This is *my* family now, *my* parents, *my* sister. Things won't get better any faster if she forces me out. "Please, Zelda. Please let me stay?" The very memory of the clown house sends an imaginary spike through my brain.

Zelda throws her head back in surrender, and then surprises me with a hug. "Well, hang in there, hmm?" After a quick confused second, I hug her back, just to stay on her good side so she won't change her mind.

. . .

Nikki must have kept her end of the bargain because I hear nothing at school about knives or Jefferson. Even better, I snag a solo for the spring concert tomorrow, playing *Sleepers, Awake* with full orchestra accompaniment!

Chloe and Faith tag along as I cruise the mall for something to wear for my official musical début. "Omigod, you're so lucky!" Chloe exclaims as I model a lacy white top and swirling black skirt. "You look so thin in that!"

"I'll do your hair." Faith fingers my curls, which are still in pretty good shape. Being Asian and all, her own sleek black hair is flawless, while Chloe's coppery red is almost as curly as mine. "A French braid would be perfect."

The word "braid" makes me remember Kenyatta's Halloween party, and I feel a queasy flood of longing just to hear Shavonne's voice. Ever since she lit into me at her mom's funeral, I haven't had the nerve to call her. Something tells me she has no plans to contact me, either.

"No braids," I say flatly. "I'm wearing it down."

As I change back into my own clothes, Chloe asks cautiously, "So. You think Danny'll show up at the concert?"

"Danny? Why? We broke up ages ago."

"Well, you know . . . people break up all the time and then

get back together. Anyway," she adds slyly, "you never did tell us what really happened between you two."

"Yes, I did." Uneasily, I try to remember the exact excuse I gave them. "We, um, just decided to . . . you know, go out with other people."

"Well, you're not going out with anyone," Faith points out, "so that means you still like him. And *I* think you should call him and ask him to come tomorrow night."

"Yeah, do it!" Chole chimes in. "What's the worst that could happen?"

The worst that could happen? Well, he could cuss me out and slam the phone in my ear. Maybe even have me arrested for stalking.

"I can't," I admit.

"Yes, you can," Faith insists. "Be assertive, Gina!"

"I said I *can't!*"

Shocked and hurt, they clamp their mouths shut at the same time—and that's when it hits me: No more secrets.

I'll tell them the truth. I'm so sick of this charade, so sick of lying to my friends. Besides, maybe Zelda's right, maybe I'm not the biggest coward on the face of the earth. But this I'm going to have to do in absolute privacy, and if they react like Danny? Well, at least I'll know where I stand.

"Sorry, guys," I say, and we do the group hug thing, and then an idea hits me. "Hey, why don't you come over after the concert? You can spend the night, and, well, I'll tell you what really happened with me and Danny." I've never had a sleepover, and I'm sure Claudia won't mind. "Be prepared," I add, scooping up my new outfit. "I have a *lot* to tell you!"

. . .

By the time morning rolls around, I'm a mental train wreck, and not only because of the concert. How the hell am I gonna explain

"Martha" to Faith and Chloe? Slightly nauseated, I toss the rest of my bagel to Taffy who snaps it right up.

Claudia stops me at the door as I head off for school. "Nikki's coming home a week from Sunday."

I force a smile. "Great! Is she okay?" This falls kind of flat. I hope she can't tell.

"She's much, much better. But I wanted to let you know because—" Claudia stops, then smiles back and gives me a quick hug. "Well, we'll talk about it when you get home."

I forget all about this by the time I get to school. I'm so excited about the concert, my thoughts spinning around in a thousand different directions. What if I'm discovered by somebody important, someone searching the world over for their next protégé? It happens in movies. Why not in real life?

And then I daydream about Danny showing up at the concert, begging me to forgive him for acting like a jerk. Okay, another movie moment, but hey, why not? He's had enough time to think it over, to remember how much we meant to each other. Maybe he misses me so much, he'll decide to surprise me. By this time tomorrow, my whole life could be different!

I put on my début outfit after school and practice my concert piece one last time. When Claudia calls me downstairs, I find Zelda waiting, too. Oh, if she screws up this night for me, I'll never let her forget it.

"I need to talk to all of you together," Zelda announces. She herds us into the living room and waits till we sit down. "I am happy to say that Martha's mother is doing well, and that she's met all her goals. She has a job, and she is renting a house on the west side. And," she adds pointedly, "she is looking forward to seeing Martha."

I gnaw my thumbnail, aware of the silence. If Momma wants to see me so bad, why doesn't she come to my concert tonight?

Zelda continues when nobody else says a word. "In fact, she has asked me to bring her home tomorrow."

Richard explodes. "Tomorrow? That's ridiculous. I thought we'd at least have until—" He stops, and I blink at him. Have until when?

Prickling with dread, I spring out of my chair to face Zelda. "Well, I'm not going! You didn't even ask me."

"Martha." Zelda uses that fake-patient voice I hate so much. "Our goal has always been to get you two back together."

"Your goal. Not mine."

"Listen, please. There was a hearing yesterday, and Mr. Lipschmidtz recommended that you go back to your mother—"

"No, no, no!" I yelp, the walls shrinking in on me. "I never even laid eyes on that guy. He can't tell me what to do!"

"Yes, he can, Martha. And your mother now has legal custody."

"How come *I* wasn't invited to that stupid hearing?"

"Because it wasn't required that you be there. At any rate, the decision has been made, and . . ." Zelda trails off, giving me a flicker of hope. "I'm sorry. There's nothing I can do."

Did Richard know about this hearing? Did he go to it by chance, and then not even mention it? Damn, he's a lawyer. Of course he knew! I bet he's known about this for days and didn't have the balls to bring it up.

I hear myself ask from a far-off place, "Why can't I stay here?"

Richard and Claudia exchange looks, but it's Zelda who

answers. "Well, unless somebody manages to pull a few strings around here—" She directs this at Richard, the champion string puller of all time. "It's already been decided, Martha. You're going back tomorrow."

"My name is Gina!" I scream.

No fair! I don't want to be with my mother. She's a drunk, she's a junkie, and she can't even remember my goddamn birthday.

"But what about Nikki? She's coming home next Sunday. She's like my sister now, you know?" I try not to think about our last conversation, the one we had on the basement floor. "You mean you want me to leave without even saying good-bye?"

Richard interrupts me, very softly, "Gina, please. Don't make this any harder." *Tick, tock.* "Nikki doesn't want you to be here when we bring her home."

The earth tilts just a fraction. "She doesn't want me here at all?"

"That's why I thought . . ." He clears his throat. "I thought we'd be able to give you another week. To kind of get used to the idea, before Nikki gets back." He aims a glare of fury in Zelda's direction, and it's the first time I've seen her look even remotely rattled. "That's what you led us to believe, and now you're telling us tomorrow?"

Claudia stands, makes a funny sound, and abruptly leaves the room. She doesn't look at me as she passes. In fact, nobody is looking at me at all.

"This isn't fair," I whimper. "This is so not fair."

"Gina, believe me," Richard pleads as he steps forward to take my hand. "If there were any other way—"

I wrench away from him, whirling on a fish-mouthed Zelda instead. All this time pretending to be my friend while she plotted and planned to destroy my life. I scream so hard, spit flies out of my mouth. "This is all—your—fault!" And then I blast through the front door and down the sidewalk, running, running as hard as I can.

## ·····  **48**  ·····

I hate them.

I hate them.

I hate them so much that when Zelda zooms after me in her car, I won't even get into it at first, and then I refuse to get out when she drives me back to the Brinkmans'. I want nothing out of that house except for my trunk, my black coat, and my Elvis posters. Nothing in my room, not even any clothes. I don't even want this crummy outfit I'm wearing.

"You can't go to your mother's without any clothes," Zelda argues.

"I said I don't want them. And if you make me take anything, I'll just burn it all when I get there."

So Zelda goes inside by herself, leaving me balled up in the backseat. I'm not even crying, I just feel hot, sick, and useless. When Richard comes outside to "reason" with me, I simply lock all the doors and hide my face, ignoring his pleas, his persistent tapping. No, I'm not going to the concert, because that's what he's asking me—among other things, like why can't we talk this through? Please, Gina, please? And when it gets to the point where I can't stand it anymore, I slam my fist into the window and scream for him to leave me alone. Scream that he's a traitor and a drunk and a fucking murderer, and how I hate his guts, how I wish he'd just die.

Then, only then, does he give up and go inside.

. . .

We ride to Momma's new place in absolute silence except for the bumping of my trunk in the hatch of the car. A tall, wide bridge takes us from the east side to the west side, a bridge named, Zelda tells me—like I care—after that old actor, Bob Hope. After passing a sign that says Ohio City, we drive down a couple of shady streets with a few pretty homes and ritzy town houses, but Momma's house isn't one of the nice ones. Neither is her street. Neither is her neighborhood.

Instead, we turn down a severely grungy alley, and I stare, unsurprised, at the used-to-be-white house with the overgrown yard and rusty fence, and the broken-down bus shelter ten feet from the front door. A chipped, dirty statue of the Virgin Mary, minus the head, rests in a sawed-off bathtub propped next to the stoop. This I find seriously disturbing.

Mamma Mia's, a bar-and-pizza joint, is conveniently located on the other side of the alley. Wow, food and booze right in our own backyard. So far the only good thing about this slum is that it's miles away from Wayne. Which, unfortunately, means I'm also miles away from Jerome.

When Momma opens the door, I hardly recognize her. She's lost a ton of blubber, and her hair is back to its natural light brown, clean and short and surprisingly stylish.

"Glory be! I wasn't expecting y'all till tomorrow." She hugs me fiercely and starts to bawl as I gaze over her shoulder at the big sloppy sign:

## Welcome Home Martha!

Home? I'll never feel at home in this piece-of-shit tenement. A shabby two-story house that might cave in on us at any second. Brown paneled walls, ratty gold carpet, and those fat Venetian blinds you might see on *I Love Lucy*. The furniture is a jumble of garage-sale rejects, and the hot, tiny living room smells like bacon grease and bug spray.

Momma sniffles and honks and then proudly takes us on a tour: long skinny kitchen, postage stamp–sized john, and two stuffy bedrooms at the top of the stairs.

I stare in horror at the one that's supposed to be mine. "Where's my old bed?"

"I sold it."

"You sold my bed?"

"Well, I wasn't gonna pay for storage. Anyhow, it was old. I didn't know you'd be so upset about it." She truly sounds amazed.

Zelda interrupts to say she'll be back in the morning with the rest of my stuff. Not sure if she's going deaf or playing stupid, I almost say, "Don't bother!" but then change my mind. Let Momma think I'm here by my own free will, not because the Brinkmans kicked me out like a puppy who peed on their Persian rug.

When Zelda's gone, Momma remarks, "Your hair looks nice. Reckon it must've cost a fortune."

And I'm not gonna tell her how much, either. "Yours looks nice too, Momma."

She pats her own head with a grin. "You want a Coke or something?"

"No thanks."

She swings open the fridge as I peek under her arm. Not much there, but at least there's no beer. "What happened to your glasses, sugar pie?"

"I got contacts, Momma." Already they feel like grit in my eyes, and an invisible nail gun seems to be whamming my head. I wonder, what're the chances of digging up any painkillers around here? Zilch, no doubt.

"Zelda tells me they're real nice, them folks that took care of you. Maybe I'll ask 'em over to supper. Think they'd like that?"

Yeah, they'd be thrilled. Nikki'd get a real kick out of Momma's Hamburger Helper. Still, I keep quiet because I'm noticing stuff now, like a man's windbreaker on the back of a chair, and a bowling ball bag on the kitchen floor. Since when does Momma bowl?

"Oh, I almost forgot!" Momma jumps up and scrambles around for a Drug Mart bag. "Happy birthday, sugar pie. Sorry it's a little late."

A "little late" is right. Listlessly I open the bag—nice gift wrap, Momma—and find a manicure set with four different shades of polish.

"I know you bite your nails, but maybe this'll give you some, um . . ."

"Incentive?"

"Yeah, incentive."

She seems disappointed when I don't shower her with thanks, but what does she expect? My birthday was two freaking months ago.

A key jangles in the door, and Momma springs up, chirpy as a bird, when a strange man strolls in. "Oh, there you are, honey. Martha, this here's Larry."

"How ya doin', Martha?" Larry holds out a big, rough hand

for me to shake. He has curly gray hair and a neat matching beard, and a very nice smile except for a missing front tooth.

"No point in beating 'round the bush. Larry and me, we been livin' together since we got outta rehab. I just know you two are gonna—"

Omigod, it's Wayne all over again. Is rehab the only place Momma can dig up a man? "Are you outta your skull?"

Instead of knocking my block off, Momma smiles helplessly at Larry. "Sorry, honey. I reckon she had a tough day."

Larry stuffs his hands in his pockets, jingling his change. "You know, Lou Ann, I think I'll go take a walk and let you two get reacquainted." Momma protests, but he shushes her up and then winks at me like we share a secret. He is so damn lucky I don't reach over and knock out another tooth with the nearest blunt object.

As soon as he's out of the house, shades of the old Momma overtake the new. "Now don't you go messin' this up for me, hear? Larry got me through a lotta bad times, and he's sweet as pie in case you ain't noticed."

"Even sweeter than Wayne?"

Man, that's all it takes. "Look, you don't want to stay here, then you can pick up that phone and tell that uppity bitch to come get you. I am not puttin' up with this crap of yours again," she shouts and then careens out after Larry.

Fine! Sweating and furious, my murderous headache growing worse, I plunder the house in search of something to take for it. Nothing, absolutely nothing, not even a crummy aspirin. Dread floods through me like a river of boiling lava as I crawl into my new bed, missing Taffy like crazy, and try hard not to think about the Brinkmans at all. But that's impossible, and before I know it I'm crying, and all crying does is make my head hurt even worse.

How did I ever imagine those people would adopt me? Gina Brinkman—what a sick, pathetic joke! Invite them for dinner? I'll stick my head in the oven first.

## 49

Momma almost faints when Zelda shows up with my stuff the next day.

"Good Lord! You sure this is all Martha's?"

No, Momma, she robbed 'em at gunpoint.

"Are you going to help me bring it in?" Zelda asks me.

Talking to Zelda is like talking to a tree trunk. "I told you I don't want it."

Momma gives me a nudge. "That ain't no way to talk. Now go help the lady."

Lady, huh? Just yesterday Zelda was an "uppity bitch." I schlep everything in, slamming stuff around as noisily as possible. Afterward, as soon as Zelda's big butt disappears down the front stoop, I ask Momma pointedly, "Does she know what's-his-face is living here, too?"

"His name is Larry. And it ain't against the law, and it ain't none of her business."

Larry himself shows up with a newspaper and a box of blueberry muffins. I eat one in my room as I unpack my stuff, and after Momma cools off, she comes in to help.

"Larry and me, we go to AA meetings every night, and you know what? They got Alateen, too, a couple nights a week."

I kick one of my twelve pairs of Brinkman shoes under the bed. "I'm not going to any meetings."

"C'mon, it'll be good for you. Kinda like a support group."

"Who says I need support?"

Momma frowns, hands on her hips. "Quit arguing, will you? Because I say you're going." So I have nothing to do with this decision, either. Why didn't she say that in the first place instead of dicking around?

I smooth the satiny lining of my winter coat as I hang it up in the musty closet. I love this coat, I adore this coat. I sniff the sleeve, smelling the Shalimar Claudia lent me for my Valentine's Day dinner with Danny, my insides snagged by a rush of homesickness.

"Martha, Martha. Let's not start off on the wrong foot. Now maybe I ain't been the best mother, but I worked real hard to get to where I am now. I've been at my restaurant job for over a month, and I'm off the booze and off the pills. But I can't do it by myself. I need you to help me—Martha? You listening?"

I drop the coat sleeve, the fragrance still in my nostrils. "Uh-huh."

"So I want you to go to them meetings so you can understand some stuff. Just give your old Momma a chance now, okay?"

Fine, whatever. I'll go sit with a bunch of creeps and listen to them whine. What else is there for me to do around here anyway?

Oh God, I want my cello . . . but no, that cello belonged to Gina, and now poor Martha is shit out of luck. How will I ever find out if I passed my audition? Not that it matters, now that I have nothing to play.

"Martha?" Momma tucks a curl behind my ear. It takes all of

my self-control not to flinch away from her touch. "Are you happy to be home?"

"Yes, Momma. I'm happy," I recite dutifully, a perfect Stepford daughter.

. . .

This is finals week, and Zelda's fixed it so I can take my exams down at the Board of Education instead of forcing me to go back to Waverly. Ha, like I'd set one foot back into that school after ditching the spring concert. I pass the tests, though not exactly with flying colors, but hey, who cares? I'll be bagging groceries in no time, or flipping burgers like Momma.

With no cello to play, I find myself plucking at rubber bands and composing tunes on any piece of paper at hand. And my journal? Forget it. I have no desire to pick apart these past few days of my life. Instead, I doodle on the cover till I notice what I'm writing—*Gina Brinkman*, *Gina Brinkman*—and gouge the name out so viciously, I snap the point off my pencil.

Who's Gina Brinkman? A finger puppet.

Nobody.

. . .

The days limp by, each one forty hours long. I'm bored without a boom box, and no cable TV. I go out of my way to avoid the other kids in the neighborhood, whose main forms of entertainment seem to be smashing bottles in the street and dodging traffic on their skateboards.

I do take long, lo-o-ong walks to get out of that crappy house every day, and today I end up down at the West Side Market. Old white ladies in babushkas, dragging their shopping carts. Old black ladies in stretch pants, dragging their screaming grandbabies. A few yuppies thrown in, dragging wheeled attaché cases. Wall-to-wall stands piled with mountains of fruit and vegetables.

One whole pig corpse eyeballs my every move, and honest to God, I may never touch another pork chop. I buy a bag of grapes from a black-bearded, beer-bellied, non-English-speaking vendor in a turban, and gobble them on the way home through the noisy, sunny streets.

The first thing I see when I hit my back door is that same old cello case waiting in the kitchen. Electricity prickles the hairs on my arms. If this is a joke, it's not funny.

"You had a visitor today." Sourer than usual, Momma scowls at the cello like it's her mortal enemy.

I unfold the note taped to the case.

> *My dear, dear Gina,*
>
> *I know you don't want to talk to me, and I understand. I only want to say how sorry I am. Even though you may not believe this, I want you to know that we miss you very much. You were an important part of our lives for a long time, so please try to forgive us, and don't hesitate to call me at any time, for any reason.*
>
> *Love, Richard Brinkman*

There's a P.S. at the bottom: *The cello is a gift. No one else plays it, and it's completely insured. Take good care of it. I wish you all the best.*

The smell of the instrument is as familiar as Claudia's perfume. I run my fingers along the strings in shocked disbelief. Why did he give it to me? Because he's sorry he kicked me out? Because he's sorry he broke his promise and told Nikki all my secrets?

"Um, did you talk to him?" I glance around, hating that he might have seen where I live. *How* I live.

Momma makes a noise with her sinuses. "He didn't bring it.

He sent some delivery guy." She shakes her head at the cello. "Well, if you ask me, that sure is one sorry-looking old instrument. You'd think folks that rich could afford to buy you something new."

Duh, Momma. It's very old, very special, and completely irreplaceable.

"You gonna call him up and say thanks?"

I should, I ought to, but what do I say? I said more than enough to him in Zelda's car, all those terrible, hateful things. So what does he do? He turns around and gives me his cello.

Does that mean he forgives me? Or am I supposed to forgive him?

## 50

My first Alateen meeting is worse than I expected. People are crammed like pigs' feet into the basement of a church so incredibly medieval, it's not even air-conditioned. Kids in one room, adults in another, and slogans, slogans, everywhere I look: Let Go and Let God. One Day at a Time. Live and Let Live.

Bite me, I think.

I pop my wrists glumly and slouch in my folding chair while everyone else recites the serenity prayer: "God grant me the serenity to accept the things I cannot change, courage to change the things I can, and the wisdom to know the difference." Somebody blabs about the Twelve Steps, blabs another prayer, and then it's time to introduce the newbies. No last names—we're a-non-y-mous, remember? Ha, I bet half these losers end up in my homeroom next year.

I sit there, duncelike, till somebody pokes me. "Martha," I mumble, and "Hi, Martha!" bounces back at me from all sides. Mortified, I unfocus my eyes and half-listen to all the same poor-little-me stories: drunk moms, drunk dads, brothers, sisters, grandmas, grandpas. One kid's dad used to beat him with a dog chain, so his mom stuck him in a foster home—get this!—for his "own protection." I bet some dim-bulb social worker had a hand in that one.

Afterward, I duck out without socializing. The night is muggy and hot, and I smack at the mosquitoes trying to kamikaze my face as I wait on the church steps till Momma and Larry come out.

"So what'd you think, Martha?" Larry asks in his annoyingly cheerful way.

What does he care? I came, didn't I? Entirely ticked off by the idiocy of this evening, I simply stalk off without a word.

"Hold it!" Momma catches up, something she could never do in the old days. "Why you gotta be so rude? Larry's gonna think you don't like him or something."

"I like him fine, Momma. Honest."

"Oh, I'm so glad to hear it." She nudges me, lowering her voice. "He's a sweetheart, that's for sure, and handsome, too. Don't you think he's handsome?"

I blink to keep my eyeballs from swiveling. "Well, except for that one tooth he doesn't have . . ."

Momma gasps like I just socked her in the stomach. I'm sorry. I can't help it. I am just so *mad* at her for making me come back, never mind that the Brinkmans would have thrown me out anyway.

And this, right here, shows you how rotten I really am. It's not Momma's fault she's sick, and if I were any kind of a decent daughter, I'd be trying a lot harder to make things better between us. I'd be nicer, too, so she wouldn't get so mad all the time, or so sad all the time, or whatever it is that makes her want to drink all the time.

A jagged streak of lightning carves a slice through the sky as Momma marches back to Larry, and I slink off by myself. Well, at least when I get home, now my cello will be waiting. The one single thing that makes my life bearable.

. . .

The idea grows like the sponge in the bottom of the goldfish bowl Larry gave me, trying to buy my affection, no doubt. Now that I have a cello, why can't I keep taking lessons? They're already paid for—why give them up?

But when I spring this on Momma, I get: "Forget it. You got Alateen those nights."

"Yeah, well. I'm done with all that."

"What do you mean, you're done?"

There is no getting through to that hillbilly mind. "I'm not going to any more of your dumb meetings, okay? *You're* the one with the drinking problem, so *you* go and pray to, to Saint Jude or whoever that guy is—"

"Saint Francis!" Momma snaps.

"—and hold hands with a bunch of weirdos and listen to 'em boo-hoo-hoo about all the shit in their lives. I'm done! The end."

Momma sends me a flaming look. Okay, that wasn't the smartest thing for me to say. Maybe I need to try a different approach.

"Oh, Momma. I'm kidding." With a syrupy smile, I rub her stiff shoulders with my fingers and thumbs. "Anyway, those meetings don't even get started till seven. If you let me take those lessons, I can make it back in plenty of time." From Shaker Square? Yeah, if I fly.

Momma, still fuming, scooches away. "No, you got your fiddle and you can fool around with that. You don't need any more lessons." A fiddle, she calls it.

"That's not fair!" I scream. "You're just being a bitch about this!"

"You watch your mouth!"

Poor unsuspecting Larry tries to stick up for me. "Come on now, Lou Ann, why don't you give the kid a break? You been listening to her play? Damn, she's good."

He winks at me, but before I can send him a vibe of gratitude, Momma leaps between us, snarkier than ever. "If I want your opinion, mister, I'll be sure to ask for it!"

"Fine. Suit yourself." Larry slams out in a huff.

I give up, hide in my room, and comfort myself with my little goldfish from Larry: Wolfgang, Johann, and teeny-tiny Ludwig. Larry or no Larry, drinking or no drinking. Nothing has changed. Nothing'll ever change.

. . .

Zelda pops in unexpectedly on Friday. I don't go to her office because Momma doesn't make me, and so far nobody else seems to care. Today she starts blathering about some program she wants Momma and me to join—family counseling, vocational job training for teens . . .

Vocational training. Translation: for kids who can't go to college.

"Do I have to do it?" I ask. "Like, is it a law or something?"

"No-o," Zelda answers, and it kills her to admit it.

"Then forget it."

"Martha," Momma butts in, but I have so—totally—had it!

"I want to be a cellist, not some factory freak!" My finger bobs under Momma's nose. "And you won't let me take lessons even though they're perfectly free, and—"

Momma whaps my hand away and launches into her usual tirade while Zelda grabs me and hustles me out of the room. "Get upstairs," she hisses. "I will handle your mother."

Trembling, furious, I make it to the top of the steps, and then press myself into the wall, listening to bits and pieces of their conversation.

". . . already had the audition. She's gifted, Lou Ann. And if the lessons are already paid for, what harm can it do?"

"Who cares if they're paid for? It ain't my money. You think that hot-shot lawyer's gonna be doing that the whole rest of her life?"

*Murmur, murmur* . . . and then I hear the word "life" again from Zelda, something about me doing something with my life, and all Momma says to that is, "You can't do nothin' with shit but make another pile of shit."

"Martha's life does not have to be a pile of shit. This isn't difficult, Lou Ann."

"I'll tell you what's difficult—it's people like you who keep tellin' her she's so special! *This* is her life, okay? Ain't nothin' gonna change it."

I decide, with a sinking chill, not to listen to any more. I slip into my room and watch my darting goldfish, remembering the day I figured out that Momma doesn't "like" me very much. Is that really because of my dad? Or is it just because I'm me?

Zelda appears about ten minutes later. "Well, I have a *bit* of good news. I think your mother may be ready to compromise."

"So what do I gotta do? Shave my head bald and wear a bone through my nose?"

"No. If you go back to Alateen, you can continue your lessons." When I don't jump for joy, she prods me with, "That's fair, don't you think?"

Sounds like blackmail to me.

Then again, when you think about it, what Zelda just pulled off is nothing short of a miracle. So . . . okay, fine, I'll do it. Anything at all to get my lessons back!

Funny thing is, when I do go back to Professor Moscowitz, he never even mentions all the time I missed. He admits, grudgingly, that I sound "not too bad for a change," which has got to be the biggest compliment that crazy dude ever gave anyone.

●●●●●● **51** ●●●●●●

After that, I make an effort to be nice. I go to every meeting, sit in the back, and pretend to listen to all the miserable stories. Maybe years from now, when I'm famous, I'll be laughing about this. Then again, maybe it still won't be funny.

Tonight, Emilio, the boy with the dog-chain-swinging dad, stops me by the punch bowl before I can make my usual getaway. He's kind of cute, in spite of his fanatical grin, with shaggy hair, dark eyes, a hint of a mustache, and the longest eyelashes I've ever seen. And I love his Rolling Stones T-shirt with the glow-in-the-dark tongue.

He blabs nonstop for a bit, then asks, "So who're you with?"

"My mom," I grumble.

"Which one's your mom?" Emilio nods when I point her out. "Oh, I know her. She's nice."

"Nice? Ha-ha. She's not nice to me."

"Is that your dad with her?"

"No, they're just living in sin."

Emilio snorts into his Hawaiian Punch. Then, "So, you got a boyfriend?"

I stab him with my eyes. "Whaddaya think? I come here to pick up guys?"

"No, I mean sorry, I mean, I'm not coming onto you, okay?" Poor Emilio turns redder than the punch, and I wonder why I'm being so mean to him.

I sigh. "Forget it. I did have a boyfriend, but we, um, broke up."

Too scared of me now to ask for any details, Emilio starts yakking about the meetings and how much they've helped him, and if I ever want to get together to discuss the program . . . y-a-w-n! Fossilized with boredom, I shift from one foot to the other till Momma's piercing "Yoo-hoo!" thankfully frees me from his clutches.

· · ·

Larry, believe it or not, is a good influence on Momma. Not only has she stopped bitching about having to hear me practice, she actually listens sometimes, but never really comments. Larry, though, always cheers me on.

"Couple more years, darlin', and you'll be charging admission," he teases.

"I hope so," I say honestly.

Momma squints dubiously. "You think she's that good? Still sounds like a bunch of screeching to me."

"Hell, yeah, she's good. She's even got a concert coming up."

I shift uncomfortably. It's not a real concert, just one of Professor Moscowitz's studio recitals. Larry only knows about it because he's been driving me to my lessons. I didn't tell Momma, and if Larry hadn't opened his trap, I probably wouldn't have bothered. What if she refuses to come? Worse, what if she shows up and acts like an idiot?

I'm almost sorry I agreed to this thing. Plus, Professor

Moscowitz's studio is so close to the Brinkmans, and to Waverly, what if I run into someone I know? I have no clue who's playing besides me, or who'll be in the audience.

"A concert?" Momma repeats, brows mashing together.

"It's a recital," I say reluctantly. "We take turns, and well, it's really no big deal . . ."

"What're you playing?"

Um, the same two things you've been listening to for the past month and a half? A section of "Winter" from Vivaldi's *The Four Seasons*—yes, the same Vivaldi who got me hooked in the first place—and the "Simple Gifts" part from *Appalachian Spring*. "Why? Are you coming?"

"Depends. When is it?"

"Next Wednesday," I mumble, half hoping she won't hear me.

"Wouldn't miss it," Larry says heartily. "Right, Lou Ann?"

Momma stalls. "What about our meeting that night?"

"Hell, we can miss one meeting. Don't you know this girl of yours is gonna be a star?"

Momma's startled eyes collide with mine. I think it just dawned on her at last that my cello is not a game, that I'm dead serious about a career, and that I'll be playing my cello forever whether she likes it or not. "Do you want us to come, sugar?"

"Sure," I say airily, never mind that the worst vision imaginable just slammed into my brain: a drunken Momma staggering onstage, belting out some hillbilly ballad, then flashing a tit at Professor Moscowitz before falling headfirst into a tuba . . . omigod, omigod, *omigod*!

Momma breaks into a brilliant smile. "Well! Then we're coming. You know, I might even have to break down and buy me a new dress for the occasion."

Wow, this is serious.

I try not to be nervous, but sorry, I can't trust her. I even go so far as to warn Professor Moscowitz, in a roundabout way, of course. "So what would you do if like this totally drunk, obnoxious person showed up and messed up your whole recital?"

He studies me from beneath his furry unibrow. "A relative of yours, perhaps?"

"Maybe."

"Then rest assured, I vill shoot them on sight."

Why do I get the feeling he's not taking me seriously?

"Oh, and could you not call me Gina that night?" Yes, that's what he still calls me, and yes, I love hearing it. I love that "Gina" can be resurrected for a couple hours each week. "My family calls me Martha, and you'll just confuse them."

Professor Moscowitz shakes his shaggy silver mane, but he's not interested enough to ply me with questions. He says (half in English, half in either Russian or Yiddish) that as far as he's concerned I can call myself Jascha Heifetz as long as I show up, play well, and don't throw my head around like a goddamn racehorse.

"Heifetz wasn't a cellist," I argue before I realize this was a test.

With a sneer of approval, he shoos me out the door.

## ••••• **52** •••••

Momma, true to form, waits till the day of my recital to run out for a new outfit. She calls in sick from work, and makes Larry drive her to Tower City because she wants a *real* dress this time, not some discount rag. It's funny to see her all psyched up like this, because I'm not used to the "new" Momma. Every day she stays sober feels like a miracle.

I decide not to wear the outfit I bought for Waverly's spring concert (bad karma!) and instead find a long ivory dress with spaghetti straps in my overly jammed closet. With no blow dryer, no conditioner, and an outdoor temperature of ninety-five muggy degrees, there's not much I can do with my crazy mop except twist it into a scrunchie and spray the hell out of it.

At six thirty p.m., an hour and a half before the recital, Larry calls me from Tower City. "Bad news, darlin'. I kinda lost your momma."

"What do you mean, you lost her?"

"We were supposed to meet in the food court, and I've been waiting for two hours. I was hoping maybe she took the bus home or something."

"Well, she's not here, and my recital's at eight!"

"Well, how 'bout if I come home and run you over, and then—"

"No, no, go look for Momma. I can get there myself, unless you think I should wait . . ."

"No, you go on ahead. Maybe we're just passing each other up." Poor Larry sounds like he wants to bawl. "Soon as I find her, we'll be there."

Crap. Where is she?

I ride the bus to the rapid transit, the rapid to Shaker Square, and make it to the studio with seven minutes to spare. My first real performance, not counting my audition, and here I am, too flustered to see straight. I glance around at the audience, at the other musicians—nobody I know, thank God—and then watch the door for Momma and Larry, waiting and wondering.

At Professor Moscowitz's impatient hiss from his seat at the piano, I jump up, trip over someone's foot, and make my way to the platform. The studio is small, with just enough chairs for invited guests, so the two empty seats are sickeningly obvious.

The second I touch my bow to the strings, the dread, the panic, instantly disappear.

Yes, I am focused.

Yes, I play beautifully.

Yes, the nutty professor is bobbing his head as he plays along, and holy shit, what's that on his face? No way! He's never cracked a single smile the whole time I've known him.

The applause rocks me, making me so giddy I practically float back to my seat. I did it, I did it—and everyone clapped! I'll never forget that sound, and I want to hear it again, and again, because *this is exactly who I was meant to be!* I know it without a doubt. Nothing will ever change my mind!

Afterward, Professor Moscowitz pumps my arm so hard he almost rips it from the socket. "That was extraordinary, Gina. Extraordinary!" And yes, other people are congratulating me, too, and shaking my hand, praising me from all sides. I'm stunned enough to forget about those two vacant seats, and all because Professor Impossible-to-Please Moscowitz called me "extraordinary" in front of witnesses, no less.

On the way home, in the back of the almost-empty bus, my jubilation fades as it hits me: *Momma had damn well better be dead!* And when I hear voices shouting on the other side of my front door, I know she's alive, but that Larry's ready to kill her.

". . . never, never understand how you could do this, Lou Ann!"

"I didn't do nothin' to you! I told ya, we just talked."

"Right, you talked!"

The door smashes open and Larry barrels down off the stoop as Momma calls, "Now don't go runnin' off on me, Larry! Larry? Come back here!"

Larry plows into me in the dark. "What happened?" I yelp. "Where was she?"

"I said I was sorry!" Momma screams through the screen. "What more do you want?"

"Go ask your momma what happened," Larry says, jerking open his car door.

"Lar-*reee*!" Momma comes flying down the steps. "Larry, please don't go!" For a moment I swear she's about to race after the car. I pull her back into the house before we end up on somebody's camcorder. "Martha, stop him!" she pleads, clawing at my dress.

"Let go of me!" I fling off her hands. "Where were you all day?"

"Oh, great," she snarls. "Now you're gonna start on me, too!" She stalks back into the house and I follow on her heels.

"You missed the whole recital!"

"I'm sorry," she says shortly.

"Bullshit!"

Momma's head jerks in astonishment, but then she just plunks onto the couch and digs her fingers into her eyes. "I am sorry, sugar pie. I really did want to see you play."

"So why didn't you show up?" I stomp my foot hard when she refuses to answer. "Where were you today?"

"I was trying on clothes, see? And I went to put some stuff back, and I saw this guy watching me, and, well—it was Wayne."

I start to say "Bullshit" again, but my throat fills with sludge.

"He's workin' down there now, cleaning and stuff. And I didn't see Larry around, so I . . . well, Wayne, he looked so down, and he was so glad to see me. So we went and took us a walk, and we had a nice long talk, and—oh, don't look at me like that! We just talked. Nothing else."

I think "rage" is a pretty good word for what I'm feeling right now.

Rage, and something worse. Something that pushes tears to the edges of my eyes, but the rage fries away like water on a griddle.

"You missed my recital because you went for a walk with *Wayne*?"

"I'm sorry," Momma rasps, hanging her head. "I swear to you, sugar pie, next time you have a concert, I promise I'll—"

"Don't promise me anything!" I swing my cello case off the floor and head for the steps on rubbery legs. "I really hate you right now."

"I know," she says sadly.

Momma disappears sometime during the night. She stumbles in close to dawn, and yes, she's rip-roaring drunk. Larry's back by then, and she won't tell him where she was, who she was drinking with (like I don't know!), or why she has sucker bites all over her neck. I smother my ears so all I can hear is the click-click-click of my ancient fan and an occasional cussword from Momma's mouth. Larry slams out again, and I drift into a jerky sleep, twisted up in my sticky sheets.

In the morning, Momma's unconscious in a mountain of beer cans. This, after all her baloney about staying clean and sober, how she needs my help, blah, blah, blah. It's bad enough that she's drunk. Bad enough she's missing work. But to be fooling around on Larry—and with *Wa-ayne*, of all people?

I stomp outside, ready to explode into jagged pieces, thinking about everything else she's done to piss me off lately. About the fact that not once did she ever ask me about Chardonnay. What happened, Martha? Why did you jump her with a knife? How do you feel about it now?

Then again, I never asked her about that overdose. Never

found out if it was an accident, or if she did it on purpose, or what she thought would happen to me if she'd kicked the bucket.

Maybe now we're even.

Abandoning Momma in her nest of cans, I practice my cello for six hours straight, stopping only to make a pot of coffee and wolf down four pieces of toast. Her position hasn't changed. I couldn't care less.

I dig up some money, drag the rickety grocery cart ten blocks to the store, stock up on essentials, and drag it back home. Larry's still gone. Momma still hasn't moved.

Eight p.m.

Nine p.m.

Except for one arm dangling off the couch, Momma hasn't budged.

At quarter to ten, a haggard Larry shows up. He stares at the couch. "How long has she been sleeping?"

"All freaking day."

Momma flails her limbs as Larry snatches her shoulders. "What'd you take, Lou Ann?" Only then do I notice the dark stain under her butt, and my jaw drops in guilty revulsion.

Not waiting for an answer, Larry tears the house up till he unearths the evidence. Momma doesn't even duck when he throws the prescription bottle at her. She just sits there groggily, saliva swinging from her lower lip.

"That's it. I'm outta here, Lou Ann."

In silent, uncomprehending horror, I watch Larry haul out a suitcase and begin throwing things into it. Momma's bottom lip vibrates as she sucks her drool back in, but she doesn't argue, doesn't cry, doesn't say a word. She simply stares with hooded, vacant eyes as Larry wraps it up and heads for the door.

"Sorry about this." He pats my rigid shoulder. "I could

almost put up with the crap she pulled yesterday. But, well, there ain't no way I can stay with her now."

"She's sick! It's a sickness. You know she can't help it." If he can forgive her for Wayne, why can't he forgive her for this?

"I know it's a sickness. Hell, I'm sick myself. But I already been down that road, darlin', and I ain't going there again. I can't live with somebody who can't stay sober. Anyway," he adds, "your momma needs more than AA. I think she needs a shrink."

Momma makes a burbling noise, tumbles off the couch, and staggers to the kitchen to gag into the sink. I wince when her face accidentally smacks the faucet. "Should I call 911?"

"Naw, if she can walk, she'll be fine." Larry picks up the brown bottle and shows me the label. Valium, twenty tablets. "Looks like she only took a few." He squints at the bottle. "Who's Wilhelmina Kirchner?"

"How would I know?" I have no idea where Momma gets this junk. Maybe she mugged some old lady coming out of the drugstore.

Larry thrusts a few bills into my sweaty hand. "You're a nice kid, Martha. You keep up with that cello."

A minute later he's gone, and that's too bad because, missing tooth and all, I really liked that guy. I suppose I can't blame him for not wanting to live with someone like Momma. Neither do I, but I don't get that choice.

· · ·

Luckily Larry's right, and Momma's fine in the morning, not counting the fat lip she got from the faucet.

"I'm sorry, sugar pie," she slurs around my homemade ice bag. "I swear I just don't know what come over me yesterday." Same old Momma, same old script.

Life truly sucks.

###### • • • • • **54** • • • • •

I love, love, love the main public library downtown, a monstrous building with marble floors and wall-to-wall books in dozens of rooms. It's my new favorite place, and I'm here at least twice a week. If I could find a bed, and a place to practice my cello, honest to God, I'd never go home.

Today, staggering under the weight of my loaded backpack, I barely make it back to Public Square to catch my bus when something bops me on the back of my head.

"Yo, Miz Martha!" Anthony falls into step. "Been missin' me, sweet thang?"

I grind to a halt, swinging my pack hard. "Get away from me!"

"Yow!" He grabs his arm and doubles over. "What the—?"

And then another voice says, "Yo, dawg. Leave her alone."

"Damn, JoMo. This ho can't even be civil to me no more." Anthony straightens up to give Jerome a shove. "You mess with me again, I'm gonna kick your ass."

Jerome is in no way intimidated by this. "Get outta my face. I wanna talk to my friend." Anthony, outraged, slinks away. I stare after him in amazement as Jerome gives me a wide grin. "How ya doin'?"

"I'm fine." I eye him up and down. He's gotten even taller in the past couple of months, and his braids are longer, bulging out of his do-rag. "How about you?"

"Cool. I'm cool." His glasses are gone, and something else is different, too. Something not very nice. "Damn, girl. You lookin' fly!"

"You, too." Whatever that means. "What're you hanging around him for?" I nod toward Anthony who snaps his teeth in my direction.

Jerome fidgets strangely. "Um, I moved in with my mom, and Anthony, he been stayin' with us."

For ten full seconds I can't even speak. "You're living with her now? Does that mean she's, you know, is she—?"

"Straight?" Jerome snorts, a disturbing sound. "Hell, no. She ain't never gonna be straight."

"But—" I shut my mouth. I have enough problems of my own. "Well, you're still at Jefferson, right?" Didn't he say his mom lives in the projects?

"Nah, I dropped out."

He pretends to cower as I shriek, "What do you mean, you dropped out? You're only fifteen."

"So? I'll be sixteen next year. Then my mom'll sign the papers."

"What're you gonna do in the meantime? Break the law?"

He smirks. "Report me, why don'tcha? Shoot. Think I care?"

It dawns on me now what's not quite right about Jerome. He sounds so much like Anthony that if I shut my eyes, I'd never be able to tell who was who. "What about MIT? What about that scholarship you wanted?"

This is not my Jerome, the Jerome I knew so well. This isn't even the same-but-not-the-same Jerome who surprised me at the Brinkmans' last spring. This Jerome stands there spouting crap about a GED, and how he'll never get into that college because he "ain't the right color."

Fuzz bristles on the back of my hot neck. "Why're you acting this way? You trying to show off for that jerk-off cousin of yours?"

Jerome blows air through his lips. "What way? I ain't acting no kinda way. And hey, what about you?"

"What about me?"

"Look at you! You think you all that?" His eyes sweep over me, and I know what he sees: me, in one of Gina's fashionable summer ensembles, glitzy brand-names displayed on both my purse and my backpack.

"No," I argue, unable to dodge the stinger in my chest. "But I'm not the one who like turned into some weird, freaky—" I stop, because there's really no word for it. Or maybe there is, and I'm afraid to say it.

"I didn't turn into nothin'," Jerome whispers, and for one second I see a flash of my old friend, and I think, No, it's okay. He's still Jerome, and I'm still me, and we haven't changed *that* much! But then he blows it with, "You, though. Ha! Livin' up there with them rich folks now, I guess you ain't used to hanging with us niggas no more."

I feel my knuckles smash into his stomach before I realize what I'm doing. His fists jerk up, and for one quick second he almost hits me back. "I'm not one of your freaking homies, Jerome. Don't you even *think* you can talk to me like that."

"Damn, girl. Who taught you that move?" He rubs his stomach with a weak grin, but when he sees I'm not laughing, his face grows hot and dangerous. "You know somethin'? I don't even know who you are. I don't remember what you look like. You ain't even Martha no more."

My arms turn to cement. My mouth and my feet don't exist. It's like his words have turned me into one giant block of nothingness.

"And if *you* wanna go to college," he goes on, "then hey, do it! But I got better ways of making money without bustin' my ass at MIT."

That's when I notice the big gold ring on his thumb, shaped like a snake with dazzling red eyes. And his flashy watch and all the bling decorating his neck and, yes, his *own* designer-name clothes. Either he's holding out on his mom as far as that money is concerned, or he's got a new source of income. I'm betting on number two.

"Yeah. Drug money." He starts to protest, and that only makes me madder. "Oh, don't lie to me, Jerome. I'm not stupid, okay?"

"You ain't stupid, huh?" he repeats, his words dripping with contempt. "You took that fucking gun from me, remember?"

Yes, and that's not all I remember. "So? It wasn't even loaded! Why'd you give it to me then, and let me think it was loaded? That was a really dirty trick, I hope you know."

"How'd I know if it was loaded? It was Anthony's piece, man. He told me to get rid of it, so that's what I did. And you were stupid enough to take it."

"You *told* me to take it! You never said it was Anthony's." I never would've touched it if he had.

"Well, I'm tellin' you now. So, yo, thanks a lot, bitch."

He's off the curb and halfway across the street before my pitifully stunned brain reacts. "Did you tell Anthony you took that money? Huh? Did you?"

"Yeah, I told him!" he yells back. "And it don't even matter no more."

"He killed your brother, Jerome. Don't you even care? *He killed Bubby!*" I scream this after him, forcing edgy bystanders to detour around me in wide circles. I keep on screaming it till he's lost in the crowd, and not one time does he bother to look back.

I cradle my backpack on the jarring ride home, sick to my stomach, sick in my heart. Okay, I know I'm different, but in a good way, right? Who could possibly like the "old" Martha better?

Jerome's right about one thing: I am so utterly stupid. Too stupid to know Gina from Martha, or Martha from Gina, and too stupid to care. But worse than that, all this time I've been too stupid to realize that the one person I thought would be my friend forever was never my friend at all.

## 55

Momma's out of a job again, out of AA, and back to cruising the bars with a bunch of scummy new friends. Nothing I do, nothing I say, makes the least bit of difference. That, I think, is the most depressing thing of all.

Me, I'm still doing the Alateen thing. I even changed my cello lessons to different days so I can get to the church in time for the opening prayer. A lot of the stuff they talk about sounds very familiar: Being afraid to bring home your friends because you never know what shape your folks'll be in. Hoping they don't humiliate you at school functions. Going out of your way to pick fights with them, just to pay them back for making you so miserable.

And again and again the sponsors try to drum it into our brains that *we are not responsible for anyone else's addiction!*

"Doesn't that make you feel, well, helpless?" I zero in on Emilio who shows up at every meeting. Either he's secretly stalking me, or he basically has no other life. "Like no matter what you do, there's no way you can stop them?"

Emilio shrugs. "I don't feel helpless, I feel—" He thinks for a second. "Free."

"Free? You gotta be kidding."

"You don't get it yet, Martha. You have to, you know, pray a lot, and keep working the program. There's a lot of stuff you're gonna find out about yourself."

"Why do I have to do the steps? I'm not the drunk in the family."

"Well, you don't have to. But it'll make you a stronger person, you know?" I shake my head fiercely, and he juts his chin at the crowd. "Hey, you're no different than anyone else in this room. You just like to think you are. Boy, are you wrong."

"And boy, are you full of it," I inform him, stalking away.

"The serenity prayer—" he insists loudly. "'Accept what you can't change, and change what you can.' It's easier than you think."

I wander home through the sticky dusk, dwelling on all that junk about prayer and acceptance and finding your Higher Power. I wish I *could* be like Emilio and blindly believe in this stuff. After what happened to Bubby, you'd think I'd be a bit more religious, knowing how easily it could've happened to me.

There's a pile of mail bulging out of the rusty mailbox. Bill, collection notice, bill, collection notice. Then I notice an envelope forwarded by the Brinkmans. The return address in elegant gold letters reads *Great Lakes Academy of Music*.

*Omigod!*

With long, ragged breaths, I open it delicately and skim the two paragraphs. The first one says that Miss Gina Kowalski has been accepted as a student for the upcoming school year. The second paragraph congratulates her for winning the *Andrew Carnegie Award for Talented Young Musicians in the Original Music Composition category for "Variation on a Theme" by Rupert Campbell*. The prize is twenty-five-hundred dollars, and this is on top of their regular scholarship!

Momma stumbles tipsily out of the kitchen when she hears me scream, "I got in! I got in!" She has to pry the letter out of my fingers because I'm too excited to let go.

"Who's Gina?" she slurs, blinking at the page.

"Never mind. Just read it!" I pirouette joyfully across the decayed gold carpet as Momma reads slowly, moving her lips with each word.

"Just in the nick of time, too! Lord knows we could use a little extra cash."

I stop dancing so fast, I practically slip a disk. "That's scholarship money. They don't just hand it to you to spend."

"Scholarship for what?"

"Jeez, you read the damn letter. It's that music school, Momma!"

She rereads the lines, and I can hear those rickety wheels turning. "Well, shoot. If you won it, you won it. It's your money, ain't it? Maybe I'll call these folks up and see if they can cut you a check." Chuckling at my expression, she adds, "Oh, good Lord. I ain't gonna spend all of it. You can take a few bucks, buy whatever you need."

"Are you crazy? I busted my ass getting into that school!"

"School, schmool. We got bills to pay."

A surge of ferocious energy springs through every inch of my body. I swear to God, even my hair starts crackling. I scream at her that she's not paying any bills with my money, and how I am sick, sick, sick of her trying to destroy me. "Why can't I go there? Why? Why? Why?"

A hand flashes out, whipping my head sideways. " 'Cause I said so, that's why." And when I shriek about how unfair that is, she shrieks back that I'm more trouble than I'm worth, and why, oh why did she ever let me back in the house?

I rub my sore cheek, refusing to cry. "Well, I don't want to be here either. I wish to God I was someplace else!"

"So go! Get outta here. Go back to your rich goddamn lawyer." And then she hauls out both barrels. "Oh, right, I forgot. He threw your ass out."

"He did not. I left." Which is technically true.

"Oh, yeah? Face it, missy, that man was plain sick and tired of you."

"Sick of me, huh? Well, what about Larry, Momma? What about Wayne? You can't even hang on to any of your scumbag boyfriends."

She slugs me again, and it's like being hit with a mallet. A warm wet trickle drips down from my nose. "You watch what you say! You ain't nobody special in this house, missy. You ain't nothin', you hear me?"

I glance at my red fingers, feeling a rise of sheer rage—and realize with an eerie thrill that I just struck a raw nerve. "No wonder they dumped you. You're just a sick, pathetic drunk!" The words spew out of my mouth, bubbling up in the blood. Yes, I want to hurt her, hurt her feelings really bad. To make *her* cry, like she always makes me cry. "And if Daddy were here, he'd never let you treat me like this. He'd throw you outta here right on your big fat—"

Momma advances. "Oh, yeah? Well, let me tell you something, missy. If I'd known then what I know now, I'd woulda taken that money his folks gave me and put an end to the whole thing."

I can't speak for a second, then, "What whole thing?" No answer. "You mean me?"

Momma stops in her tracks. "Forget it," she says abruptly, but it's too late to take it back, and now I know the truth. I was never meant to be.

"You should have." Probably the worst lie I ever told. "I don't know why you didn't."

"'Cause I wanted him," she says, quieter now. "Never mind that he never wanted me, or that if his folks had had their way, you'd a been—" Momma chokes.

Toast, I think darkly. A blob at the bottom of a drain.

Recovering, Momma adds with a feral sneer, "You wanna know why I burned that fiddle of his? 'Cause that's all he cared about. That, and the gambling, and all his lady friends, too. Not me, missy. And he never cared nothin' about you."

My vision blurs. I'm having trouble catching my breath.

"All I ever heard was how I tricked him into marrying me, and how his family hated me, how I wrecked his damn life. You wonder why I drink? I was just a kid when I married him! And he treated me like shit from day one."

This is not my mother. As drunk as she is, as crazy as she can be, my real mother would never talk to me like this. My real mother would never tell me these lies.

"I hate you!" I blurt out. "You are the most fucking insane person I've ever known!"

A blotch of color appears at the base of Momma's neck. Billowing up into her hair, it turns her face as scarlet as the blood on my T-shirt. When she moves forward, I'm sure it's to clock me again, but she heaves me aside and clumps upstairs. A split second later the lightbulb goes off: *No! Not my cello!*

I spring up after her and, yes, she's in my room. But instead of my cello, she's holding my little round fish bowl, and before I can stop her, she tosses it through the door. Three helpless orange bodies with gaping mouths skid wetly down the steps in a spray of colored gravel.

"For your information," she says ferociously, "Wayne *didn't* dump me. I been seeing him regular, and he already asked me to move back in. I might do it, too."

That's when I lose it. I smash into her so hard, she flips over my trunk and lands on her spine with a humongous crash. For one endless second she lies perfectly still, and then she says, disbelievingly, "I think you done busted my back, sugar pie."

Sick with shame, unable to believe what I just did, I squat beside her. "Momma, I'm sorry—"

"Don't—you—touch—me! Get the hell outta my house!"

So that's what I do. I rush outside and across the alley to Mamma Mia's where the flashing neon light—All U Can Eat—makes me feel woozy and sick. Holding my nose to the sky to slow the red dribble, I sink to the sidewalk under the blacked-out window.

A guy in a green apron comes out for a cigarette. "Wow. What happened to you?" When I ignore him, he adds, "You know, you shouldn't let people smack you around."

"No shit, Sherlock. Got any more brilliant advice?"

He disappears, and brings me back a wet towel. I mop my face, turning the cloth a bright pink. He has stringy brown hair and a sweet homely face with teeny wire glasses at the end of an extremely large nose. His shirt tag says "Josh" and when he asks me my name, I automatically say "Gina"—but how lame is that? Gina would never be sitting on a sidewalk in front of a beer joint, hemorrhaging into her lap thanks to a smack from her old lady.

"You want to come in and have a Coke? I'm still on my break."

"A beer would be nice," I say thickly. "But could you bring it out here?"

"Uh, are you old enough to drink?" He jumps back as I spit out a glob of bloody snot, and then goes back into the bar for a couple of brewskies. "Man, you look awful. Why don't you go home and go to bed?"

"I can't. My mom'll kill me." I remember my cello, waiting helplessly inside, and pray, pray, pray Momma doesn't decide to *really* teach me a lesson.

"Well, go lie down in my van." Josh points to the parking lot and then gets mortally offended when I give him my not-so-humble opinion of this lame-ass idea. "Hey, take it easy. I'm not gonna molest you. I'll wake you up when I get off."

I think about this while I work my way through the beer. Oh, why not? I can't sleep on the sidewalk.

A grimy-looking mattress covers the floor of the van. I glare suspiciously, but Josh merely shrugs. "See ya later."

I roll up in a ball, head wobbling, nose aching. Twice I lean out the door to spit blood onto the gravel, and it dawns on me now why my vision's so bad: Momma clobbered me so hard, she knocked out a contact. I pop the other one free and flick it outside. Who cares? Those were Gina's, and Gina is dead.

Next thing I know, Josh is shaking my shoulder. I wipe a pool of pink slime away from my neck. "Time is it?"

"Going on three. You okay?" I nod sluggishly, watching him rummage around till he comes up with a J. "Want a toke? It's an awesome painkiller."

Guiltily, my mind flashes to Emilio. "What is this? Some devious plan to get me stoned?"

"I already told you, I'm not gonna bother you. But if you ever want to, you know, do it, we could just, like . . . do it."

"Do it?"

"Yeah. Mess around."

I am not about to make the same mistake twice. "I'm only

fifteen, not that it's any of your beeswax." When he makes a grab for my illegal beer, I add quickly, "But I like older men."

"Yeah?"

"Yeah." Omigod. Am I flirting?

He puffs on the doob, then passes it over and I stare at it for a moment like I'm holding a stick of dynamite. Oh, what the hell? How can this possibly make anything worse?

The bitter smoke burns as it snakes down my throat. I choke and splutter, but finally get the hang of it, and Josh is right—it does take my mind off my throbbing nose.

"So, how much older?" Josh asks nonchalantly.

I suck harder on the joint. "How old are you?"

"Twenty-one."

The street is dark and quiet, with only an occasional passing car, as we dangle our legs out of the back of the van. I watch the lights go out in my house, so at least I know Momma made it up from the floor. My body feels like it's floating . . . floating . . . and Josh looks cuter and cuter with every puff. "Well. I guess that's old enough."

He breaks into a goofy smile, and we polish off the joint in silence. Then he shuts the van door, whips off his glasses, and kisses me so passionately, our noses clank.

"Ow! Watch it," I complain.

Apologetically, he pulls away and then gets back to business. Between the beer and the pot and the rancid blood, my breath smells funky, but Josh doesn't care, and his is almost as bad. My shorts are off in like two seconds flat, and I feel his hands groping me, feeling me, touching me . . .

And now I remember, clear as crystal, why I loved being with Danny, how good it feels to be hugged and kissed, to have somebody say they love you, whether they mean it or not.

But as wasted as I am, I remember one thing. "Wait, wait. You gotta put something on."

It's almost too late, and he stops with a gasp. "Huh?"

"A rubber," I snap.

"Oh, man!" he whines, still trying to get in me. "I don't have one."

I shove him off. "You think I want to get AIDS?" Not to mention everything else that could happen.

"Jeez, do I look like I have AIDS?"

"I don't know what AIDS looks like," I tell him, trying not to think about Mrs. Addams.

Josh isn't happy, but he gets over it fast. Instead, he takes my hand and shows me what to do, and the whole time I'm doing it, I'm thinking about other things. Like how I could really go for an iced mocha about now—frosty cold, double espresso, with whipped cream and drizzled chocolate . . .

When it's over, it's over, and he falls back, panting. I yank up my shorts, jump down onto the gravel on shuddering legs, and teeter across the alley. Stoned, stoned, I am oh—so—stoned! Maybe it's the pot that makes me feel so brave, or maybe not. Maybe it's just me. But one thing I know that's the absolute truth? No matter what happens, no matter how drunk she gets, I will never let Momma hit me again.

Not like that. Not ever.

She's still awake, sitting in near-pitch darkness at the kitchen table. "Lucky for you I didn't break my back. I can't hardly walk now, it's achin' me so bad."

Can hardly walk, Momma. It's *can* hardly walk, not can't hardly walk.

"You lay a hand on me again," she continues, "you ain't gonna live to tell about it. Got that?"

I bite my tongue because I don't trust my voice, and anything I say will only make her madder. But I mean it this time—I have *so* had it up to here! Now if only I could figure out a way to say this out loud, to her face.

As I turn to go upstairs to make sure my cello's in one piece, Momma, without warning, lets out a watery sob. "I didn't mean it, sugar pie. I swear I didn't mean it!"

Something twists deep in my stomach, and yes, I halfway give in. "Momma, come on. Don't cry about it, okay?"

"I coulda busted your nose! I didn't mean to hit you that hard."

She wants me to tell her it's okay, and that I forgive her for what, like the thousandth time? I chew my tongue, sweat dribbling down my back.

"I tried so hard to get you back," Momma blubbers. "And first chance you get, I know you're gonna leave me. Then what'll I do? What'll I do without my sugar pie?"

Okay, *okay!* I can't stand it anymore.

"Oh, Momma." I hug her briefly, hoping I don't smell like somebody who smoked dope and had semisex with a perfect stranger ten minutes ago. "Come on. I'm not going anywhere." My voice cracks, and I wonder what she'd say if she really knew how badly I don't want to be here. How I'd do anything, anything, to get away forever.

I know she's sick. I know she's an alcoholic. I know she can't help the way she acts sometimes. But if she'd—just—quit—drinking! She's done it before, more times than I can count. So why, why, why can't I make her stop drinking now?

Because nobody can do that, not even me. The sponsors say that, and Emilio, too, over and over till I'm ready to scream.

So when will I believe it? Tomorrow? Next week? Ten years from now?

And will it make me free, like Emilio says?

"I never woulda done it," Momma adds hoarsely, and I know what she's talking about. "I wanted you, sugar pie. And I did love your daddy. I loved him a whole lot. And maybe he didn't love me, but he sure did love you."

I guess I believe her. This time, anyway. It's better than believing what she told me before.

She cries and cries till she's all cried out, then honks her nose and lights up a cigarette. I don't mention Wayne and neither does she. We sit there together thinking our own private thoughts till the sun crawls into the sky, turning the kitchen a muddy gray.

When it's light enough to see, I throw out the plastic fish bowl, clean up the colored rocks and the water, and scoop up the shriveled bodies of my poor murdered fish. One by one, I drop them into the toilet and watch them swirl, swirl, swirl till they disappear forever in a gush of rusty water.

## 56

The rest of the summer, I stay as far away from Momma as humanly possible. She hasn't hit me again, but she's sinking fast. Her pathetic new pals hang around night after night, drinking and toking and even snorting coke. Momma joins right in, not caring that I can see her, not worrying for one second that I might blow the whistle.

I try to talk to Emilio, but I think he's losing patience with me. He says *I* have to be the one to change the way I react, to worry about myself instead of obsessing about Momma. Ha, easy for him to say. It's not his mom spending twelve hours a day in a burned-out coma.

And it's not his mom, either, who's keeping him out of the school of his dreams. No matter what Momma says, to me or to Zelda or to anyone else—my life will *not* end up a big pile of shit. Now I have to think of something fast because I have to register for Great Lakes in person, and a parent or guardian has to go with me. Forging Momma's name on a piece of paper won't fly this time, and now that Larry bailed, she doesn't even pretend to care about my music.

I wait for a morning when she's less hungover than usual and butter her up with a box of chocolate-filled donuts. Overjoyed, she digs in, and I casually announce, "You know, I do have to register for school this week."

"I already did that," she says with her mouth full.

"I mean for Great Lakes."

The donut stops in midair. "I thought we settled all that."

"Zelda said—"

"I don't care what Zelda said. *I* said you could take lessons, and you're doing that, right? What more do you want?"

"*God!* I want to go to that school, Momma. *That's* what I want!"

She bangs down a fist, squirting chocolate across the table. "Jesus H. Christ, I am so sick of hearin' about that school."

"And I'm sick of you screwing up my life!" I scream back.

"Oh yeah? Well, living with you ain't exactly a piece of cake, missy."

"Ha! Then maybe you'd like it better if I dropped over dead."

"Oh, don't go startin' that psycho crap on me. You wanna die so bad? Stop whining and go do it." Wham! Out she slams.

Grabbing the donuts, I throw them on the floor and then jump on the box and kick it across the room. Forks and knives and spoons fly through the air as I jerk the silverware drawer out of the cabinet. Pawing though the mess, I search and search, but the most lethal thing I come up with is a rusty potato peeler. I even go so far as to poke it at my wrist, but I'm too much of a wimp to even nick my skin.

I fling it at the wall and sink to the floor, wishing I had the nerve to do something so horrible it'll haunt her forever, for the rest of her life. But then I think about my cello and how Momma'll sell it on eBay, or maybe trade it for drugs if I drop over dead, and I know for a fact: I will never let her do it.

. . .

When Momma's not back by chow time, I refuse to worry. I help myself to a beer, burrow into the couch, and skim through the few lousy channels we have. I do find a chopped-up version of *Blue Hawaii* but it hurts too much to look at Elvis's sulky, gorgeous face. Damn Danny, anyway. He even ruined Elvis for me.

*Twilight Zone*'s on, and a lady named Nan is driving her car cross-country. Somewhere along the line she gets into a crash, and from that moment on, everywhere she drives, this strange-looking hitchhiker pops up ahead of her. Problem is, only Nan can see him, and the more she runs into him, the more creeped out she gets.

Well, it turns out Nan *died* in that accident and didn't even know she was dead. But what's truly bizarre is, after a few beers, I start to wonder if that's what happened to me. Did the cops really blow me off the fire escape that night? Did I imagine everything that's happened to me since?

Maybe I never lived with the Brinkmans. Maybe I never met Danny at all. Maybe Bubby's alive, Shavonne likes me, and Jerome is still my geeky best friend. Maybe my whole pathetic existence from the second I was born has been nothing but one endless *Twilight Zone* marathon.

I hunker down on the couch, trying to put a name to this funny sensation. I know what I must look like, sprawled on the couch, chugging Momma's beer, trying to analyze the whole point of my pointless life. And then when I think about Josh and what we did in the van, I'd like to rip every inch of skin off my face. What was I thinking? How could I do something that stupid?

Easy. Because I was mad. Because I was sad.

And because, like Momma, I just had to get high.

The doorbell jangles, knocking the scary thoughts out of my head. I lurch to my feet and kick the empty cans under the couch. It might be Zelda. She's *way* overdue for a visit.

I open the door and nearly fall over from shock.

"Hi, Gina." Nikki's hair is now chin length, pale and smooth. And get a load of mine: tangled, overgrown, with an inch of dark roots. I should be standing in flip-flops in front of a trailer, roasting wienies over a rusty oil drum. "Is this a bad time?"

I trip down onto the stoop, shutting the door firmly behind me. "Yeah. Kind of." My flesh blisters with embarrassment as I watch her eyes roam, taking in the details of the yard and the front of my house. Overloaded trash cans. Screens dangling from the windows. Newspaper tumbleweeds hurtling across the lawn.

She spots the headless statue. "What's that?"

"It's a Bathtub Mary."

"What happened to her head?"

"She came that way." Along with the rest of the decor, of course. Nikki's yellow Mustang is parked at the curb, and I'm happy to see she left the motor running. Clearly she doesn't plan to hang around very long. "What do you want?"

Nervously, Nikki plays with her hair. "Well, I was gonna write you a letter because I have some things to tell you, but my sponsor said I should do it in person. I'm in AA now, you know? And there are these twelve steps we have to follow, like—"

"I know what the steps are." I don't need a whole dissertation.

"You do? Oh. Well, I'm trying to work through my ninth step. To make amends, you know, to all the people I hurt." I wait, saying nothing, wondering where this is going, and why, oh why can't somebody fix those damn screens? "Well, I want to apologize for some of the stuff I said."

"You don't have to apologize," I hear myself say. "Although I never did appreciate you calling me a slum rat."

"I'm not doing it for you, Gina. I'm doing it for myself."

Yep, same old Nikki. "Fine. Go for it."

"Okay, I've got four things to say. First of all, I'm glad you called my dad when I got, um, sick that night. Yeah, I was pissed because you promised not to tell, but, well, you did me a favor. So, thanks. I mean it."

Somehow "you're welcome" seems incredibly lame.

"Okay, number two. Do you know why my dad made you leave?"

"Duh. You told him to."

Nikki nods. "I was so mad at you for turning me in. Plus, you were right, I *was* kind of jealous. I mean, you're always so sure of yourself, so strong, and everyone liked you so much."

Me? Strong?

"Especially my mom and dad," she continues, cheeks pinking up. "I mean, I kinda thought they loved you more than me because you were like all they cared about for a while. Kinda like Rachel, you know? Daddy always loved her more even though he'd never admit it. That's what it felt like, anyway."

I remember the fury on her face when she caught me and Claudia singing in the kitchen. "Well, I would've had to go anyway," I mumble. "Not like I had a choice."

A typical Nikki sigh of impatience. "Number three: what I did to you and Danny. Okay, I know he liked you, but you were just faking him out, and—well, it was wrong for me to tell him all your personal stuff. That should've been your decision. And I'm sorry it hurt you." She halts for breath. "It hurt Danny, too."

Hurt Danny? My muscles grow rigid as I remember our last date. Danny knew all about me before he even picked me up that night. He made me sit through that crappy movie, wondering what was wrong. Then, instead of asking me point-blank if what Nikki had said was true, he just tap-danced around it till he had me backed into a corner. Why didn't he dump me when he first found out? Talk about fake outs.

I shift to the other foot. "So what's the fourth thing?"

Nikki snakes her French manicure through her hair, and glances around, probably expecting a mugger. "This is really, really hard, but—well, my dad never told me about you. You were right. I lied."

She stops and waits, and I wait, too, wondering why I'm so astonished at this last piece of news.

"When that friend of yours from that picture showed up, I knew you were lying. I even tried to get back into your trunk, but you'd locked it by then. So I looked around your room, and found this."

She reaches into her sleek white clutch, and drops Shavonne's mood ring into my hand. My eyes bug out. Funny, I never missed it.

"I'm the one who found it in Daddy's car, in the backseat, so I gave it to him so he could give it back to Mrs. Addams. Then when I saw it in your room, I was like, God, that was *you* I saw in the car that night!" Pause. "Hey, pretty good costume."

I squiggle the ring onto my finger. Almost immediately the black stone turns orange, and I hold it up to the sunlight, wondering what it means.

"Anyway, I was gonna ask Daddy about it, but I knew he'd never tell me. So I poked around in his office and found some stuff out about you, and—well, he leaves his computer sometimes, so I went into it, looking. It wasn't hard to find out who you really were. But he never said a word to me. Cross my heart."

Why did I believe her? How could I not have known?

Avoiding my chilly stare, Nikki draws an invisible line with the toe of her woven sandal. "I heard Daddy tell Mom what you said to him that day. All those names you called him? You really hurt his feelings."

"So? He hurt me first." But without any venom, the words mean nothing.

"It's my fault he hurt you, so don't blame him. Blame me."

I sneer. "So now what? Is this the part where I'm supposed to say, 'Aw shucks, Nikki, thanks, I feel so-o-o much better!'?"

Nikki's flush deepens. "No. But if there's something you want me to do, something to make things right, will you let me know? 'Cause I'd still like us to be friends."

I almost do it, I almost say okay. After all, this must've been positively hideous for her. But why put it all on me?

"I gotta go," I say instead. "And you better get out of here before somebody rips off that car."

Before I can slink off, Nikki steps forward to pull me into a hug. She sniffs once, then twice. "Gina. Are you drunk?"

I shake myself loose. "Bye, Nikki."

"Wait! You, like, reeeek of beer!"

"Why don't you mind your own business, Miss Queen of the Ninth Step?"

"It doesn't help anything, okay?"

"It makes me feel better!" I shout.

"It doesn't change who you are."

"Hey, it just so happens I know exactly who I am. Now do me a favor and get your stick-butt off my porch." I swing open the door, but she grabs the handle.

"You think you know who you are? So who are you, huh? Just think about it for a second." As I force the flimsy door out of her grip, Nikki's own hot antiseptic breath hits me through the flapping screen. "Oh, and that cello he gave you? He'd never let us touch it." Her lips curl in a fierce knot. "Not even his precious Rachel."

I slam the door, knocking loose that last hinge. I force down another beer, hoping to pass out and wake up when I'm twenty. Instead, I keep replaying that scene in Zelda's car: *Traitordrunkmurderertraitordrunkmurderertraitordrunkmurderer!* How I told him I hated him, that I wished he were dead.

For once it feels good to let myself cry, to make all the noise I want without anyone hearing me. Rejuvenated, I jump up and march to the fridge, and snatch out every beer, every wine cooler, anything I can find.

My mom's an addict. My dad was an addict. I may suck at statistics, but one thing I know? The chances of me growing up to be exactly like one of them are a whole lot better than me winning that scholarship.

Every bottle, every can, I pour down the drain.

I won't let it happen. I swear on Bubby's soul.

## ••••• 57 •••••

Momma's been AWOL for two days, and now I'm spazzing out. Is she back in the hospital? Was she busted for drugs? Is her dead, battered body stuffed in a sewer pipe? There could be a thousand reasons why she hasn't come home and none of them any good.

Zelda leaves a note on the door while I'm at the library: *Just wondering how you are. I'll stop back soon.* Then children's services pops up on the caller ID. Zelda again, but what do I do? If I answer, I'll have to fake my way through a lie. If I never pick up, she'll get suspicious for sure. I let the machine take over, and she leaves message after message, commanding Momma to call her back ASAP.

Emilio leaves a few jumbled thoughts of his own, wondering why I haven't shown up at any meetings. But I'm too afraid to leave the house, even for my lessons. What if Momma comes back while I'm gone? What if she's hurt, or in trouble, or deathly ill? Not only that, but I'm running out of food and the smell from Mamma Mia's makes me want to crawl into their Dumpster and scavenge for leftovers.

I hate, hate, hate this! And I hate being alone.

The third morning, Zelda tries again. "Lou Ann, this is Zelda. I got your message."

Message? What message?

"Are you there? Hello? Um, Gina?"

*Now* she remembers my name, now that pigs are flying.

"Well, please, one of you call me back as soon as you get this, hmm?" She leaves her cell phone number, and it's easy to remember because the last four digits make up the year I was born. A minute later, though, she calls back. This time her tone is sharp and her accent even sharper. "Never mind. I will be there by noon. I want to know what's going on, and one of you had better let me in!"

I don't budge, I just stand there, my brain sharp as glass and vibrating with ideas. Can I hide under the bed and wait till she leaves? Unless, of course, she brings legal reinforcements. I picture myself on *Cops* with my face fuzzed into tiny cubes, hustled into a cruiser, news cameras flashing. I can't go to Emilio's because I don't know where he lives, and all he'll do anyway is start spewing that prayer.

No, that's not fair. At least he has more sense than me.

Ten fifty-five on my digital clock—one hour and five minutes till Zelda shows up. Would Josh help me out, let me hide in his van? Maybe. But how will I have to pay him back?

*WhatdoIdowhatdoIdowhatdoIdowhatdoIdo?* Will it be a group home again? Another foster home? I highly doubt that the clown house wants me back, seeing as I didn't exactly leave there on the best of terms.

*Bang!* Momma stumbles through the doorway, a jug of Jack Daniels in one hand, a bag of goodies in the other. Her filthy entourage follows close behind.

"Hey, Lou Ann." One biker dude—Virgil or Verne or possibly

Vermin—jiggles like a kindergartner who can't find the potty.
"You said we'd get the place to ourselves today."

"What are you doin' here?" Momma seems truly, incredibly,
undeniably stunned to see me, and that's when I know—she
thought I'd be gone! *She's* the one who tipped off Zelda, hoping
Zelda might pick me up before she got back.

I crunch my teeth. "I live here, remember?"

"Lou Ann!" Vermin whines impatiently as the other maggots
set up shop on my perfectly polished coffee table. I see a huge vin-
tage bong, tidy plastic Baggies loaded with, well, whatever, cigarette lighters, homemade pipes, and—

I stop my mental inventory when Momma hisses in my ear,
"Go somewhere, you hear me? I got stuff to do, and I don't want
you around."

"Better listen to your momma," says a familiar voice behind me.

With a knot of dread, I spin around and bump smack into
Satan.

"Hey," Wayne greets me, looming unsteadily in the doorway.
"Long time, no see." I stick my arm out to send him a seriously
significant finger, and he cocks his head in surprise like, oh gosh,
I hurt his feelings. "Aw, c'mon. That any way to greet an old
friend?"

Momma slaps my arm down. "I said beat it, Martha. *Now!*"
"Make me!"

As her mad-dog eyes glaze over, I dash for the stairs, knowing she's too sloshed to follow. Breathing hard, I hover in my
puny room, thinking and thinking, and then gather up all the
spare change I can find. I flip open my black trunk and pick out
my most recent journals, jamming as many as I can into my
backpack. If Momma decides to throw another bonfire in my
honor, at least my latest memories will be safe.

I peer back at my alarm clock—11:03—and stick my feet into sandals, sling my pack over my shoulder, pick up my cello case, and move slowly back downstairs. Everyone's huddled around the coffee table, smoking and snorting and doing whatever else professional stoners do. I think of all the beer I've had over the past couple of days and how great it made me feel, at least for a while. Now it scares me to death, only because I can see why they do it.

For one second I'm tempted to smash their bong into the wall. Ha, what could they do? Call the cops on me? But the expression on Momma's face is the one thing that stops me. Leaning into Wayne, who already has a greasy hand on her thigh, she sucks in smoke, releases it, and then shuts her eyes with a dreamy, satisfied smile.

I can't make her smile. But she's smiling now.

She mumbles when she senses me standing by her shoulder. Something like, "You still here?" Or maybe it's, "See you, dear." But she never calls me dear. Only sugar pie.

Momma, Zelda will be here in less than forty-five minutes. Hide the drugs! Make everybody leave! You'll end up in jail, and then they'll put me someplace again, and you can't let that happen, you can't, it's not fair!

But I don't say it out loud. I don't even want to try.

With my free arm, I hug her clammy neck. "I love you, Momma."

She answers vaguely, not bothering to look up, "Why, I love you too, sugar pie."

Leaving the house, I hit the sidewalk and walk block after block, street after street, on and on till I lose track of time. At one point I notice a stray dog with one ear, and I think of Luther Lee Washington and his missing mutt, Ole Marvin.

I whistle once. "Here, doggie, doggie." That one ear pricks up as he dangles a happy tongue, but he won't come any closer. It's just as well.

I continue my trek till I'm almost downtown. The clock on the tower of the West Side Market says 1:33, so whatever was going to happen must have happened by now. Hoping nobody sees me and thinks I'm planning to jump, I study the muddy water of the river as I trail across that same Bob Hope bridge. How far would I fall if I jumped—maybe a thousand feet? And do you really get to see everyone who died ahead of you? Are they surprised when you show up, or were they waiting for you all along? Watching you your whole life, knowing exactly when it would happen.

I never thought I'd say this, but if I see Emilio again, I think I'll tell him about Bubby. Then, while I'm at it, I'll let him know that, yes, I'm gonna do the twelve steps after all.

Not in order, though.

Leaving the bridge, I zigzag the streets till I find a phone booth that miraculously works. I think about Zelda and how she tries to be so nice, even when she'd like nothing better than to knock me to the moon. Man, you'd have to be crazy to have a job like hers. Whatever they pay her, it's not enough.

My cello case is silent as I plant it to one side. A small *woof* makes me swing my head around, and I spot that one-eared dog creeping up from behind. I call, "Hey, I thought you were dead!" He cocks his head, tail wagging fiercely. Cute as hell, but I bet he's loaded with fleas.

I pick up the receiver and dial my birth year. When Zelda answers, I don't even have to explain. She just tells me to stay put so she can come pick me up.

Jerome, I'm not ready for. I bet he wrote me off forever and thinks I did the same to him. Did I? I'm not sure, but there's no way I can do this now. Maybe someday. Or maybe real soon.

So I try Shavonne next, but her phone's out of order, probably for good this time. Maybe she went to live with her Aunt Bernice, and I don't know her aunt's number or even her last name. But I bet I know somebody who can help me find out.

I squash the button and release it once more. Guess old Ninth-Step Nikki did a number on me, for real. I pop in another coin and dial slowly, and listen to the ringing over the thunder of my heart.

By the time Richard answers, my tongue is glued to my tonsils. "Hello? Hello?" Then, "Gina, is that you?"

I suck in my breath, scared he'll hang up before I can utter one word—and then finally, finally, I find my voice.

"No," I say into the mouthpiece. "It's Martha."

# Acknowledgments

So many people have been involved in the creation of this novel, and I'd like to thank each of them, for many different reasons.

My fabulous agent, Tina Wexler, of ICM, for falling in love with Martha and making my lifelong dream come true. Jill Davis, my editor at Bloomsbury Children's Books, for her endless dedication, advice, and support, and for miraculously keeping me sane throughout the editing process. My husband and life partner, Clarence Garsee, for helping me raise an unbelievably "normal" family, and for all his love and patience. My daughter, Elizabeth, my first reader and biggest fan, and my son, Nathan, who always cheers me on.

Karen Margosian, my sister and best friend, who can always make me laugh even when we're crying. My brother, Milan Nerad, the first person ever to hear my stories—and, more important, the first to beg for more. My extended family: Leah Koson, Matthew Margosian, Mary Nerad, Mary Nerad Junior, Kenneth Johnson, and Tom Nerad for reminding me what a "real" family is. Genevieve, Sophia, and Lydia Koson, for allowing me to steal their names. Ruth Ward, my "adopted" sister. Don't forget:

"We're gonna make it . . . !" My dear friend Melody L., for her unconditional love, and for helping me better understand the twelve steps of AA. Janet Walsh, for her support, motherly advice, and the occasional well-aimed kick. Tangela Lindsey, for teaching me the true meaning of "soul sister." My crit group members and online friends who have supported me over the past several years: Holly Farriman, C. J. Parker, June Phyllis Baker, Donna, Tinny, Sher, Kate Harrington, Kat, Jade, Laura, Yvonne Grapes, Sharolyn Wells, Kathie Carlson, Nadine Laman, Jenny Mounfield, and Pamela Reese, my first face-to-face writing buddy, who deserves a special thanks for her generous help with the social-service advice, and for all our parking lot conversations about psychotic mommas and "nekkid" elfs.